M000289376

A Spy Among Us

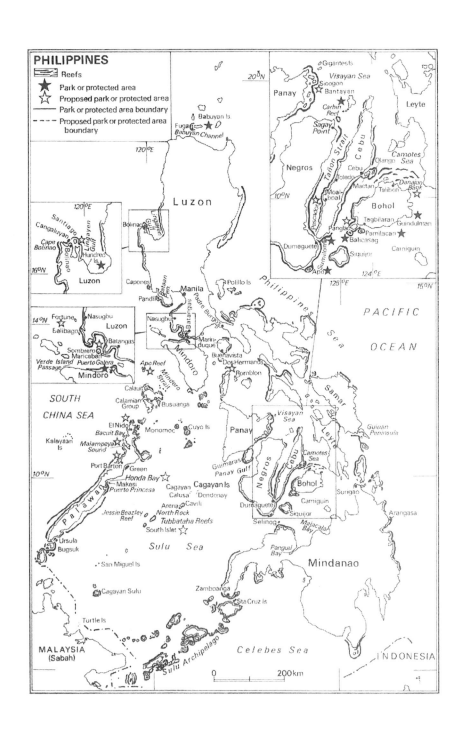

PHILIPPINES

- Reefs
- ★ Park or protected area
- ☆ Proposed park or protected area
- — Park or protected area boundary
- - - Proposed park or protected area boundary

20°N

120°E

Babuyan Is.
Fuga
Babuyan Channel

Luzon

120°E

Santiago
Cangaluyan
Cape Bolinao
Bolinao
Hundred Is.
Linayen Gulf
Lingayen Gulf
16°N
Luzon

Bolinao

Capones
Pandili
Manila
Polillo Is.

14°N
Fortune
Balibago
Nasugbu
Luzon
Batangas
Sombrero
Maricaban
Verde Island Passage
Puerto Galera
Mindoro

Nasugbu
Marinduque
Buenavista
Dos Hermanos
Romblon

Mindoro
Apo Reef
Mindoro Strait

Calauit
Calamian Group
Busuanga

El Nido
Bacuit Bay
Monomoc
Cuyo Is.
Kalayaan Is.
Malampaya Sound
Port Barton
Green
Honda Bay
Makesi
Puerto Princesa

SOUTH
CHINA SEA

Palawan

Cagayan
Calusa
Cagayan Is.
Dondonay
Arena
Cavili
North Rock
Jessie Beazley Reef
Tubbataha Reefs
South Islet

Panay
Guimaras
Panay Gulf
Negros
Cebu
Visayan Sea
Camotes Sea
Bohol
Camiguin
Dumaguete
Siquijor
Selinog
Majacalar Bay

10°N

Sulu Sea

Ursula
Bugsuk
San Miguel Is

Cagayan Sulu

Turtle Is

MALAYSIA
(Sabah)

Zamboanga
Sta Cruz Is

Celebes Sea

Sulu Archipelago

Panguil Bay
Mindanao
Surigao
Arangasa

Samar
Leyte
Guiuan Peninsula

INDONESIA

0   200km

PACIFIC

OCEAN

15°N

Gigantes Is.
Visayan Sea
Sicogon
Bantayan
Panay
Carbin Reef
Sagay Point
Leyte
Negros
Tañon Strait
Cebu
Olango
Camotes Sea
Toledo
Cebu
Moalboal
Mactan
Talibon
Danajon Bank
Bohol
Tagbilaran
Gundulman
Panglao
Pamilacan
Dumaguete
Balicasag
Siquijor
Carniguin
Apo

125°E
124°E

Philippine Sea

A Spy Among Us

By Dorothy Fleming

Brandylane Publishers, Inc.
Richmond, Virginia

Copyright 2009 by Dorothy Fleming. No portion of this book
may be reproduced in any form without written permission from
the publisher.

ISBN: 978-1-883911-80-5
Library of Congress Control Number: 2008937601

Brandylane Publishers, Inc.
Richmond, Virginia
www.brandylanepublishers.com

To my friend, Ruth, who encouraged me to write this book.

Author's Preface

A *Spy Among Us* is fiction, however, some of the street names, places, and personalities are real. The story is based solely on my dramatization of events. It is also spiced with some unconfirmed tales and opinions exchanged among the people in the streets of Manila and the various provinces.

In mid-January 1941, Lieutenant Colonel Bill Walters, chief of a small intelligence unit in Manila, sent a secret letter to Colonel Polson, a special liaison for the Philippine Unit in the War Department in Washington. In his letter, Walters mentioned the murders of three American Army intelligence officers in Manila, as well as increasing sabotage and espionage activity. He further stated that he suspected a German spy, Boris Meissner, to be guilty of the heinous crimes. He elaborated that Meissner had also aided the Japanese in forming an extensive spy network in Manila. Walters asked Polson to help him and the War Department in the replacement of the three dead Army officers. But instead of three replacements, only one officer, Major Jacob Victor McCord, was selected and dispatched to the intelligence unit in Manila.

McCord arrived in June 1941 and joined the intelligence unit, code name "Quest." The small clandestine group soon learned that, although the spy network was successfully in existence, apprehending Meissner and the leader of the spy network would be difficult.

The intelligence that had been available prior to Pearl Harbor and the occupation of the Philippines was negligent on nearly all levels. There had been a misuse of information, a lack of know-how and the ability to interpret reports with clear understanding. It showed what could happen when sound reports were ignored and not properly analyzed or used. Insights failed.

The Philippine Investigation Bureau (PIB) and the clandestine group Quest caused this failure and mishandled the intelligence obtained through telephonic eavesdropping, wiretapping and careless surveillance. The ineffective management and use of these materials temporarily placed them in a difficult position.

Introduction

Japan's audacious international political behavior and inclinations presaged the sentiment and apprehension of the United States. It confirmed what many world leaders suspected; Japan was convinced that she had divine signals from heaven to change the social structures of Asia into a new and important period of economic prosperity, a "Greater East Asia Co-Prosperity Sphere." She had gained several territories earlier and in 1931 insolently seized several countries: Manchuria, Korea, Formosa, the Pescadores Islands and the Ryuku Islands from China, as well as the southern Sakhalin and the Kuriles from Russia. Any speculations about Japan's intentions certainly stopped. By 1937, Japan proved to the world that her expansionist objective was not to be taken lightly. A commercial treaty with Siam in 1938 helped Japan accomplish some of her adventures in Southeast Asia, giving Japan an important foothold. (Siam was renamed Thailand in 1939.) The Japanese Empire laid claim to French Indo-China in mid-1941. Meanwhile, the Imperial Empire looked upon other nations in Southeast Asia with further objectives; the Philippines, then an American colony, which she long coveted for her strategic locations; Burma, the Netherlands East Indies, Malaya and several other southeast Asian countries for their raw materials.

While the war in Europe raged, Germany, Italy and Japan signed the Tripartite Pact in September 1940. The pact referred to sometimes as the Axis Alliance or Axis Military Powers exacerbated the United States' dilemma over Japan's intention to expand her reach in Asia, justifying her blatant propaganda of "Asia for Asians."

In the meantime, tension between the United States and Japan increased due to Japan's policy in China and Southeast Asia. During that time, Japan sent Ambassador Nomura on a peace mission and later in November 1941 Ambassador Kurusu was dispatched to the United States to aid Nomura in negotiating with the United States to improve relations with the two countries.

On December 7, 1941, however, Japan bombed Pearl Harbor. The following day, December 8, they also attacked the Philippines. That same day President Franklin D. Roosevelt declared war on Japan, bringing the nation into World War II. Four days later, on December 11, Germany and Italy declared war on the United States. By January 2, 1942, the Japanese had occupied Manila, the capital of the Philippines.

CHAPTER 1

It was February 1941. The Army captain's arms swung in cadence with his soldierly footsteps as he made his way through the munitions building, a temporary place built during World War I and current home of the War Department, located on Constitution Avenue and 20th Street in N.W. Washington, DC. His face was serious, his lips were tightly closed and his back was ramrod straight. He was on his way to a very specific section of what was known simply as the WD.

Securely held in his right hand was a large brown envelope. He quickly passed the conference room with its many chairs, maps and a big blackboard but slowed his steps as he passed the Secretary of War, Henry L. Stimson's office, with its large and well-appointed reception area. He gave it a brief but respectful side-glance and continued on. A moment later he neared an equally unostentatious room with shiny brass letters carefully nailed to the door—Office of the Chief of Staff (OCS). The door was wide open, and a junior officer was intently talking to someone on the telephone. In an adjoining room was the office of General George C. Marshall, Chief of Staff, United States Army. The captain had heard earlier that morning that General Marshall was scheduled to attend a briefing about Japan at the White House.

The captain's chest swelled with pride and patriotism. An American flag attached to a shiny brass flagstaff stood behind Marshall's wide and impressive desk. Every time he saw the American flag or heard the national anthem, his eyes became misty.

"God Bless America," he murmured and took a deep breath.

He had now reached that part of the WD where the highest leaders of the US Army held their offices. Framed photographs of some of the country's most famous military men—both dead and alive—lined the

1

walls of the corridors. A sense of tradition filled the air. They were the faces of brilliant men, some of whom were tough, uncompromising, arrogant and vain strategists. And those gone for centuries still silently demanded respect from their graves. Those who were still alive and active in their duties demanded—sometimes not so silently—such respect in order to reach the General officer's lofty height. Young Army officers must be proficient in all things—military science, discipline, and social and political correctness.

The corridor had an uncanny air that evoked heady dreams and high-level aspirations to follow in the footsteps of those military leaders whose greatness emanated from steel-like bravery, deep devotion to duty and love for their country regardless of personal flaws. Most of all, they were men with unshakable visions and purposes.

Without words, their eyes told the stories any up-and-coming officer could only hope to tell. George Washington. Andrew Jackson. Ulysses S. Grant.

The large portrait of George Washington occupied a special space in Marshall's office behind his desk. Carefully drawn on the wall above the picture was an impressive flag of the first thirteen colonies. A similarly large portrait of President Roosevelt was on the opposite wall.

As the captain walked on, he glanced at the large photographs of some current generals—Brigadier General Leonard T. Gerow, Major General George Grunert, Major General Walter T. Frank, Lieutenant General Walter A. Short, and Major General Douglas MacArthur.

Near the end of the corridor, the captain stopped to admire the framed photograph of a distinguished looking man, Brigadier General Brehon B. Somervell. He had heard rumors that the dynamic general was impatient and stubborn. General Somervell was in charge of building a permanent facility to house the growing War Department. With the war in Europe worsening, Japan's aggressive behavior in China and Southeast Asia no longer could be ignored, and the lack of space for the growing military and civilian government employees' presence in Washington was becoming intolerable. For years, rumors of a single complex to accommodate the entire department flooded the ranks. First it was talk, and now a reality. The captain was told by some of his officer friends that construction was to begin in about eight months.

As the captain stood there, he was elated about the prospect of a single headquarters for the WD.

"I wonder what they'd name the building?" he whispered to himself as he headed toward his destination. "I must ask Colonel Polson."

He relaxed slightly after leaving the area around Marshall's office and told himself how much he admired and respected the Chief of Staff for his demeanor and decisive mind. He slowed his steps as he approached the third door on his left with the name, Colonel Samuel Polson, Special Liaison Office, United States Army, engraved on a piece of Philippine mahogany. He pushed the door open and the smiling blond secretary, seated behind a large, well-polished desk greeted him with a patronizing smile.

"May I be of help, Captain?" she asked, while trying to read the name on the metal plaque pinned above the pocket of his uniform.

"May I help you Captain...Deaver?" she inquired, this time more graciously.

"Yes ma'am," he answered politely. "I've a message for Colonel Polson."

"Please wait here," she told him.

Shortly a voice boomed from behind the slightly closed door.

"Come in, Deaver." Polson's voice reverberated through the room.

Deaver went inside. He had had dealings with Colonel Polson before and liked the gray haired, tough-talking senior Army officer. He had heard that Polson had fought in France in World War I and received a medal for his bravery.

"Sit down, Deaver. How's the message center doing?" Polson asked with genuine interest, but he realized there had to be a reason for Deaver's visit.

"Busy, Sir," Deaver said as he handed him the envelope marked "Confidential." Polson opened it and read the message aloud.

"One of Chiang Kai-shek's Army generals, on a top secret assignment to the Philippines, was found dead in the streets of Manila with a dagger wound on his neck. His briefcase was missing as well as his personal papers. It appears to be murder. A separate letter has been dispatched to OCS with details of the incident. An investigation by the Army Intelligence Division, G-2, is ongoing. We need your help." Colonel

Polson finished with a hard sigh. "I'm sure they'll bring this to the immediate attention of General Marshall."

"Looks like trouble, Sir," Deaver said.

"Another goddamned problem! What in the hell is going on in that damn colony? They need my help? How? If G-2 and the military police can't find this asshole, how can I? Nothing seems to go right anymore. All the great scenery and all those damn nice people, you'd think people would grab a San Miguel beer and just relax. A month ago two American soldiers were ambushed and killed while on a group training on Bataan Peninsula."

He glanced at Deaver.

"You see why I'm so goddamn bald headed? It's because all the time I get warm and loving messages such as this. Ever since we moved to this damn Munitions Building, I swear. First the Germans invaded Poland and ever since I've heard nothing but trouble in Asia. Were you here then, Deaver?" Polson shouted.

"No, Sir. I was at Hawaiian Department G-2."

"Anyway, the offices of WD moved here from that large building just west of the White House on Pennsylvania Avenue. We shared it with the State and Navy Departments," Polson said, rubbing his head and smiling. "I tell ya, it was the most goddamn disorganized decision. But it was enlightening. Everyone was just too glad to get away from the Navy and especially the State Department. WD created a real sweet title for me, Special Liaison Officer." He paused. "You're an insightful and smart officer. Tell me what's not being said in this goddamn report and don't give me any bullshit!"

"With due respect to you Sir, I've given it some thought," Deaver said, shuffling his feet. "Here's the first scenario. You, as WD's liaison for the Philippine Department, the officials in the Philippines and the American Army brass here, and probably some members of Army intelligence will initially have to face Marshall and Stimson. If the Army leadership and G-2 can't solve it, then the State Department will have to carry the ball about the murder of the Chinese Nationalist general because of political repercussions. And if you all fail to appease Chiang Kai-shek, then President Roosevelt may be forced to enter the picture."

"I'm going to forward this message and a cover letter to Marshall suggesting that the State Department be kept out of this incident. God forbid. They seem to muddy the water when it comes to military affairs," Polson said, still clutching the letter. "Instead I say we have an American Army general sent immediately to China with the deepest of apologies to Generalissimo Chiang Kai-shek and a promise that guns and food be provided ASAP. I believe that will do it, Deaver. What's another dead general to the generalissimo? But I know he could certainly use more weapons and food for his troops."

Polson set the letter down on his desk and adjusted his chair.

"I'll alert Major Alba at Army intelligence of this letter. As G-2's front office staff officer, his opinion is highly regarded in General Marshall's circle."

"Good move, Sir. He's a fine officer to know," said Deaver, nodding his head in agreement. "I truly believe, Sir, that the real story behind the killing is spy related. My gut feeling tells me that Japanese spying in the Philippines is pervasive. I've mentioned that to a G-2 friend of mine sometime ago but I couldn't convince him of the seriousness of the situation. I'm basing my belief on continued Japanese expansionist behavior in Asia exacerbating tension not only in Europe but as well as in the United States," said Deaver, scratching his head. "With due respect to you, Sir. I'd like to hasten my belief that Japan is a rogue nation."

"Yes!" Polson said. "I especially found it troubling when the Japanese occupied Manchuria in 1931, and then very shortly thereafter, I believe in 1932, established that damn puppet government of Manchukuo. Japan moved vigorously in exploiting that country. And, of course, the Japanese-Chinese war in 1937, which Japan called an 'incident.' They're still at war with each other.

"And don't forget of their hold on Korea and Formosa," Polson said, now riled up. "How about their sly way of obtaining the French governor of French Indo-China in August of last year, for freedom of passage in the country and the use of the colonial territory's bases."

"They want to dominate that part of the world with the slogan of Greater East Asia Co-prosperity Sphere. Add all the Southeast Asian countries to that," Deaver said. "They like to make people there believe that their slogan is objective and purely economic, which I don't believe. So how can they take or invade a nation? First, through spying. Learning about their weaknesses and strengths. While I was on temporary duty in Manila to help revamp Clark Field's message center, I began hearing about a certain Japanese spy ring, but no one could really tell me that it actually existed.

"It's probably frivolous, but my second theory is this, Sir: perhaps the Chinese general stole someone's wife or he was killed because he was Chinese. As you are well aware, Sir, there are many Japanese in the Philippines."

Colonel Polson lit a cigarette.

"Deaver, your first theory is sound, but the second one is weak. The reason for the killing must have been deeper than the general just being Chinese or stealing someone's wife. I'm theorizing that the murdered Chinese general may have secretly come from the United States but stopped in Manila to discuss various matters," Polson said, with a deep exhale of smoke. "He may have been carrying important papers containing Order of Battle, strength and composition of the Nationalist Army and a signed agreement of a promise of mutual assistance and military and economic alliance between the United States and Chiang Kai-shek.

"I understand he was to meet the commanding general of the Philippine Department with a letter and instructions from Chiang to discuss the agreement and to specifically talk about the Philippines's role regarding military support in any way against Japan. Or, perhaps a Chinese communist killed the general. Don't forget Chiang and Mao Tse-tung, the leader of the Chinese Communist Party, despise each other. You may recall old Chiang refused to go after the Japanese, and instead he relentlessly went after the communist Chinese for a long time. He reasoned that Mao's communism was worse for China than Japanese expansionist activities. Of course, Chiang was eventually forced to reverse his policy about Japan."

"I like your theory, Sir," Deaver said nodding

"Deaver, if a spy killed that Chinese general, they'll never catch him," said Polson thoughtfully. "He would be too clever to be caught. There are spies in the Philippines because of the frequency of sabotage occurring in the Army bases there. It's a dedicated plot to destroy our American forces in the Philippines.

"Our military intelligence there, with the help of PIB, will have to deal with spies there and not continue to have security-myopia by ignoring reality. Also, it's easy to be indolent in paradise."

Captain Deaver concurred with Colonel Polson, who continued.

"Deaver, you seem to know what's going on among our intelligence groups. I guess being in the message center keeps you in the midst of things. How's the Far East Intelligence Division doing at Tempo H at Buzzard Point down there off M Street?"

"You mean in regard to Japan, Sir, or China?" Deaver asked.

"Not the Chinese Branch but the Japan-Watch Branch," answered Polson.

"They're both pretty active, Sir. I had lunch with a J-W Branch analyst just yesterday," Deaver said nonchalantly. "He told me, not giving away any secret information, that since Japan concluded a treaty with Germany and Italy several months ago, the whole division has been very busy. The J-W Branch has been placed on alert."

"I would imagine. That treaty affects China as well," Polson said. "Japan certainly admires Adolf Hitler. That pact makes me nervous. It appears to have certainly emboldened Japan to widen her scope of future dominance."

"Sir, do you have any plans regarding our conversation about the message?" Deaver said.

"Yes. I've a friend in Manila, Lieutenant Colonel Bill Walters. I'll drop him a letter and ask him to give me a report on the Chinese general's death and what he thinks the reason was," Polson said. "Bill is an intelligence officer and a good one. The last time I saw him he was on some hush-hush job about a spy in that city. I believe he said it was a German spy, but he wasn't quite sure then.

"It could be the same spy that killed the Chinese Nationalist general," Deaver said.

Polson looked into the distance and said in almost inaudible voice, "I have an uneasy feeling that this murder portends difficulties for the Philippines." And as Deaver was leaving, Polson called him back. "Did the Far East Division get a copy of this message?"

"Yes, it did, Sir," Deaver said.

"Send a copy of this message also to Colonel J. W. Duncan over at

Tempo U. He's a great fan of the Philippines."

"Right away, Sir," Deaver said.

He was nearly out the door when he turned around.

"I beg your pardon for asking, Sir, but hasn't Colonel Duncan been in meetings with G-2 about sending an intelligence officer to Manila?" Deaver asked hesitantly.

"Yes, he has. Glad you mentioned those meetings," Polson said. "Walters's letter mentioned that damn German spy. They've been trying like hell to catch the son of a bitch but with negative results."

Polson directed his gaze on Deaver and then lowered his head.

"The war in Europe is already in full effect. Hitler's march is sweeping, bloody, uncontrollable and devastating. Meanwhile Japan's dream of an empire in the Asian continent is being taken seriously by the United States and the Allied countries," Polson said grinning. "And here we are talking about a goddamn spy in Manila. Unbelievable."

Deaver's ears perked up. He enjoyed reading stories about spies, but it was the idea of real spies that got him going.

"You mentioned during our conversation a while back that your friend was, at that time, working on a hush-hush job about a spy. What was the spy's name?" Deaver asked with a boyish excitement.

"Yes," Polson said. "His name is Meissner."

"Sir, do you know the officer they're sending?" Deaver asked.

"Major Jacob Victor McCord, a staff officer in Colonel Duncan's group."

"Good choice," answered Deaver. "Mac is a good friend. He and I were at West Point together. He was a year ahead of me. I knew Mac before West Point."

"Not one word of this must escape your lips, Deaver," Polson said. "WD is treating McCord's assignment with the utmost secrecy. There are so many spies lurking around in Washington. Someone might pull a trigger and kill him."

"Not a word, Sir," Deaver said reassuringly. "Mac told me and another friend, John Stone in the FBI, of his difficult assignment in France. He's highly qualified for the job."

Deaver paused to clear his throat.

"Sir, on a separate subject. You know the superstructure General

Somervell is designated to build for the War Department?" Deaver asked. "What are they going to name it? Is it going to be something like the Kremlin?"

Colonel Polson looked directly at Captain Deaver.

"I don't know! I'm sure they'll all come out with a good one!" said Polson, somewhat annoyed.

The telephone rang on Polson's desk. It was Deaver's cue to leave the office. Polson nodded as Deaver saluted on his way out the door.

On his way back to his office, Deaver pondered about his friend Mac and felt deeply disappointed for him that his request for reassignment to a California intelligence group was not to be.

Jacob Victor McCord, Jr. was the only child of Helen and Jacob McCord. He was born in the small and conservative town of Kilmarnock in a house that his father built on the banks of Indian Creek, one of the many tributaries of the Chesapeake Bay, in the Northern Neck of Virginia.

Jake senior was a waterman. He taught his son, whom he and his wife called Mac, all there was to know about his trade and, above all, to love and respect the waters. He used to tell his son, "Mac, love the water, but also respect it. It could help you or destroy you."

Mac was tall for his age, and by the time he was nine years old, he was already an excellent swimmer and proficient in his father's trade. Crabbing did not make the McCords rich, but it made them a comfortable living, like Mac's father and grandfather before him. At times the bad weather would cause the family some financial problems, but as a whole it was a good life for them and among those in that part of Virginia society who proudly cherished their inherited trade. The watermen were a close knit and fiercely independent social group, who stubbornly clung to their way of life. But some who chose not to follow in their father and grandfather's footsteps, nevertheless, carried with them that independence and stubbornness often found among watermen.

One day, when Mac was two months away from his graduation from the Kilmarnock high school, tragedy struck his family. His father, Jake, had quietly died in his sleep from a massive heart attack. After his father's death, Mac informed his mother that he was dropping out of school and picking up what his father had left behind. But Helen would not hear any of it. She was resolute in her insistence that he graduate from high school while she made the living for both of them. First, she sold their boat and applied for work with Mr. and Mrs. Elmer Brock of neighboring Irvington, Virginia. She became the hostess to their popular and successful Irvington Inn, on Carter Creek. The Brocks knew the McCords well and had a high regard for them. Mr. Brock had been, for many years, the principal buyer of the McCord's live blue crabs. Also, through the help of the influential Brock family, Mac, shortly after his graduation, was accepted to West Point.

After his graduation from West Point as Second Lieutenant, the young shavetail was immediately sent to an Infantry unit, where he stayed a year. As an Infantry officer, his next assignment took him to Panama for three years. There, he not only learned to read, write, and speak Spanish, but an officer in Army personnel advised him to make intelligence his primary specialty. When he came back to Washington, he applied to the War Department for an Army intelligence position, and within a short time, he was accepted.

Mac was happy as an intelligence officer, assigned to G-2 headquarters to coordinate the flow of intelligence on Europe. His grasp of Hitler's surging dominance and of European affairs attracted the attention of Colonel J.W. Duncan, Chief of Army Group1/Europe at Tempo U. Duncan needed an officer of Mac's caliber who could also write current and political articles for the War Department's publication about Europe and Adolf Hitler. Duncan was a strict officer who took intelligence very seriously. From him, Mac learned the value of not believing every piece of report he read or any information he heard as valid

CHAPTER 2

In another part of Washington, an Army major bounded up the stairs two steps at a time. He could hear the telephone ringing loudly and incessantly. He slammed through the halfway-open door to his office and scampered to his desk. But of course, it stopped ringing as he was about to pick it up. He had been working long hours for three straight weeks and was already on edge.

"Hell! I bet that was WD Publications," he murmured. "Demanding bastards! I told them they'd have their article by this evening. I swear those editors work around-the-clock."

The telephone started ringing again. He reached across his desk and grabbed it. "Political and Subversive Section," he answered tersely but politely.

"Is this Major Jacob McCord?" the female voice on the other end of the line inquired.

"Yes, it is, ma'am."

"I'm sorry, Sir. I didn't recognize your voice. This is the FBI Foreign Documentation and Espionage Section. Mr. John Stone asked me to get you on the line. He had to step out of the office for a minute," she paused. "Oh. Hold on, please. Here he is now."

"Mac. John here. I had a feeling you'd be in early this morning. You told me a couple of days ago you had to turn in an article today. Had your morning coffee?"

"Nope! Wilson isn't here yet. What gives, old buddy? It's 0530. What're you doing up with the chickens?" Mac said reclining in his chair.

"We're on graveyard shift, Mac. Been here since midnight. I understood from the boss there'd be more of it coming. That war in Europe has us going like crazy ducks. Lots of subversives are infiltrating the US via

Canada and Mexico. How about you? Why so early? Your 'pubs's branch nipping you at the heel?"

"Yeah. The chief editor is a relentless tyrant. I've a deadline at 1700 hours," said Mac, stifling a yawn. "What's up?"

"Mac, do you have today's Times Herald?"

"No. Why?"

"On page eleven is a horrible murder story. Since you're in the intelligence business and you've been in Europe helping the French find that spy, I thought the article might be of interest to you. You might even know what asshole committed that awful crime." Stone muffled the phone on his chest.

"Hello?" Mac said.

"Okay, Mac? I've got to go. My boss just stuck his head in the door. He wants to see me again. Take care," Stone said, slamming down the phone.

Mac looked strangely at the phone and then set down the receiver.

"Shit," he said under his breath and shrugging his shoulders. "I don't know what the hell he was talking about. But I probably need to read the article."

He jumped up from his chair, went downstairs, passed the guard and opened the entrance door to the street. He stood there momentarily enjoying the early morning fresh air and the still uncrowded streets. He was on his way to buy the Times Herald when the traffic light turned red.

A streetcar stopped in front of the two-story wooden structure located on the corner of 12th and Constitution Avenue, N.W. On the front of the building were the large painted letters—TEMPO U. To the left side of the wide entrance was a thick square piece of honed and stained cypress wood nailed to the siding, UNITED STATES ARMY etched into it. The building was one of several temporary structures built in Washington during World War I. This particular one was given the letter U and officially identified as the Temporary U Building.

Compared to the fortresses of the United States Post Office Department, the Interstate Commerce Commission, the Federal Communication Commission and the Federal Bureau of Investigation, Tempo U looked out of place. Beyond fleeting curiosity, nobody gave it a second thought. Only those in the secret world of intelligence knew that the drab-looking building was occupied by "spooks."

Among the spooks elite, Tempo U was known as the "little house by the road." Despite the humbleness of the temporary building, all the spooks were cognizant of their importance in the vast mosaic of governmental affairs. It was a divine calling whose role was vital to the security of the nation, regardless of in what building their desks were located.

The doors of the electric streetcar opened wide and several people, some civilians and some military stepped down and carefully avoided the puddles of water left by the melting snow. The past two or three days had been uncommonly warm for February. Mac could not remember what last year was like. He wished that he had on civilian clothes instead of the regulation uniform, as the sooty water soaked the cuffs of his pants.

He scuttled across the street to a newsboy standing in front of the Interstate Commerce Commission and watching over his stack of papers.

"Read all about it! Read all about the war in Europe!" he shouted in a staccato monotone. Mac handed the newsboy a dime and stuck the paper under his arm and hustled back across the street, disappearing through Tempo U's doors.

"G' morning, Major Mac," greeted the friendly civilian guard, who had just come on duty. Looking sharp in his special issue blue uniform, the guard sat alertly behind the wrap-around counter under the commanding sign—ARMY GROUP 1/EUROPE—the counter in shimmering silver and the sign in big black letters.

"Good morning, Mr. Wilson," Mac returned the greeting as he displayed his identification pass clipped neatly to his necktie.

Mr. Wilson gave Mac's ID a sharp scrutiny as he always did the IDs of those who entered the building, regardless of who they were, and nodded his approval.

"Thet thar ring's sure hantsome, major," the guard said noticing Mac's left hand resting on the counter. "Furst time t'wearin' it? I ain't seen it 'fore. A precious stone's it? Must've cost ye a hunk."

"It's a blue sapphire and those are diamonds on each side," Mac answered self-consciously. "I brought it back from France." Mac paused and then continued in his pleasant and distinctly Tidewater, Virginia accent. "Warm enough for you yet, Mr. Wilson?"

"I likes it warm. S'matter of fact I wish it were summer hot," Mr. Wilson said, this time giving Mac's ID just a glance. "Okay, Sir."

The guard nodded his approval again for Mac to go inside and then pulled out his pocket watch.

"Ye must truly be a early riser. Ev' since my transfer here, ye'd been comin' in real early as some 'em others."

Mac nodded. "Yeah. Always lots to do."

"Thet 'em Chemical Industry 'n Weapons Sections 'ave real been burnin' t' midnight oil."

"I know," Mac answered. "They've been working around the clock for some time."

Mac sniffed the air and smiled.

"I know why I come this early, Mr. Wilson. I like the way you brew that coffee," Mac said. "Strong!"

"Yeah. Navy strong. Not many 'n TEMPO U like my coffee," Wilson said, taking a sip from his own mug. "Ye sure always welcome t' all cups ye need all day. I keep thet there java pipin' hot for ye knowin' ye prefer my coffee t' thet there Post Office Department's cafeteria's coffee. Weak!"

"Thank you. I believe I'll have a large cup now. I need it," Mac said. "I'll drop a silver dollar in your box as my contribution for the next two week's coffee, cream and doughnuts."

Before going back to his office, Mac made a point to pass by the Railroad, Terrain and Area Studies Section to pick up some data on Nazi Germany, which he would incorporate into his report. The files were neatly arranged and waiting for him.

Back at his office, he left the door wide open, turned on all the lights in the room and placed the doughnut wrapped in a paper napkin and cup of coffee on his desk. He proceeded to open several windows to let fresh air in the stale room. Not satisfied, Mac turned on the old fan sitting on top of a safe in the corner.

He quickly made himself comfortable by removing his olive-drab topcoat and jacket and hanging them on the rack behind his chair. After taking a big swallow of coffee, Mac placed the pile of papers on his desk.

He grabbed the rough draft of his article and began editing. Aside from a few misspellings and one major grammatical mistake, he was pleased with what he had finished. He then sat there for a good ten minutes, but no inspiring thoughts came to him immediately. Instead, he wondered what Colonel Duncan, his boss and Chief of Army Group 1/Europe, research division, wanted to discuss with him.

Yesterday, the Colonel had accidentally bumped into him in the hall.

"Oh, McCord," Duncan said to him nonchalantly. "I'll have my secretary, Mrs. Ottis, call you tomorrow."

Mac shrugged his shoulders and wistfully hoped that it would be about the reassignment to California that he had put in nearly a year and a half ago, shortly after his tour of duty in France ended. He was anxious to give Deaver a call if anything about his reassignment to California had come in. He glanced at his watch, but it was still too early. He would have to wait another two hours. Deaver rarely came in before 8 a.m.

Meanwhile, he was going to concentrate on his work, and maybe if he finished, he told himself, he could leave the office a little early and look at the car he had been admiring at District Auto Sales. The car would be great for the drive to California.

Pleased with the thought, he picked up his fountain pen and was poised to begin writing, when he suddenly remembered the news article. He grabbed the paper and began scanning the front page. Like most days, the war in Europe was the major topic, and there was an analysis on the fall of France. After truce was signed in June of last year, the seat of government was moved to Vichy on the Allier River in central France, which was still unoccupied by the Germans. But, according to rumors, it wouldn't be that way for long.

Mac started to reminisce about his assignment in France. He learned two valuable lessons as a covert intelligence agent on the trail of an elusive spy: do not take your adversary for granted, and sometimes hard work and long hours did not mean a successful operation.

In 1937, Army Intelligence sent Mac to France. He had been there before with his parents, touring through most of Europe shortly after he finished high school. But it was his first time in France for the military that year.

McCord was assigned to spend a two-year tour of duty with a small

American Army intelligence group stationed in Paris. The group was assigned to work with the French military intelligence unit on a special, top-secret assignment.

The team of four Army officers was to help their French Army officers counterparts, under the leadership of Colonel Fabre, gather intelligence on a clever German master spy, Boris Meissner. The infamous Meissner was known all over Europe as a notorious killer and saboteur. It was their job to ferret him out. Meissner's existence was known only by hearsay and had never actually been clearly identified by either intelligence unit. The French group believed that he was responsible for killing a French general and his aide and dynamiting two of France's weapons arsenals in the little-known town of Etampes, about thirty-one miles outside Paris. Yet those were just a few on a long list of sabotages that Meissner was suspected of carrying out. They wanted Meissner dead or alive.

Colonel Fabre and a French civilian secret agent named Duvalier visited the headquarters of the American team often. Duvalier was introduced to McCord and the other officers as a highly influential and trustworthy man, according to the French military intelligence circle. After the first dozen or so visits, Duvalier and Mac sparked a special bond with each other.

"I like your dedication to work," the French agent told Mac one day within earshot of Lieutenant Colonel George Cooke, the head of the US intelligence team. "We in France have worked very hard to catch Meissner.But we are not lucky. I do not know if we will ever catch him. He is a chameleon. Catching Meissner is like trying to catch a shadow. He stays in one place only long enough to wreak havoc, then disappears. But who knows, you Americans might succeed one day."

Duvalier then looked squarely at Mac.

"You are stubborn, intelligent and perhaps luckier than I. Maybe it will be you who will catch Meissner. Oui, mon ami?"

Mac vividly remembered asking Duvalier during that conversation, "You seem to know this German spy well. What makes him tick?"

Duvalier then laughed at the word, "tick."

"Tick?" he asked Mac. "Tick. You mean, why does he kill? Why does he destroy? Let me see if I can explain to you what makes Meissner tick. A spy discovers some weakness of his enemy. But this Meissner is more

A Spy Among Us

than a spy. I have analyzed him and his activities for many years."

Duvalier then walked dramatically to the window overlooking a narrow and busy street below. Mac followed him.

"What makes Meissner tick, my Yankee friend, is his obsession with Adolf Hitler," Duvalier said, gazing down on the rainy Paris streets. "His fanaticism drives him to deep dark hatred towards anyone who criticizes Hitler or Nazi Germany. To him, Nazi Germany is Hitler. He will attack and kill anyone. Vous comprenez?"

As time passed, Duvalier began to confide in Mac, who in turn kept careful notes, passing them to Lieutenant Colonel Cooke.

One bit of story contained in Mac's report that interested Cooke was, although Meissner was German-born, he was educated in the United States for most of his young life. Meissner spoke near-fluent Japanese and fluent, unaccented German, French and English. He truly was a chameleon.

As months passed and the sabotage grew bolder and more destructive in France and other parts of Europe, the search for Meissner became intense and dangerous. However, to the chagrin and frustration of the two teams, they had no idea what the German spy looked like. There was no accurate description of his appearance.

The teams trounced all over France, Holland and Belgium after numerous complaints of espionage and sabotage from those countries. All evidence recovered pointed to Meissner. Soon, other countries lent their resources to help catch him, but the tight security networks that were set up in France, Holland, Belgium, Luxembourg and Switzerland proved useless.

"Looking for someone whom no one can identify is futile," Colonel Fabre once said to Mac. "Boris Meissner will continue to be elusive. He is invisible."

"Sir," Mac said one day to Cooke, "Why did the French bother to ask for our help? We don't know who it is we're looking for, except by name. And we're not even sure of that."

"The whole thing is crazy," answered Cooke. "The French have had a high regard for our Army intelligence ever since we blew the cover of a German spy posing as a staff member in the French Embassy in Washington. They had a clever spy in their inner circle and didn't know

17

it. There was a lot of hoopla about that on the radio, thanks to Walter Winchell and the newspapers. Now they think we can do it again."

One evening there was a knock on the door of Mac's apartment. The messenger handed him a note from Lieutenant Colonel Cooke.

"Mac, come quickly to apartment 121G at 12665 La Rue du Seine. It's a block from that Chinese restaurant, Le Dragon. Duvalier was just stabbed." Mac read the strangely scribbled handwriting aloud. "No one knows how much longer he'll live and he is refusing to talk to either Fabre or me. He keeps on asking for you."

Mac reached Duvalier's apartment without difficulty. The French secret agent had invited him there a number of times to join him and his mistress, Michelle, for dinner.

A disheveled Colonel Fabre met Mac at the door and led him to Duvalier, lying in a bloody heap of towels on the bedroom floor.

Mac got down on his knees and began talking into the dying man's ear. Fabre said he would go outside for a smoke.

"Bon soir, Duvalier," Mac whispered. "I'm here, your Yankee friend, Jake McCord. Mac."

Duvalier's eyes fluttered for a while then showed recognition.

"Mac, I do…not have…much time left. I'm dying," Duvalier whispered unevenly. "I…am a double…agent…for France…and Germany. Fabre does not know it…nor anyone…in the…French…intelligence or government."

Duvalier stopped and began breathing heavily.

"I am…a smart…Frenchman, no?" Duvalier said trying to conjure up a smile.

"Yeah, you're smart," said Mac, supporting the agent's head with his hands. "Who did this to you?"

"Meissner," Duvalier said in a barely audible whisper. "He might still be out…down…the hall."

Mac gasped upon hearing the name and quickly turned his head in the direction of the door. He thought he had seen a man standing in the doorway watching him and Duvalier. He barely caught a glimpse of the man. He ran to the hallway, but no one was there.

"Duvalier, what do you know about Meissner?"

"Little, and most from rumors. He…is…a loner. He hates spies against Germany and hates…anyone…who dislikes Germany," Duvalier said, repeating information he had already told Mac many times. By then Duvalier's face was serious and stared directly at Mac.

"He tracks them down and cuts off…their heads, legs or fingers…his style of killing. Like a signature," Duvalier said.

"Why did he not just cut off your head?" Mac asked, counting all ten fingers on the agent's bloody hands. Mac then began to wonder if Meissner was watching in on them. And was it he who opened the door to the room? Fabre never came back to the room.

"He did not have time…to cut off my head…or my legs or my fingers. We struggled." Duvalier paused. "I scared him…I told…him the police were on their way…here. Michelle was…with me…here. She…escaped and went to get Fabre. But he was too late."

Duvalier's breathing was becoming shorter and more difficult.

"Can Michelle identify him?"

"No…everything happened…fast. I do not think she got a good look at him. She was too frightened."

Suddenly, someone was shouting outside the room. A French soldier whom Mac asked to guard the corridor to Duvalier's room shouted, "Halt! Halt or I'll shoot!"

Then the noise of running footsteps were heard and two gunshots rang out. And then there was silence.

The French soldier ran to the room.

"I was coming around the corner when I saw a man peeping in the room. I am sure he saw both of you and everything that went on in there. I am sorry he escaped, Sir."

Mac thanked the soldier.

Meanwhile, there was more urgency in Mac's voice. "Duvalier, who else knows about Meissner?"

There was no response from the dying man.

"Duvalier. What does Meissner look like?" Mac asked.

Duvalier's voice was getting softer and faltering, more difficult to understand.

"Tall…over six feet. Blond, thinning hair…about forty-five years… old. Maybe more…"

"How about his eyes. What color are his eyes?"

"Eyes?" Duvalier managed to shake his head. "But he has a birthmark that…looks like…a…tattooed…swastika on…the back of…his left shoulder."

"Who else knows about the birthmark?"

Duvalier did not answer.

"Do you hear me? Who else knows about the birthmark? French intelligence? British intelligence?" Mac asked.

"I…don't know. Perhaps from rumors."

"How'd you know about it?" Mac asked and noticed that Duvalier's left hand was clenched.

"In…a health spa in Strasbourg. I heard…a messenger boy called out his full name…he had a message for him. This…irritated Meissner. He cursed out…the messenger and told him…to get out. Then Meissner looked around. He thought…he was alone. He did not become aware of my presence…until a little later…I was called to the…telephone on the intercom."

"Is there anything else? Anything?"

Duvalier's breathing was becoming very heavy. "Very difficult to catch…him. He is an expert on disguises. Everyday he is…a different person."

"How would you know that, Duvalier?" Mac asked.

"He told me. He…informed…me because I believed that he already… planned to kill me." He took one deep breath. "Mac…promise not…to tell Fabre…or anyone that I…am a double agent," Duvalier said as tears traced paths on his blood-stained face. "My wife…my ten year…old daughter, Simone. They will be…harmed…and ridiculed. Best they…do not know."

"I promise," Mac whispered in Duvalier's ear, wiping the tears with a clean towel.

Duvalier took a deep breath again. "Mac…in my…hand. It…is for you. It is Meissner's. During the struggle…" His fist opened and a ring fell into Mac's hand. Duvalier took a long breath and whispered, "Mac… Japan…Japan is…"

And, just about then Fabre and Cooke ran into the room. Fabre bent down and placed his ear close to Duvalier's mouth and then gave his face two quick gentle slaps.

"He's not breathing," Fabre said.

"Duvalier! Can you hear me?" Mac asked, shaking Duvalier's shoulders.

There was no response.

Mac rose to his feet and turned to Colonel Fabre and Lieutenant Colonel Cooke and opened his hand.

"Colonel Cooke. Colonel Fabre," he said, displaying the ring to them.

"Keep it," both officers told him.

"Duvalier gave it to you," Cooke said.

"I saw him drop it in your hand," Fabre said. "It was his dying wish that you should have it." Fabre sighed.

"Did you understand what he said?"

Mac shook his head.

Two weeks after the murder of Duvalier, a man was found dead floating on the Seine minus his head and legs. He had a swastika tattoo on the back of his left shoulder. However, French authorities could not determine whether it was really Meissner. It was even difficult to guess the height of the dead man. But the French police, urged quietly by French intelligence, distributed the story of Meissner's death to the French newspapers. They had speculated that with the release of the news, the master spy would get cocky and carelessly show himself.

As his memory turned back to Europe, Mac felt lucky to be sitting at his desk at that moment. He remembered vividly how worried both the American and French intelligence teams were when on September 3, 1939. France and Great Britain declared war on Germany, and less than four weeks later, on September 27, Warsaw, Poland fell to the Nazis. They all agreed that Belgium, the Netherlands, Luxembourg and France would not be too far behind. During that period of conquest by the Germans, the hopes of finding or capturing Meissner were stomped out.

"There is always tomorrow," said Colonel Fabre during a somber meeting with the two teams. He turned around and faced them all. "Hopefully Meissner will disappear in this war."

A few months after his return from Europe, Mac ran into Lieutenant Colonel Cooke in Washington. Cooke told him that when the Germans occupied Paris on June 13, 1940, Colonel Fabre's team fled and eventually joined General Charles de Gaulle in London.

Mac reached for his coffee cup and became aware that his hands were shaking.

"What the hell is the matter with me? I have to get out of Washington before I go nuts," Mac said to himself. "All at once I'm a bundle of nerves."

He took a deep breath and another swallow of coffee and began flipping through the Times Herald. Either because Mac forgot all about his request for a transfer to California, or his 1700 deadline was postponed for another hour that afternoon, he began to relax. Now and then he would stop reading and again thank his lucky stars that he had left France before the German troops took Paris.

After the Herald's analysis of the fall of France, there was an especially heavy spread of articles and photographs on the almost nightly bombings of London by the German Luftwaffe. The blitzkrieg caused unbelievable destruction, according to the newspaper. Then he turned to page 11A, a UPI article with the strange title: "Who Was He?"

The item, accompanied by a photograph of two cars barely recognizable amongst the flames and smoke enveloping them, immediately aroused Mac's interest.

(UPI, London, Feb 1941) Tuesday evening in the tiny town of Huntingdon, about 59 miles north of London, two automobiles were totally destroyed in an explosion that witnesses said was thought to be another German bomb.

Huntingdon police rushed to the scene and managed to bring the fire under control. The driver of one of the cars was unrecognizable, but police were unable to locate the second driver amongst the piles of twisted metal. After hours of searching, a man, estimated to be about 5 feet 8 inches, was discovered lying on an embankment 200 meters away from the debris. His head and his ten fingers were missing. Police are searching for a person of interest, described as a tall man, in his mid-40s, with

balding blond hair. The man was last spotted talking to
the police at the scene of the accident around 3:45 a.m.

Mac set the paper on his lap and rested the back of his head on his
hands.

"I wonder who was talking to the police?" he mumbled to himself.
"The description of the man in the ditch sounded like what Duvalier
told me. Only Boris Meissner kills that way."

He shivered slightly and unconsciously removed the blue sapphire
ring from his finger. He reached for the magnifying glass on his desk
and for a hundredth time read the tiny inscriptions inside the ring—To
Sonny, Love, Mother.

Mac had been back in Washington over a year and until a few minutes
ago had not given Meissner a second thought. He started to get up from
his chair, but something compelling tugged at his mind. Strange that he,
Mac, should remember clearly what Duvalier had told him not long after
Mac had joined the US intelligence team.

"Catching Meissner is like trying to catch a shadow," Mac said to
himself. "What the hell. It can't hurt."

He picked up a telephone on an isolated desk—a secure line—and
asked for John Stone. A male voice answered.

"Stone speaking."

"This is Mac. Thanks for your suggestion. The article in the Herald is
very interesting," Mac said. "How's your section coming along, John?"

"Keeps me busy. I'm collating a barrel of info coming in from the FBI,
the military intelligence groups and our friends in Europe," Stone said
before cutting the small talk. "The stranger in the newspaper. Do you
think he could have been the murderer?"

"Yeah. I've a gut feeling it was Boris Meissner," Mac said. "However,
every heinous crime such as that can't be Meissner's fault, or can it? Got
a folder on him? I'm curious."

"Funny you should ask about his folder, Mac," Stone said. "My boss
told me yesterday to transfer the folder from Inactive File to Watch
File. And you're the second person to inquire about him today. One of
our own requested data on Meissner just yesterday. I believe he said his
name was FBI Agent Edward Martin. This Meissner must be wanted for

murder or sabotage on American soil. Give me a little time while I get the folders."

"Okay," Mac answered.

Stone was back after a few minutes.

"Have your pencil and paper ready," Stone said. "You might want to make some notes while I read it to you. It's pretty short."

Meissner is believed to be the illegitimate child of German native Claus Meissner and an American woman. The mother's name is unknown, and her area and place of residence in the US is unknown. Another report suggests Baltimore. His mother is believed to be alive. No known description of her. Except for mother, no known relatives in US or Germany. Father dead. Boris Meissner believed to be his real name. Some unconfirmed sources say he occasionally uses his mother's maiden name, but reports fail to identify her name. He also uses many other aliases that the Bureau thinks he borrows from obituaries. Probably has many passports. One name used and known to our European friends and shared with the FBI is Leon Barclay. He uses the Christian name Leon often and couples it with a different family name.

"Got all that down, Mac?"

"Anything else, John? Got anything from the Brits? They always have a leg up when it comes to intelligence."

"Wait a minute, Mac. Let me take a quick look at these reports we haven't filed yet. A lot of them are real dogs, mostly from unreliable sources," said Stone, quickly flipping through a folder marked "Unreliable Sources" and lifting out three pieces of paper.

"Hey, Mac. Here are three that seem to jive."

"I've got my pen ready."

"These are from French agents and marked; sources cannot be confirmed. I'll read them."

Meissner has been known to express great love for his American mother. He is such an expert on disguises, you would think that you have met two or three different men that day.

This third one is from the Brits.

Meissner's boyhood friend, Franz Linz, now living in Liverpool, made a comment to a covert British intelligence agent one day in a pub when the name Meissner came up. According to Linz, the Meissner he remembered had a great love for his mother. He constantly talked about her and bragged that when he grew up, he would like to be with her in the United States. Without any prodding from the agent, Linz continued to say that he believed Meissner would risk his life to be with her, even for just a short while. Boris had a habit of violence when something was taken from him that belonged to him. "One day I picked up his toy and took it home. When he discovered what I did, he came to our house and almost choked me to death, but luckily my mother was present. I was only seven, and Boris was six years old when I knew him. He lived with his father's sister. I don't remember now what he looked like, but those things I do remember about him."

"Source seems very good," Stone said. "Got all that down, Mac?"

"Yeah. Do you have anything about him attending school in the US? I was told he did. I just want to confirm it."

"Nope."

"Say, John, remember the ring I brought back from France? Remember the inscriptions inside the ring?"

"I do."

"John, could the name 'Sonny' be one of Meissner's aliases?"

"I don't know. I've never seen any reports on it."

"Have you tried Navy's Office of Naval Intelligence, John?"

"Yes! ONI has zero info!"

"Another thing, John, before you go. Is there any info on Meissner having a birthmark on his upper left shoulder? Reliable human intelligence, perhaps?"

"Yes, I do have some info regarding a birthmark, but from unreliable sources…rumors. Nothing has been confirmed. But the FBI and several sources have confirmed that Meissner has an obsession for women but tends to hurt them and may even kill them if they shatter his fancy. He strikes me as a sadist and a compulsive killer."

"Thanks. You have been a great help." Mac paused. "I'll ask Ellen Haggarty, our chief of biographics, and see if she has anything on Meissner. I'll send you a mimeographed copy for your file. But if I don't, it means her data are the same as yours."

"Great," Stone answered. "Any info you can provide will help us."

Mac heard the click on the other end of the telephone. He reached for The Times Herald but did not even glance at the article. He just sat there. He did not move.

CHAPTER 3

Mac finally pushed himself up from his chair and walked to the window behind his desk and looked down on Constitution Avenue. Throngs of people milled around and cars, taxicabs and trolleys sped along. Amazing, he thought, that he should be getting additional information on Meissner now that he was no longer in Paris. He didn't envy anyone who was assigned to search for the German spy.

He enjoyed his present work but conceded that humans were curious animals and that being in intelligence had a way of satisfying that curiosity.

He drained the rest of the coffee from his cup and was flabbergasted when he realized that the time had inched up on him. It was already seven o'clock. In an hour, he reminded himself that the rest of the office would start reporting for work. Typewriters would start banging and telephones ringing.

He had to at least finish the first article in his two-part series on the rise of Adolf Hitler and his political impact in Europe in the coming years. Next week, he planned to start with part two—will Hitler's maniacal visions of domination change the face of the world?

Mac hoped no one would disturb him, at least for the next few hours. He started writing, but the article in the paper kept distracting him. Just as he finally willed himself back to work, the telephone rang.

Captain Jones, who had just arrived at his desk in the room adjacent to Mac's desk, answered the telephone.

"Hey, Mac. On the double," Jones said loudly. "The old man wants to see you ASAP."

Mac raised his hand without looking up from his article to indicate that he had heard Jones. A frown appeared on his face. He just knew

Colonel Duncan was calling about the study. He shook his head in frustration. For the last week, WD's Publication Branch had been pushing him for the first part of his article in order to publish it in the widely-read magazine, Army Talk. It had been difficult to write because of the complexities that had been quickly evolving in Europe and the paucity of reliable intelligence information. Mac wished his information from radio and newspapers were from more definitive military sources. However, he was comfortable in that much of the information contained in his report was confirmed by British intelligence. He was certain that he would finish it by the end of the day.

Mac drew a deep breath and reluctantly eased himself out of his chair and stretched his long wiry body. He hoped that the colonel's call would be about his reassignment to California. In that case, he would not have to call Deaver. He straightened his necktie and tucked it inside his shirt, grabbed the olive-green service coat from the rack and hurried out of the room. In his mind, things were turning on the plus side for him. He was elated, but still had some suspicions.

He ran down the steps, turned an abrupt left and entered the open room with a large sign above the entrance door—Chief: Colonel J.W. Duncan, Research Division, Europe. He cleared his throat loudly several times to attract the attention of the division's secretary who was busily filing folders into the gun-colored metal safe. Waiting to be recognized, he let his eyes wander around the room and let them settle on a large picture of FDR staring directly at him from the other side of the office. He admired President Roosevelt and liked that photograph of him. There was one just like it at the War Department, Mac thought, clearing his throat again to get the secretary's attention, but who obviously was unaware of his presence.

"Excuse me, Mrs. Ottis. I…"

"Oh, Major McCord. I did not know you were standing there," the attractive blond woman apologized. "Please, be seated. Colonel Stewart of the US Army Corps of Engineers is still with Colonel Duncan. He has had a wave of visitors since he came to work early this morning."

"Would you want for me to come back, Mrs. Ottis?"

She shook her head as the telephone rang. "Research Division, Europe," she answered. "Yes, Sir, Senator Sidel. I shall tell the colonel that he should join you and the French Military Attaché at the Occidental Restaurant tomorrow for lunch at twelve noon."

She looked at Mac.

"It is like this from Monday to Friday and sometimes even on Saturdays. I'm so sorry you had to wait," she said, glancing at her boss's closed door. "I think Colonel Stewart is coming out now."

A short, burly man came out of the room and thanked Mrs. Ottis for giving him the time in Duncan's schedule.

"It was important that I see him today," he explained as he walked out of the room.

"You can go inside now, Major McCord," she said, hurriedly jotting down the senator's message. She went ahead of Mac and gave the yellow message slip to her boss.

"Shut the door and sit down, McCord. We've something important to discuss," Duncan said, wiping his spectacles with a handkerchief he drew from his back pocket and then passing it across his florid, perspiring face. The big ceiling fan was whirling around.

"Thank you, Sir," Mac said and sat down, planting his feet wide apart on the carpeted floor and looking directly at his superior officer.

"I'm going right to the point," Duncan said brusquely, studying the strong face and stubborn eyes of the younger officer. He leaned across his wide desk. "Know anything about Southeast Asia, specifically the Philippine Islands?"

Mac shook his head slowly, his straight eyebrows raised ever so slightly in surprise, but his unflinching steel-blue eyes remained on the colonel's face.

"Well, Sir," Mac replied. "I had read way back that the US and that country have had close ties since Admiral George Dewey's victory against Spain in Manila Bay. That was during the Spanish-American War, Sir."

Mac felt uneasy being questioned about a country he had little knowledge about, and he resented that he was not given an opportunity to brush up on it.

"The Philippine archipelago has about 7,100 islands," said Duncan, "and Luzon, where Manila is located, is the largest. Mindanao, way down south, is the second largest island."

"Sir, I am embarrassed to admit that I know very little about the

Philippines. Those Southeast Asian countries are kind of remote and exotic places." He shook his head again. "What I know about the Philippines could fit in a thimble."

"It's obvious. But there's always time to learn, McCord. How about the Philippine Department? Have you read about it?" Duncan persisted.

"Yes, Sir. I understand it is the highest US Army command in the Philippines," Mac said with an increasingly puzzled look on his face. "If I may ask, Sir, what is all this about?" He passed his fingers through his crew-cut reddish blond hair while his steady eyes continued to look directly at the veteran officer.

Duncan took out a box of matches from his shirt pocket and reached for the pack of Camel cigarettes on his desk. He deliberately tapped the bottom of the pack until one was halfway out and extended his arm to Mac sitting across the desk from him.

"Cigarette?"

"Yes. Thank you, Sir."

Colonel Duncan lit his own cigarette, inhaled deeply and let out a cloud of thick, gray smoke towards the ceiling.

"I'm glad they finally made a decision. It has taken the War Department six weeks to the day to find a suitable Army intelligence officer," Duncan said. "Late last evening a courier from the department handed me an envelope stamped 'Confidential'. In it were your Orders."

Mac remained silent, but his face showed puzzlement.

"I realize that I'm not making any sense, McCord."

There was a momentary silence.

"It's about you! Your Manila assignment!" Duncan said with a grin.

Mac straightened his back and tapped his cigarette gently in the ashtray on the desk in front of him.

"WD okayed my Manila assignment?" he said, more puzzled than ever.

"Yes, the War Department did, McCord. Didn't mean to keep you in the dark. I've been so damn busy, it escaped my mind a number of times. This war in Europe keeps me running at full speed."

Colonel Duncan dragged deeply once more on his cigarette and let out the smoke slowly from his nostrils. He began to explain that four weeks ago, G-2 had called him to come to the headquarters at Munitions

Building with Mac's and Captain Jones's performance ratings. Three other office chiefs, with performance ratings of their own men, were given a two-hour secret briefing by Major Alda, a G-2 staff member.

"Ten names of Army officers ranging from lieutenants to majors were submitted to G-2 for determination. And after much discussion, your name was pulled out."

"What was the purpose, Sir?"

"It seems that Lieutenant Colonel Walters, who is in charge of a small intelligence group in Manila, had written a letter to the War Department requesting three Army intelligence officers to replace the officers who were murdered in Manila," Duncan explained.

"WD said no at first, and for good reason," Duncan said. "There are soldiers and sailors who get killed every day and WD probably won't be able to replace each dead soldier or sailor. I suggested that Manila should take care of its own problems."

Duncan further explained that another, more detailed letter from Walters explained why he thought the officers were killed, by whom and provided more information about the spy network in the country.

"And more importantly, why they might need to be replaced," Duncan said. "This time, the military leadership was sympathetic and expressed great alarm regarding Walters's suspicions, but only agreed to send one officer because of the war," Duncan said.

He added that the department told Walters to get the other two from their own personnel pool in Manila or elsewhere in the Philippines and train them.

"To do what, Sir?" Mac asked.

Duncan pursed his lips.

"To help find a spy and a murderer!"

Mac put out his cigarette in the ashtray. "No one there knows who did it?" he said, as his California dream quickly melted away.

"It was my understanding during the briefing that neither the Philippine Department nor the Philippine Investigation Bureau, PIB, their version of our FBI, knows who the spy is, despite extensive investigation," Duncan said.

There was a gentle knock on the door. It was Mrs. Ottis.

"Colonel," she said in a sweet voice. "General Clayton, G-1, is on line one, and the British Embassy is on line two."

Duncan thanked Mrs. Ottis and told her that he would take Clayton's call immediately. He turned to Mac. "Let me take these two calls, McCord," he said.

Mac pushed back his chair and went to a small room adjoining Duncan's office to wait. He was irked that obviously his request for reassignment to the West Coast was denied for an assignment to a country that, to him, no one could find on the map. As he sat there, a truly deep frustration took hold of him. As much as he loved the military, for the first time in his career, Mac wanted to put in his resignation and simply walk out. And why not, he asked himself. He was alone now with no family responsibilities. His frustration slowly turned to anger. He got up from the comfortable sofa and was pacing the floor of the room, trying to calm himself, when Duncan stuck his head in the door.

"I'm sorry you had to wait, Major. You and I were discussing the Philippines," Duncan said.

"Yes, Sir," Mac answered, following the colonel back to his office.

"Why don't they send FBI agents to Manila?" Mac asked. "After all, it is an American colony. It's their responsibility to go after saboteurs and criminals."

Duncan, a tall man from San Antonio, was a no-nonsense type officer. He had brown eyes that twinkled even when he talked, but on serious matters, they became serious. He leaned back on his chair and gave Mac a hard look.

"It seems to me that they should, but the Manila unit wants you," Duncan said. "I suppose in time the FBI will be involved in it, too. McCord, when you get there, use the reason 'why' in your pursuit. That 'why' is the key to that Manila puzzle. What is motive! Why were those American Army officers brutally murdered?"

Mac nodded his head.

"I will certainly try, Sir," he said wearily, convinced that he might just as well accept his fate. After all, he had dedicated his life to the service of his country. And he just might like the Philippines, he told himself reassuringly.

"Walters is forming another Army investigative unit," Duncan said. "That's the group you're going to join. Alda called me last evening and said that you're WD's candidate. Evidently, Walters, who's continuing to run the show there, insisted that you're his choice based on your outstanding record as an intelligence officer and your special assignment in France. I don't know how in the hell he knew about you or your record, but someone did! I know that my friend Polson did not tell Walters. It's all very strange."

Mac was silent as he watched Duncan twiddle the cigarette between his fingers.

"Anyway, McCord, Walters suspects that the person they're after is not only the murderer but is also a spy involved in a lot of subversive acts in the Philippines," Duncan said. "I've got so much on my mind; I can't recall the spy's name at this moment. Telephone calls about you must have burned the wires between here and the Pacific."

"Colonel, would you mind if I read the letters?" Mac said.

"I don't have them," answered Duncan.

According to Duncan, Walters sent two letters to the War Department but were shown to neither him nor his colleagues. Alda did, however, brief them on the contents.

"They probably got placed in the same office managing the whole undertaking. But there's a copy of Walters's letter to Colonel Sam Polson. Ask Mrs. Ottis to let you read it. It's been some time since I've seen it. G-2 also has a copy of the same letter."

Mac's eyes were fixed on the senior officer across from him.

"Do you think those murders could have been committed by foreign agents instead of just one person?" Mac asked.

"I don't know. Walters doesn't think so. But you may be right," Duncan said. "Could be willful ignorance and near-sightedness on the part of our American intelligence in Manila."

"That would be unfortunate," Mac said. "The spy situation there must be prevalent throughout Manila. Japanese agents, perhaps. Yet we haven't read or heard of any overt intents or signs of aggression in that country."

Duncan glanced at McCord and snorted, "Perhaps they're just being quiet about it. French Indo-China is already under her influence, and she demonstrated her aggressiveness in 1939 when she brought Hainan Island under her control. Japan is up to no good, McCord." He passed his handkerchief over his perspiring face. Visibly angry, Duncan blurted out, "The world is turning upside down. Look what's happening in Europe!"

Duncan went suddenly silent for several moments. When he became aware of Mac's uneasiness, he apologized for his outburst, adding softly that his wife's parents still lived in Poland, and she's been calling for information twenty times a day. "And as for the Philippines, McCord, I spent two happy years there as a young lieutenant, and I was there a whole month last year," Duncan said. "There was a Filipino agent at the PIB, Agent Chavez, who briefed me on how active foreign spies are getting to be in the Philippines. Now and then I hear from him to tell me what's going on in Manila. You'll probably meet Chavez when you get there. You, too, will like the Filipinos and the Philippines."

He made an opening on his crowded desk for a brown folder and took his time to read certain paragraphs on the typewritten papers.

"I looked at some data copied from your military personnel file given to me by Major Alda," Duncan continued without looking up. "Aside from having a fine scholastic record at West Point, you excelled in athletics, especially in swimming."

"Swimming?" Mac asked, wondering if the colonel had lost his train of thought.

Duncan shrugged his shoulders. "I don't know if being an excellent swimmer has anything to do with being a smart intelligence officer in Manila. I think the whole country is more water than land," he said, smiling ruefully. "Who knows, you might need that ability. Being a smart man and a good swimmer may come in handy."

"I have not finished the articles for Army Talk," Mac said, refusing to give up hope of lying on California's sandy beaches.

"That'll be okay, McCord. The division's editor, Major Muzak, and I have discussed it," Duncan said. "Give your papers to Captain Jones. He'll finish your articles and give them to the branch chief editor and then forward them back to Muzak. Clear your desk by the end of the day. You needn't report for work at all. Do what you've got to do for your journey to the Philippines."

"Sir, how about my request for a transfer to California?" Mac asked, now sounding desperate.

"I'm very sorry, McCord! That's out! You're going to the Philippines!"

Duncan shouted. "But that's not enough to quit the Army, is it?"

Duncan's eyes twinkled.

"The Army needs your caliber, McCord," Duncan said. "It has lost many good men because of their impulsiveness. Hang in there, McCord!"

"Yes, Sir," Mac answered almost disconsolately.

"After you leave my office, go to the Green Room and see Jean Cisco. I think she said there's a Top Secret/Special Eyes Only document written by a naval intelligence officer about the Philippines," Duncan said, taking a deep breath. "Your badge there shows you've got TSSEO clearance. She has set aside the document for you."

"Anything else, Colonel?"

"Yes. WD has already contacted Dr. Zinka at Georgetown University. He's holding a seminar on Southeast Asian history and politics in a week. I suggest that you register for the course."

"This is so sudden."

Duncan nodded. "Everything in this great military institution of ours is Expedite! Expedite!"

"How about the language? I don't speak…"

"Tagalog?" interrupted Duncan, once again studying the contents of Mac's personnel folder. "It doesn't matter. English and Spanish are spoken in the Philippines. According to this excerpt from your file, you're fluent in Spanish. But pick up a Tagalog-English pocket dictionary at the library. It wouldn't hurt."

Mac nodded.

"Good thing to know, Sir," Mac said clearing his throat. "Do you know when I'm supposed to leave for Manila?"

Rising to his feet, Duncan lit another cigarette and walked to the window. The conductor of a streetcar was impatiently clanging the bell at automobiles to move.

It was some time before Duncan finally answered.

"They'll be happy to see you there by July 1, but they'd prefer that you arrive there a few months or so earlier," Duncan said. "I'm sure they'd like for you to have time to get acquainted with Manila and some parts of the islands. It's a beautiful country with beautiful and friendly people. I'd like very much to visit it again before I retire. But it is sure hot."

Mac slipped both of his hands in his pants pockets and calculated aloud that it would probably take a month and three weeks to arrive in Manila by Army transport.

Glancing at Mac, Duncan walked to his desk and picked up an envelope. "Here are your Orders. I'd say you should leave from New York about 1 March and get to Manila by the end of April."

"Sir, I was at Fort Myer the other day and was told you may be leaving Washington?"

"Yes, in May, to start a new Army intelligence group in San Antonio, and then I'm retiring," Duncan said. "I've kept you in my office long enough. Good luck, McCord." He patted Mac gently on the back. "I hate to see you go," Duncan said. "You're one of the best in this business, but it's time for you to move on."

He waited a few seconds before he spoke again.

"I'd like to offer you something to remember," Duncan said, giving Mac a serious look. "It doesn't matter how much covert, overt or human intelligence an analyst collects; it's how he sifts through those raw materials. I visualize all intelligence information on a certain subject as part of a big puzzle. Sometimes it's the most minute and innocent report or object that completes the puzzle."

"I'll remember that, Sir."

Mrs. Ottis was standing by the door. She waited until Mac had left the room, and then quietly told Colonel Duncan that Agent Edward Martin at the FBI had just called.

"He said to remind you that he'd like to see you before he departs for Manila to temporarily join an agent Chavez at the Philippine Investigation Bureau," Mrs. Ottis said. "He's bringing his partner, James W. Kagan, to meet you. He wondered if you could brief them about Manila and the bureau, as neither of them has been there. He'll call you as soon as he gets back from Baltimore this afternoon."

Duncan had learned earlier that morning that Martin had to identify the mutilated bodies of two FBI agents who used to work for him. The bodies were discovered at Baltimore's Sparrows Point shipyard.

"Oh, yes," Colonel Duncan muttered absent-mindedly. "Yes, Chavez. A good man. I told McCord about him. Get hold of his office, or tell Martin that I'll be happy to brief him and his partner."

Before Mac left Tempo U, he stopped in Mrs. Ottis's office and read

Walters's letter to Polson. As he was reading it, all at once a sharp sound of surprise escaped from his lips and his eyes became glued on the name on the letter—Boris Meissner.

No matter how much he willed for them to move on to the next line, his eyes remained frozen, unable to move. Mac shook his head vigorously, breaking the spell.

"Son of a bitch! So the spy in Manila is Boris Meissner! What a shit!" he murmured to himself as he continued to read the letter, recalling vividly that Duvalier's description of Meissner's appearance differed from that of the Chinese agent's.

"Son of a bitch!" Mac murmured again.

Mac immediately called Major Alda at the WD to ask permission if he could make a copy of Walters's letter plus some copies of classified documents he would like to take with him to Manila. Major Alda approved, but insisted that Mac should also clear it with Colonels Duncan and Polson.

Before Mac left for New York where he was to await the Army transport, he had lunch with Stone and Deaver. Since it was their last day together, they decided to splurge and went to the Occidental Restaurant instead of their usual lunch at the Post Office Department's cafeteria. Mac turned to Deaver and asked if there was any breaking news coming through the message center.

"Mostly routine stuff," he answered, but mentioned the dead Chinese general and his conversation with Colonel Polson regarding the overall spy situation in the Philippines. The conversation turned quickly to the war in Europe, and Boris Meissner came up.

"Mac, ever since you called to inquire about Meissner, I've been keeping a close tab on that guy," Stone said. "I've been dropping bits and pieces of info into his folder whenever I find reports about him."

"Anything new since we talked on the phone, John?" Mac asked, taking a bite out of his t-bone steak.

"Yeah. I've been meaning to call you about that," Stone said, lowering his voice almost to a whisper and bringing his head closer to Mac's. "I won't mention his name, okay? We've upgraded his file from Unclassified to Secret."

Mac's interest perked up.

"He's gaining importance?" Mac asked.

Stone nodded.

"Yesterday, the data section handed me a message from an unknown source, not real reliable info, but rather interesting," Stone said. "According to US Naval Intelligence at Zurich, the guy's mother's name was Ann Wollos. She was an infant when her American parents moved back to the United States from Switzerland. As an adult, Wollos went back to Switzerland for a visit and, while there, she met Claus Meissner, a German. She later came back to the United States. She's presently believed to be married to a wealthy realtor in Baltimore."

"How do you spell her last name?" Mac asked.

"W-o-l-l-o-s. Wollos," John said, looking pleased with himself. "Isn't that a doozey for an info? But don't bother looking in the telephone directory. The name's not in there. Must be her maiden name."

"Must be," Mac said. "Realtors are not in the habit of keeping their names unlisted. I would imagine they'd like to have them in great, big letters. Any more data you can think of, John?"

"Yeah. I think you've asked me to confirm whether he attended school in the US. The answer is yes, from an excellent source, Army intelligence in Switzerland. And, I've a couple more, but both are unconfirmed. As a young man, Meissner became involved in a fight and injured the upper part of his right ear. He now has prosthesis."

Stone took a sip of water.

"Mac. Deaver. I've got to run. I've a 3:00 p.m. meeting with my boss," Stone said, reaching to shake Mac's hand. "Good luck. If I come upon something interesting on Meissner, I'll give it to Deaver to send to you.

"I'll send you my address when I get to Manila," Mac said. "I'll keep in touch."

CHAPTER 4

Mac's Army transport, coming from New York, was a day late in her scheduled arrival in Manila. The ship was somewhere in the South China Sea, having difficulty reaching Manila Bay for docking. The vessel's time of arrival was to be at 0800 hours Friday, June 6, but that had become impossible to meet.

The pilot, who had boarded the transport to steer into Manila harbor, had radioed the harbormaster that day.

"The vessel is having engine trouble and can't go full speed," he said. "We'll have to limp along. Her problem appears minor. Your mechanics can easily repair it when we get there this evening."

Meanwhile in downtown Manila, a tall Caucasian wearing sunglasses and a white visor cap entered the moderately priced La Rosa Hotel. He approached the desk clerk and grunted a greeting.

"Good afternoon, Sir," said the Filipino clerk. "Oh, my. You are wet. But it is not raining?"

The tall Caucasian gave the clerk a sharp look.

"I fell from a fishing boat," he said tersely. "Where's the regular desk clerk?"

"He had to take his wife to the hospital."

"The key to my room, then," he mumbled.

"Your name, Sir?" The clerk asked politely, meanwhile opening the hotel's permanent guest book.

"Barclay. Leon Barclay."

"Here it is, Sir. Room 225," the clerk said, extending the key to the guest.

After opening the door to his room, Barclay glanced at his watch. 1:00 p.m. He walked to the window overlooking Manila Bay and stood there for some time, motionless. Then, mechanically, he placed his visor cap and sunglasses on the table and took off his wet shirt, exposing an arresting birthmark in the shape of a swastika on his upper left shoulder. On a quick glance, the birthmark could have been mistaken for a tattoo. Slowly, he turned away from the window and went to the bathroom. He grabbed a towel and dried himself, pressing it on his thick blond hair. His eyes, one gray and the other blue, took in every inch of his face, reflected in the bathroom mirror. After a few moments of staring, Barclay began to blot his face and neck with another towel and adjusted his whole disguise.

"Ah, Leon Barclay, I like your disguise. I would like for you to once again meet your creator, yours truly, Boris Meissner," and took a bow. "I have another creation, an interesting man by the name of Sonny Sollow. Now, would you like to see the real me?"

His voice changed to a falsetto, as Barclay.

"Yes."

Meissner's voice changed to his regular deep voice.

"You're a naughty boy! Of course you would! But I won't let you."

He paused.

"It's been a long time since we have spoken to each other, Barclay," he said to the disguised face in the mirror. "Listen, you've done a splendid job, blowing up that US naval ship in Manila Bay early this morning. Good luck on your next mission! We must continue to aid our Japanese friends!"

He gave his reflection a hard scrutiny, and then kissed the mirror.

"Goodbye, Barclay. Now, go sabotage the Cavite Naval Yard."

He turned away from the mirror and at the same time removed the blond wig. He went to the closet and came back to the bathroom mirror and meticulously rearranged his face with a dark brown moustache and beard and put on his glasses. He stared at his new appearance and proudly told the face in the mirror, "I'm dazzled with my own genius." He paused and whispered vainly, "I want you to kill McCord."

Meissner's diabolical laughter rang out in his hotel room.

This time his voice changed to the deep, stammering voice of Sollow.

"Give me the reasons why I should kill McCord."

Meissner turned abruptly around, away from the mirror. His voice changed to his natural deep voice. "I have four reasons why I want you, Sollow, to kill Jake McCord. First and foremost, McCord is an American, and the Americans are siding with countries that are intent on destroying Nazi Germany. Second, McCord helped the French intelligence in trying to find me. But they were unsuccessful, of course. Third, he is now helping the Americans find me. And fourth, McCord has the blue sapphire ring my mother gave me. I want it back." He paused and turned around to the face on the mirror. "Should you fail, I shall have Barclay go after McCord."

He wasted no time going back to Barclay's disguise, putting on his blond hair, white visor cap and dark glasses. Barclay exited from one of the side doors and soon disappeared into the busy, crowded streets of Manila. He was in a hurry. First, he had to drive to a place in south Manila and deliver guns to a Japanese spy ring, then he had to drive back to Manila Harbor, Pier 1. He had heard that the General Paul Burns Army transport was due to arrive in four to five hours.

He had been waiting for the ship for over twenty-four hours.

Time passed. The Army transport had now entered Manila Bay. The tugboats Paul Bunyan and Babe guided it slowly and expertly to South Harbor's Pier 1 at past 1600 hours, a little later than the pilot's estimation the previous day.

After the usual ritual of docking all large vessels, the gangplank was lowered in place for the passengers to disembark.

Mac, among those viewing the pier from the vessel, was mildly surprised that the ship's arrival should attract hundreds of people who gathered on the pier. It was bustling with energy.

As Mac wobbled down the gangplank, he was almost overcome by the heat and the humidity of Manila.

His attention was quickly drawn to a newsboy holding up a paper, evidently trying to attract the crowd's attention.

And before he touched dock, Mac heard the newsboy shouting in English, "Extra! Extra! US Naval ship blown up on Manila Bay!"

Two men in Army uniforms were intermittently searching the faces of those who were disembarking. A Filipino sergeant would now and then study a small black and white photograph in his hand. He would shake his head in disgust, but continued to scrutinize the faces as they stepped off the gangplank. The other man, a tall lieutenant colonel with an aquiline nose and thinning sandy hair, would now and then turn his head in the direction of the harbormaster's three-story building with a look of anticipation.

The second man approached the sergeant.

"Sergeant, that Army transport was certainly late coming in. Actually, very late. Must have had some kind of engine trouble," he commented.

"Yes, Sir, it must have. She is a day late. But they are always late," the slim, short Filipino soldier answered, looking up at the tall American Army officer. "That was quite a blast we heard early this morning. Did you hear it?"

The lieutenant colonel shook his head. "No, but a friend told me about it. I was out of town. Probably foul play. I heard someone say it was a survey ship from the Rock," the lieutenant colonel said. "We must both be waiting for someone."

"Yes, Sir," replied the sergeant hesitantly. "I...I am here to meet Major..."

He thought better and cut himself abruptly. The soldier became suspicious of the lieutenant colonel. He told himself that he and two other men were the only ones who were supposed to know of McCord's arrival in Manila. Once again the lieutenant colonel turned his head in the direction of the harbormaster's building and then made a move, as if he were going to walk towards it, when all at once a loudspeaker blared.

"Major Jacob McCord, there is a telephone call for you at the harbormaster's office."

A smile curled on the corner of the lieutenant colonel's lips when an Army officer stepped out from among the military personnel on his way to the harbormaster's office.

"That's him," The Filipino sergeant shouted above the noisy crowd, pointing at Mac while studying the photograph. "That is him."

The lieutenant colonel raced ahead of the sergeant and grabbed Mac by the arm.

"You must be Major McCord," he said brusquely.

"Yes. I am Major Jacob McCord."

"Forget the telephone call. There was no telephone call. The rouse was my idea to see who would come forward as Major McCord," said the lieutenant colonel.

Suddenly, Mac staggered and, losing his balance, fell, dropping both of his suitcases. Someone had pushed him. When he was able to look up he saw a man in the crowd running away with one of them.

"Stop him! Stop him!" Mac shouted and at the same time trying to get up to go after the thief. "He has my suitcase."

The next few minutes were chaotic. A male civilian was hopelessly wandering, calling across the pier in search of his wife and daughter. Next, a woman in the crowd let out a deafening shriek. Several people rushed to the woman. Simultaneously, a passing Filipino stevedore stopped near the woman and shouted in alarm, pointing to a man lying on the dock five feet from where Mac had fallen.

"That man is dead! That man has been murdered," he shouted. "The person who stole the American's suitcase stabbed him," he said, pointing to the dead man. "I saw his dagger."

In all the confusion, the tall Army officer extended his hand to Mac and helped him to his feet.

"What the hell is going on here?" Mac said, noticing the silver leaf insignias on the collars of the officer's khaki shirt.

"Sorry, I didn't mean to push you. I thought I saw something flash from over there," the lieutenant colonel said apologetically. "And I'm sorry about your suitcase.

"I'm Sonny Rhoades, but please, call me Dusty. I insist. I wanted to be the first to meet you."

"Glad to meet you, Colonel," Mac said, wiping the dust off his clothes. "Should I feel lucky you came along? Do you think that was meant for me?"

"Possibly," Rhoades nodded, scratching the bald spot on his head and glancing sideways at Mac. "You touched ground less than an hour ago and already someone hates you. You're now in the orient, where I'm told the threat of death is part of breathing, and daggers are as plentiful as the bugs. You must be hiding a secret. Why would someone want that dagger through your heart?"

Mac shrugged his shoulders and murmured, "Why? I just got here," he said. He turned to Rhoades and thanked him again for saving his life. Glancing at the dead man, a stranger to them, he could not help but noticed the colorful handle of the dagger, a checkered red and black.

"Fancy and deadly!" he said aloud.

"Yes!" Rhoades agreed. "I hear you're an intelligence officer. I suppose you'll be going to Fort Santiago, headquarters of the Philippine Department."

"I don't know. I haven't been told what my assignment will be," said Mac with intentional vagueness.

"Hmmm. I knew mine before I arrived," Rhoades said.

He burst into a hearty laugh when he noticed that Mac was gazing somewhere else.

"I guess you expected a chauffeured limousine to meet you," he added jokingly.

Mac pursed his lips. "No, I thought that a Lieutenant Colonel William Walters was to meet me. Do you know him?" he asked.

"No. Anyway, welcome to Manila, the exotic city of intrigues," Rhoades declared with great flourish. "I can tell you wanted this assignment."

"I was so overjoyed to be here, I kissed the ground and gave away a suitcase full of clothes," Mac said. "But thanks for the welcome mat, Colonel."

"Why all the formalities, McCord? I'd rather you call me Rhoades or Dusty. I'll even tolerate you calling me by my first name, Sonny, but not Colonel."

By then the Filipino sergeant had finally weaved himself through the heavy crowd to where Rhoades and Mac were standing.

"I'm glad the sergeant is here. He knows the city," Rhoades said. "Sergeant, this is Major Jake McCord."

The sergeant straightened his back and saluted.

Mac returned the salute and murmured, "At ease, sergeant."

"I am Sergeant Delberto Pocodillo. My wife and friends call me Poco, Major McCord," he said with a pleasant accent. "Is it not obvious that my name is Poco?"

The small soldier smiled his tight-lipped, friendly smile, alluding to his short stature. "And if I may say in Tagalog, mabuhay, Sir."

Mac came forward and extended his hand for a handshake. "Poco, it's good to meet you, and thank you for welcoming me to Manila," Mac said.

"We expected you a couple of months ago," Rhoades said.

"Yes, we did," Poco agreed.

Smiling ruefully, Mac explained that a couple of unfortunate things occurred before leaving New York and upon reaching Los Angeles. "We were scheduled to arrive here yesterday but the ship again developed some difficulties. And here it is already June 7. The month is going at a fast clip," Mac said.

Rhoades smiled, showing discolored front teeth. "Frustrated? Join the club, McCord. You should never have left Washington if you wanted to get promoted. You've just boxed yourself into oblivion. The Philippines is such a place. Out of sight, out of mind."

"I don't discourage easily, Sir," Mac said as he wiped away the beads of perspiration running down his face.

"Colonel Rhoades, Sir. I think we should get away from this hot sun. I am afraid we will all drop dead from sun stroke," Poco said apologetically. "I will go and find transportation."

Rhoades nodded. "Good idea, sergeant. Major McCord and I will wait here."

Poco came back after a few minutes.

"I am sorry, I could not find a taxi. But this karetela will get you to the military center," Poco told Mac. "You have been billeted at the Bachelor Officers's Quarters. Do you wish for me to go with you, Sir?"

"Of course. I guess the driver can drop both Lieutenant Colonel Rhoades and me at the BOQ," Mac said.

"No! I'm on my way to the railroad station. I'm still at Fort Stotsenburg," Rhoades explained hesitantly. "I come to Manila now and then. I heard about your arrival from a friend, and as I told you earlier, I wanted to be the first to meet you. I understand you're from Washington. I know the place well. I'll be moving to Manila next Monday. San Marcelino."

Poco and Mac hopped on the karetela, which zigzagged slowly through the overcrowded narrow streets on its way to the military center. Poco, ramrod straight on his side of the seat, would give Mac a side glance once in a while. Mac, with his long legs in a stretched, relaxed position, complained to Poco of the intense heat and high humidity. Now and then, Mac massaged his temples. It always seemed to relax him.

Suddenly, the driver slumped forward and rolled out of the horse carriage, falling to the ground.

"What's going on?" Mac shouted, lurching forward to pull back the reins bringing the horse to a stop. Both he and Poco jumped out of the carriage to see what had happened to the driver.

The incident had snarled the traffic and a big crowd had gathered. Meanwhile, Poco felt the driver's pulse.

"This man is dead," he said, looking up at Mac.

"I see. There's a dagger through his neck."

Mac asked around if anyone saw who killed the driver of the carriage, when, out of the crowd a tall man with a dagger hidden in his hand lunged at Mac, sending him to the ground. The man then ran away and disappeared into the crowd.

Poco rushed to Mac's side. "Are you hurt very badly?"

Mac shook his head. "It's only a scratch," Mac said inspecting his wound. "Some mercurochrome and a bandage should stop the bleeding."

"Major Mac, did you see who stabbed you?"

"Not really. He was a Caucasian, but that's all I saw. It happened so fast," Mac said.

Feeling something beneath him, Mac leaned on Poco and whispered, "I'm lying on the dagger. Pick it up and hide it. Give it to me later. And let's get the hell out of here."

There was fear in Poco's voice when he spoke again. "I am used to horses. I will drive the karetela while you lay flat on the floor. When we get to the officers's quarters I want you to run in as fast as you can. I will follow behind with your things. I fear that whoever that was is still after you."

"Can you give me a guess why someone should want to kill me, Poco?" Mac said. He crouched on the floor of the carriage behind the driver's seat, clutching his shoulder.

"I do not know, Sir. Maybe it was meant for someone else."

"How about the first incident at the pier, Poco?"

"I do not know about that either, Major."

They left the crowded street behind and were only three blocks away from the military center in the Walled City when they heard the sharp sound of a gunshot. The horse stumbled forward, then its two front legs folded, almost toppling the karetela.

Poco jumped out of the horse-drawn carriage, followed by Mac. After quickly examining the horse, Poco discovered that it had died of a bullet wound between its eyes. "Let us better run to the center. We will be safer there," he said, carrying both the brief case and the suitcase.

A taxi driver came roaring up to them, its horn blowing incessantly. Then the taxi stopped and the door swung open.

"Hop in Mac. Sergeant."

It was Dusty Rhoades.

"We were a short distance away from your carriage when we saw what happened to the driver and then to you. We couldn't get to both of you fast enough through the traffic. Then we heard the gunshot and the horse dropped."

"You seem to be around whenever I need help," Mac told Rhoades with a slight suspicion in his voice. "Thanks again."

"I'm convinced that you're on someone's black list," Rhoades murmured, eyeing Mac calmly.

"I thought you were on your way to the station," Mac said

"I was, when I saw what happened," Rhoades answered, staring at Mac's bloody shirt. "How's the shoulder?"

"It's just a scratch. I heal fast," Mac said.

The taxicab stopped in front of the BOQ. As Mac was about to leave the car, he noticed that a button was missing from Rhoades shirt, revealing the handle of an Army Colt .45 pistol in his belt. Mac also observed the tip end of a dagger's sheath tied to his right leg.

Poco carried Mac's belongings to his room. He placed the suitcase on a luggage stand and slipped the briefcase under the bed. "Have a good night, Sir. I hope you will feel better tomorrow."

"Poco, wait. I feel well enough. I think we could both use a couple of strong drinks and some hot food. Where's a good place?"

"Major Mac. But the Army regulation, Sir," Poco said. "Officers are forbidden to fraternize with enlisted men."

"I know that. We'll both wear civilian clothes," Mac said. "Anyway, aren't we both going to be assigned to the same outfit?"

"I think so, Sir."

"That group, I'm pretty sure, is going to be rather small, and you and I will be thrown together on many occasions, if not all the time. I'm certain the commanding officer will understand, but I'll discuss it with him if it comes up," Mac said, searching through his bags. "Pure luck. That damn thief didn't steal everything," Mac mumbled. "He left me my tooth brush and other important items," he said, throwing two aspirins into his mouth.

"What time do you wish for me to come by, Sir?"

"About 7:00 or so. That'll give me a chance to clean this wound and soak for a bit in the bathtub. I didn't have such luxury in the Army transport."

"Okay, Sir," Poco answered.

As he was leaving, he turned around and added, "I placed the dagger on the table by your bed. I will bring back a bottle of mercurochrome, cotton and bandages."

Before he sank into the bathtub, Mac turned on the ceiling fan and the small Philco radio, some of the BOQ's minimal furnishings. The teasing voice of Wee Bonnie Baker singing 'Oh Johnny,' to Orin Tucker's orchestra floated through the room.

The warm bath was relaxing, and his shoulder wound started to feel better. Mac put on his robe and stretched himself on the bed, studying the dagger with a chilling thought that it could have stabbed his heart. He recalled the dagger that killed the man at the pier had the same red- and black-checkered handle. He opened the credenza's drawer and dropped it in. He made sure the door was locked and dead-bolted, and then fell asleep.

A loud knocking awoke him. He rolled out of the bed and rushed to open it. "Sorry, Poco," he apologized, glancing at his watch. "I must have fallen asleep. The bath relaxed me. Give me five minutes."

"No problem, Sir," Poco said, placing the drugstore paper bag on the credenza. "I borrowed my brother's Chevy."

Mac marveled at how adroitly Poco drove in the heavily congested downtown Manila traffic. Again, Mac complained about the weather. It was already past 7:00, and it was still scorching hot.

He never imagined that downtown Manila could look just like so many other big cities in the United States—modern, glittering and crowded. Soon they passed a huge billboard of a smiling Shirley Temple next to an equally large billboard of a man and a woman advertising Jantzen bathing suits. Another billboard displayed a Coca Cola girl in a bathing suit. Some other displays showed cigarette brands such as Camels, Chesterfields and Lucky Strikes. But what dominated the skyline was a well-lighted billboard with the seductive and exotic Scarlett O'Hara in the arms of Rhett Butler.

Mac closed his eyes and swore that he was in Tampa, Florida, and under his breath stated, "'Gone With The Wind' in Manila?"

"Yes. It is a premiere in the city. The women wear evening dresses and the men have on coats and ties. Manila has class, Major Mac," said Poco with a pleased smile.

Mac looked at his watch and whistled. "I don't believe this. We've been in this awful traffic for over two hours. It's already past nine."

Poco began blowing the horn of the car and waving his right arm for pedestrians and karetelas to move on.

A little later he announced, "We are here, Major Mac. The Manila International Club."

Poco jumped out of the car and lifted his head to the sky.

"Look at those dark clouds rolling in. Let us hurry inside. It is going to rain. This is June, you know," the tiny sergeant said

"It got dark so quickly," Mac said.

"A dark night like this always reminds me of a poem, old Filipino folklore I used to hear and recite when I was in grade school—

'Wickedness and darkness go hand in hand

And men of evil thoughts go in a band

With intentions to kill and pillage the land.' All at once loud thunder and lightning broke out, anticipating rain.

CHAPTER 5

Mac and Poco had barely entered the club when the heavy downpour started.

Inside, the large and exotically decorated Manila International Club was semi-dark and pleasantly cool. Its low, indirect lighting added to its sensual atmosphere.

Neon signs outside were pulsating from bright to brighter to brightest, casting a glow of red, green and orange rain-streaked light through the thick maroon velvet and white Chinese silk curtains. It was invitingly cozy in the room, aside from being unusually quiet.

Poco was pleased that it was still early enough to have his favorite table. He always liked to be near the exit but close to the dance floor. He enjoyed watching people dance. A waiter who apparently knew him came hastily to their table as he and Mac sat down.

"Hello, Sergeant Pocodillo. What will you and your friend desire?" he asked with a flourish.

Poco ordered a pitcher of San Miguel beer and a bowl of peanuts fried in garlic.

"Alberto, before you leave I want for you to meet Major McCord. He just arrived from America," Poco said, looking rather stiff. He thought that keeping his back straight, especially when seated, made him look taller.

"How do you do, Sir," the young waiter greeted Mac with friendly enthusiasm. "You will like Manila if the heat does not kill you the first week. But also we have lots of rain, like now. Did you know June is the start of our rainy season? I hope that you are a good swimmer."

"Know him well?" Mac asked Poco.

"My wife and I come here often. We like him. He is a good waiter, but

I wish he would tell the visitors good things about the Philippines. The bad things they will soon find out," Poco said.

Poco turned to Mac and said proudly, "The club will start filling up by 10 o'clock."

"We have the best band in the entire city," Alberto added, returning with their orders.

"Now, that is good salesmanship, Alberto," said Poco.

When they were left alone, Mac turned to Poco.

"On a more serious subject." His steel-blue eyes held Poco's dark ones. "Who knew of my arrival?"

"I thought only three people—Colonel Miller, Major North and myself. I was surprised to see that Lieutenant Colonel Rhoades was also waiting for you. I have not met him before," Poco said, giving Mac the photograph he had with him at Pier 1. "I used it to recognize you with."

"Where in the hell did you get this photo?" Mac snapped.

"Colonel Miller found it on Lieutenant Colonel Walters's desk."

Mac was beginning to realize the severity of everything that happened so soon after his arrival. He felt uneasy about Dusty Rhoades. But he concluded that he had to keep his suspicions to himself until he could prove them.

"I can tell you are thinking about what happened to you," Poco said.

"Yeah. Makes me nervous. I don't see any assailants and yet I get attacked. But why?"

The sergeant shook his head. "I do not know, Sir," explained Poco.

Mac wondered aloud again if all three of the incidents were meant for him: the dagger on the pier, the karetela driver's murder, the horse. Once more Poco answered that he did not know, but he added quietly, "It appeared that the killer fully intended to get you." Poco paused. "The body of Lieutenant Gibbs was recently discovered floating on Subic Bay with a bullet wound in his head. Gibbs, who had a girlfriend nearby in Olongapo, had only been with the group a very short time, since March."

According to Poco, Gibbs's killer was never apprehended, and, like the others, no one knew who had killed him.

"After his death, we were down to only two agents: myself and Major North, until now, of course," Poco said, then lit a cigar. "By the way, Major

North has a thing about being called Major or Sir. He wants to be called Charlie."

"Okay, I'll be sure to call him Charlie. Will there be others in the group besides us?"

"Yes, Sir. They are already here. We will be six again."

"When were the first three officers killed, Poco?"

The sergeant moved his head closer to Mac's and lowered his voice.

"Mid-September. It has all been strange, Major Mac."

It appeared that Majors Haggarty and Summers were killed the same day but in different parts of Manila. Summers's body was found with all ten fingers missing, washed up on a beach at Sangley Point where the Cavite Naval Base was located.

"Cavite is southwest of Manila," Poco added.

"The killer or killers worked pretty fast," Mac said.

Poco nodded. When he continued, his voice dropped to a whisper.

"Major North thinks Haggarty was killed while he was fishing. He loved to fish and would often rent a boat from old man Kawazaka. The day after he disappeared, Major North and I rented a boat from the boat livery and searched around the Army/Navy Club off Dewey Boulevard and as far as Cavite. No clues. We finally gave up after three weeks."

"Haggarty's body was never found?" Mac asked.

Poco wiped his lips with his hand and noted that, according to the police, a week ago two little boys found a skeleton without a head somewhere on a beach.

"It could not be identified, however. I think the cops are still working on it. Major North later told me and the police that he thought it was Haggarty's skeleton because of the proximity to where he generally anchored to fish, near a deep cove." He took a big swallow of beer. "Major North knows that cove well and had gone fishing there with Haggarty once or twice."

"You know where it is, Poco?"

"Yes."

"How about Stein?" Mac was curious.

"Two weeks later, Captain Stein disappeared. We could never find his body. We all assumed that he also was murdered. It was strange. There were several stories, but they were never substantiated."

"How did Walters's mission begin, and how did you get in with the group?"

It did not take much prodding from Mac for Poco to relate how it all began. He took another big swallow of his beer and removed the foam from his upper lip with his tongue. He began his story from the beginning. He was assigned to an Infantry detachment in Baguio. But more than a year ago, he had a hush-hush call from a Lieutenant Colonel Walters, whom he did not know. Walters told him that he had cleared his release with his commanding officer in the 57th Infantry, Philippine Scouts, and to pack his bags and immediately come with his family to Manila to join a group that needed his help. He was not told his job was to be with intelligence until he had arrived, but a background investigation had already been completed, and getting his clearance would just be in a matter of a week or so.

Poco made it known that he had never been in intelligence, but that did not seem to matter to Walters. After he had received a month's training from a Major Charles J. North, Jr., he reported to Walters, who introduced himself as chief of the intelligence detachment in a small office at Fort McKinley, not far from the city.

Walters explained to Poco that he had orders from the Army high command in Manila for his small group to pop in anytime at any Army base and give reports on the conditions of transportation, weapons, morale and discipline of that base or camp. The idea was that, since they were unknown to any of the Army bases, and their visits were unannounced, their reports would be more impartial. They were to take the places of Army inspectors for two or three months to determine where things could be improved.

"That was our mission," Poco said.

"Why so? Didn't the military inspectors do their job well?" Mac asked.

It seemed that before an inspector could get to a base or a garrison to do his evaluation, the date of his arrival had already been leaked out. So, even before he could get there, everything on the base or the garrison on the list would be in tip-top shape. The inspector's report would naturally be favorable. But the Army leadership began to question the generally favorable reports.

Mac wondered where the story would lead to as he watched Poco throw some peanuts in his mouth.

It appeared that not long after that, Walters decided that they go in pairs and criss-cross most of the country, not just Luzon. They traveled extensively throughout the big islands—Luzon, Visayas and Mindanao—doing the same mission. But they were always reminded and briefed that along the way they were to continue to keep their eyes and ears open for any unusual activities carried on by an individual or groups and to report unusual references to names of animals or flowers. Poco continued that one day, Charlie North pointedly asked Lieutenant Walters why they should report such unusual references. Walters demurred momentarily at the question but obliquely answerd the major that as soon as he found out the answer to his unusual request, he would let him know.

Mac lighted a Chesterfield. "The whole assignment sounds like a pretext," he said, tasting a few of the peanuts.

"We all thought so at the time, especially Major North. He told me once that Walters was paranoid about spies," Poco told Mac.

"Who was your partner?"

"I did not have one," Poco said, explaining that he traveled along with Majors Haggarty and North, who were partners. "Since they were seniors in rank, I was to go with them as an interpreter in case Tagalog or Visayan was needed. I speak both dialects. Although Tagalog became the national language not too long ago, 1937 or something like that, other natives in other parts of the country do not readily speak it or other island's dialect. That was probably the reason Walters chosed me."

"How about the others?"

Lieutenant James Gibbs, the sixth member, Poco continued, had not yet joined them, but Captain Abe Stein had been paired with Major Woody Summers. And in retrospect, the data they brought back were the same as before—loose discipline among Army units, lack of modern weapons within the Army itself, lackadaisical attitude among officers and their men and poor transportation systems. Poco paused and smiled his closed-lip quick smile.

"I have often times heard American servicemen say that if they want to go on a long vacation, they ask for an assignment to either Hawaii or the Philippines. One can be on a continuous vacation here. You will soon learn that it is very easy to do as little as possible in this high heat and high humidity," Poco said.

Mac did not make any comments, but instead he asked how Poco liked being in intelligence.

"It is okay," Poco frowned. "We continued to travel extensively all over the islands gathering information not any different from what we had before. Nor did we hear or see anything unusual. It became extremely boring."

"Fortunately," Poco mused, "in May, Lieutenant Colonel Walters quietly told us to reconnoiter Bataan and Corregidor and to report any strange activities there."

"Why all at once such an assignment? Did Walters suspect something?" Mac inquired, taking a swig of his beer.

Poco nodded and told Mac that they were sure Walters suspected something but would not tell them until he had all the facts.

"He was a fine officer and a conservative man. He used to complain to us that the security at the Rock is too lax, vulnerable to sabotage from foreign agents and Filipinos who do not like Americans."

Poco continued to explain that since situations in Bataan were copesetic, the intelligence officers drove to Subic Bay and borrowed a motorboat from the naval station to investigate Corregidor, always with the idea of reporting anything unusual.

"Walters fondly called us his special intelligence detachment emergency ring (SPIDER)." He cleared his throat and took a fresh Tabacalera cigar from his shirt pocket, lighted it and went on to elucidate their plan. That night, they made their way towards Corregidor and anchored the thirty-five foot cruiser close to the island with a plan that in the morning they would also give it a thorough survey.

"I take it SPIDER did find something unusual while anchored," said Mac, intrigued.

"Yes," said Poco.

He began explaining what occurred before dawn the next day. An early riser, Poco was having his cup of coffee on the stern of the boat when he observed that a heavy, thick fog had rolled in from the South China Sea during the night and settled like a blanket over the bay. In the quiet of the morning, he thought that he heard the sound of a motorboat, but he was unable to see through the fog. But the hot daybreak sun and strong eastern wind soon burned and lifted the fog. Looming on their starboard was a fishing boat with three men.

"It was eerie to suddenly see a boat nearby when there was none there before. From an area where it was easy for me to look out with a pair of binoculars but be difficult to spot, I saw one of the men, also with binoculars, surveying the Rock. He had his back to me," Poco explained with excitement in his voice. "He must be describing something, I murmured to myself. That second man was taking down notes. The third man was pretending to be fishing, but I think he was really the lookout man. There are, however, three fishing poles in the boat."

"Didn't they see your boat?"

Poco explained that it was not so unusual to see a navy boat full of sailors and civilians anchored near there.

"They probably thought we were still asleep from too much boozing the night before. Nor is it unusual to see fishing boats in that area. That fishing boat stayed there for a couple of hours," he said.

"How about North, Haggarty, Summers and Stein?"

"Major North was not with us in that particular assignment. He said that he had a very bad summer cold," Poco said. "I went below, awoke the officers and notified them of the fishing boat."

"Did any of you recognize those men?"

"No. But Major Haggarty, who watched them through his own binoculars, described one as Caucasian with a moustache and a beard, and confirming my previous description of the other two as Asians. We all recognized the boat belonged to Kawazaka, owner of a small fishing livery in Manila."

"Are all his boats recognizable?" Mac asked.

"Yes. They are all painted black with large white letter K's on each side of the bow. Haggarty, Summers and Stein became suspicious; the next day they went to Kawazaka to obtain the men's names, but Kawazaka only had their address."

"Where were you and North?" Mac inquired.

"I could not go. My father was dying, and Major North's cold had worsened, so he was forced to stay in bed," said Poco, who paused for a while, then went on to say that Haggarty, Summers and Stein went to the address in Quiapo but only found two men. The Caucasian had managed to escape. When they demanded the sketches and the notes, they were attacked, and they had to kill their opponents in order to save their own lives.

"Major North and I read their report before it was submitted to Walters."

"That's too bad. They could've taken them as prisoners and pressured them to talk. Who were they?" Mac inquired.

"Paid informants. From the officers's report, one was a Filipino, and the other was Philippine-born Japanese."

"How could they have known?"

"Abe Stein, who understood Tagalog but could not speak it, interpreted what transpired between them before they were killed. One said, 'Do not give them anything. These notes and sketches are only for the eyes of Big Iguana and Red Rose.'"

"Big Iguana? Red Rose? Who are they?"

"I do not know, but I believe that Stein and Walters knew. And Major North thinks they are cover names."

A suspicious look came across Mac's face.

"How could North even think that?"

"He is a very smart man," answered Poco.

"Perhaps he had heard the names from someone."

At that moment, Mac was more interested in knowing more about the names Big Iguana and Red Rose but decided to drop the subject for the time being and instead asked, "Were any more papers found on the two men?"

Poco nodded. He explained that, aside from the detailed description of what approaches to the Rock a sailor could see and of the types of weapons visible, they also found a rough sketch of the navy's coastal area at the entrance of Subic Bay in a desk drawer.

"Were you close to Walters, Poco?"

"No, but Major North was."

"You seem to like this Major North."

Mac's statement needed an answer, but Poco merely shrugged his shoulders and murmured hesitantly, "He saved my life several months ago."

He glanced at Mac and debated with himself whether or not to disclose his true feelings about the incident. He thought a while, then lifted his glass of beer and took one or two swallows, meanwhile studying Mac's face. Warmth and kindness was hidden somewhere in the strong face, the unblinking steel-blue eyes and the straightforward way he talked. Poco decided to relate it.

He and North were investigating a certain place in Olongapo, which North had told Poco earlier was a house of foreign spies. A rather friendly Filipino man started to run after them while they were walking on the main street. The stranger shouted for North to stop, that he wanted to talk with him.

"He sounded like he knew the major and was trying to get his attention, but Major North started to run away from the man and instructed me to do likewise, but while so doing, I stumbled and fell. The major opened fire and was wounded. It could have been me. A Coast Patrol came along and killed the Filipino stranger, whom I later learned from the US Navy was Agent 25, a Filipino spy for the Japanese," said Poco hesitating momentarily. "I believe to this day they knew each other well."

"That's rather a strange thing to say," Mac said thoughtfully. "I would not mention that to anyone again. A strict Army disciplinarian might think that you're intimating North was cozy with that spy. You could get into trouble for such a statement."

Suddenly, he tapped Poco on the arm.

"At that table over there is a Filipina with extremely bright dyed red hair; she is with two Japanese men. Do you know them?"

Poco craned his neck and shook his head. "But I have seen her before. She is a waitress at Uncle Billy's Girls, a topless nightspot in Kapalaran. I have heard some customers call her Cookie. I suspect she is also a prostitute."

After a short conversation with the Japanese men, Cookie opened her large handbag, took out a brown envelope and handed it to the taller of the two men, who immediately left the club. She, however, stayed and was soon joined by a Filipino, presumed by Poco to be her pimp.

"I wonder what she gave them," asked Mac.

"Maybe a secret document on the Cavite Naval Yard, Sir. I suspect she is also a spy. That is not the first time I have seen her friendly with

Japanese men," said Poco. "The one to whom she gave that envelope was tall for a Jap."

"Do you think she was spying for the Japanese?" Mac asked.

"Why not?" Poco answered, "considering the amount of sabotage on US Army ships that has occurred, not to mention the murders of US Army personnel." He paused. "You may be right."

The next time they looked around, Cookie had also left. The band was in full swing and the club was getting noisier, so Poco and Mac were shouting over the noise.

"Is there a Japanese community here in Manila?" Mac asked.

"Yes, a large and affluent one. Many of the residents came from Davao."

"Is Davao a Japanese community?"

"It is more than a community. It is the capital of Mindanao, the southernmost and second largest island," Poco explained, his brown eyes shining with pride. "Davao is a modern city and the chief port of the island."

He was his proudest when discussing the beauty of his country.

"There is a heavy concentration of Japanese in Davao." He was silent for a while. "I have no problems with the Japanese. They are industrious and are good citizens."

Mac's eyes were intense on Poco. "And, have you ever thought of some Japanese-born here may be in cahoots with the motherland and sent here to spy? Considering Japan's objective in Asia, it's probable she is deep enough in espionage here to get a toe-hold." Mac lowered his voice. "Have you ever thought of a war in the Philippines?"

Poco placed his cigar on the ashtray and a serious look came to his face. He contended that he had not given it any thought nor heard anyone mention it. "As of now, the US military here does not act like it is totally energized for war, unless I am blind. But, I have been hearing rumors of Douglas MacArthur coming back to improve the defense of the Philippines." He took a deep breath. "I can see that there are foreign agents here. They might even have killed the American Army officers."

He moved his chair closer to Poco. "Why do you think foreign agents killed them?"

"Perhaps they knew too much about the spy system here."

Mac asked Poco to tell him about Lieutenant Colonel Walters. Poco took a big puff from his cigar. "He will not be our boss anymore. He drowned in the Army/Navy Club's swimming pool, which I questioned. I believe he was murdered. A good friend of his at the Philippine Investigation Bureau, Agent Chavez, believed he was also."

Poco described Walters as an excellent swimmer who would jump into Manila Bay and swim for hours, disregarding the bay's strong currents. In November 1940, eight months in advance, Walters announced that he would be retiring in July 1941.

Unfortunately, the day after Gibbs was murdered, Walters drowned. "They were both killed about a week before your arrival, June first and June second, respectively."

"Sounds like a bad omen for me," murmured Mac. "You've already mentioned Colonel Miller, Walters's replacement. Have you already met him, Poco?"

"No."

"Does he live at the military center?"

"No, somewhere on Dewey Boulevard."

"Is that an Army area?"

"No, Sir. It is a civilian community with beautiful and expensive homes."

"Really? How can he live there even with his colonel's salary?"

"I do not know, Sir." Poco took a long pause. "I heard from some of the men at the Army center that he is unfriendly. No one seems to know anything about Colonel Miller."

"What happened to all those reports that were submitted to Walters?"

Poco told Mac that no one in his group knew the whereabouts of the reports. However, they were all aware that Walters kept them all intact until he could present a complete package to the Philippine Department G-2 shortly before his retirement.

"Do you think Miller has those reports? Someone should ask him on Monday if he knows anything about them."

"You are right. One of the officers should ask him about those reports," answered Poco. He then told Mac that Miller's assignment with the group was only temporary, and that eventually he was slated for a high position in the Philippine Department. According to rumors, Miller was alarmed at the killings and requested the assignment to form another unit to go after the murderers and find out their true motives. Poco added, "He wants all six members to be in his office Tuesday morning at 9:30. He will not be back until that day from Clark Field." He grabbed a paper napkin and wrote down the address of their new office—170 Olivia Street, in the Escolta, Manila.

Poco described the building to Mac as a one-story wooden structure located behind the Nagoya Emporium, the largest variety store in Manila and easily recognizable by a large framed picture of Emperor Hirohito hanging visibly on the wall inside. He paused momentarily. "There is an alley and a tall wire fence between our office and the emporium. And our building has a large shingle with Land Surveyors, Inc., painted on it, probably to keep our anonymity." Mac and Poco's voices became louder. At that moment, the bandstand's floodlights turned on, and the drum began to beat with increasing crescendo, alerting the packed nightclub that the show was about to begin.

"Ladies and gentlemen," the master of ceremony announced into the microphone, "Welcome to the Manila International Club. And for those of you who have just arrived," continued the Filipino MC, "welcome to Manila, the city that never sleeps." He paused and appreciatively looked around at the large, crowded room. "And now, ladies and gentlemen, our one and only Julia, the most sensational singer in all of Southeast Asia."

A sultry-looking woman dressed in clinging silver-sequined long dress with revealing neckline appeared from behind the curtains and walked gracefully toward the microphone. Accompanied only by the pianist and the guitarist, Julia began to sing "Besame Mucho." Her singing style was appealing and provocative. The crowd was wild and demanded an encore. "More! More!" They shouted. Julia acceded to their demand. "I am going to sing for you, 'Heart and Soul.'"

Mac became aware of a well-dressed man three tables away from them escorting an exotic and beautiful woman to the dance floor. His eyes followed her graceful movements. He could not take his eyes away from her. Finally, the beautiful woman looked up and saw Mac staring at her. She returned his stare and their eyes met. His heart began to race and his blood rushed to his face.

Meanwhile, Poco became aware of Mac's interest. "We have many beautiful Filipinas," he told Mac. And, for the first time he smiled widely. A gold-filled front tooth twinkled at Mac in the semi-dark club.

"She is beautiful! Do you know her?"

"I have met her. I know her uncle, Jose Zaldivar. A captain in the Philippine Army."

By then the music had stopped, and the woman and her escort went back to their table. "How about the tall man with the moustache, beard, and eyeglasses? He appears to be with them. Do you know him?" Mac asked.

"No, Sir." Poco shook his head.

"I want you to introduce me to her."

"When?"

"Now!"

Poco was surprised at Mac's answer. "Now? She has two men with her. They may not like it."

"Jeez. I'm not going to sleep with her. I just want to meet her."

"Okay. Let us go out and come back in, and I will accidentally bump into their table."

They did as planned. Poco bumped into the table of the woman and her escorts, spilling champagne and ash trays on the floor. "I am so very sorry," he apologized.

"Sergeant Pocodillo," exclaimed the woman, with a look of surprise. "How good it is to see you again. How is your wife, Teri?"

"She is fine," Poco answered stiffly. "Oh. Ah. I want you to meet Major McCord, he arrived yesterday afternoon from the States."

"Hello. I am Miguela Molina," she told Mac. "And this is Manuel, my cousin, and Mr. Sonny Sollow, also an American."

"Hi," Mac murmured. Her soft brown eyes and low, accented voice thrilled him.

Manuel shook Mac's hand but Sollow refused and declared, "An... another lazy soldier b...b...boy on an...an...extended vacation. All you bas...bastards do is...is lay around and f...f...fuck."

"Mr. Sollow!" admonished Miguela.

Mac's face turned red. He grabbed Sonny Sollow by the collar and hissed on his face, "I don't like dirty words spoken in front of ladies and children," and pushed him to the floor.

Sonny Sollow pushed himself from the floor and told Miguela and Manuel that he was leaving.

"I think we should also leave, Major Mac. It is 2:30 a.m.," suggested Poco.

"Yes." He turned to Miguela and her cousin and apologized for his behavior and told Poco that he would call a taxi to take him home.

"No. I insist on driving you back to the BOQ, Major Mac." Poco said.

On their way out of the club, Mac and Poco simultaneously noticed a man standing by the main entrance, appearing to be waiting for someone. As they came closer to him, he raised his arm. But suddenly a person, like a flash of lightning, bumped hard into Mac, causing him to fall to the floor.

"I am so sorry," Mac heard a female voice apologizing. It was the small Filipina with the dyed red hair. Her dress was extremely tight and short, and the belt she had around her waist was wide with many stones of varied colors. "I am so sorry," she apologized again and quickly disappeared in the heavy rain outside.

In the meantime, Mac had sprung to his feet. "I hope today isn't going to be like yesterday."

"Manila is full of intrigues," quipped Poco. He moved closer to Mac and whispered, "Major, I think that woman saved your life. I think she bumped into you on purpose to distract the man by the door. I could have sworn I saw a dagger flash in his hand."

"The woman who bumped into me. Wasn't she the same person whom you called Cookie?" Mac asked.

"I did not see her face. It happened so fast. I had my eyes on the man."

The rain had not subsided. They ran to Poco's car and quickly got inside. Neither said a word for a while. Much later, Mac inquired what Poco thought of Sonny Sollow. Poco pursed his lips. "I found it curious why he had such an immediate dislike for you, like he already knew you."

"True!" Mac murmured, a perplexed look on his face.

CHAPTER 6

At about that same time in another part of the city, a black Chevrolet was speeding from Paranaque; it slowed upon reaching Taft Avenue, sped up again when it turned eastward, then stopped in front of a large stucco house in a fashionable residential area in the vicinity of Santo Tomas University, where many Filipino-Japanese and Japanese resided. Manilans referred to the place as Little Tokyo.

The driver reached for his raincoat, jumped out of the car, and ran to the door of the house. He knocked and waited, aware that the thunder, lightning, and the heavy rain made it difficult for people inside the house to hear his knocks. He knocked again, this time much louder. The door opened. "Oh, yes. Come in, Martinez," invited the tall and slender Japanese man. There was a quick exchange of conversation between them. "I think the general said that you would be coming from our Paranaque cadre. Is that right, Martinez?"

"Yes, but I was expecting to see General Tanaka."

"Oh, he is not back from Baguio."

"That is all right, Lieutenant Ikeda." Martinez was disappointed. "I am sorry I am thirty minutes early. But I think it is better this way. I wanted to take advantage of the rain."

"Yes. You have less of a chance of being followed. People generally sleep sounder when it is like this. By the way, Martinez, the general told me before he left to be sure to tell you how pleased he is with your work. And he remembers well what a good job you all did with that torpedo-loaded barge near the Cavite Naval Yard last November." Ikeda paused. "I am sorry that you have to travel such a distance, but the general wants you especially on this project."

Martinez was pleased with the compliment and thanked Ikeda.

"Here is the envelope. General Tanaka's instructions are inside. Give it to Sergeant Haleso in Olongapo. I understand you have worked with him before."

"Yes, Lieutenant." Martinez took the envelope, placed it inside his shirt, and left. He was soon out of Manila and on Route 3 going north, but in San Fernando, Pampanga, the car veered to the left on Route 7 to Olongapo, a navy town near the Subic Bay, about forty-five miles northwest of the city. When Martinez finally arrived on Subic Street, he parked the Chevrolet behind a house near Tony's Bar and Grill.

Martinez was a Filipino secret agent, highly regarded among the Japanese.

He got out of the car and knocked on the door. The flap to a small square window on the door opened, and a man peered out. Recognition came to his eyes, and instantly he opened the door for the short and heavyset Martinez.

"Good morning, Martinez," greeted the sleepy guard.

Martinez returned the greeting and hurriedly climbed the stairs, entering the room. Inside, three Filipino men were studying the Lingayen area on the map while the other two were exchanging views with one another as to the importance of Lingayen Gulf for their cause. They were all evidently waiting for someone. One of the men in the room, the only Japanese, approached Martinez with a pleased look on his face. "We did not know what to expect, so we all decided to stay awake. Do you have the instructions?" asked Sergeant Haleso, undercover military personnel in civilian clothes. He was like many Japanese military spies in the Philippines, posing as vendors, storekeepers, cabinetmakers, and gardeners.

Martinez nodded, taking out the legal-sized brown envelope from inside his shirt and handing it to Haleso, who opened it, took out two pieces of paper, and quietly read them. After a short while, he began to brief Martinez and the four other Filipinos in the room.

"General Tanaka wants us to do a job that must be accomplished tonight! According to him, the US cargo vessel Richmond is on its way here from Hawaii and will drop anchor tonight at Lingayen Gulf. In that ship are hundreds of 37-mm guns, Garand rifles (M1), revolvers, small shell ammunition, and many vehicles of various types—trucks, jeeps and even passenger cars."

Martinez raised his hand, and Sergeant Haleso acknowledged him. "You have a question?"

"Do you think our big leader, Red Rose, knows about that job order from General Tanaka?"

Haleso looked at Martinez for a long time. "He must," he answered hesitantly. "It is only logical that all orders should flow from his office to General Tanaka and down to all of us. Therefore, these papers I have in my hand must have come from Red Rose."

"I heard the big chief of our national spy organization is someone with the cover name of Big Iguana. Do you know who he is?" one of the Filipino agents in the room inquired.

"I do not have the slightest idea," answered Haleso.

"Well, do you know who Red Rose is?" the same Filipino inquired.

"If I did, I would not tell you. You Filipinos are too inquisitive and ask dangerous questions," Haleso answered tersely.

"What does Red Rose want for us to do?" Martinez asked, a deep and sincere fanaticism on his face and in his voice.

Haleso began to explain the instructions to the men. "We are to dynamite the cargo vessel Richmond. It must not reach Manila Harbor. There is a boat livery in the town of Lingayen where we can rent two native fishing boats so that we will be like the boats fishing the bay or the South China Sea. We must all be careful and not cause any suspicion or get caught or questioned."

Martinez interrupted Haleso. "Suppose I get caught. What then?"

Haleso's eyes narrowed. "I will kill you! It is too bad Agent 25 was killed by the Coastal Patrol. He had more brains than you," he said sarcastically.

"Sure. He had more brains, but I am still alive," laughed the tough Martinez. "What if you get caught, Sergeant Haleso? Do I kill you?"

"Don't bother. I will blow out my own brains," Haleso answered, giving Martinez an angry stare. "We have too much to do to waste time, so pay attention! US coastal patrols and Philippine Army units are all along the coastline of Lingayen Gulf. Those military groups are especially well trained. When we finish the job, we are not to go back to Olongapo; we will instead take Route 13 out of the town of Lingayen and drive as far as Tarlac. Then we are to take Route 3 in Tarlac to Manila and stay in the Pasay cadre with Agent 10, Captain Kondo, whom we all know." Haleso paused momentarily and looked at everyone in the room. "Understood?"

They all nodded.

"Good," Haleso said. "I am going to mention now this next assignment in Pasay because I may not have time later on. It will take all we can do to try and get out of the town of Lingayen after we sink the vessel Richmond tonight."

He paused. "We will be contacted in Pasay by someone from Red Rose's office for that next assignment, except for Martinez."

He looked at Martinez. "You stay in Lingayen and wait for an American by the name of Sonny Sollow. You are to help him destroy a US supplies convoy of ten army trucks coming from South Harbor in Manila going to Clark Field. You and Sollow will interdict the convoy between Manila and Angeles."

"Why me?" Martinez asked.

"Because you know Luzon better than anyone here, and you speak both English and Tagalog. No one will suspect you or the Americans," Haleso explained.

"I do not know this Sonny Sollow," Martinez said.

"It doesn't matter. He knows you! Besides, your role is not to question anything, Martinez." Haleso paused. "This Sonny guy is easy to anger. He cut off Colonel Matsumuto's little finger when he disagreed with him." Haleso yawned. "We are all tired. Let us get some rest."

"One last question," Martinez said. "Is the guard coming with us?"

"No. He stays here," said Haleso.

A couple of hours later, Haleso and his five Filipinos left Olongapo in two cars in accordance with the instructions. They parked the cars behind a small beer tavern by the side of the road near Route 13—an easy getaway from the coastal town.

They first reconnoitered the area, and then Martinez and another Filipino in the group walked to the boat livery where they rented two boats, complete with fishing poles and nets. They told the owner of the fishing marina that they, along with some friends, were going to use them for that night's fishing. Satisfied with the deal, they went back to the tavern and had a couple of beers.

Before dark came, Haleso and Martinez got in one of the cars, and this time they reconnoitered the western coastline of northern Luzon, from Lingayen to San Fernando, La Union.

About halfway to Vigan, they decided to go back to the tavern in Lingayen and joined the rest of their group. Not wanting to appear conspicuous, Haleso signaled his men to mingle with the other customers at the bar. The main topic of conversation there was the arrival of the US cargo vessel Richmond.

Haleso glanced at his watch. 11:30 p.m. He approached Martinez and whispered, "Go outside and see what you can learn about that ship."

Martinez did not have to do that. Everyone in the bar, including the bartender and the owner of the tavern, rushed outside. "The ship dropped anchor," shouted one jubilant man. "It is here! It is here! The American sailors are here! They are going to spend lots of money."

Martinez asked the owner, who was standing next to him, "How long will that ship stay?"

"About noon tomorrow, for Manila," answered the tavern's owner.

"Are the sailors going to stay in the vessel tonight?" Martinez again asked.

"Oh, no," answered the owner. "What for? No one is going to hijack her. Besides, I want for them to come ashore and spend money in my tavern. I have owned that place for fifteen years." He smiled. "Many of the women along this coastline have been waiting for the Richmond's arrival. I assure you, that ship will be empty within an hour. It has always been like that every year. Those sailors really enjoy themselves."

Martinez scratched his head. "Are they going to guard that ship?"

"Oh, maybe two or three sailors will stay in. Then after a while they are replaced by two or three other guards." The owner paused. "Why are you asking me all those questions? You must be a spy!"

"No. I am not a spy," answered Martinez nervously in Tagalog. "I am just an ignorant Filipino from Manila" Then he reverted to English. "I have never seen a big ship like that before."

The owner gave Martinez a hard suspicious stare and left.

A few minutes later, Sergeant Haleso and his five Filipinos went down to the boat livery where he and two of the men jumped in one boat, and the other two joined Martinez in the second boat.

Martinez waited for the go-signal from Haleso.

At 1:30 a.m. the last sailor had reached shore and disappeared inside the tavern. Haleso gave his signal. The two fishing boats left the marina and approached the anchored cargo vessel noiselessly. Haleso's boat approached the starboard of the vessel while Martinez kept his boat on the port side. They all sat there for five to ten minutes until they were certain there were no signs of life inside the Richmond.

Two men, one from Martinez's boat and the other from Haleso's, slipped into the water. With extra lines tied around their waists, they swam to the stern and pulled themselves up into the ship via anchor lines. Once they were in the ship, each man quickly threw down a line to his group and fastened the other end to a cleat for the men below to climb aboard. Four of the six men went to work immediately, planting dynamite in strategic places from bow to stern. Meanwhile, Haleso and Martinez rushed below to plant dynamite in the engine room.

Two of the American sailors guarding the vessel surprised the four Filipino saboteurs who had just finished their job and were sliding down the lines on their way down to their respective fishing boat. The American sailors opened fire, killing all four spies instantly. In the meantime, Haleso and Martinez, alerted by the shots, rushed out of the engine room. But all at once, the big cargo vessel exploded, followed by two more explosions. The fiery blasts shook the western hills of northern Luzon, and the orange and black smoke spiraling to the sky could be seen for many miles.

It took Richmond less than an hour to sink. There were no survivors. Shortly after it exploded on Lingayen Gulf, Sonny Sollow in Manila found a note under his door—

"Large Panamanian freighter, Flores, accompanying large ship to the Richmond will nose its way to Manila Bay, to dock at South Harbor around 5 or 6 p.m. tomorrow. Sorry about Martinez's death. He was a good agent. You will have to be on your own. Give this assignment your fullest attention. Contents are rifles, some 75-mm guns on self propelled mounts, medical supplies, signal equipment, 30-caliber machine guns and .50-caliber guns, ammunitions, and American Jeeps. Freighter contents will be unloaded into 10 Army trucks slated for Clark Field and Fort Stotsenburg. The Army convoy must not reach those bases. Destroy all Army trucks in the outskirt of Manila. Signed: Big Iguana."

He was tired and refused to react to the note. The following day, however, Sollow again read the message and carefully noted the signature of the sender and then carelessly threw the note on the table. He sat down on the sofa.

"Ah, Iguana," he said aloud angrily. "Let me count the ways of my hatred for you—you are an intolerable imbecile, a sycophant, and inept in managing the most wonderful spy network I created without your help! I'm a brilliant man, and I despise you for giving orders to me, Boris Meissner!" He pushed himself from the sofa and began pacing the floor, enraged.

"Oh, I wish that I had not promised the Fuhrer's chief of intelligence officer before I left Germany that I not harm any of Emperor Hirohito's officers or Mussolini's men."

He went back to the table where he laid Iguana's instructions and again read it. He then tore the note and burned it in the kitchen sink. Without hesitation, he called for a taxicab to pick him up and grabbed a small briefcase before he left the house. He walked to the end of the street and discretely waited. When the cab finally arrived, Sollow told the driver to hurry to South Harbor.

Among the small cafes Sollow selected was the one with the best view of the pier and a table in the far and quiet corner of the restaurant overlooking the pier. According to workers at the terminal, the freighter Flores would be docking there. From his seat, he would now and then direct his gaze on the busy pier. Many stevedores were busily carrying barrels of dried fish from ships to their receivers while others carried goods such as sacks of rice en route to Macao, Hong Kong, and Formosa. There were some stevedores pushing carts with heavy household equipments slated for the Visayan Islands. Two or three long empty carts pulled by horses waited on the side for other incoming cargoes.

Sollow fidgeted with his food and asked the waitress for his second cup of coffee. Time slipped by quickly; and still there were no signs of the Flores. So as not to invite any more suspicions from the waitress (who had already inquired earlier whether he was waiting for someone), he decided to leave the café with his briefcase but stay within distance of the terminal.

Sollow sat under a shady tree, closed his eyes and slept.

He was suddenly awakened by the rumbling sounds of empty trucks on the streets. And that was when he began counting Army truck after Army truck passing in front of him. There were exactly twelve trucks, two more than the number Iguana had indicated in his instruction. Like some Filipino children and adults, he too began following the Army vehicles as they wound their way into the now congested Manila Harbor.

He glanced at his watch and was surprised at the time: 8:00 in the evening. Turning to the young man running next to him, Sollow asked what the trucks were all about. "You don't know?" answered the man.

"No. I don't know," said Sollow.

"They are going to pick up something at the pier. Maybe food," explained the Filipino.

"How long will the unloading last?" Sollow inquired.

"Oh, maybe three or four hours. Perhaps longer. And then it will take them forever to deliver them. You know how slow convoys travel. I heard they are going to Clark Field and Fort Stotsenburg."

"How do you know so much?" Sollow asked.

"My older brother is a Philippine Scout," answered the Filipino running ahead of Sollow.

Sollow went back to the same café. This time he ordered beer. While being served, he asked the waitress how long the unloading operation would take.

"I often see how much time it takes to unload those freighters. They probably will not finish tonight. And just moving those Army trucks out of here will take a very long time," explained the waitress.

The passing of many hours confirmed what the waitress had said. Deep darkness had overtaken the unloading process. Sollow approached one of the stevedores and inquired if the Flores would soon finish its commitment to the Army. He answered that the last Jeep had just been unloaded and that the lead truck appeared to be heading out of the shipping terminal.

Darkness became Sollow's advocate. He picked up a sack of rice from among the stack on the ground and carried it on his shoulder. Confidently, he walked to where the lead Army truck stood, making certain that he would be seen just as another worker. With the sack of rice still on his shoulder, he lifted the tarpaulin that covered the rear part of the vehicle. To his surprise, neither the contents nor any of the trucks were guarded. Having established that, he slowly looked inside the cab of the lead truck. The driver, a young corporal, had a rifle on his lap and was sound asleep next to his partner. With agility, Sollow took the head of the driver in his large hands and twisted his neck. He dragged the lifeless body out of the truck and dropped it into the bay. Looking carefully to be sure he was not being watched, he walked to where the military police sat on the passenger seat and awoke him. "Hey, wake up," he told the startled soldier. "I just killed your buddy. Unless you do exactly what I want you to do, I'll also kill you," Sollow told him while at the same time taking away the rifle from the guard. "Understood?"

"Yes, Sir," answered the guard.

"Are there any more military police guarding the trucks?"

"Yes, sure," said the military police. "There are three of them. They are in a separate truck. They'll be guarding the rear of the convoy. They're armed with rifles."

"Here's what I want you to do," said Sollow. "I want you to approach the driver of each truck and tell them this—'Upon reaching the outskirt of Manila, we are to park in a row, one truck behind each other, and stop. It'll probably be midnight and we'll all be tired. We all need to rest a couple of hours. Some of you might want to go to the all-night nearby bar and restaurant and have a couple of beers. I'll give you all a signal when it's time for us to proceed with our journey." Sollow paused. "Understood?"

"Yes, Sir," answered the military police.

"Now go. Tell the drivers and the guards," Sollow commanded. "And remember, I'll be right behind you with this dagger. Any funny move and I'll slit your throat. When you finish, we'll go back together to your truck. I'll drive, but I'll tie your hands and feet. If you're asked where your buddy is, tell them he was supposed to report to the Philippine Department for another assignment."

"Yes, Sir," answered the frightened military police.

They had reached the outskirt of Manila. All the trucks parked according to instructions and the men all went to the bar and restaurant.

Now alone, Sollow grabbed the military police by the neck, twisted it, and left his dead body in the truck. Meanwhile, the tired regular enlisted men were only too willing to spend a couple of hours drinking beer and exchanging stories. For some, it was meeting women in the all-night bar. Sleep was immaterial to all of them. It was great not to be working. The nickelodeon was loud with popular American music, and they were joyous at their unexpected liberation from their daily tedious duties. While the men were blissfully enjoying themselves, Sollow's plan of destruction formulated in his mind. Actually, he did not have to think long. He had already planned it, and he was aware that the success of his plan depended on one very, very simple strategy—speed! He had an important thing to do first. He enticed each of the three military police outside guarding the convoy to accept three bottles of whiskey that he had purchased from the bar. While they slept from excessive drinking, Sollow strangled the intoxicated men. They never knew what hit them.

Sollow then sat down on the ground beside the lead truck and opened his small but deep suitcase. Inside were twelve clusters, three sticks of dynamite to a cluster. Each cluster was attached to a long, twisted, finger-like cotton cloth soaked in gasoline, which he carefully extended from the lead truck to the next truck until he reached the last of the vehicles occupied by the now-dead military guards. His scheme of madness did not stop until he had lighted a match to the twisted cloth which would carry the ignition from end to end.

The explosions reverberated throughout the stunned outskirts of Manila. Sollow entered the restaurant at the same time of the explosions. One of the soldiers standing by the door had witnessed the violent noise. Turning to him, he said, shocked, "Hey, mister. Did you see anyone who could have set those trucks off?"

"Nope," answered Sollow. "I just got here." He nonchalantly walked away from the soldier and went to the bar and ordered beer, hardly able to contain his elation over his evil triumph. Fire trucks and police did not take long to arrive. People came from everywhere to gawk at the wild flames and smoke rising towards the darkened sky that shattered the serene night. Thousands of pieces of metal objects had catapulted beyond sight, only to come down with unmitigated, undirected force. The fire from the burning trucks continued to spiral upwards and

73

hungrily emblazoned the black sky with red and gray. While chaos was everywhere and the mangled trucks offered evidence to the heinous crime, Sollow disappeared into the darkness of night, pleased with another of his masterpiece of destruction. The breadth of his obsession knew no bounds.

CHAPTER 7

Mac found his door unlocked when he returned from the club. He swore he had secured it before joining Poco. Shrugging, he let himself into his room, turned on the lights, and stared in bewilderment. What the hell? Why would anyone try to kill me, steal one of my suitcases and now, ransack my room? he murmured angrily. He rushed to where Poco had deposited his other luggage and saw the lock broken. He quickly examined the contents of the luggage and found them to be intact, and remembering where Poco had placed his briefcase, Mac got on his knees and searched under the bed. Fear gripped him. "It's not here! It's been stolen! Where are you! Whoever you are? Come out from hiding and confront me!" He shouted angrily. Mac stopped shouting abruptly. "Could it be you, Meissner, who has been trying to kill me? Come out from hiding and confront me," he said loudly.

Exhausted and frustrated, he kicked the door shut and sat on the sofa, mentally reviewing the contents of the stolen briefcase—there were the data on Meissner that his friend John Stone at the FBI had provided him including some unclassified reports obtained from newspapers and rumors; a copy of Lieutenant Colonel Walters's letter to Colonel Polson at the War Department; an insightful report written by a navy commander on the Tripartite Pact, given to Mac by Jean Cisco, librarian of Army Group 1/Europe at Tempo U, before he left Washington. A copy of his Orders was also in that briefcase, including his Army Colt .45 pistol.

Despite the rain, the temperature in the room was almost intolerable. Mac got to his feet, turned on the ceiling fan, and opened all the windows in the room. Every muscle in his body ached. Going with Poco to the Manila International Club and staying out all night did not help. He could not remember where he had eaten a good meal but at the moment he would rather sleep than eat. He took off his shoes, left the radio and light on, and slumped on his bed, still wearing his clothes, and was soon fast asleep.

The exteremely bright Manila sun streaming through the windows of his room awakened him. The radio blared about a US cargo vessel, Richmond, exploding very early that morning on Lingayen Gulf. "It's too soon to tell, but the natives in that coastal area suspect it to be foul play," the radio commentator explained.

Mac quickly turned off the radio. He was not in the mood to hear any more bad news. But the Richmond incident occupied the airwaves. "Hell, I'm in a hostile environment!" he murmured, rolling out of bed.

He showered, changed, and hailed a taxicab for downtown Manila, walked around the Escolta, bought a newspaper and soon discovered a Manila café, where he ordered a late lunch and coffee. The headline about the cargo vessel's explosion attracted his attention. But his thought process continued on into another avenue.

Mac began to think through the attacks on him. Why am I being followed and attached here in the Philippines? Is Meissner really in this country? If he is, as Walters had stated in his letter, is it because Meissner believes that I'm able to identify him? But I don't know what he looks like! I can't identify him! I've never seen him in person! I've never even seen a photograph of him. He paused mentally. But Meissner doesn't know that! he told himself. He must think that I saw him peeping in the room while I was attending to Duvalier. Could it be Meissner who's after me? Mac reasoned that suspecting the German spy may or may not help, but that it was a good start. All he had to do now was to find him. He knew it would be difficult, if not almost impossible. He recalled what the dying Duvalier told him. Meissner is a shadow.

But, I'll find him! Mac gritted his teeth.

He took the thick ring off his finger and held it up against the bright sunlight streaming in through the glass panels of the café, turning it on several angles and squinted to read the words inside, which he already knew by heart: 'To Sonny, love, Mother.'

Mac slipped the ring back on his finger and facetiously wondered if it had voodoo power. He lifted his eyes in time to witness a taxicab weaving and heading towards the front door of the Manila café. The cab lurched, jumped on the cement sidewalk, and stopped, barely missing the glass panels of the restaurant. Suddenly, the back door of the taxicab opened and a man in an all-white suit got out, entered the café, and dropped dead at Mac's feet, a dagger deep in his back.

Mac shouted to the waitress serving him to call the police as he searched the dead man's pockets for identification. He found a wallet with a driver's license and a card with the dead man's picture and name, James. W. Kagan, and his FBI badge.

"Jesus Christ," Mac said under his breath. "Miss," he called the waitress, "Were you able to call the police?"

"No, Sir," she answered. "The line is busy."

Mac pushed himself up from his crouched position and took the telephone from the waitress. "Let me try." After two tries the police department finally answered, whereupon he reported the murder. Mac immediately went outside and looked in the taxicab and found the driver slumped forward on the wheel, his head and face were bleeding. The driver was trying to say something.

"How are you, old timer?" Mac asked, at the same time wiping the blood off the old man's face with his handkerchief. "Do you speak English?"

The taxidriver lifted his head and looked at Mac. "Weer aam I?"

"An inch away from the Manila café's front door," explained Mac.

Although he was still dazed, the Filipino driver made motions of trying to get out of his cab. "Eep I could haab a glass op waater, I weeel bee ukay."

Mac got some water and gave it to the old man who emptied the glass and told Mac that he had to move his taxicab before the police arrived and charge him for reckless driving. "Eet waas naat my pault." Just about then, they could hear sirens in the distance. "Dey are caaming. I maast leabe."

The only way to know the whole story was to go along in the cab and listen to what the old man had to say. Mac doubted that he knew the murdered American was an FBI agent. Mac told the driver to wait. He quickly paid for his breakfast and jumped into the cab. "You had better press on that gas if you don't want the police to catch you."

The cabdriver kept driving until he reached the Walled City and stopped in front of a Catholic church, hastily making the sign of the cross. "I am saape here in Intramuros."

"The police won't find you in the Walled City. Did you know that man in your cab was murdered?"

The old man shook his head. "No. Weets waan?"

"The man in the white suit. He was an American," was all Mac said.

"Baat dey were bot Americanos," the cabdriver told Mac.

"Could you tell me what happened?"

The cabdriver slowly explained that he was on his way back to downtown Manila when he saw two men standing on Dewey Boulevard, evidently waiting for transportation. The man in the white suit flagged him down, and both got inside. According to the cabbie, they seemed like two friends until the man in the white suit directed him to stop at the nearest police station. "I guess he wass guuing tuu turn hees preind een."

"So, what happened next?" Mac inquired. The cabdriver answered by explaining that, suddenly, the two men started fighting. The man in the dark clothes commanded the driver to keep on going and cross the Pasig River Bridge to the Escolta. "I deed, baat he heet me uun my head enyway weed hees gun."

Mac took a deep breath. "I guess you had better take me to work. 170 Olivia Street."

"Studying Mac's face in the rear view mirror, the cabdriver declared that he had delivered an Army officer to that same address not too long ago.

Mac remained silent.

"New to Mayneela?" the cabdriver asked.

Mac nodded.

"I can teel. Yuu are pale. Waan week here and yuu weel be brown like me." The driver noted and paused. "Wat ees going uun een dat uuld house?"

"Nothing. Just a meeting."

"Dat uuld beeldeeng ees baad lack."

"What do you mean it's bad luck?" Mac asked with interest.

The cabdriver explained that, for a long time, the house was a bar called Sergio's Bar and Grill, where people spent many hours drinking during their off days from work. He further explained that Sergio's was a very rough place but was popular with Filipinos as well as with American soldiers and sailors. "I teenk ebery seex months der waas always saamwaan muurdered der. Suum times a Peeleepeeno, baat suumtimes Amereecan suuldier bouys."

"Why would they kill American soldiers? Slow down a bit, old timer. I got a little time. Drive around a couple of blocks. Mac leaned forward from the back seat and brought his face closer to the driver. "When was the bar closed?"

Encouraged by Mac's attentiveness, the driver related that last year after an American Army officer was fatally shot and carried away, his body was never found again. He paused. "I waas dere. I saaw eberyteeng. Baat a mont ago saamwaan reets bouut de house and made eet luukeeng nice."

"Wait a minute. Did you say you were there and saw an American Army officer murdered?

The cabdriver nodded but added in his simple way that he didn't mention the incident to anyone for fear the same man who killed the officer would also kill him.

"Then why are you telling me?" Mac asked suspiciously.

The cabdriver smiled widely. He had very few teeth. "Yuu were kind tuu me. Anywaan kind tuu cheeldren, uuld people and aneemals, ees kind. I trasst kind people," he explained, wiping with the back of his hand the saliva that had dripped to the sides of his mouth. He elaborated that it was time for him to tell someone, because the secret had been heavy in his heart. He kept looking on and off, from the rear view mirror to the road until his brown eyes locked with Mac's steel-blue eyes. "Uunly yuu aand de Bleesed Beergen Mary knuu about dees."

"I appreciate your confidence in me, and the Blessed Virgin will bless you for it," Mac said and tapped the cabdriver on the shoulder. "What's your name?"

"Teadore Ruuseebelt Panganeeban."

"Theodore Roosevelt Panganiban?" Mac repeated and spelled the last name.

"Yees, baat yuu caan cull mee Ruusee," the old cabdriver said. He told Mac that his father was a great admirer of Roosevelt during the time of the Spanish-American War. His father also thought that Teddy Roosevelt was a fine president for America.

"Thanks, Roosie. Teddy Roosevelt was a fine president. By the way, where were you in the bar that you should say no one saw you?"

Without hesitation, the cabdriver related that it was his day off, and by early that afternoon, he had already drank too much San Miguel beer. The regular customers did not come until maybe 6 or 7 o'clock that evening. There was only himself, Sergio, two other civilians, and the American soldier in the Bar and Grill.

"Go on," Mac prodded.

Roosie laughed loudly and related that he must have eventually blacked out from having drunk too much beer. He was certain that Sergio dragged him behind the counter and let him sleep it off on the floor. With pride in his voice he told Mac that he and Sergio were good friends, and Sergio took good care of him whenever he got drunk. And anyway, when he felt better and was about to get up and go home, he saw a tall white man in a cream colored suit standing by the exit door. Although a straw hat was pulled low over his face, he could see that the tall man had blond hair. "I saaw heem tek a gaan prom hees waistband aand shuut de Amereecan suuldier aas he waas leebeeng. De gaan deed naat make any nuuise." Roosie paused to clear his throat.

"How could you have seen the murderer if you were behind the counter?"

Roosie explained to Mac that the bar counter was near and in line with the exit door and that his eyes had a clear shot of the door.

Mac asked where Sergio was at the time.

"I duunaat knuu. Baat he haad a habeet op stepeeng next duur tuu see a friend."

Furthermore, Roosie said that the murderer had signaled two men to carry away the dead American officer. He then paid the two men. They were Japanese, said Roosie .

"How did you know they were Japanese?"

He became indignant. "Leesten, suuldier buoy. I aam aan uuld maan. I haabe seen a lot op Hapons, and know a Hapon ween I see waan." He paused and cleared his throat. "Yes, dey weer Hapons. Dey luuk deeperent pram Peeleepeenos. All hapons luuk de saame."

"Sorry about doubting you, old timer." Mac lighted a Chesterfield cigarette and offered one to Roosie, who immediately placed it behind his ear.

"Did you know the American Army officer's name?" Mac asked.

Roosie related to Mac that he had heard from several people later that his name was either Abe Stone or Steiner, and that he was a Jew. He ran his tongue on his lips, and then continued. According to the old man, he had seen him in the bar many times, but he was always by himself and always asked many questions, usually regarding the murders of two Army officers.

Mac was startled with the revelation. That was probably Captain Abe Stein, Mac said to himself. Poco had told him about Stein last Saturday while they were at the Manila International Club.

"Would you recognize the tall white man who killed the American Army officer if you saw him now?"

Roosie replied that he would not, but the tall man was wearing a wide belt with a large, gold buckle that had an imprint of a cobra head. The old man stopped the cab in front of a building where Mac was to meet his group for a meeting. He charged Mac 50 centavos for his fare.

"Say, old timer, I'd like to keep in touch with you. Where can I find you?"

"I oopen wait puur riders een pront uup de Mayneela Eenternational Claab."

"Is there someone there who would know you in case I needed to see you?"

Roosie told Mac that his grandson Alberto worked as a waiter at the Manila International Club. He then handed Mac a card with his name and telephone number and that he would pick him up any time he wanted a taxicab.

"Good." Mac carefully placed the card in his wallet. "I'm Major Jake McCord, but call me Mac."

CHAPTER 8

Mac's gut told him that Roosie was truthful, regardless of the fact that his story sounded a bit fictional. He was so convinced of Roosie's veracity that he wanted to see the proximity of the exit door of the former Sergio's Bar and Grill to the backyard's fenced gate of the Nagoya Emporium. He estimated that from where he stood there was about ten to twenty feet distance between the two buildings.

It was a narrow alley, much narrower than many of the alleys he had seen in his native Virginia. It separated the former Bar and Grill from the large Japanese bazaar that was enclosed by a six-foot barbed-wire fence. It was still early in the morning, but the heat and humidity were already unbearable, and Mac wondered how the trees, shrubberies, and animals were surviving the unmerciful weather.

He had a strong urge to go into the backyard of the Japanese bazaar, but since it was broad daylight, and nearby streets were busy, he decided a more appropriate time would present itself later on. After all, he did not wish to be accosted by the emporium and questioned about his intentions.

There was one object that almost escaped him. Behind some dying shrubberies was a five-foot by eight-foot cement slab laid near the back door of the emporium and facing the fenced gate. Next to the slab was an unusually wide doghouse. Mac turned away when he saw a fawn-colored Boxer sniffing around and digging at the hard surface on the edge of the cement slab. It appeared from the appearance of some loose earth that the Boxer had been successful earlier, but became discouraged from further digging by the presence of rocks that had been placed strategically underneath the slab.

Big fellow, Mac thought, and decided to leave the alley and walk around to his soon-to-be office. He believed Roosie's story, and now he must be careful with whom he shared it. He was glad he still had a few minutes left to himself.

He turned the knob and opened the door. "Hello! Is someone here?" Mac called out. No one answered. He closed the door softly behind him while his alert steel-blue eyes made quick assessments of the room. The floor was highly polished and the four walls were of mahogany. The two new ceiling fans and two big floor fans were whirling away, circulating cool air. To the right side of the main entrance was an enclosed office with the name, "Col. Bradford Miller" painted on the door. Not far from the colonel's office was another door with iron bars. Above the door was the red sign—Exit. That must have been the place from which Roosie saw the tall, blond man shot Stein. It pleased him to know that no one was yet in the building.

Mac noticed that at the center of the perfectly square room were six desks and chairs, and close to each desk was a metal safe with a bar and a lock. Facing the desks were two wide windows with bars and black painted glass panes. On the wall were two large framed photographs that dominated the entire room, that of President Franklin D. Roosevelt and a picture of another dignified and handsome man whom Mac recognized to be the president of the Commonwealth of the Philippines, Manuel L. Quezon. Below the framed photographs was a blackboard with chalks neatly placed in a row. The room looked clean and comfortable. He assumed it was also used as a briefing room. He walked towards the blackboard, and to the right of that were three enlarged maps—one of the Philippines, one of Manila, and a separate map of Luzon, which primarily occupied his interest. On the left side of the blackboard were maps of Japan, Germany, and Europe.

Mac had earlier noticed where Colonel Miller's office was located in the large room. But approximately six feet to the right of his enclosed office was a desk, a metal safe, and a window similar to the others. A cardboard taped to the front side of the desk read—Deputy: LTC Sonny Rhoades.

"I'll be damned," Mac said under his breath. "Dusty Rhoades!"

He opened the door to Miller's office. His window had no bars, nor were the glass panes painted. It vulnerably looked out on Olivia

Street. Shutting the door quickly behind him, Mac became aware that, between Miller and Rhoades's offices, was the secretary's desk next to an Underwood typewriter.

Mac heard the front door opened and closed. He turned around. It was Dusty Rhoades.

"I see you got in," Rhoades said.

"The door was unlocked," answered Mac.

"I unlocked it before I went to get a cup of coffee," said Rhoades. "I figured someone would get here before I returned. There aren't any classified papers yet in this room." He glanced at his watch. "Excuse me, Mac. I've a telephone call to make."

Mac gave the map of Europe a cursory look and became interested once again on the map of Luzon. He heard footsteps, and, turning around, he heard Poco tell an Army officer with him, "That is Major McCord."

The barrel-chested officer was making strides toward him. Despite his large frame, he was agile and extremely self-confident in the way he moved. He was over six feet tall; his dark brown hair was thinning. A rugged, tan face sported a walrus-like moustache. Mac apprised the major as looking fit and strong but old for his rank; he must have been around fifty years old.

"Hello. You must be the anointed one sent from Washington, DC. I'm Charlie North, and do call me Charlie," he greeted in his deep voice, while extending a large hand to shake Mac's own extended hand. "I respect a man with a firm handshake," Charlie said, nodding his head in an approving and friendly manner.

Mac smiled. "I'm Jake McCord, Sir," he said and was quick to notice the studied, laid-back manner and suppressed arrogance of Charlie. Despite his critical appraisal of Charlie, Mac liked his manliness and easy humor.

"You were studying the map of Luzon when we came in. Looking for a particular place?" Charlie inquired with curiosity.

"Oh, I was just trying to locate Clark Field," Mac answered.

"You've your finger on the Clark Field area," Charlie said.

"What mountain is this?" Mac inquired with interest.

North snorted. "That'll cost you lunch. That's Mt. Arayat. It's over three thousand feet high and Clark Field's most distinguished landmark. The town of Arayat is southeast of the mountain." Charlie paused momentarily and, playing serious, said, "That'll be your first lesson today on Philippine geography. Anyway, McCord, welcome to vacationland. Poco hasn't left out anything about you." Charlie paused again, this time studying Mac's face. "Jeez, Mac," he said jokingly, "you're awfully white." His weather-beaten face cracked into a wide smile, displaying a slight gap between his two front teeth.

"Strange. A cabdriver also told me that," answered Mac sheepishly.

"Don't tell me his name. I bet it was that outspoken Theodore Roosevelt Panganiban. I like the old codger." Charlie paused.

"I know you're calling me "Sir" because of my age and not my rank. I'm probably the oldest US Army officer in Manila, but don't make me feel any older. I'll be your friend if you call me Charlie. Come on, I want you to meet the rest of the team," Charlie said.

"Wait a minute, Charlie, I'd like to talk to you and Poco outside," Mac said, leading the way towards the front door. Once they were by themselves, Mac related to them the murder of the American FBI agent that morning at the Manila café.

"Mac," Charlie asked, "did the FBI agent say anything to you?"

Mac shook his head.

Charlie took a deep breath and sounded remorseful. "I'm sorry to hear that he died. Poco told me about the incident at the pier and the subsequent incidents you encountered. How's your shoulder?"

"Fine," Mac murmured and proceeded to mention his room being ransacked after coming home from the club with Poco.

"My briefcase was stolen. It contained important and some classified papers and my pistol."

"Listen up, Mac. You had better be careful. You could be the next victim," Charlie advised. "Someone out there wants to kill you."

"You sound so adversarial, Charlie," Mac said, surprised at the older major's intonation.

They joined the group, and Charlie announced loudly, "Gentlemen, this is Major Jake McCord. Mac arrived three days ago from Washington DC. He's joining our team."

A slight-of-build young lieutenant with wavy hair, thick eyebrows, and a slight under bite, came forward. "Mac, I'm Saul Golden." There was a friendliness in his voice and on his intelligent face. "I can see you just got here. This Philippine sun will soon take care of that," he said pleasantly. "Where're you from, Mac?"

"Kilmarnock, Virginia. Not far from Richmond."

"Oh, yeah. That's in the Northern Neck. I used to have a friend who lived in Irvington. He and I used to go fishin' on the Rappahannock River around Urbanna. Sometimes we'd go to Gwynn Island and do some fishin' there." Golden paused. "I'm from Jersey. I bet you knew the minute I started talkin' I was from Jersey." He smiled. "We've been expectin' you."

"The transport ship took in some problems," Mac said.

"We heard you're from an Army intelligence group in Wash'ton, DC. You like intelligence work?" Golden said.

Mac nodded. "I do enjoy cloak-and-dagger-type work. I think I'm good at it. Besides, even if I didn't enjoy it, the Army has been super to me. I'd give it my best shot."

Mac lit a Chesterfield cigarette. "How about you, Golden? What's your outfit?"

"Philippine Division, Major General Jonathan M. Wainwright, 31st Infantry, at the Post of Manila, downtown. Ammo supply unit."

"And now you're here doing some intelligence."

Golden shrugged his shoulders. "Beats me. My knowledge about spy work is zilch. Major North has been briefin' and applyin' the cram style on me, Czestochowa and Delgado when Colonel Walters died. I un'derstan' from him that our new boss is Colonel Miller." Golden sighed. "I'm glad I'm a short timer. My two years'll be up by the end of this month. This hot, humid weather's too much for me. I bet it's already a hundred-thirty degrees un'er a shade."

"Okay, Golden," another second lieutenant said, elbowing the genial Golden from monopolizing Mac. "Give me a chance to introduce myself to our newest member," he said rudely. "And for chrissake, stop telling anyone that'd listen to your sad story about missing the good ol' USA. I should be the one complaining. I've another year left." Then he lowered his voice. "Jew boy, your problem is you can't make it with those women in Olongapo and Cavite. Your prick is too short."

"You dumb, big Minnesota Polak! Stop payin' those pimps to look up girls for you! One of these days your balls are gonna fall off from gonorreah," snapped the feisty Golden. "At least I've a better plan for my organ."

Charlie North removed the thick cigar from his mouth. "Don't mind these two pups, Mac. They're good friends. They're just trying to get rid of their aggression," he explained, his hand on the Minnesotan's shoulder.

"Mac, this young giant is Stanislaw Czestochowa. Inside his tough exterior is a cuddly bear, and being of Polish descent, I bet he hates the Nazis. Don't you, old buddy?"

"With a purple passion, Sir," he answered and went on to introduce himself. "Hi, Mac. Czestochowa." And, adding good-naturedly said, "My last name stops everyone's thought process. He suddenly stopped talking. "Hey, Mac. Where'd you get that ring? Have you robbed a bank? Us lowly and underpaid characters can't afford that."

"Czestochowa." Admonished Charlie, "you're embarrassing our newly-arrived friend." He paused. "Don't be too hard on him, Mac. He and I are friends."

"It's okay, Charlie. And I don't embarrass easily. But it's an old ring," Mac told those around him. And since he did not think Czestochowa needed an explanation, he quickly changed the subject. "Are you with Golden at the Post of Manila?"

Czestochowa nodded. "But in a different outfit. I'm with training."

"I can see the team is well-represented," Mac mumbled.

Charlie lead Mac away to another part of the room and explained that although Walters believed that diversity in specialities would make their mission more effective, nevertheless, Golden, Czestochowa, and Delgado were given intelligence briefings. Poco following behind, voiced that Golden would replace Summers and Czestochowa would take Haggarty's place. Delgado and Mac, respectively, were assigned to replace Gibbs and Stein. Poco further mentioned that Delgado and Golden were soon to leave for the US at the end of June.

All the faces in the room turned when the entrance door opened and closed. Dusty Rhoades announced, "Gentlemen, Colonel Miller."

"That is Delgado walking behind Colonel Miller," Poco whispered to Mac. He is from Brownsville, Texas." Czestochowa overheard what Poco told Mac and added sarcastically, "The Mex is probably one of General Santa Anna's descendants who got left behind in Texas."

"Grow up, Czestochowa," snapped Charlie.

Following Delgado was a pretty Filipina who kept on walking until she had reached the secretary's desk and then raising her eyes looked directly at Mac. "Who's she?" Mac asked Poco with a start. He was not certain, but he thought he had seen her before.

"I do not know her," said Poco.

There was a sudden hush in the room when Rhoades announced, "Gentlemen. Please. The meeting is now in session." He paused. "This is Colonel Bradford Miller."

"Hey, Mac," Czestochowa said in a low voice, "let me try that ring on my finger. I've a thing about beautiful rings. That one might give me luck. I sort of feel that lady luck is deserting me."

Mac ignored him, but not for long. Czestochowa insisted to the point of being obnoxious. "Come on, Mac. Let me try it on."

"Okay. But it might not fit. You're a bit heavier than I," Mac said, handing Czestochowa the ring just to quiet him.

Czestochowa forced the blue sapphire ring in his left index finger and soon discovered he could not remove it and began to fidget with it.

Colonel Miller was a tall man with a fast gait when he walked. His face was expressionless with a mouth that looked small for his wide countenance. His receding hairline was blond, and his eyes were furtive. He had an air of readiness about him. "Good morning, gentlemen," he greeted and glanced to where the secretary stood and acknowledged her presence by a nod of his head. "Miss. Please be seated. You all know why you are here. I've been told that everyone has been briefed. However, I think that we should first get to know each other," Miller continued. "Gentlemen, this lovely young woman is Miss Purita Aquino. She's going to be the team's secretary and will report to Lieutenant Colonel Rhoades. Miss Aquino is on leave from the Philippine Department to help us. Colonel Rhoades has spent a lot of his time looking for the right woman and was able to convince the Army command of our need. Miss Aquino came highly recommended."

The thirty-year-old secretary acknowledged Miller's introduction and gave the group a self-conscious smile.

"Now, I shall introduce myself, and the rest will follow in descending order of seniority." Miller stopped and then continued, "Several months ago, while I was still assigned in Washington, DC, the War Department handed me a letter signed by the Army Chief of Staff. The department advised me of my new assignment at the Philippine Department, G-2, here in Manila. Then when Lieutenant Colonel Walters drowned, I requested that I form an investigative operation expressly to catch the spy who, we believe, murdered Major Haggarty, Summers, and Captain Stein. As you all know, that's our mission—to catch a spy and a murderer. Included in this plan, of course, will be the recent murder of Lieutenant Gibbs. Both civil and military investigators were unsuccessful under Lieutenant Colonel Walters. Hopefully, this new team will be! You answer only to me." Miller paused. "And I will answer only to the commander of the Philippine Department, the United States's highest Army command in Asia. This undertaking is top secret, and our findings are considered sensitive, in that they could mean danger and even death for one or more of us if they get in the wrong hands." Miller proceeded to tell the team that there were only two or three people who knew about their clandestine operation, and no one must know about it if they were to make their particular mission successful.

He went on, "Now, you might ask, why were you not given training in detective work but, instead, a quick study in intelligence?" It was because the killer was believed to be not only a very clever spy but also a murderer. If they caught the spy, he emphasized, they would catch the murderer. "I understand the FBI will be investigating this also because American lives are involved, and the Philippines is an American colony." He looked at everyone in the room but gave Mac an especially careful scrutiny. "My superiors have given me only about six months to accomplish this particular job. We should have results by October and definitely by 1942." He walked to the blackboard and wrote down the names, Golden and Delgado. "I was told that these two officers will soon be leaving—"

His words were cut short by a sharp sound of an object bouncing off the highly polished wooden floor. All eyes watched as the object settled into a rolling action, gaining momentum, going on a fast straight path, and stopping at Colonel Miller's feet. He picked it up and studied it intensely, closed his hand over it, and finished what he started to say.

"The reason these two officers were sent to us was, I was told, that our mission has a low priority. And they will not be replaced." Miller studied the ring again and quickly placed his finger on his lips to stop a nervous twitch on the left side of his mouth whenever something excited him. "When this work is finished, I'll report to my superiors for my future assignment. Thank you." He glanced at Rhoades. "Let's start with you, then North, McCord, Delgado, Czestochowa, Golden and Pocodillo."

Rhoades jumped to his feet. "I'm Sonny Rhoades, Fort Stotsenburg. I personally applied for this assignment. I wanted the opportunity to work with an intelligence expert like Colonel Miller," he paused. "I want all of you to call me Dusty." He turned to face Miller. "Sir, I'd like to take this opportunity to thank you for taking me in your team."

Miller nodded his approval and pointed to Charlie, who introduced himself, whereupon Miller inquired whether his family was in Manila. "No, Sir. My wife went back to Chicago several months ago. She could no longer stand the extreme heat and high humidity. Plus the US Army and the High Commissioner in Manila wanted the American civilians to leave. One reason—only speculation on my part, Sir—I think is that the US is getting edgy about Japan's exploitation in Asia." Charlie paused. "Really, Sir. I think it's Japan's overall designs in Asia that could worsen and cause problems for Uncle Sam. Just listen to what Japan is propagandizing every day, Asia for Asians."

Miller began pacing the floor and without looking at Charlie, asked, "North, do you have children?"

"Yes, Sir. A boy and a girl. They left with my wife," answered Charlie.

Miller abruptly stopped pacing the floor and faced Charlie. "Do you still have your parents?"

"No, Sir. Just my mother." A pained look flitted across his face. "She's a widow. My father died about five years ago."

"I understand this is your second tour of duty in the Philippines," Miller said.

"Yes, Sir. This tour will end in six months of this year," Charlie answered.

"Why two tours of duty? You must enjoy Manila." Miller began pacing once again.

"I want to help find the spy and killer, Sir. Lieutenant Colonel

Walters's death was unfortunate," Charlie patiently answered, and then cleared his throat. "Sir, may I inquire respectfully what your intentions are for asking all those pointed questions?"

Miller looked a long time at North. "Because you have the longest tour of duty here among all of us. We can all learn from you about this country." Before he nodded to Mac to introduce himself, he inquired, "To whom does this blue sapphire ring belong?" He raised the ring towards the light and read aloud the inscriptions inside. 'To Sonny, Love, Mother.' "Does this ring belong to you, Lieutenant Colonel Sonny Rhoades?" Miller said, emphasizing the name "Sonny."

"No, Sir," Rhoades answered.

"To me, Sir," Mac said, pushing himself up from behind his desk.

Miller turned around and faced Mac, who was now standing by the side of his desk with his hands behind his back. "Tell me, McCord, how can a major's salary afford such an expensive ring as this?"

"I can't, Sir," Mac answered. "It was given to me by a dying French intelligence agent, Duvalier, who had earlier befriended me. His work and his intellect were highly appreciated by the French government and French intelligence. While I was in France, he helped me and offered me some advice in the processes and purposes of intelligence. One day Duvalier, and Boris Meissner were in a life and death struggle and, according to Duvalier, Meissner stabbed him."

Miller stared at Mac. "I see," he said, and began pacing the floor again. "When were you assigned in France?"

"Paris, France, '37-'39, US intelligence unit assigned to the French Army intelligence group headed by Colonel Fabre, Sir."

Miller found Mac's explanation interesting and invited him to brief the team regarding his assignment in France. "We might all learn something from you," he said.

"Very well, Sir," answered the surprised Mac. He knew Duvalier's name was bound to come up during the briefing. He did not believe that he would violate his promise by telling anyone that Duvalier was a double agent. Almost two years had passed, the war in Europe had deepened, and Mac was in the Philippines among other Americans. Mac cleared his throat and began to relate his experience to his colleagues, from the beginning of his assignment to that of helping the French intelligence in finding the German spy, Boris Meissner, until the time he went back to the States. They listened with interest. Mac mentioned that what perplexed him then and now were Duvalier's last dying words, "Japan...Japan..."

He never finished.

"Too bad Duvalier died," Charlie said aloud. "He could have helped you."

"Yes," said Mac. He continued that he learned from the French something useful: sometimes gathering intelligence on someone did not always yield dividends. Obtaining good intelligence information could sometimes be difficult and elusive. "And many times," Mac added, "the information is unreliable."

Miller placed his forefinger on the left corner of his lips, trying to stop the twitching. "Was it a successful mission, McCord?"

"Most unsuccessful for all of us. And Hitler's attack on Poland, exacerbating chaos in Europe, made it that much easier for Meissner to elude us and continue his espionage work," Mac explained.

"What do you know about this master spy, Meissner?" Czestochowa asked.

"Hardly anything. Just from intelligence reports and a little from human intelligence," Mac said. He explained as much as he could recall of what Duvalier had told him about Meissner. Mac paused momentarily and added that, while he was attending to the dying Duvalier, he thought he saw someone looking in from behind the door, but when he turned around, there was no one there.

"Sir, regarding Japan, this is just my own opinion. I agree totally with Lieutenant Colonel Walters. Before he died he wrote a letter to his friend at the War Department voicing his suspicion that Meissner could be both the spy helping Japan and the murderer of those Army officers."

"Do you have any idea what this Meissner looks like, McCord?" Miller asked.

"No, Sir," Mac answered.

Charlie raised his hand for recognition.

"Major North," Miller said.

"I'd like to ask a question of Major McCord," Charlie said. "Major, didn't you say that you saw someone watching you while you were attending to the dying Duvalier? Surely you must have seen the man's face." Charlie paused momentarily. "It was Meissner who was watching you, wasn't it? Tell the truth, Major," Charlie said tersely, "so that this team will know that it's Meissner we're really after."

"I did not see who it was." Mac answered emphatically.

"Listen, Mac," Charlie was now friendly. "It would make our job much easier if you describe to us what this Meissner looks like. Stop denying that you didn't see him."

Mac locked his steel-blue eyes on Charlie. "Major North, believe what you want. You're asking me to say that I saw something I did not see." It angered him that someone should question his honesty.

Miller changed the subject. "Are you regular or Reserve, McCord?"

"West Point, Sir."

"I don't have any papers about you," Miller said.

"I'm sorry Sir. My briefcase with my Orders in it was stolen. If you wish, I'll wire Washington today for them," Mac answered.

Miller's voice was crisp. He told Mac that he would contact the War Department in Washington about Mac's papers. He then pointed to Delgado, who stood up and introduced himself. He was followed by Golden and then by Stan Czestochowa, who gave his name and where he was from and added that he wished he was in Europe fighting the Nazis.

"I wouldn't let one Nazi soldier stay alive." Czestochowa glared at Rhoades.

"Are there any questions?" Miller inquired after Poco had introduced himself.

Czestochowa raised his hand. "Colonel Miller," he said, "if I may offer an opinion. I believe those officers were murdered by a foreign spy."

A sudden hush came over the room. Miller inquired what made Czestochowa so certain about the murderer. He reluctantly related about a fisherman in Olongapo who had told him about two men he recently saw fighting in a fishing boat in the middle of Subic Bay one early morning. According to his informant, one of the men shot the other and pushed him out of the boat.

Miller inquired whether the victim and the attacker were Filipinos.

"No, Sir. Whites." Czestochowa cleared his throat. "The victim could have been Lieutenant Gibbs. I understand from some of my drinking buddies at Fort Wint on Grande Island that Gibbs had a girlfriend in Olongapo and was there often." Czestochowa cleared his throat again. "It's rumored that the murderer was a tall man." He laughed. "Like Lieutenant Colonel Rhoades or me," and added, "or like you, Colonel Miller."

Miller stared at Czestochowa; his face remained immobile.

Charlie jumped to his feet. "Colonel Miller. Colonel Rhoades. I'm sure Czestochowa didn't mean anything by what he just said." Charlie smiled. "He's outspoken and often puts his foot in his mouth, but I don't believe he means any harm."

"Well, I take exception to it!" Rhoades growled and gave Czestochowa an angry stare. "Why in the hell didn't you report this before, Czestochowa?"

"Hell! I'm not crazy. I'd have been the killer's next victim," answered Czestochowa, and grinning asked Rhoades, "Colonel Rhoades, Sir, did I hear correctly that you're half German? Your mother, I heard." He paused for a moment and then good-naturedly, "Sprechen ze Deutsch?"

"What of it, you fucking Polak! You should be court-martialed for insubordination. You've let everyone in Manila know your grandparents and your father's brother were killed by Hitler's troops. Don't blame me for their deaths. I wasn't there, you fucking asshole. And stop airing your goddam innuendo that I may have killed Gibbs." The angry Rhoades paused and pointed his finger threateningly at Czestochowa. "You had better watch your loose tongue, Polak, or your head will roll!"

"Jeez, Colonel Rhoades. You needn't be so angry. I was only kidding."

"The hell you were," Rhoades snapped. "Just watch yourself Lieutenant! You're not in the US! You're in Asia, where killing is an art and intrigue a daily meal!" He paused momentarily, Glaring at Czestochowa. "Do you understand what I mean, Polak?"

"Gentlemen. Please! Settle your personal problems outside." Miller snapped. "Here's what I want done. I want all of us to fine-comb Manila, Cavite and Olongapo as a starter. You will work by twos—Golden and Delgado, North and Pocodillo, and McCord and Czestochowa. Lieutenant Colonel Rhoades, of course, will manage the office with the help of Miss Aquino." Miller glanced at Rhoades. "Is there anything you wish to add?"

"How about a good layout of Corregidor?" Rhoades promptly answered.

Miller began pacing up and down the briefing area before he answered. "Why do you think we need that layout?" His eyes were now darting from face to face in the room.

Rhoades explained that it would familiarize people like McCord who did not know the area. "He doesn't know a damn thing about Corregidor, and neither do I. If I may guess, before they were murdered, those officers must have gone to many military camps in accordance with their mission." Rhoades continued to explain that along the way the officers encountered their killer. He believed that the present team should go to several of those places and do some inquiries about those murders. "Is it not our job to find out? Corregidor is an excellent place to start."

Charlie North did not think so. He jumped to his feet, and his otherwise unruffled face appeared disturbed. He asked Miller's permission if he could differ with Rhoades's reasoning.

Having gotten Miller's permission, Charlie explained, "Having the layout of Coregidor is dangerous. And I suppose you'll also want the information on weapon positions, type and number of weapons, and number of soldiers there. As careful as we all are, it could get into the hands of foreign spies."

Charlie was adamant that he did not think whoever would be doing the layout would get away with it regardless of rumors that the area's security was too lax. According to him, the commanding general had set up all kinds of security on that tadpole-shaped fortress. "It's a restricted base. You can go inside other installations, even take pictures, but not there. I know. I was on duty at Fort Mills on Corregidor on weapons training program for Filipino recruits when Colonel Walters pulled me out to join this little outfit. I can truly say that anyone caught with that layout will be court-martialed."

Czestochowa voiced his opinion. "Colonel Miller, I agree with Major North one hundred percent."

A tomb-like silence pervaded the room. All eyes were on Dusty Rhoades, who stated that he was aware of the area's security and lack of security in other Army bases. But he convincingly told them that he had already spoken to the deputy commander of Corregidor. "He okayed the idea. After all, who's going to use the layout? Spies?" Rhoades paused and glanced at Miller. "We are!"

Miller agreed that it was a fine idea. "I like your plan. I will rearrange the team. I'd like for Pocodillo with McCord in case the Tagalog language comes up. I understand from Rhoades that the rest of you, more or less, know a little Tagalog." Miller paused. "McCord. Pocodillo. You may proceed with the investigative work in Manila. Golden and Czestochowa can do the layout of Corregidor. You're both familiar with the island fort."

"Yes, Sir," answered Golden. "We've a lot of friends there."

"North and Delgado can do Cavite and Olongapo. Delgado, I understand you've a brother who's an airplane mechanic," Miller said.

Delgado nodded and said that his brother was stationed at Nichols Field just outside Manila.

"How's our island defense? Does your brother know?" Miller forced a smile. He wanted to give the group, especially McCord, who showed an innate and suspicious behavior towards him, the impression that he was not really that interested in the Philippine military condition. In addition, he was curious to see who in the small team would indicate a sign of interest in the Philippine defense.

"He has often said to me that the entire country has less than three hundred airplanes, and most of them have been deemed obsolete." Delgado paused. A serious look crossed his face. "I think they are still servicing the P-36 at Nichols. As my brother Dom told me, the P-36 would never get off the ground to protect the Philippines in case of an attack. Of course, that was just his opinion."

"Why is that, captain?" Miller persisted.

"Because, the aircraft is just no damn good, and it hardly gives the pilot any protection." Delgado quickly added, "Dom believed, however, that Clark Field is bound to get some heavy bombers one of these days, maybe two hundred aircraft and hundreds of fighter planes, which he called P-40's. Clark is the only airfield large enough for those bombers."

"That's good news," Mac and Rhoades stated simultaneously. "I agree," Charlie chimed in.

Miller paced up and down the floor and then turned around. "Delgado, the information you just gave the team was very enlightening. Before you leave, I want you to write down what you've just told me and let Miss Aquino type it for you." He turned to the secretary, trying to hide his excitement. "Miss Aquino, leave the paper on my desk."

Czestochowa raised his hand. "Sir, there's a strong rumor in Manila that General MacArthur is going to be recalled to active duty and reorganize the US and Philippine armies."

"I have heard that too," Delgado said. "He will be on duty in late July."

Miller looked around the room, intensely studying the faces in front of him. "It's not a rumor. It's a fact," he snapped. He appeared frustrated. "I want Corregidor's layout by the end of this month, and I want the investigations as soon as possible. Hopefully by then we will have found the culprit. I'd hate for the MacArthur group to interfere with what we're doing." He inhaled deeply, picked up a piece of chalk, and wrote on the blackboard: QUEST. "'Quest' is this team's code name. There must not, repeat, there must not be any leaks in our mission. I want Quest to accomplish this mission." He glanced at Mac. "Hopefully we'll find this faceless spy called Meissner."

"Colonel Miller, do you know when the FBI agents will get here?" Charlie inquired.

"Negative," answered Miller. "For all I know, they could be here already."

Rhoades stood up and announced that, as of tomorrow, all military personnel in the room must wear civilian attire.

"Excellent idea, Rhoades," said Miller. "While we're on this job, we don't want to call attention to ourselves. Office hours will be from 0900 to 1700 hours."

Mac noticed that Miller was left-handed, but he also observed that, for some strange reason, the colonel had, more or less, been staring at him. That's the second time he's given me a hard look. The first time was when he greeted the team. There's something about him that I don't trust, Mac thought.

"Is there anything else anyone would like to mention?" Miller looked around the room. "I'd like for us to adjourn early. I've another meeting to attend."

Mac made an instant decision that he was going to report the murder of the FBI agent to the rest of the team. "Sir, before you leave, I've something to report," Mac said, and related the death of FBI agent James W. Kagan.

"Unfortunate," murmured Miller, glancing at Rhoades. He placed a Camel cigarette to his lips, took out a fancy-looking box of matches. From where Mac stood, the box seemed to be aqua green with something silver on the cover. Mac was not certain, but he could have sworn the colonel's hands were trembling. "This finishes our session," Miller announced, removing the cigarette from his lips. He turned to Czestochowa. "I want you to zip your lips about what the fisherman told you in Olongapo and your opinion about the dead man being Lieutenant Gibbs, or you'll find yourself with a dagger in your back. That's an order."

"Yes, Sir," Czestochowa answered.

"I want to emphasize something before we leave, if I may, Sir," looking directly at Miller. "The man we're after is wily and extremely intelligent. He may even be listening to what we're discussing," Mac said, this time glancing from Miller to Rhoades.

"Before Mac left the building, Rhoades approached him. "Did the FBI agent say anything to you before he died?"

"No. He was already dead when he fell. It was probably better that he couldn't tell me who killed him, Sir," Mac said with a suspicious tone in his voice as he looked at Rhoades. He excused himself and closed the door behind him.

CHAPTER 9

Colonel Miller decided not to immediately leave the building as he had earlier intended. Instead, after the introductory meeting was over, he waited until everyone in the Quest team was gone. He then locked the door and left.

Miller had a natural way of walking at a fast pace, but as soon as he was on the street, he walked even faster. Three blocks later, on a quiet one-way street, an unmarked black car stopped, and he got in on the passenger side next to the driver. The car stopped again in front of a Philippine bank not far from the impressive Marsman Building, and Lieutenant Colonel Rhoades slid behind the driver and immediately tapped him on the shoulder.

"What's your name, son?"

"Private Malloy, Sir, United States Army," he answered.

"Drive to the outskirts of the city. There's a large warehouse in the vicinity of Tutuban Railroad Station. Stop behind the warehouse. A Filipina is waiting there for us," said Rhoades.

"How will she know us, Sir?" Malloy inquired.

"She'll know us," Miller interjected.

It did not take long to reach the warehouse, despite the heavy Manila traffic. The soldier, dressed in civilian clothes, stopped the car at Miller's signal and alertly opened the car door. Miss Purita Aquino climbed in next to Rhoades. Promptly, Miller turned to the driver and told him to take them to the Philippine Department's headquarters at Fort Santiago.

They were then met at the door by an Army captain.

"Please follow me," he said, and then led them to an office. He knocked. A voice inside answered, "Come in." The visitors at Fort Santiago were ushered into a large, sumptuous room that was probably the Philippine Department's war and briefing room. On one side of the room was a large wooden stand with a large map of Southeast Asian countries, and the Philippines, with all of its seven thousand islands, was encircled in red. A straight line, drawn also in red, crossed between the two Asian capitals. The distance from Tokyo to Manila, eighteen hundred miles, was written in black.

Two men, an American colonel, wearing the US Army uniform, and a Filipino civilian were discussing something serious. They were both studying a map of northern Luzon spread out on the table. The captain cleared his throat respectfully to inform the colonel that his visitors had arrived and were in the room by the door, waiting. The colonel and the civilian both turned around simultaneously. "Colonel Danbury, Sir," said the captain, "your guests, Colonel Miller, Lieutenant Colonel Rhoades, and Miss Aquino are here."

"Thank you, captain. Please tell the guard that we're not to be disturbed for a while," said Colonel Danbury, who strode towards his visitors. "I'm delighted that you were all able to get away from your busy schedules. Colonel Miller, Lieutenant Colonel Rhoades, allow me to introduce Agent Chavez. He's from the Philippine Investigation Bureau, otherwise known as the PIB. Chavez, I'd like for you to meet two men and a woman who dared do what they're doing. I realize you already know Miss Aquino."

"Yes," said Chavez. "Miss Aquino is the only female agent we have at the PIB, but she is excellent. We are all proud of her ability as an agent." He glanced at Miller and Rhoades. "However, we have made it widely known that she is an employee of the Philippine Department and on temporary assignment in your small group, Colonel Miller," he explained. "Colonel Danbury of G-2 and we at the PIB wanted it known that she's one of many Filipinas working as clerks and typists in the department."

"Fortunately, Miss Aquino is also a fine typist. We wanted to keep the PIB below the radar. It has helped us quietly and effectively in the most frustrating situations," explained Colonel Danbury.

"For your information, Miss Aquino is most often accompanied by a covert PIB agent in some duties, excluding your office, Colonel Miller," Chavez explained, glancing knowingly at Danbury.

"Really!" Both Miller and Rhoades simultaneously voiced their surprise.

Chavez realizing that Miller and Rhoades were politely questioning why Miss Aquino had to have a covert agent with her, answered quickly that the PIB did not wish for her to be abducted by an enemy spy.

It was then that Danbury decided to change the subject. "Are there any more questions?" He asked.

"Yes," answered Rhoades. He gave Danbury and Chavez a quick glance. "Miller and I have a small problem that both of you might help us correct."

"And that is?" Danbury asked.

"Among the members of Quest is Major Jacob McCord, Army intelligence, Washington, DC. He's here for a different reason from ours, Colonel Duncan told us before we left Washington to help Lieutenant Colonel Walters find the spy and killer of those American Army officers," explained Rhoades.

"Walters recently drowned," Danbury said.

"We're sorry to hear that," said Rhoades. He glanced at Danbury and Chavez. "I'm sure that you both know McCord. Our problem is serious. We are aware of his suspicion of us. He briefed the team on his assignment in France. A French intelligence agent knew the spy's name, and we surmised that it could be the same madman you've been searching for, Boris Meissner."

"Yes," said Chavez. "There are many stories of how he got to the Philippines. We gather that he left Germany, went through China, and then traveled to Malaya, where he boarded a ship at Singapore for the southern island of Mindanao, Philippines. From there, he escaped to central Philippines—Negros, Cebu, then to Panay, and on to Mindoro. From Mindoro, he slipped into Manila."

"Your undercover acts are clearly working," said Danbury. "Continue to feed McCord's suspicion. It's a diversionary tactic that might draw out our culprit. Miss Aquino, you keep up being a good secretary. Colonel Miller. Lieutenant Colonel Rhoades. Continue to do your work to keep things in perspective."

"I am almost certain," Chavez said, "that McCord is being watched by this Meissner because of what McCord had learned in France about him." Chavez mentioned that Walters was convinced, and so told the PIB and G-2, that the man they were tracking down was Meissner. "McCord, I see, has confirmed Walters's analysis."

"McCord also reported to the group the death of, Kagan. Besides being tough, he's also a dedicated and excellent intelligence officer. He'll go far," said Rhoades. We'll help you search for Meissner."

"You're doing well," Danbury said. "It appears everything seems to be going as planned. We all know where we stand. I'll discuss some important things to Chavez later on." Turning to Chavez, he told him to befriend McCord as soon as possible. And to Rhoades and Miller he added, "We in G-2 must pretend that we know nothing about you or your team. Before McCord left Washington, the Philippine Department made it known it would not interfere with his work. Walters wanted it that way. But we are monitoring who his enemies are, but so far, all we're suspecting is a name." Danbury reached into his shirt pocket and took out a telegram. He explained to them that the Philippine Department, G-2 evidently intercepted the recent wire for McCord sent by Colonel Sam Polson, WD's special Liaison, Southeast Asia Section, Philippines Unit, Washington, DC. "The information contained in the message appears innocuous but if it gets into the hands of a clever spy, it could be dangerous." He read the message slowly to punctuate its seriousness. 'McCord, your friends Stone in the FBI and Deaver in WD insisted I send you this message.' By the way, Deaver has since been transferred to Panama. 'The subject we discussed while you were in Washington is in Manila under various assumed names. No alias is known to us. Goes around in many different disguises. Info confirmed by FBI and WD's intell.' Signed: Polson." Danbury glanced at Rhoades. "Do you know this John Stone?"

"Yes, he's a good man," answered Rhoades. "He compiles and indexes names of people and groups engaged in espionage, crimes, and subversive activities."

Danbury sounded exasperated. "I don't know if we'll ever find this man. If the whole continent of Europe couldn't find him, how could we?"

"There is someone, Sonny Sollow, an influential American whom I suspect is a spy for the Japanese, but it's very difficult to prove," added

Chavez. "That sort of information could get into Sollow's hands."

"It would, indeed, be dangerous," Rhoades said. He explained that McCord, a couple of days ago, was physically attacked when getting off the Army transport from Los Angeles to Manila Harbor. I don't believe that he was able to retrieve his belongings." He glanced at Miller. "I suspect his orders were also stolen."

"I understand," said Miller.

"How unfortunate," Danbury stated. He then inquired whether there were any further questions or comments.

"Yes," said Miller. "Two Army officers in our team, Golden and Czestochowa, are going to do a layout of Corregidor very soon. The purpose is for bait to attract a certain spy. We don't want the two officers to be shot or incarcerated." Miller paused, smiling. "Incidentally, in front of Quest, Rhoades and I hate each other."

Chavez laughed heartily and praised the two officers for being such good spies and added that he liked the idea of their planned layout of Corregidor. "That is another red meat to entice our favorite spy to come out of his hiding."

Danbury agreed and that he would alert Corregidor about the plan and to give the two officers access to the island base in order to accomplish their assigment. Meanwhile, Chavez wondered aloud if he could ask the colonel a question on another subject. Danbury nodded.

"You mentioned several months ago that military weapons and ammunitions are due to arrive in Manila," Chavez said. "You promised then that the PIB was going to be allotted some guns and ammunition."

"I do remember, and yes, I did clear it with the Philippine Department and it got approved." He reminded Chavez, however, that all of the weapons, ammunition, and everything that was slated for Fort William McKinley, other military camps around Manila, and the PIB all went down with the cargo ship Richmond. "However," Danbury stated, "a Panamanian freighter, the Flores, will soon arrive. Hopefully this time those weapons slated for Clark Field and Fort Stotsenburg will reach those bases by truck convoy. I'll see what I can do for your bureau."

Chavez inquired whether the PIB could help guard the receiving trucks.

"I don't believe that will be necessary," Danbury answered. He elaborated that the convoy would be guarded by well-armed and well-trained military police, and that the unloading procedure would be done at night. Danbury got up, and the rest did also. "Miller. Rhoades and Miss Aquino, keep up the good work with our plan of deception. This is the last time we'll see each other for a while. It's too dangerous for all of us to do otherwise. There are so many covert foreign agents prowling around. Contact Miss Aquino when you need help. She'll know where to go."

Danbury paused and turned to Rhoades. "I almost forgot. I'm assigning you to contact a certain woman from whom Chavez and I get a lot of help spying on the Japanese and their intentions. She reports to Chavez directly. Her name is Cookie. She's a lady-of-the-night and a waitress at Uncle Billy's Girls, a nightspot in Kapalaran. You are to help her in every way you can. Whenever you need aid regarding this particular assignment, discuss it with Chavez. Befriend Cookie as soon as you find time. Your work is Top Secret. Good luck!"

As Miller, Rhoades, and Aquino were departing from Fort Santiago, Charlie, who had invited Mac and Poco to join him for lunch, was at his favorite Manila café. They were there to discuss Mac's request to move to another place in the BOQ, since his room had been burglarized. At the café, Mac, with the help of Poco, called Miguela at the Zaldivar-Molina Corporation. "May I speak to Miguela Molina, please?"

"This is she," Miguela answered in that melodious accented English.

"This is Jake McCord. Mac. Major McCord." He unsuccessfully kept himself from stammering. He was so smitten with Miguela when he saw her at the Manila International Club, he could hardly speak.

There was silence on the other end of the line.

"Hello, are you still there?" Mac asked.

"Yes," Miguela answered.

"Ah. Ah. Will you have supper with me tonight?" Mac felt all at once that his voice box was impaired.

"Tonight? I cannot. I have made plans."

"Please," was all Mac could squeeze out of his throat.

There was another moment of silence on the other line. "Actually," Miguela finally told Mac hesitantly, "I have invited some friends tonight for supper at my parents' place, Buenavista, 2200 Dewey Boulevard. I would love for you to join us, Mac. Supper is at nine." There was a slight pause. But before Miguela could hang up the telephone, Mac, elated, accepted her invitation and quickly added that he would be at her parents' house, Buenavista on 2200 Dewey Boulevard at 9 pm for supper.

After talking to Miguela on the Manila Café's public telephone, Mac went back to the table where Charlie and Paco were waiting for him. Mac repeated his concern to Charlie about staying in his assigned quarters at the BOQ.

"Yes," said Poco. "I think Major McCord should be moved to another room."

Charlie agreed and told Mac that Major Nick Evans, in charge of billets, was a good friend of his. "We were in ROTC together at Chicago College. Room 121, next to mine, is vacant. Charlie glanced at his watch. "I'll call him right now. I'll use the café's telephone." Charlie returned smiling. "You can move in today. And I'll also see about another Colt .45 pistol for you. But I can't promise you the gun."

Mac was pleased. He glanced at his two companions. "There's something I want to tell both of you, but this isn't the place."

Charlie cocked his head to one side. "How about my room?"

"No, I'm afraid someone might hear what I have to say," Mac insisted.

"Hmmm," Charlie murmured and began stroking his moustache. "I don't think our office is that private. Miller may be there."

"Is it that serious?" Poco voiced his concern.

Mac nodded.

Charlie and the Filipino sergeant looked at one another. Charlie, again stroking his moustache, said, "I've an idea, Mac. The sergeant and I have good friends who'll give us privacy. Several months ago we saved Ruby Redd from being beaten to a pulp by two bad guys who were going to steal money from the restaurant's cash register. Her husband was out of the city when that happened. Ever since then they can't do enough for us. The place is a favorite to American servicemen. And there are a number of rooms where we can talk privately."

Poco agreed that it was a good idea and that Ruby and her husband, Big Redd, were loyal and would walk through a mine field to aid a friend. With such a sincere recommendation, Mac was satisfied. They stepped out of the café and Charlie whistled to a taxicab standing by.

"Place?" the cabdriver asked as his passengers climbed in the car.

"Sampaloc. Kapalaran strip," Poco said.

"Where in K strip?" asked the cabbie.

"Ruby Redd's," answered Charlie.

"Yes, Sir. Fine restaurant." The cabdriver smiled. "Big Redd certainly has a lot of woman to take care of," he said knowingly of Big Redd's wife, and turning to Mac, who had taken the passenger seat next to him said, "You new in Manila?"

"Yes," Mac answered.

"Where're you from?" the cabbie inquired without glancing at Mac.

"Virginia," Mac murmured.

"I've never been there. You must be in the Army. I can tell by your haircut. You know what I mean. Short!"

There was a silence in the cab for a little while. Meanwhile, Mac noticed that the cabbie was nervously chewing on his left hand fingernails. "Do you always chew your fingernails that way?"

"I do. I get nervous, especially when I'm driving. Strangely enough, I don't bite my right hand nails."

"Here, have a Chesterfield. It'll keep your left hand busy," Mac told him.

The cabdriver thanked Mac and reached for the box of matches on the dashboard with his right hand. "First time on the strip?" Mac nodded and said, "That's a fancy match box you have." He was certain that during the introductory meeting that morning, Colonel Miller had lighted his cigarette from an identical looking matchbox.

The cabdriver thanked Mac and stated that he liked the aqua green match cover with the silver periscope sticking out of water. "I picked it up at the Periscope Club. Here, take this. I've another one."

As the cabdriver reached for a box of matches on the dashboard to put in the pocket of his sleeveless shirt, Mac saw blue marking on his upper arm. "That's an interesting tattoo you've got—birds over a mountain."

"Thanks, I got drunk one night in Cavite and when I sobered up the next morning, there it was," the cabbie explained a little nervously, tugging on his short sleeve. "You speak Tagalog?"

Mac shook his head. "Just got here a couple of days ago."

"Are you a Filipino? You speak like an American," Mac told him, studying the driver's face.

The cabbie explained that he was a Filipino, but that he was an American citizen, born in San Francisco, and finished high school there.

Mac inquired about Ruby Redd and Big Redd and if the cabbie knew them.

"Everyone knows Ruby and Big Redd. Good people. She's an American from New York. Her husband, Big Redd, is a Filipino-American. She's friendly but becomes a tigress when anyone tries to harm her Big Redd." The cabbie added, "The restaurant is one of the best in Manila, if not the best. She's the cook and an excellent one at that," he declared enthusiastically as he expertly went through the heavy traffic while pushing down on the cab's horn.

The taxicab was zooming away from the congested areas of the city. "Instead of going through the regular shortcuts to the strip," Charlie told the driver, "go the longer route, by Malacañang Palace. We want to show Major McCord where President Manuel L. Quezon and his family live."

After another long silence, Mac turned to the driver and asked his name. "Jim," he answered hesitantly. "Jim Wanabe."

The taxicab wound its way through and around the city, crossing the Pasig River that divides Manila several times. They passed hundreds of billboards advertising Coca-Cola, Carnation Milk, Ponds Face Cream and most products that were familiar to Mac. Poco pointed out the many different government buildings, Catholic churches built by the Spaniards, a muslim mosque, and Malacañang Palace which Mac declared loudly was impressive. "And several miles from here, we also have the San Miguel Brewery where the best beer is made," Poco said proudly.

They reached their destination. The entrance to Kapalaran strip was emblazoned with a thousand red and green blinking lights from one end of the wide and tall arch to the other end, with words, also in bright lights, "Welcome to Kapalaran strip." Neon lights flicked on and off, enticing gamblers' appetites. Not too far from the gaudy entrance, many people were standing in line to get inside a seafood restaurant called Anna's, while cars were parked along the road in haphazard ways, creating an awful traffic snarl.

"The strip looks active," Mac stated, glancing at his watch. "It's only four o'clock in the afternoon."

"The strip never sleeps," Jim Wanabe answered, now and then glancing at Charlie and Poco in his rearview mirror.

As the taxicab rolled on slowly, Mac turned to glance at a gaudy-looking front door with hanging tinsels. Next to it was a glass window, on which was painted a large red hibiscus. There were a couple of women in heavy makeup and tight short dresses leaning against the door.

Wanabe sensed Mac's curiousity. "That's Fat Mama's whorehouse. She and the girls will be missed around here when they move to Intramuros, or the Walled City. The red hibiscus is Fat Mama's trademark." He smiled lasciviously and added, "There's a real pretty girl there by the name of Monieca. In case you get interested tell her I sent you." He continued to point out the different businesses. Near Fat Mama's was Billy's Girls, a popular club that featured nude dancers every night at around ten. Across the street from Billy's was the Periscope club. "See their logo? It's like the cover of this matchbox." With great relish, Wanabe explained to Mac that the Periscope had an excellent band for dancing, and the singer was a talented and beautiful blond from New York. From eleven to twelve every night, the club had a real eye-stopping show. "The striptease dancers are men. They dance and parade around stage, slowly removing their clothes. And, at the finale they have nothing on except a G-string. They drive the women crazy. American sailors like to go there because lots of women go there." He paused and lit the Chesterfield cigarette Mac had given him.

"What's that tall building next to the Periscope Club?" Mac inquired.

"The Far East Hotel. It's lavish and very expensive. Many wealthy tourists to Manila stay there," Wanabe explained.

They passed many other businesses adjacent to each other with names like Lucky Star, Solo's, or El Oro, all of which, Mac surmised, were gambling casinos. "I've occasionally played at some of those casinos but came out poorer," Charlie snorted. "Are you a gambling man Mac?"

"I've tried it. I was never lucky."

"Every Sunday the church pulpits go into high gear in condemning Kapalaran strip," Poco said, adding to the conversation. I—"

Poco was interrupted by Wanabe, who announced loudly, "Ruby Redd." He parked and jumped out of the cab. "I'm also having lunch here," he declared after Charlie had paid him.

A small skinny man with a large Adam's apple greeted them at the door. "Charlie North! Poco! It is real good to see both of you again," he exclaimed pleasantly.

Charlie shook the small man's hand and placed his arm around his shoulder. "How's business?

"Excellent. Lots of tourists. Many Europeans. Probably escaped Hitler," Big Redd answered, smiling broadly.

"Big Redd, I'd like for you to meet Major Jake McCord. Mac is our friend," Charlie stated proudly, inhaling deeply, causing his big chest to appear even more impressive.

"I always like to meet another potential customer, especially a big spender," Big Redd said, giving Mac a good look. "You must have just come in."

Mac smiled and said that he would do some sunning as soon as he could. Meanwhile, Charlie was looking around the restaurant and noticed Wanabe sitting at a table, watching them and listening to everything they were saying while presumably waiting to be served. Charlie approached him and talked to him angrily. Not wanting to have any problems in his restaurant, Big Redd took Charlie aside and in a soft voice told him to take it easy.

Charlie asked Big Redd to send two pitchers of San Miguel to a small room where they could talk.

"It will have to be upstairs, Room Number Four, where you held Stein's birthday party before he was murdered," Big Redd said. "All the smaller rooms are occupied."

"That would be fine," Poco interjected. "We will just have to speak a little louder to each other."

Big Redd was leading his guests up the stairs when he asked Charlie if the skeleton found recently on a beach could have been one of the American Army officers. Charlie said that he did not know. Suddenly Charlie stopped and nonchalantly said, "There's a certain ring in your voice. You've never been that curious before. What gives?"

Big Redd chuckled. "I've an American civilian customer who often eats here."

"What's so special about that? Obviously he likes Ruby's cooking." Charlie said tersely.

"That is not the interesting thing. What's interesting is that he invariably asks me if I've heard who killed those officers. A couple of days ago, he inquired if the police had identified the skeleton. He is sort of a strange duck but gives excellent tips. Must be rolling in the dough," Big Redd explained.

"What's his name?" Mac asked.

"Sonny Sollow, I think he said. He wants us to call him Sonny," Big Redd said.

In the privacy of Room Number Four, Mac related to Charlie and Poco Roosie's claim that he saw the man who killed the Army officer. "His description of the man killed sounded like it could have been Stein." Mac paused. "Roosie said that he thought he had previously heard him being called Abe Steiner."

"Wow!" Charlie exploded. "We've got to make sure as hell that Roosie stays healthy. Would he recognize the killer?"

"No," Mac simply answered. He held back the detail of the killer's belt buckle with the imprint of a striking cobra. "Poco," he asked, "did you know that Alberto, the waiter at the Manila International Club, is Roosie's grandson?"

Poco shook his head and asked Mac if Alberto knew what his grandfather knew. Mac glanced at his two companions. "Roosie said that he had never told anyone about it. Why would he lie?"

Charlie lit a Tabacalera cigar. "I doubt he did. He's too damned scared." He looked at Mac. "That's such a break for our mission. You've got to let Miller and Rhoades know. We can't keep this information to ourselves."

Mac stared at his two companions. "Let's wait a while. I've misgivings about Miller and Rhoades."

Charlie blew grey smoke up the ceiling. "I don't blame you, Mac. Miller is odd. He's like a jigsaw puzzle." Charlie went on that, although Miller did not introduce the idea of a layout plan on Corregidor and appeared almost afraid of the subject, after Rhoades mentioned it, he enthusiastically accepted it. Charlie took a short puff of his cigar. "Maybe in time we'll understand Miller." He then went into a tirade about Rhoades. "I think I know him. I grew up in the streets of Chicago." He began to describe Rhoades as an intense man who seemed to always have something on his mind. "I don't trust him! I was watching him and Miller while Mac told us about the murdered FBI agent. Miller flinched like an electric needle had hit him, whereas Rhoades showed no emotion. I question the intentions of people like that. Sick!"

"Jeez, Charlie. You surprise me. I didn't know you could be so analytical. You know, I don't like them either, but I believe I will share my information with them. Perhaps tomorrow." Mac suddenly stood up and gestured to Charlie and Poco to be quiet and tiptoed to the door.

He quickly opened it. "How long have you been standing here?" Mac asked Wanabe.

"I just got here. Honest," Wanabe said, nervously chewing his left hand fingernails. "I was just about to knock on the door and ask if you guys are going back to the city."

Angrily, Charlie charged toward Wanabe. "You son of a bitch! Don't you ever spy on us again!" he told him and flattened him to the floor.

CHAPTER 10

The cabdriver slammed on his brakes in front of the military center and Mac hurriedly paid him. By his watch, it was already 7:30 p.m. He had exactly an hour and a half to get ready and have another taxi take him to Miguela's house by nine. Mac allotted himself only a few minutes to transfer what worldly possessions he had left from his former room to the room next to Charlie's.

The trip from the Kapalaran Strip back to Manila was long and arduous. Despite his fatigue, however, Mac knew that a warm shower and seeing Miguela again would invigorate him.

After searching his pockets, he soon found Miguela's address. He quickly called Roosie to pick him up at the military center in thirty minutes. Mac walked outside the center and waited for the taxi on the corner of the street. It was the first time he was by himself on the streets at night since arriving in Manila, and it made him rather apprehensive. Poco had warned him time and time again that American servicemen were easy targets for muggers and pickpockets, especially at night. 'Hide your money inside your shoe and hold onto your watch.'

His trepidation, however, was soon diverted. There were no imminent signs of malevolence. As far as he could see, the streets were lined with hundreds of neoned advertisements, street lights, street signs, and flashing neon signs from nearby all-night shops, bars and restaurants. The unusually bright June moon also contributed to the luster of the streets. And when he sniffed the air, the strong breeze from Manila Bay carried to his nostrils the different odors. The whole place pulsated with activity, nightgoers coming out of one nightclub and going to another. Taxicabs, cars and horse carriages were impatiently trying to get through the narrow and crowded streets. From a saloon across the streets, Clyde

McCoy's tuneful and exciting "Sugar Blue" drifted through the air from a Juke Box.

A quick smile curled around the corners of Mac's lips when he saw five American sailors enter a nightclub adjacent to the saloon. They reminded him of when he was only a Second Lieutenant. He and his friend, John Stone, a junior at Georgetown, used to frequent a small Bar and Grill in Waldorf, Maryland, called the Bloody Bucket. He wondered how he and Stone could have sat at that bar listening to that Juke Box, eating peanuts and guzzling beer like there was no tomorrow, watching people dance on a postage stamp of a dance floor. How they enjoyed themselves. He remembered pleasantly, on another time, one Friday evening after work when he, Stone and their mutual friend, Deaver, drove to Richmond to celebrate Deaver's promotion to First Lieutenant and he to captain, at a nightclub called TGIF. And, how sorry he was to learn that night that Deaver was to leave for another assignment in Georgia in two days.

Mac placed his hands in his pantspocket and sighed. It seemed the gods disapproved of him having a good time. Every time he began to enjoy a place, he was transferred, or his friends received another assignment.

He failed to notice a taxi stop in front of him. A voice said, "Get een, Major Mac." This time the taxi driver stuck his head out the window. "Hey, Major Mac, get een," he said loudly and, at the same time opening the back door of the cab with his left hand.

"Sorry, Roosie, my mind was down the pike," Mac said, getting in the cab. "Take me to 2200 Dewey Boulevard."

Roosie guided the taxi through the heavy traffic. After a very long silence he inquired if the Molinas were Mac's friends. Without waiting for an answer, he asked, "What part of Amereeca are you prom, Major Mac?"

"Virginia."

"Beergeenia?" There was a long pause. "Beergeenia?" Roosie repeated. "Ees dat near Deetroit whure cars are made?"

"Well, Virginia is closer to New York." Mac did not wish to hurt Roosie's feelings.

"Oh, yees. I heerd of New York. I habe a coosin whuu works een de keetcen of Waaldorp Astuuria hotel."

"Yeah. Waldorf Astoria," answered Mac.

"Een hees letturs he seeys people whuu eat een de restaurant are suu reets dey geebe heem laats op maney by just remuubeeng dee deerty plates prum dee tables." Roosie said.

The taxi had now left the downtown traffic and was heading south of Dewey Boulevard on the other side of Taft Avenue. Roosie then made a right turn and entered a place, which to Mac looked like a public park. As the taxi continued to glide slowly through the heavily forested area, its high beams caught a large white board nailed to a coconut tree standing near the road. It answered Mac's perception of the area. The bold black letters, one side in English: PRIVATE PROPERTY. NO TRESPASSING. The opposite side in Spanish: PROPEIDAD PRIVADA. PROHIBIDO PASAR.

The taxi moved slowly on the narrow asphalt road, made darker by tall acacia, palm, and coconut trees. By the time the tall trees and the thick overgrown shrubberies were left behind and the high wrought iron gate was in full sight, the landscape changed dramatically. Had it been daytime, Mac would have had the treat of seeing a lush green garden with well-manicured oleanders, ixoras, and hibiscus, with the artistic frangipani, also in full bloom, planted here and there, giving the garden that exotic tropical atmosphere. A number of Manila palms, with their narrow fronds, dancing to the whiff of wind from Manila Bay, added to the splendor of the garden. While the explosive grandeur of the flowering plants tried to best each other, a tall, widespread gardenia bush, sitting by itself in the center of the large circular driveway was generously permeating the night air with its aphrodisiac scented white flowers.

Periwinkles, begonias, lantanas and geraniums placed around to cover roots of large shrubberies dominated the approaches to the house while rumbling honeysuckles and morning glory vines and bougainbilleas, with their glorious flowers, had found their way around some well-placed trees.

"This is a mammoth garden of Eden. This place is huge," Mac said.

"Yes. De Moleenas cull eet Buenabeesta. I habe been here meeny times," Roosie said proudly.

"They must have an army of gardeners to maintain these acres of growth."

"Dey are bery reech. Der Chaupper, Gregorio, and me are priends.

We used to dreenk togeder at Sergio's bar and greel. He had tuuld me dey own halp of Mayneela and propeertees een de Beesayan Islands, baat dey are nice," Rosie explained as he guided the taxi through the open gate and slowed it when they neared the wide circular driveway of the palatial stone and stucco house.

After telling Roosie to come back in a couple of hours, Mac knocked on the door. A young uniformed Filipina maid appeared and stared up at Mac with a puzzled look. "I'm Major McCord. I'm a friend of Miss Molina."

Then he heard Miguela's voice. "That is all right, Cecilia. Major McCord is my guest," she said in her melodious and accented English as she approached the door.

"Miguela!" Mac's voice was almost inaudible. "I'm Mac!" He could feel his face getting red. His pulse raced.

"Mac, how…how good it is to see you again," Miguela whispered. "Welcome to Buenavista. Please come in." She paused and turned to the maid. "Cecilia, tell Claudia and Tilde to hold off on supper for thirty minutes. I would like for Major McCord to meet my other guests." Miguela paused again. "Please come in, Mac," she repeated, blushing.

Mac just stood there feeling as if his feet were encased in a ton of cement. "I didn't realize you're such a rich lady, and you're beautiful." Mac blurted out. He felt stupid and embarrassed. He wondered why he said those things to that soft-spoken, gentle, shy woman whom he hardly knew. His heart pounding loudly, he hoped that she did not hear him.

Miguela smiled, ignoring what Mac had said. Meanwhile, he steadied himself and ran his dry tongue across his lips. He found his voice. "This is an elegant house."

"Thank you."

They remained standing by the open door, their eyes locking on each other's. They were unaware that the maid Cecilia had come back and was telling Miguela that supper would be held up for a while.

"Unfortunately," Miguela said to Mac, "My parents, my brother, Ernesto, and my sister, Agrifina, are vacationing in San Francisco. We have a house there overlooking the Pacific Ocean. They left as soon as school closed. They will be back in late August. I promised to look in on the house now and then," she explained, smiling.

He liked her smile. "Don't you live here?"

"No. I have my own apartment," Miguela said, shutting the door behind her. There was momentary silence. "Mac, I would like for you to meet some friends of the family. They are in the library having champagne before supper."

She introduced him to Dr. and Mrs. Longo, as well as Senator and Mrs. Magal, who were delighted to meet an American Army officer. "My nephew is talking about joining the Constabulary when he finished college," Mrs. Magal said.

"Mac," continued Miguela, "this is agent Chavez. He is with the Philippine Investigation Bureau."

"Yes, we are very proud of Chavez. He is the Commonwealth Government's internal nemesis to the foreign spies in this country," chimed in Senator Magal. The senator was a dignified-looking man and tall for a Filipino. A graduate of the University of the Philippines, he had great respect for the Americans in the Philippines and held high regard for many of their programs, especially regarding education. He studied Mac for a long time, without being discourteous. "Major, are you familiar with the Philippine Commonwealth Government?"

"Yes, I am, senator," Mac answered. "I've somewhat of a limited knowledge about it. I have heard conversations about President Quezon on the ship coming from the United States and read articles about him in magazines when I arrived here."

"You must be interested in the Philippines, Major McCord," said Senator Magal.

"I am, Sir," Mac said.

"Major, did you know that General McArthur had been military advisor to President Quezon since 1935? He was to establish and develop a program for the Commonwealth Government's national defense," said Dr. Longo whose brother was in the Philippine Constabulary.

"I was not aware of it, Dr. Longo," Mac answered. "However, I knew that he was Chief of Staff of the US Army for sometime, I believe since 1930. Then, I lost track of him. I suppose that was when he accepted the assignment to be the Commonwealth Government's Military Advisor."

"Major, are you of Irish descent?" Mrs. Longo asked.

"No. Both my parents are from Scotland," Mac answered.

"Did you know," Mrs. Longo continued, "that 85 percent of Filipinos are of Malayan stocks? The doctor and I and our parents and grandparents are all of Malayan descent. There are many who are Chinese-Filipinos, and not as many Japanese-Filipinos."

Later, the supper conversation turned to Chavez, a short, muscular man with graying temples. "Chavez, asked Senator Magal, "Have you discovered the identity of the body recently found by the cove near Buenavista?"

There was no immediate answer from Chavez. He was staring at Mac, who was seated across the dining room table from him. "No, senator," he finally answered. "We heard some allegations that it could be that of Major Haggarty. But the PIB could not accept it. We need better identification."

Mrs. Magal entered into the conversation. "How about the killer?"

"We do not know that either," answered Chavez. He explained that even if the PIB was able to identify the skeleton, he did not think they could find the killer. "There have been no clues, but it is not a closed book."

"Who found the skeleton?' Mac inquired with interest.

Chavez looked at Miguela. "Tell him."

Miguela sighed. "My brother, Ernesto, his eight-year-old friend, and the family dog discovered it a couple of weeks ago."

"I heard about it from Sergeant Pocodillo, but I don't believe he mentioned who found it," Mac said. "It must have occurred before I arrived."

"It was front page news and on the radio, but the names of the two boys were never mentioned," Chavez explained.

Miguela leaned forward and looked at everyone at the table. "I am sure everyone heard that loud explosion on Manila Bay last Saturday morning."

Everyone nodded except Mac. "The ship arrived from Los Angeles late that Saturday."

"What about that explosion, Miguela?" Chavez inquired.

Miguela related to her guests that she got up very early that Saturday, before everyone in the house was awake, and decided to go for a walk on the beach. She remembered throwing a stick on the water for her dog,

Swimmer, to fetch. As the dog was swimming towards the floating stick, a motorboat, at top speed, came roaring out of nowhere causing such a wake that almost drowned Swimmer. Suddenly, the boat stopped, and the man in the boat turned around and gave her a look as if he knew her and then went on his way at high speed.

"An hour or so later, there was that terrible explosion. I have been wondering ever since if that man had something to do with it," she said.

"Chavez, do you know anything about that?" Senator Magal asked.

"Although we work very closely with the Philippine Department, the Navy investigated it alone. We have not yet heard of their findings."

"Do you think they will find out who did it?" Dr. Longo asked.

Chavez shook his head. "So many crimes in this city go unsolved." He softly tapped the table with his fingers. "We know there are a number of spy cells and a national spy organization in Manila. The news media suspects it. And we at the PIB think we know who's running it, but we cannot prove it," Chavez explained. "We believe that an American, if he is an American, formed it and is helping the spy ring, but we cannot prove that either. Furthermore, it is also our belief that Haggarty and the others killed were all spy-related. But, we are working to prove that also."

"Who is the American, Chavez?" Senator Magal asked.

"I am sorry, senator, I cannot tell you. Do you wish for me to lose my job?" Chavez said, smiling. He looked at Mac. "The senator is Chairman of Governmental Security and Intelligence Committee in the Commonwealth Government of President Quezon."

"Would you recognize the man in the boat? Was he by himself?" Mac asked Miguela. She answered that the man was alone and that she would fail to recognize him. But she described him as having a white visor cap, dark glasses, and blond hair.

The ornate grandfather clock standing against the mahogany paneled wall struck twelve times. Senator Magal, Dr. Longo, and their wives thanked Miguela for the lovely evening. Meanwhile, Chavez was telling Mac that he was sorry he had to leave, mentioning that he had to get up early tomorrow morning and drive to Clark Field to attend a briefing on foreign counterintelligence.

"I would like for you to join me. It would give you a chance to see that part of Luzon."

Mac politely declined the offer until a more propitious time presented itself. Chavez looked disappointed. "In that case, pass by my office whenever you can find time. Just ask for me at the entrance of the PIB building."

"Thanks, Chavez." Mac smiled. "I'll drop by as soon as time permits."

Alone with Miguela, Mac asked if he could stay a bit longer while he waited for his taxicab. She liked the idea and suggested that a short stroll on the beach would be refreshing. "If we are not back before he gets here, Tilde will bring him in the house."

Mac agreed. Somehow, he trusted her and hoped that she trusted him also.

They walked in silence for a couple of minutes, enjoying the gentle breeze, the bright moonlight, and the beach. But the wind suddenly changed from gentle to a strong, steady blow. Miguela pointed to the sky. "The moon has disappeared. I do not know who said that if you stare at the moon covered with black clouds, you will meet your enemy face to face."

They continued to walk, neither saying a word. The only sounds were the high wind whistling through the trees and the now heavy surf, sloshing back and forth on the shore. "I knew when I got up this morning that it will rain tonight," she told Mac.

"How'd you know?" Mac shouted over the gale.

"The beach reveals many secrets when you live near it." She paused. "When you see the lighter underside of the leaves, it most often presages a storm with heavy waves. This is also the beginning of the rainy season."

Mac stretched his right arm and touched Miguela's elbow. "Let's walk closer to each other so we won't have to shout to be heard." His touch made Miguela's blood tingle, giving her that same feeling as when they shook hands at the Manila International Club.

"Is there a place on the beach where we can sit and talk?" asked Mac.

"There is a broken down boat on the north end of the shore that was beached by a typhoon several years ago. It is deeply buried in the sand, but we can still sit on it comfortably. The surf will not reach us." Miguela paused momentarily. "I also found Swimmer after that storm. Do you mind if he joins us, Mac?"

"Not at all."

Miguela called loudly through the strong wind. "Swimmer. Come here, Swimmer."

Soon, Mac felt a friendly nudge on his leg. He dropped his hand and petted him on the head. Swimmer responded by licking Mac's hand. "I think he's been following us all along. I love dogs. I used to have one when I was a young boy. His name was Curly. He and I went everywhere together."

Miguela laughed and asked Mac if his dog had curly hair. "Yes," answered Mac. "All Chesapeake Bay retrievers have sort of reddish curly hair. He was a handsome dog, just like Swimmer." Mac talked freely with Miguela. He was comfortable with her. He told her about himself when he was a boy growing up in Virginia's Northern Neck, and about his parents. On Saturdays and Sundays, he and the dog would accompany his father in his workboat, and they would chug out of Indian Creek, going full speed ahead until they reached the deep Rappahanock River, where his father had for many years dropped his crab traps.

Mac paused momentarily and, saddened, talked about his wife. "Joanie and I got married when we were rather young. We were very happy and planned on having children. One Saturday while I was on duty she decided to visit her mother in North Carolina. Late that night, I got a call from my mother-in-law that Joanie was killed in a car accident. I was devastated." Mac took a deep breath. He told her about his assignment in France, from Duvalier to Meissner and the sapphire ring. He did not hold back on the incidents that occurred at Pier 1 upon his arrival.

"Oh, Mac. I am so sorry," was all Miguela could say.

"It's okay. Let's change the subject. What was the name of that guy at the Manila International Club with you and Manuel?"

"Sonny Sollow."

"All I can recall about him was his bad manners," Mac said.

"Well, he is tall with thick reddish brown hair; he wears eyeglasses and has a beard and moustache. Sonny also has a speech impediment. He stammers." Miguela paused momentarily. "Sometimes Papa discusses his work with me. According to him, Sonny Sollow is a very wealthy businessman from the United States, I believe from Baltimore, Maryland."

"What's his business with your father?"

Miguela explained that her father owned a number of houses on Dewey Boulevard, which was a little farther north from Buenavista. It seemed Sonny leased one of the houses for a year since the previous November. "Sonny Sollow really wanted to buy it as early as September, but Mama put her foot down. He comes here now and then to talk to Papa. I guess he still wants to purchase it. Mama wished he would go to the Zaldivar-Molina building instead of coming here."

"Will your father sell?"

"Not as long as Mama is alive. She loathes Mr. Sollow and often tells my father not to trust him, for he is an evil man. Mama has a fine intuition about people and has proved it a number of times."

Mac wondered aloud why Sollow was with Miguela and her cousin at the club. "He does not affect me one way or another. I guess he likes us. He invited Manuel and me to the club as his guests."

There was a short silence.

"Tell me about yourself, Miguela," Mac said at last, placing his arm gently around her waist.

Miguela, feeling limp and unable to clearly think, had some difficulty at first. She was twenty-three years old and had a brother who followed her but died at birth. She reluctantly mentioned her future plans that she had recently discussed with her parents. "After I received my Bachelor's Degree from the University of the Philippines, I thought about going to Stanford University in California to take up law."

"Oh. That's wonderful…." Mac sounded disappointed that he would not see Miguela again. At that very moment, Miguela felt faint of heart.

Miguela moved closer to Mac. "But…meeting you," she said shyly, "seems to have, all at once, altered many things that I had planned. You… you make me feel so special in your life."

"You are! The first moment I saw you," Mac whispered in her ear while tightening his arm around her. He inhaled deeply. "I like your perfume."

"Thank you." Miguela paused. "Mac, we had better get back to the house. It is about to rain."

Suddenly, strong winds swept across Manila Bay, bringing with them thunder and lightning. They ran towards the house, Swimmer ahead of them. But in seconds, as if displeased with the rhythmic imbalance of the atmosphere, the gods became angry and cracked open the sky above them, causing a torrential downpour. Miguela shouted through the wind that they would not be able to avoid the rain. "Over here," she said, running to the dressing room of the swimming pool house and turning on the switch. "I think the electricity is out."

After they dried themselves with the dressing room towels, Miguela guided Mac to the sofa in the small salon. "The rain will stop for a while and then start again. We will quickly run to the house as soon as it stops," she explained.

Mac pulled Miguela up from the sofa and placed his arms around her. "Would you think too badly of me if I kissed you?"

"No," she answered tentatively, biting her lower lip and crossing her arms to keep her body from trembling. Mac took her arms and placed them around him, and kissed her. At first Miguela did not reciprocate. But slowly, she returned Mac's intense kisses with the same ardor.

His strong arms held her closer to him. The softness of her body and her warm lips engulfed him. He could feel her nipples hard against him as he kissed her neck.

The myriad sweet and sensuous scents of salty water, sand, and sun-baked odors carried by the night's bay wind became mixed with the flowering plants. Jasmines wrenched from their stems by the willful and angry wind added to the exotic and delicate fragrances in the air.

CHAPTER 11

Ever since Roosie's story and the happenstance of the Boxer sniffing around a cement slab, Mac's suspicion of Nagoya Emporium's backyard as a place where Stein could possibly have been buried continued to be heavy on his mind. He became more determined as days passed to do a little investigating and convinced Poco to join him.

One day, after the Quest session was over, they walked around the emporium to the main street of the Escolta and stopped at a shoe shop, where Mac asked an elderly female clerk whether she knew how long the emporium had been doing business in Manila.

"I cannot recall exactly when, but perhaps in 1937. The Japs who manage that store are unfriendly. And there are too many men going in and out, mostly Japs. They act strange. They keep to themselves and are always in a hurry," the clerk explained. "A Filipino who cleans the building told me about it." She paused. "Watch out for that big dog. I understand he bites. They keep it upstairs most of the time, like it's guarding something important. Sometimes it is seen loose in the backyard." She told Mac and Poco that she did not like anyone at the emporium. "Ask around at any of the stores in the Escolta, and they will tell you the same thing."

"Have you met the owner of that emporium?" Poco asked.

"No," answered the female clerk. She informed them that many of the stores around the business area, including the emporium, opened at 7:00 a.m. and closed at 4:00 p.m. "If you want to know more about that store, talk to Mr. Calderon. He owns the Fishing Tackle Box across the street."

At the tackle shop, Mac told Mr. Calderon that he needed a shirt and wondered if he could purchase it from the Japanese emporium.

"Did you just get in from Cavite, sailor?" Mac tried to explain that he was in the Army, but Calderon interrupted him. "Let me tell you something, sailor. Anything made in Japan is inferior. My advice is for you to purchase that shirt from any clothing store other than from the emporium. There are Filipino and Chinese stores next door. They sell shirts."

"Do you know the people running the emporium?" Poco inquired.

Calderon gave him a disgusted look. "I do not care to know them. They act strange. They have a meeting every night on the second floor. I know because I watch them." He paused. "Excuse me, I have another customer."

"Major Mac, I will wait for you outside the emporium. Dogs do not like me," Poco explained. He voiced his uneasiness about Mac going inside the store and cautioned him to be very careful. "I will call Colonel Miller if you do not come back in fifteen minutes."

Mac went inside the emporium and was soon aware that, directly above him, a burly, stern-faced Japanese man, sitting on a high stool on the small second floor balcony, was watching him and other customers. His hands were resting on the banister of the balcony. The little finger was missing on his right hand. Sitting next to him was a large fawn-colored Boxer with a white, star-shaped marking on his chest. "By damn. That's the dog I saw in the backyard," Mac murmured.

Pretending not to notice the intense and watchful eyes of the man and the dog on the balcony, Mac casually told the sales girl that he wanted to purchase a shirt.

There were hundreds of men's shirts on display on four long hanger stands. Mac, away from view of the watchful eyes of the Japanese on the balcony, parted a couple of the hanging shirts in front of him, enabling him to see and make mental notes of the shop. First, he saw the exit door leading to the emporium's fenced backyard. Near that door were stairs. He reasoned that at the top of the stairs would be an entrance to other rooms, and one of those rooms would lead to the balcony.

At the other end of the building, on the ground floor, was a room that he surmised could either be a storage or electrical room. He turned his eyes once more to the exit door and stairs. He wanted to be certain that the exit door was adjacent to the stairs. He did not know when he would do it but fully intended to browse inside those rooms on the second floor one dark night just to satisfy a strong curiosity.

Deep in his thoughts, Mac was startled to see Sollow in the store with a large envelope in his hand, standing at the foot of the stairs, talking to the four-fingered Japanese man. Mac could not determine how long Sollow had been there, but from the seriousness of their faces, he guessed that they were discussing something significant.

To avoid Sonny Sollow recognizing him, Mac quickly picked a white shortsleeved cotton shirt and paid the cashier. As he was hurrying to leave the store, he glanced back. Sollow was following the Japanese man up the stairs, where they disappeared in one of the rooms.

Outside, Mac convinced Poco that they wait for Sollow to come out of the emporium. "That son of a bitch is up to something."

Inside the building, meanwhile, the Japanese with Sollow following him from behind, knocked on the door, and a younger Japanese man opened it. "Ikeda, is General Tanaka in?" The four-fingered Japanese man inquired.

"Yes, Colonel Matsumuto. I shall tell the general you are both here," Ikeda said and left. He returned with a slight-of-build, gentle-looking Japanese man.

"Ah, Mr. Sollow. It is good to see you," General Tanaka greeted.

"L-Likewise, Tanaka," answered Sollow. "I've brought you updated photographs of Manila Harbor, the naval base at Sangley Point in Cavite, Clark Field, and Fort Stotsenburg in northern Luzon."

"Excellent! We need them. Please sit down, Mr. Sollow," Tanaka said.

"Thank you. I will." Sollow paused. "I must congratulate you on your timely destruction of the cargo vessel Rich…Richmond. I-I'm certain Matsumuto and your other l-lackey, Ikeda, didn't do it," he added scornfully.

Tanaka ignored Sollow. "Yes. We took care of her. Unfortunately, we lost six people, particularly two men, Sergeant Haleso and Martinez."

"Let's not be ungrateful, Tanaka. Aren't you going to thank me for destroying the Army convoy with all those military supplies from the cargo ship Flores?"

This time Tanaka stared at his visitor, a look of displeasure came to his face. "Mr. Sollow, I am happy that you dropped in," he said, clearing his throat. "It was brought to my attention by our underground network that three FBI agents from the United States had quietly arrived in Manila two weeks ago. Late May. Our intelligence informed me that their names, we are not certain, may be William Lucas, Edward Martin, and James Kagan. Of course, Kagan is dead, which leaves two FBI agents. For lack of information and photographs, these men remain unknown to us. Do their names sound familiar to you, Mr. Sollow?"

"I too, was…in-informed of their arrival, but I have yet…yet to know them. Their names are unfamiliar to me, but in time I will know them, and I'll…I'll then inform your efficient spies," he added sarcastically.

Tanaka continued, "What might their purpose be for being in Manila? Do you think the American government has become aware of our network?"

"Why don't you ask your spies?" Sollow said sarcastically again.

"General, allow me to raise another subject with Mr. Sollow," Matsumuto said, bowing.

Tanaka gave his approval by nodding his head.

"On another American activity," Matsumuto said, his voice unfriendly. "The Japanese espionage network in the Philippines have recently reported that, since Lieutenant Colonel Walters's death, another Army officer, a full colonel, has replaced him with the sole purpose of finding the killer of those three American officers."

"There…there are such rumors," Sollow said, shrugging his shoulders. "There has certainly been…been enough written in the newspapers about those dead men."

"You know Mr. Sollow," Tanaka interrupted, "I have a deep-seated feeling that you are not working towards Japan's goal, but your own personal agenda."

"Think what you…you wish, g-general," Sollow hissed and abruptly left his chair and was about to leave.

"Mr. Sollow! Wait! I have something else to impart to you," Tanaka's eyes and voice were cold and unfriendly.

Sollow returned the cold stare. "Do you now, Tanaka?"

"Yes. Matsumuto and I know who murdered those officers. It came from a most reliable source." He paused. "You murdered them!"

"Really! Does it matter who killed them? You should be pleased.

Three less Americans," Sollow said and left.

Outside the emporium, Poco shifted from one foot to the other. "Major Mac, we have waited for almost an hour for Sollow to come out," he said wearily.

Mac glanced at his watch. He suggested that he and Poco hurry over to the alley where he thought Sollow could have parked his car. They ran to Olivia Street, turned abruptly to the right, and they reached the alley. There was no car in sight. They ran a little farther past their office and saw Sollow get inside a white and blue taxicab. They immediately hailed a red city cab passing by. Once inside the cab, Mac directed the driver to follow the white and blue cab. "But don't get too close."

The white and blue cab left the Escolta, crossed a bridge, turned left on Rizal, then stopped in front of Ruby Redd restaurant, where Sollow and the cabdriver went inside. In the red city cab Mac instructed the cabbie to stop behind a building, and he paid him. After waiting a while, he and Poco also went into the restaurant but through the kitchen, in time to see Sollow and a companion take a booth. Mac and Poco, meanwhile, chose a table near the booth and paid the waiter in advance for two bottles of beer with the instruction that they were not to be disturbed.

The booths were divided from the dining tables by a row of flimsy floral cutains to give customers some privacy. After some time, Mac discretely parted the curtain ever so slightly to see who Sollow's companion was, and with his pen wrote something on a paper napkin and gave it to Poco to read, 'Sollow's friend is Jim Wanabe. If you remember him give me a thumbs-up and destroy the napkin when you've finished reading.' While Poco followed the instruction, Mac whispered that he was going to jot down as much as he could of their neighbor's conversation on another paper napkin. It was then that they both overheard Wanabe asked Sollow a question. "Did you see some different birds over a mountain last weekend?"

"No. The same species of…birds as…as before. They continue…to remain small," Sollow answered and stopped as their waiter approached to pour some more coffee. "It's…it's best to wait for the big ones." The conversation between Sollow and Wanabe continued to be audible, thinking perhaps that they were by themselves. Wanabe asked Sollow whether he had given to T the data on the flats one, three, and five. "They are very important."

Sollow nodded. "A week ago. Did you in…include in the package ab…about the hot iron?"

"Yes," Wanabe said. "The G-owned in L is 704 single T. I also included that from the very wide H_2O, the southern entrance to the CP and M is through the U-shaped and smaller H_2O."

Do you have a pac…package for me now?" Sollow asked.

"Yes," said Wanabe. He reached into his pocket and gave an envelope to Sollow. "The photo is in there. It is of two hundred ants at Bpen with fire, thunder, and lightning."

"I'll contact you. Don't contact me," said Sollow, giving Wanabe a stern look.

When Sollow and Wanabe left the restaurant, Mac and Poco followed them in another taxicab. Sollow's taxi stopped in front of the Far East Hotel, where Sollow disappeared through the foyer, and Wanabe turned his cab around, back to the city.

As soon as Mac was back in his quarters, he copied what he had written on the table napkin on to a piece of paper and then read what he just transcribed. He could not make any sense out of it, but he carefully folded it and inserted it in his wallet. Later that evening, he knocked on Charlie's door. "The door is unlocked," Charlie answered. He was stretched out on his bed.

"Charlie, you look all in. I didn't expect you to be back from northern Luzon."

"I didn't go. I had another errand to do." He rolled to his side and sat on the edge of his bed and lighted a cigar, taking several deep puffs. "I'm flattered with your visit, Mac. What's so important?" Charlie asked testily.

Mac handed to him the blue sapphire ring. "Read what's inscribed inside the band and see if you know of anyone by that name."

"You're just here for me to read the writings in that ring? I've heard the inscription. Miller read it to us. Remember? You've got to be crazy," Charlie said grumpily. But instead of reading the inscription, he slipped it on his finger. "By damn this ring fits well. Can I purchase it from you, Mac? Any man would be proud to wear this handsome jewelry."

Mac said the ring was not for sale, and Charlie declared jokingly, "I'll just have to take it from you one of these days." Charlie got up and went to his closet and came back with a magnifying glass. He sat down on the edge of the bed again and read the writings inside the ring. He looked up at Mac. "It reads, 'To Sonny, love, Mother.'"

"Charlie, you sounded so sentimental just then," Mac stated, rather amazed at his rugged-looking friend. "There's a heart inside that hairy chest of yours."

Charlie laughed heartily, forgetting his grumpiness. "Just reminded me of my own mother." He took another puff from his cigar and abruptly asked Mac who the owner of the ring was.

"Boris Meissner. I believe that I mentioned it to the team during our first Quest meeting," Mac said.

"Yes, come to think of it, I believe you did."

Mac picked up the magnifying glass and read the inscriptions in the ring like so many times before. "I find it almost eerie that I feel compelled to even wonder why the name Sonny should occupy my mind." He recounted having met a guy some time ago by the name of Sonny Sollow at the Manila International Club. And then saw the same man at the Nagoya Emporium earlier in the day having a serious conversation with a Japanese man. But Mac, somehow, without any conscious reason, held back that he and Poco followed Sollow and Wanabe to the Ruby Redd restaurant and listened to their conversation.

"No crime in that, Mac," Charlie said.

"Did you hear Rhoades introduce himself as Sonny Rhoades at our first meeting?" Mac persisted.

Charlie nodded. "He did. That's his name, Sonny Rhoades. What's wrong with that, Mac?"

Mac sucked in his breath and exhaled loudly. "And, this ring! Strange how the name Sonny keeps popping up."

Charlie rubbed his balding head. "Strange indeed! How about a beer, Mac?" He went to the bathroom and took two bottles of San Miguel from the bathroom table. Upon coming back, Mac asked him if he thought Sonny Sollow and the Sonny in that ring could be one and the same. Charlie's eyes narrowed. "I don't know. Now you actually know three men with the same name: Sonny 'Dusty' Rhoades, the Sonny in that ring, and Sonny Sollow." He paused and gave Mac a hard look.

"What are you driving at, Mac? It's a flimsy reason if you are inferring that Sonny Sollow is a spy simply because you saw him talking to a Jap or that Lieutenant Colonel Rhoades is a spy simply because his name is Sonny, or that the Sonny in that ring could be either Rhoades or Sollow. You're getting off-track." He reminded Mac not to forget what their sole mission was. "We're looking for a murderer who may also be a spy. Remember? I doubt if Sollow, whom I don't know, is either of those. Why don't you zero in on Rhoades? Perhaps he's Boris Meissner. Perhaps he was at the pier when you arrived, and it was he who tried to kill you." Charlie paused. "But my advice is for you not to get on your high horse and charge just yet. You might get your tail caught in a crack, especially if the Sonny you'll be accusing has friends in high places."

Charlie explained further that the name Sonny was not so uncommon and made a bet with Mac that he would probably find several hundred men named Sonny in the US Army. "My history teacher at Chicago State was named Sonny Petrovsky." He walked to the bathroom and carried back two more bottles of beer. "What else do you know about Meissner?"

Mac expressed regretfully that, among other things in that briefcase stolen from him, was a letter from Walters to a friend of his in Washington pinpointing Meissner as his prime suspect as a spy for the Japanese and the murderer of the Army officers.

Charlie glanced at Mac nonchalantly and took a sip of beer. "I've just made a decision," he said, changing the subject. "I think that I'll change Miller's game plan a tiny bit, just till the end of June."

"Oh?"

"Mac, I'm going to pull rank on Delgado. I'll tell him to forget about being partners with me and enjoy himself before he leaves for the United States at the end of this month."

"Can you trust him not to divulge your plan to Miller?" Mac asked.

Charlie explained to Mac that he knew Delgado's brother, Dom, and that Delgado often talked of spending some time with Dom and his wife. "My plan will give him that opportunity." Charlie further explained to Mac that the two brothers were close to each other and had not seen each other in a year until the younger brother, Delgado, was pulled out from an Army unit in Mindanao and told to report to Quest. Some weeks later,

Dom was transferred to Clark Field to service aircraft bombers planned for Clark base. Charlie took a big gulp of beer. "Delgado shouldn't have talked about the rumored arrival of B-17 bombers. Christ, a foreign spy would eat up such info." He shrugged his shoulders. But hey. What the hell? Rumors are flying like flies in Manila."

"How will you convince Delgado?"

"That I should stay here and help you, McCord, get to know the place. After my investigations, I'll write the report. He can sign his name on it along with mine when it's finished. He's not to tell anyone about my plan, and I'll keep my mouth shut about him spending almost the entire month of June near Clark Field with Dom and his wife. Delgado isn't going to jeopardize his chance of going back to the States."

"What an absolutely weird idea. What made you decide to do that?" Mac studied Charlie's face. "You could be court-martialed for insubordination. I'd drop the idea like a hot potato."

"Listen up, Mac. My gut tells me that I should be with you and Poco." Charlie went on to complain about the foolishness of Rhoades for assigning Czestochowa and Golden to come up with a layout of Corregidor. He continued to discuss, with animation at times, that the plan could get in the hands of foreign spies and fifth columnists. "Anyone in Quest can tour the Rock. We don't need any layout plan, and added to all the stupid things I've heard, the Meissner story convinced me that I must stay close to Manila and find the criminal."

It was apparent Charlie was riled, but Mac did not wish to hear any more complaints about Delgado and the layout plan. He himself would not mind having a layout plan of Corregidor. Besides, he would much prefer for them to discuss their mission and improvements on their investigative system. Mac walked to the window, conveying his intentions of changing the subject. Charlie opened the door of the credenza by his bed and took out a fresh cigar and forgot to shut the drawer. While Charlie was lighting his cigar, Mac had turned around and accidentally saw a dagger with a similar handle to that which he and Poco picked up earlier. There was also a matchbox identical to the one that Wanabe had given to him, with the Periscope Club's logo.

Mac immediately assumed that Charlie had gone to the Periscope Club. But he became curious about the dagger. "By the way, Charlie, I couldn't help but notice that dagger in your credenza. May I see it?"

Charlie handed it to Mac.

"Is this yours?"

Charlie hastily shut the drawer and told Mac that he could not remember where he found the dagger, and added, "It's a handsome weapon."

"It's deadly!" Mac said, giving it back to Charlie and quickly changing the subject to the murders of the officers and what Delgado had said during Quest's meeting, that foreign spies could have murdered them. "I've had the same thoughts and from various whispers I've been hearing, Walters was also murdered," Mac added.

"I believe that." Charlie sighed. "And I believe also that espionage in the Philippines has increased significantly in the last few years. Walters used to tell me that if you scratch Manila's surface hard enough, you'll find hundreds of squirming foreign spies."

During the course of their conversation, Mac mentioned rumors about Walters's papers being stolen. "I wonder if they contained incriminating evidence? Haggarty, Summers, and Stein may have zeroed in on the spy ring, hence their demise."

Charlie looked a long time at Mac, and a quick smile appeared on the corners of his lips. "I'm certain of it." He voiced his belief that, according to his own analysis, Walters, on his own investigations, had gathered evidences on a certain spy or someone belonging to a spy ring in Manila as the killer of the officers. Charlie took a puff from his cigar. "I don't have any idea who killed those guys, but you said Walters's letter to a friend in Washington names Meissner as their murderer. Is that right, Mac?"

Mac nodded.

Charlie offered Mac some glimpses into Walters's behavior. He related what a friendly and open man Walters was, but when it came to revealing any information he had about those officers, he kept things close to his chest. He paused. "That's probably the reason why he got murdered. He knew too much and had the evidence to prove it."

"What makes you so sure, Charlie?" Mac asked.

"Here's what he said once to me: 'North, I've got something to tell you that'd curl what few hairs you've got, but not until I've collated all reports. It'll blow up someone's cover.'" Charlie expressed his many disappointments that Walters never did tell him the identity of the person he was alluding to. He learned from Walters that he compiled everything SPIDER had reported to him including his own findings, in a large blue three-ringed binder. "Christ," he said wistfully, "how I wish I could have gotten hold of that blue binder before Walters died."

"So would the Philippine Department G-2," Mac said.

Charlie pursed his lips. "Poor devil, he never got to see retirement."

"Did he at any time tell you the nationalities of these foreign spies in the Philippines?" Mac asked.

"Yes," Charlie answered, "mostly Japanese."

"Interesting," said Mac. "It's Japan's belief that Southeast Asia should be under her umbrella, a concept of a Greater Asia Co-prosperity Sphere." He told Charlie that it would not surprise him if there were Germans and Italian spies in Manila. "I suppose it's because of Japan's political admiration and understanding of Germany. As you well know, the political admiration and understanding ended in the Axis Powers, creating a united military front in Europe and Asia."

"Jeez, you're brilliant, McCord."

"It's all been in the newspapers," Mac answered dryly. "You said a few minutes ago that Walters kept things pretty much to himself. But, did he ever voice any pet theories. Surely he must have done that."

"Yes, he had a pet theory that Japan would eventually attack the Philippines for all the reasons you just told me. It's nothing new for Japan to be mother Japan to all Asians. It's in her plan to conquer all of Asia sooner or later. But she always has a special affinity for the Philippines."

"What was Walters's timetable, Charlie?"

"Never had a chance to ask him." Charlie shrugged his shoulders. However, the Philippine Department must not be anticipating any attack soon," he added sarcastically. "Just look at the military weapons. Mostly obsolescent."

"Mac urged Charlie that they go back and discuss the murdered officers. "I think all members of Quest believe they were murdered, but by whom? That's why we've got to change our investigative system. Let me sound out an idea to you."

"Let's hear it. I'm curious!"

Mac explained that perhaps they should stop going to the same places they had been going before, to forget Olongapo, Cavite and Corregidor. Instead, they should go underground and mingle with the people there.

"What underground place do you have in mind, Mac?"

"Kapalaran Strip. As I recall, Poco called it Sodom and Gomorrah."

Charlie smiled. "It's that, all right! All wrapped up into one. Sin city!" Charlie said, reaching for a thermos bottle on the floor by his bed.

"What's in the bottle? Gin?" Mac inquired.

"No. Cold coffee," said Charlie. "I carry it everywhere I go. Gives me a lift."

The discussion became animated, particularly when Mac aired his conviction that most things happening in Manila eventually became known in the strip, and they would have better luck there in their investigations. Charlie gave Mac a thoughtful look and this time poured himself a cup of cold coffee from his thermos bottle. He offered Mac some coffee, but Mac declined. Charlie then began to recount how he grew up in the rough side of Chicago and could have stayed there had he not pulled himself up by his bootstraps, with the help of his mother, of course. "Those people at Kapalaran Strip, like in Chicago, those people won't talk to you, Mac, until you've gained their trust first." He paused momentarily. "How in the hell are you going to do that?"

Mac grabbed a chair and faced Charlie. "I'm a pretty trustworthy fellow, and I think I should live in Kapalaran. I'm convinced that staying in Manila will never produce results. It's a blind alley. What did it bring Walters's group?"

"Sounds good," said Charlie, "but it could be very dangerous. For one, you don't know the area and the kind of people who live there." Charlie began stroking his walrus-type moustache. After a while, he conceded that Mac's idea might work. "We'll discuss it in depth at the end of this month. I've a feeling Miller and Rhoades won't hold us to report to the office every day once Golden and Delgado leave to go back to the States. We can make plans then. Meanwhile, just keep your idea to yourself. It'd be best if only you, I, and Poco know about it."

CHAPTER 12

The end of June came quickly, and Quest was scheduled to give their final presentations on their investigation. Before their meeting that morning, Delgado and Charlie turned in a ten-page description of their trip from Cavite to Olongapo, with dozens of short interviews with several people about the murders of the Army officers. The first page was a background about the officers, and the rest contained substantial information on the alleged Japanese spy ring in Cavite. According to the report, many had long suspected that particular area—which is very close to the Navy Yard—to be a breeding ground for foreign spies, due to its proximity to Manila and the importance of the Navy Yard. Based on their findings, both men believed that someone, possibly a Filipino civilian employee of the Navy, was spying for the Japanese. Furthermore, there were rumors that there could be several spies who took part in the murders. Charlie footnoted the report, saying that he would have to continue to monitor that part of Cavite for more evidence.

Another paragraph of the report also attracted Miller's attention, and he began to read it to the group. "While I was in a nightclub in Pampanga one night, I overheard two Filipinos mention the words 'Sun' and 'Arayat.' I approached them and inquired what the words meant. They said they did not know, that they only heard it from a Japanese-Filipino who had since left the area. I became so intrigued with the words that I began asking around town for the significance of the two words. No one knew. I began to do some analysis and came to the conclusion that the words may be code names used by spies for Japanese occupation of the Philippines. The 'Sun' is Japan, and 'Arayat,' the mountain, is the Philippines."

Miller applauded Charlie and Delgado for the fine report.

"I will personally submit your papers to the Philippine Department

135

G-2," Miller said looking squarely at Charlie. "You seem to have an in-depth understanding of spies in this country."

"Just a lot of deductive reasoning, Colonel Miller," answered Charlie tersely.

The layout of Corregidor presented by Golden and Czestochowa particularly pleased Miller.

"A detailed piece of work. I didn't realize Corregidor was so small," Miller said, reading the dimensions. "You've both done a splendid job. I see you've also indicated barracks on this paper.

"How many soldiers are there at Corregidor?"

"I believe Golden and I showed it on the footnotes—five to six thousand, Sir," Czestochowa said proudly. "The waters around Corregidor are heavily mined, according to one of the off-shore patrolmen who guards the beach."

Mac and Poco, meanwhile, could only report that they had tried but found nothing of substance. Despite urgings from Poco and Charlie to use Roosie's story in his report, Mac refused. Miller wasn't happy.

"I thought that surely you, of all people, McCord, would have already captured the killer," he said sarcastically. "Maybe you should stop spending all of your time in Manila and start acquainting yourself with the provinces in Luzon."

Before he closed the meeting, Miller made it clear that Quest's mission had to be pursued relentlessly, and any new information they gathered were to be reported to Lieutenant Colonel Rhoades immediately. He reminded them again that their mission had to be kept top secret.

"I've already received permission from Colonels Danbury and Bass to continue with this work until the end of November. Danbury and Bass are going to be important members in the McArthur reorganization. They assured me that we'll be left alone until then."

He announced that he would be out of town the entire month of July. But before he left, he wished Golden and Delgado a safe trip back to the United States.

"And as I had mentioned earlier, their billets will not be filled. Are there any questions?" Miller said.

Mac raised his hand and Miller acknowledged him.

"Sir, I understand that, before his death, Colonel Walters was preparing to present to G-2 a collection of intelligence data he had placed in a binder. Have you heard anything about it?" said Mac with his eyes fixed on Miller.

There was an immediate silence in the room. It was several seconds before Miller answered Mac.

"What are you trying to say, McCord? No! I haven't heard! I don't know anything about it." Miller looked at Charlie. "You, North. Know anything about that?"

Charlie shook his head. "No, Sir. He told me some things, but he did not give me the binder. Is that what you're alluding to, Sir? That he gave it to me?"

"Yes. I understand you were close to Walters?" Miller continued as he turned to Rhoades.

"Do you have the binder?"

"I've heard about it and had looked around for it," Rhoades said.

Miller closed the session by handing the layout of Corregidor and the North/Delgado report to Rhoades and suggested he keep the items in his safe, particularly the layout plan of Corregidor.

"It's an important document. Corregidor is, after all, a very strategic area and the primary defense area of Luzon. Heavens forbid if it gets in the hands of an enemy spy."

Miller emphasized that the plan was for everyone in the group to use as a reference to the Rock but that it should never leave their office. He encouraged everyone in the room to memorize Rhoades's safe combination.

After the session, Mac stayed behind and told Rhoades that he would like to take a look at the map.

"So soon? Just itching to know the area, huh, Mac?"

With sarcasm, Mac answered that he might find the murderer in Corregidor and continued to study the schematic for about five minutes before giving it back to Rhoades. He then joined Poco, who was studying the town of Lingayen on the Philippine map.

"What do you think of the Rock?" Poco asked Mac.

"I didn't realize Corregidor lays right at the entrance of Manila Bay." Mac answered.

"Yes. The Rock will be our best salvation if the Philippines get attacked. At least that is what we have been told to believe," Poco said as he glanced at his watch and then at Mac.

"I've promised some Filipino friends I'd join them for supper tonight. But tomorrow, for your first field trip outside Manila, how about us going to Clark Field for a starter? It would be good for you to see other places," Poco said. "Miller was right. You need to get out of the city. We will stay on the base. While we are there, you might request a short briefing about Clark Field. From there we will go to the town of Lingayen."

"Sounds great," Mac said. "I've been curious about that place. Let's scratch around and find out why the Richmond blew up."

"That is why I suggested Lingayen," Poco said. "There is a small hotel there where we can stay."

"What's for transportation?" Mac asked.

According to Poco's plan, they were to take an Army supply truck that left the Philippine Department at Fort Santiago for Clark Field every morning at 7:00 a.m. From Clark, they would catch another supply truck going to an Army post in the town of Lingayen and then hitch a ride to San Fernando, La Union.

"You need to see other parts of this country besides Manila. I'll be your tour guide during this trip," Poco said looking pleased with himself. "It will take us several days to visit all those places."

Promptly the next morning, Mac and Poco climbed into the Army truck and were on their way to Clark Field.

"We should get there in a couple of hours, long before that hot sun starts bearing down. July in Manila is oppressive," Poco said.

They stayed on the base for a couple of hours that first day and were briefed on the Army Air Corps program, the number and the condition of airplanes in the Philippines, and the number of trained pilots.

"We have pilots who are trained in light bombing and gunnery. In addition, the Air program has selected air force students who are given flying and technical training in the United States," the briefer said proudly. "This air base is the only one that can take heavy bombers."

The Lieutenant then shifted to a lighter subject, Mt. Arayat.

"It's Clark Field's distinctive marker from the air," he said pointing to a large map. "The mountain stands there, looking mighty and invincible, guarding the area and Clark Base," he said. "I personally find Mt. Arayat mysterious. Whenever I come in from flight maneuvers I talk to it to guide me in and land safely."

Mac thought that Poco's idea of him staying in Olongapo for a day or two longer had merits and told him that from Olongapo, he was going south to Cavite and would stay there three or four days.

"What transportation should I take?" Mac asked.

"Have someone from the Subic Naval Station drive you to the Malolos railroad station and get on the train for Cavite. Later, you can hitch a ride from Cavite to Manila.

At the end of ten days, Mac was not any closer to solving the crime than before he left Manila, but the trip made him that much more determined to find the murderers. His trip to Cavite, however, was in many ways fruitful. One American sailor quietly reasoned with Mac, "Just count the number of naval ships destroyed a year or two years ago. And look what happened to the Richmond. How about those military weapons from the transport Flores? They all got blown to bits, including the truck convoy," the sailor said, looking unhappily at Mac. "American soldiers and sailors get ambushed and killed. Of course there are spies in Manila. All over the Philippines."

A Filipino civilian working for the Navy insisted that rumors were rampant on the base that a spy killed the Army officers who were found dead. Or they were killed because they were getting too close to identifying the members in the spy ring. But no proof could be found.

It was during that time when Mac definitely decided he was going to the cove near Buenavista and look around where the skeleton was found. He was also anxious to pay Chavez at the PIB a visit.

Back in Manila, Mac called Miguela first and asked her if she would like to go for a boat ride in the morning.

"I'll rent a motor boat from Kawazaka," Mac said. "Bring your bathing suit in case we should decide to go swimming."

The next day, Mac, Miguela, and Swimmer went aboard the eighteen-foot motorboat for a leisurely ride on Manila Bay. The bay was beautiful and placid.

Mac gave Miguela an admiring look. "I like your bathing suit. The blue looks good on you."

"You think so, Mac?" Miguela asked shyly.

Mac slowed the boat and suddenly grabbed Miguela by her slender waist with his right hand and drew her very close to him and passionately kissed her mouth, her neck, and then her breasts. Miguela responded with passionate kisses of her own.

There they sat engulfed in each other's embrace.

Mac whispered in her ear. "Let's go back to your house. I'm too distracted to handle this boat," Mac said hoarsely, his kisses and ardor becoming more demanding.

"Mac. No! Not here!" Miguela pushed Mac away from her. "Remember, we were to go for a boat ride and possibly go swimming later on." She kissed him lightly on the cheek. "Let me be your tour guide," she quickly added and began pointing out some of the more interesting places along the bay, such as the Army and Navy Club on Dewey Boulevard, the Manila Hotel, and the North and South Harbors. Mac had slowed the motorboat to admire the magnificent Manila Hotel, when Miguela screamed.

"Mac, look out! It is going to hit us!" Miguela said ducking down in the boat and grabbing Swimmer by the collar.

Mac turned around to see a large cruiser coming very fast.

In a split second he automatically turned the wheel to starboard and shouted to Miguela. "Jump!"

The strong and boiling wake from the cruiser dashed them against South Harbor's barnacled pilings while sending the small motorboat one hundred feet away from them. After they had caught their breath and had regained their bearings, Mac swam to where Miguela was treading water and told her, "There are some half-submerged rotten pilings over there," he said pointing. "Hang on to them and see if you can keep Swimmer with you. I'll swim after our boat."

On their way back to Kawazaka marina, Mac asked Miguela if by chance she had caught a good look at the person behind the cruiser's wheel. Miguela thought a while.

"I do not remember what he looked like. He had blond hair, wearing a white visor cap pulled low over his face and dark sunglasses. Perhaps it was the same man on the speed boat whom I told you and my other guests during dinner at my parents' house, Buenavista."

Without answering, Mac asked, "Would you say that was a deliberate effort on his part to run us down?"

"Yes. The bay is very wide, and there was no other boat on either side of him to keep him from veering to his port," Miguela said, staring at Mac. "Do you think he was trying to kill me?"

"No, darling. I've a feeling he was after me," Mac said.

Miguela sighed and told Mac that they were almost back to Buenavista. Mac cut down on the boat's speed and asked her if she would lead them to where Ernesto and his friend found the skeleton.

"I understood from Poco that one of the murdered officers, Major Haggarty, liked to fish near a deep cove not too far from Kawazaka's," Mac said.

"Ernie and Gordo found the skeleton near the cove near the north end of Buenavista. Poco was probably talking about that cove. As you know, Kawazaka is just around that bend," she said pointing. "And there is the cove."

Mac slowed the motor even more and was moving towards the cove when Miguela cautioned him.

"Do you see those huge boulders piled up against that part of Dewey Boulevard and near that high wire fence? On low tide there is about ten feet of beach in the cove along those rocks."

She continued to tell Mac that although the cove looked beautiful with coconut trees hovering over them, it was very dangerous. The current, she said, was very strong and could suck a swimmer in.

"Our parents have been warning us since we could walk to never go near it. But, needless to say, Ernie and Gordo often play between those rocks and the fence," Miguela said rolling her eyes.

Mac found a half of a broken fishing pole in the boat and threw it into the swirling water, and it immediately disappeared.

"Very strong current," he murmured.

He noticed a five-foot concrete balustrade stretched about a half-mile on the narrowest part of the boulevard above the narrow but deep cove. Across Dewey Boulevard and going for some miles were some of the loveliest homes he had seen.

"Who lives in those houses, Miguela?"

"Wealthy American businessmen, Chinese merchants, Syrians, those who can afford it. Everyone calls that area the International Row for the many different nationalities who reside there," she said.

Mac admitted that International Row had a fantastic view of Manila Bay. "On a clear day they can probably see for many miles." Miguela was quiet for a brief second. "Mac, do you remember Sonny Sollow?"

"How could I forget?" he said.

"He lives in that two-story white stucco house, directly facing this cove." She paused. "I understand that he is leaving the Philippines at the end of December to go back to Baltimore. I can move into that house then. My parents are giving it to me. The Zaldivar-Molina Corporation owns it and the brick house across the street from it."

"Interesting. Who lives in that brick house?" Mac inquired.

Miguela answered that an American Army colonel from California had been renting it. "Do you want me to find out his name?"

"No, thanks," Mac answered absentmindedly. His thoughts were on Haggarty. "Miguela, where exactly did Ernie and Gordo find that skeleton?"

"Between those rocks and that fence. I guess the heavy rains and high tides had washed the skeleton to the surface," she said.

Mac asked whether Ernie and Gordo had found anything else aside from the skeleton. "Like these, for instance," he said, showing her the dog tags around his neck.

"I do not think so," said Miguela.

"Let's pull the boat to the beach. I know the cops had fine-combed that area but I also would like to scratch around," Mac told Miguela.

While she tied the boat to a coconut tree, Mac, with the help of Swimmer, found a strong piece of driftwood. He began poking around on the ten-foot sandy ground between the big rocks and the fence down the beach. Back and forth they went but found nothing. Meanwhile, Swimmer was sniffing around in a certain area and began to dig vigorously. Soon his head disappeared into the three-foot deep hole, and when he did finally raise his head, Swimmer was clutching what appeared to be a chain in his mouth. He dropped it at Mac's feet.

Mac picked up the chain. "These are dog tags," Mac said, surprised. "You're a good boy, Swimmer."

He patted the proud and happy dog on his head. Then suddenly, Swimmer whirled around and growled.

"What's the matter, fella?" Mac asked, still leaning against the wire fence, rubbing the sand from the dog tags with the corner of his shirt that he had removed. Swimmer's growl, in the meantime, became louder and more vicious.

"Be quiet, Swimmer!" Miguela commanded, holding her pet back. "Sit and stay!"

The dog obeyed but was showing his fangs, a behavior Miguela had not see before. Then, in a surprised muffled tone, she told Mac, "I think that's Sonny Sollow coming towards us."

"What the hell is he doing here?"

Sollow was upon them before Miguela could answer.

"Good afternoon, Miguela," he greeted. "Your…g-gardener told me… I'd find you on the beach."

"Sonny, how are you?" Miguela greeted back politely.

Without answering, Sollow quickly pivoted and kicked the growling Swimmer hard in his stomach. Swimmer fell on his side, whimpering in pain. Miguela rushed to her dog's side.

"There, there, Swimmer," she said, petting him.

She angrily approached Sollow and castigated him. "How dare you kick my dog! If I ever see you do that again, I will have you jailed for cruelty to animals!"

"I…I hate for dogs to growl at me." Sollow said as he looked around. "Do you re…re…member asking me several mon…months ago if…if…I had brochures on New York?"

"What about it?" Miguela asked icily, still infuriated about Swimmer.

"I have them," he said. "How about supper tonight? We'll discuss the beauty of New… New York."

Miguela answered that she already had a previous engagement. Sollow pointed to Mac who had been watching the goings-on.

"I suppose with him?"

"Yes! With me!" Mac answered without lifting his eyes to look at Sollow while continuing to clean the dog tags.

"What are you doing, soldier boy? Playing in…in the sand?" Sollow asked sarcastically in his stuttering voice.

"No. He is not! We found the skeleton's identity!" Miguela explained angrily. "Mr. Sollow, I think you should leave."

"Interesting," Sollow muttered. He went closer to where Mac was sitting. "Those...those look like dog tags. What...what do they say, soldier boy?" Sollow suddenly grabbed the dog tags from Mac's hands and read one aloud. "Michael J. Hag...Haggarty, Maj. US Army. Wh...what happened to...to him? Did he drown while playing truant, McCord?"

Mac jumped to his feet and grabbed back the dog tags from Sollow's hand. "You're really a very rude fellow," he murmured and gave Sollow a very hard jab on the jaw, flattening him to the ground.

Sollow got up and began to fight back, hitting Mac on his head and stomach. They stopped fighting only when Miguela got between them. Sollow wiped the blood from his lip and walked away. Miguela and Mac hugged and walked back to the house.

Later that evening, after calling Charlie and Poco about the dog tags, Mac decided he had to infiltrate the Nagoya Emporium again to see if he could find anything about Sollow's ties with the Japanese. Mac had been very suspicious of him since the day he saw Sollow there. He also made up his mind that before he submitted his report regarding the dog tags to Purita Aquino, he would pay agent Chavez a visit at the PIB. Tomorrow would be a good time, he told himself.

Mac could not sleep that night. It was hot and humid, and the ceiling fan in his room was only distributing the sticky unpleasantness around the room. He crawled out from under his mosquito net and groped around for his watch on the night table near his bed. It showed 2:00 a.m. He lackadaisically put on his clothes, slipped on his tennis shoes, and, with a flashlight, sauntered out of the walled military center hoping to feel cooler air. Then, an absolutely intriguing idea suddenly entered his mind.

"Yes! Why not now? There's a moment in time when one must bite the bullet and that moment and time is now!" He murmured under his breath and hailed a passing taxicab, directing the driver to drop him downtown.

He walked to Olivia Street and stood in the alley between his office and the fenced backyard of the Nagoya Emporium. There appeared to be no one around, but he had to be certain. Mac picked up a handful of stones and threw a couple of them into the dark backyard to determine if the Boxer was in the yard asleep in the doghouse. No one rushed to greet him. He threw another stone, this time into the doghouse. Again, there was no response. Encouraged by his luck, Mac pushed the gate, and it opened. Someone forgot to lock this gate, he told himself. He tried the exit door to the emporium and found it locked, but with the aid of his pocketknife, he jiggled it open.

Save for the Exit light, it was very dark inside the building. Initially, Mac was tempted to use his flashlight, but his gut told him not to use it just yet. Slowly, he went up the stairs and began to go from room to room, this time giving each room a quick inspection with the help of his flashlight, but none yielded anything of interest or importance. Upon reaching the last room, he turned the doorknob. It was locked. Again, he used his pocketknife to successfully open the door and turned on his flashlight. It immediately struck him that it was a briefing room.

The first thing that appeared was a huge map of the Philippines on the wall with various places circled in red. Next to the big map, on each side, was an equally large map of Luzon and on the other was a detailed map of Manila. There were enlarged photographs with the name printed on a piece of paper and neatly pasted on each of the photographs—Clark Field, Fort Stotsenburg, Fort Wint on Grande Island, Corregidor, and nearby forts—Fort Hughes, Fort Drum, and Fort Frank. There were other photographs of places such as the Manila Hotel, as well as the Manila Harbor.

Mac pulled open the top-drawer of an imposing mahogany desk and searched for items of interest. In his determination to find some data that would identify the proprietors of the emporium to the Japanese espionage system and Sollow's connection with them, he failed to hear neither the car door open and shut in front of the bazaar nor the opening of the front door of the building.

From the corner of his eye, he spotted a filing cabinet in the far end of the room. He pulled out two folders, one contained several photographs of Cavite Naval Yard, and he was in the process of examining the second folder marked, Northern Luzon, when he heard a very low, intimidating growl at first, and then a loud bark.

"Lucky me! That damn dog is in the building!" Mac said to himself.

And immediately following the bark, he heard a male voice, shouting,

"Hoshi. Be quiet!"

But the Boxer barked even louder and bounded up the stairs, sniffing each room along the corridor. The same man who tried to quiet the dog was following close behind.

Watching from the slightly opened door of the briefing room, Mac recognized the four-fingered Japanese man.

As the Boxer sniffed the room, the Japanese man turned on the light and looked inside, then turned off the light. Hoshi and the man followed the same routine until they were a room away from the briefing room.

Mac took out one of the stones he had dropped subconsciously in his pocket earlier that evening while he reconnoitered the backyard of the emporium, and waited for Hoshi, who was by now behaving with increased viciousness. The dog had spotted his enemy and he was, by training, going forward for the kill. Caught between the apparently trained-to-attack Boxer and the Japanese, Mac definitely preferred to tangle with the man. But that would not be the case.

Lacking any type of weapon to protect himself, he knew he had to use a strategy that would enable him to escape Hoshi. And any mistake or miscalculation on his part was unthinkable. At that intense moment, he became certain that the Japanese man was not with the dog.

"He probably went back downstairs to search around," Mac told himself under his breath. "It's now or never!"

Hoshi now stood between the open door of another room and the slightly opened door of the briefing room. Mac now had a clear view of the Boxer and became fixated with its physical components: the strong jaws and neck, the solid, sinewy shoulders. With his arm poised back, Mac steadied his aim and threw the stone across the room. Hoshi instantaneously bounded into the room, barking viciously and running round and round, searching for the intruder.

Mac, in the meantime, rushed across the room and quickly closed its door, shutting the Boxer in. Mac quickly turned around and began to run away from the rooms, but on his way down the stairs, he encountered the Japanese man.

Mac swung his arm and with a force hit the surprised man on the jaw. But as he tried to get to the exit door, the man tripped him, and a long struggle ensued. After a while, Mac thought he had the upper hand. He was going to finish him with a good, clean uppercut to his chin when the Japanese made a quick whirl, kicking Mac in the chest, sending him back to the floor. He moved to finish it with a lethal kick in Mac's stomach.

Mac rolled slightly to one side, grabbed his opponent's foot with both of his hands, and flipped him against the wall. With alacrity, though feeling the pain in his chest, Mac bounded to his feet, took the Japanese by his collar and gave him a right hook to his jaw. The Japanese man slumped to the floor, unconscious.

CHAPTER 13

Mac went to the PIB where Agent Chavez met him at the entrance of the building. The two men were obviously glad to see each other since they were guests of Miguela's small get-together at Buenavista.

"It's good to see you again, Chavez," Mac greeted.

"Likewise, Mac." A smile appeared on Chavez's strong but friendly face. "I am glad you have decided to pay us a visit. Let's go into my office. I have something to show you and a number of things to discuss."

Agent Chavez's small office was neat, and the only picture to be seen was a framed photograph on his desk of himself, his wife, and his two daughters. There were two filing cabinets in one corner of the small office. He walked behind the desk and sat down. "Please make yourself comfortable, Mac," he said, pointing to a chair across from him. "I think I know why you are here. Would it be about the murdered American officers?"

Mac smiled wryly. "Yes, I thought I'd go to the person who knows the whole story. I want you to clarify a number of ideas popping in my mind. But before I start firing questions at you, I've got something to show you."

He pulled out from his pocket the dog tags Miguela's dog, Swimmer, had found near the cove and gave them to Chavez.

"I felt obligated to show you these since you helped investigate the case. But I hope you'll understand that I can't always be this forthright with you on some other things," Mac said. "I've a good reason."

Chavez gave the dog tags a careful scrutiny, and when he lifted his head, his soft brown eyes were hard on Mac. "They definitely identify the skeleton, but we still have no clues as to who killed Major Haggarty, and for that matter nothing about the others," Chavez said as he reflected for a moment, his eyes still on Mac.

"I know you were told by Colonel Bradford Miller that your job is top secret," Chavez said leaning over his desk. "I know you cannot divulge anything about your work or your findings to anyone other than to your group. I understand that. We have the same stringent rules here. But let me tell you something, Mac. Long before Lieutenant Colonel Walters died, he, a female agent and I worked very closely together, with the blessing of the Philippine Department."

Chavez said it was he and his female colleague who had informed Walters very early on that a German spy had entered Manila under an assumed name of Leon Barclay. They initially received the information from two Filipino covert PIB agents in Shanghai. Later, a Nationalist Chinese intelligence agent in Singapore confirmed the data to Walters. But he was certain that the man's real name was Boris Meissner.

Chavez told Mac about Walters's interesting theory that, long before the Tripartite Pact, Japan had requested that Nazi Germany send a Nazi master spy to Japan to discuss forming a spy organization whose headquarters would be in the Philippines.

"According to that theory," Chavez continued, "there were dissenters in the group who had insisted the spy network be formed in Singapore. After long debates, however, the Philippines received the nod; after all, it was a country most coveted by Japan. Chavez further explained that Walters believed that there were probably a couple of prominent German spies vying for the position, but one German was given the approval—Boris Meissner.

While in Japan, Walters theorized, Meissner offered a blueprint for a national spy network in the Philippines, sharing the plan only with one very high-ranking Japanese general. It was accepted. Meissner then proceeded to mastermind one of the largest spy operations in Southeast Asia. With the Japanese espionage nucleus already in the Philippines, the organization became operational, with Meissner employing over a thousand spies. Rumors had it that, because of his obsession for anonymity, Meissner refused to be the prime figure in the system. And he had, for the most part, been successful in staying anonymous.

Until one day, Walters, sounding excited, requested that Chavez meet him in his bungalow. At first he had thought that Walters was acting too strangely, but he met him anyway. There, Walters confided that in another day or two, his work would be completed, and he would then go to G-2 and present his papers on the spy activity in the Philippines. Chavez paused momentarily.

"Walters also told me this: 'I'll disclose to G-2 who Meissner is. I know him and he knows that I know, but he's masquerading as someone else in our midst. I'm certain beyond a reasonable doubt who he is, but I won't identify him to you, Chavez, because that information must come to you from the Philippine Department G-2. I'll make sure they include you and Director Romero in on it.'"

"Pretty mind-boggling. But you've lost me, Chavez," Mac said. "Are you trying to tell me that Walters knew Meissner was the spy and the killer?"

"Yes." Chavez nodded.

Mac wanted to know if Walters pointed out Meissner to the Philippines Department G-2.

"Unfortunately for us at the PIB, and I suppose G-2 also, Walters died the following day," Chavez said, toying with the pencil in his hand for a second. "Now we do not even know what Meissner looks like and have not found any connection with the spy and the killings. We were anxious to know more about that possible connection and surmised then that the other officers must have also discovered something big about the spy for him to commit such heinous crimes."

Mac gave Chavez a quizzical look. "You seem to know a great deal about me and what my mission is."

Chavez pretended not to hear Mac. "Walters told me what a fine intelligence officer you are, Mac. He called Washington from this office and talked to your boss, Colonel Duncan, at great length about you."

"Why here? Why not from his own office phone?" Mac asked suspiciously.

"Walters was certain his telephone was being tapped. Towards the end he never used it to discuss important matters," Chavez answered.

Mac asked if Chavez knew Walters well. Nodding, Chavez explained that he and Walters had mutual respect for each other's capabilities.

"There was an unwritten reciprocal consent to exchange data between ourselves ever since we were assigned to this case. And even before those horrible incidents occurred, Walters was frequently in this office, and my female colleague and I were often invited to his office at Fort William McKinley."

"Go on."

Chavez expressed how really glad he was that Mac was in Manila. He emphasized the fact that they at the Philippine Investigation Bureau had real problems with seeing to it that the national security of the Philippine government was not threatened or compromised, knowing that foreign spies were everywhere in the country.

"I, for one, feel frustrated that I cannot solve the mysteries of the killings, but what frustrates and worries me more is the increase in espionage and subversive activities on Manila," said Chavez, then pausing for a moment.

Chavez continued that he and his female colleague had earlier warned Walters to put a stop to Stein's frequent visits to Sergio's Bar and Grill. Chavez looked at Mac dispassionately and added that the PIB had long suspected that the place was a hangout for many subversives.

"Three months before Stein's complete disappearance, a PIB agent arrested a Filipino civilian passing classified military documents to another PIB agent posing as a taxi driver," Chavez said.

"Did you put him in jail?" Mac asked.

"The little spies down the line seldom know who their big bosses are," Chavez said. "The PIB has used another strategy on lesser spies. We have decided not to jail them but follow them, hoping that they would eventually lead us to the big boys."

Mac looked gravely at Chavez. "Evidently, Stein must have discovered something important earlier. Is that what you're saying? Do you think he had the time to report to Walters what he found before he was killed?"

"Maybe," Chavez answered.

"Who owns the old Bar and Grill now?" Mac asked.

"An American. He is innocent."

There was a short pause. "What's on your mind, Chavez?" Mac said.

"Mac, we do know at the PIB that the code name of your group is Quest and also what your mission is. But you, personally, are searching for Meissner because he may be the murderer. How much do you know about Meissner?"

"Perhaps slightly more than you do," Mac answered and told Chavez what he had already reported to the Quest group. "But I've this bit of evidence I've not told anyone, but I'm going to tell it to you."

He then told Chavez about the unusual birthmark on Meissner's upper left shoulder.

"When you find the birthmark, you'll have Meissner. But keep that to yourself. You and I are the only ones who know about it. The man who told me about it is dead."

"It will stay with me," Chavez said clearing his throat. "Now, back to Walters. I know all about Walters's letter to his friend Colonel Polson in Washington. And I know that you read his letter." Chavez gave Mac a broad smile. "We also have our own spies, but they are the good guys."

Mac's steel-blue eyes widened. "Touché. But what're you trying to tell me, that along the way I should share classified information with you? I can't do that!"

"Mac, your mission is my mission. We are both searching for that particular spy and killer. We need you at the PIB, and you need us. There is a great urgency to find this monster," Chavez said. "I know all about the near misses in your life since you arrived here in Manila. I can help you, Mac. I know every nook and cranny of this city and you do not. I am not asking you to report to me. And you look very capable of protecting yourself. All I ask is that you share with us all of your findings. Quid pro quo. I am not asking the others in your office to help us. I am only asking you. I am not even going to mention this request to any of your colleagues. I realize that undercover work is dangerous, especially this favor I am about to ask of you. Think about it while I get us some hot coffee."

Chavez stood up and excused himself. When he came back he had two cups of coffee in his hands and a thick folder under his arm.

"Okay, Chavez. What exactly do you want from me?"

"Remember supper at the Molinas' some time ago?" Chavez asked, going behind his desk and sitting down. "I mentioned that we think an American is spying for the Japanese?"

"I remember. You didn't give Senator Magal his name," Mac answered impatiently. "That reminds me of something else. Do you know anything about an American business man from Baltimore by the name of Sonny

Sollow?"

Chavez stared at Mac in pure amazement. "It is odd that you should mention his name. He is the guy I had in mind at that supper. He is the favor I was going to ask you. We know very little about Sonny Sollow."

Chavez described him as appearing to be a rich man who lived in an expensive house on Dewey Boulevard and who had many influential friends in both business and government. "I heard from rumors that he even knows President Quezon rather well," Chavez said. "Why did you ask me about Sonny Sollow?"

"I met him a couple of times, and each time he showed belligerence and an unfounded great dislike for me. Why, I can't comprehend," Mac said. "I saw him at the Nagoya Emporium a couple of weeks ago giving an envelope to a Japanese man."

"No law against that, Mac. It could have contained pornography. We cannot make an arrest without tangible evidence," Chavez said.

"Correct. However, it made me suspicious," Mac answered and began to brief Chavez on what he did later at the Nagoya Emporium, describing what he saw in what he was certain was a briefing room. He mentioned to Chavez that he searched the room for the brown envelope, but he ran out of time.

Chavez praised Mac for his bravery but warned that he could have been killed. "You are probably wondering why, with such information you just gave me, the PIB does not go in there and arrest everyone. But it is a complex situation. Our seeming inactivity is really a waiting game until we are ready to ferret out the leader or leaders of the spy operation."

"Yes, I am," Mac said.

Chavez conveyed that the PIB had an undercover agent assigned to the emporium for several months. "You see, Mac, if we give them the slightest indication of our suspicion, it will tip them off. They will disappear into the night and open shop somewhere else. This way, we know who they are."

"I understand. I imagine you'd not want for me to slack up on Sollow," Mac said sheepishly.

Chavez scratched his head and cleared his throat. "Sollow is the favor I was going to ask you. This idea came to me when I met you at Miguela's."

"Chavez, is Sollow the spy and the killer?"

"I am not certain, Mac. But while you are tracking down those responsible for the murders, you might also want to consider keeping Sollow under surveillance. He is a meticulously clever man who covers his tracks well. He might surprise all of us, though. And, perhaps, you will be luckier than we have been."

Mac stared at Chavez quizzically. "That's a really big favor you're asking me."

Chavez looked seriously at Mac. "I only want to know about Sollow, and only my boss, PIB director Romero, will know what we have discussed."

"That sounds good," Mac said.

Chavez cautioned Mac to keep their conversation to himself. "Strange who could be your enemy. Perhaps your closest friends."

Mac took a sip of his coffee and looked directly at Chavez. "I heard what you said, Chavez. I've implicit trust on Charlie North and Poco, if they're whom you were referring to."

"No. Only Major Charlie North," Chavez said emphatically.

"You just don't like Charlie. He's okay. But he can be a real son of a bitch."

"You are probably right," Chavez cleared his throat. "Mac, have you ever shot craps?"

Mac looked quizzically at Chavez.

"A couple of times in high school. Why?"

"North is snake eyes!" Chavez said. He told Mac that he had a couple of things to show him about Sollow. He opened the folder on his desk, flipped through several pages and handed to Mac five newspaper photographs. "You may notice that Sollow appears in these Manila News photos. And the occasions have all been Japanese functions," he explained.

Mac scrutinized the newspaper photos. "He looks like a bystander."

"A bystander on five occasions? Three at the Manila Hotel and two at the Manila International Club?" Chavez pointed out. "Come on, Mac. Those are not coincidences."

Mac studied the newspaper photographs again and conceded that perhaps Sollow needed watching. "He must be awfully sly for you not to be able to catch him in the act."

Chavez began flipping through the folder again. He handed Mac a long Manila envelope. "Take a look at these. Walters gave them to us to keep. He said he had two more like them."

Mac carefully examined the two pieces of paper. Scribbled on one was the word "Iguana" and on the other piece of paper, "Red Rose."

"Where'd he get these?"

"As I recall, from Stein. Ever heard of them, Mac?" Chavez inquired.

"Poco mentioned them to me."

"They are cover names. We learned about them through our telephone surveillances of people whom we suspect as spies and fifth columnists," Chavez said, glancing at Mac. "We are after the big ones."

"Who's Iguana, and who's Red Rose?" Mac asked.

Chavez's large brown eyes narrowed. He quietly proceeded to explain the PIB's theories and mentioned Walters's affirmation of their theories. "Let me start from the very beginning."

According to Chavez, when the PIB and the Philippine Department G-2 first became aware that the Japanese had established a nationwide spy based in Manila, they were alarmed and immediately went to work to finding information about its existence. They learned that their code name was allegedly "Network." However, they later believed that Network was not its code name because their wiretapping and human intelligence activity had not yielded anything.

"We had all concluded that it must be something else. But since we did not know what that something else was, we just continued calling it that."

Then he proceeded to explain to Mac that Iguana, known also as Big Iguana, could be the cover name for the man in charge of the entire Japanese spy operation. Network, PIB theorists believed, was divided into three divisions—Luzon, Visayan Islands in central Philippines, and Mindanao in the south. Each division has a leader and each leader had a cover name. The PIB believed that "Red Rose" was the head of the Luzon division, also headquartered in Manila. The cover name of the chief of the Visayan Islands' division in Iloilo was "Gardenia." Later, the PIB agents in Iloilo had verified that they had caught one Japanese spy mistaking one PIB agent, Philippine-born Japanese man from Cebu, as one of them and identified himself to the agent as working for Gardenia.

"Reportedly, Gardenia is a woman. A beautiful Eurasian with a German father and a Chinese mother," Chavez said the agent was immediately arrested and jailed, but during interrogation the spy refused to talk and committed hara-kiri before the guards could stop him.

"That's too bad," Mac quipped. "He was a big spy. How about Mindanao? Who runs that big southern island?"

Chavez pursed his lips. "Our telephone surveillance in Mindanao had reported the word 'Orchid' mentioned in coded conversations. Meanwhile, other PIB agents there are gathering human intelligence and sending them back to us. Their sources are generally the Moros. We do not know who runs Mindanao."

Mac asked Chavez who the "Big Iguana" could be in Manila. The Filipino agent shook his head and answered that no one in Philippine Department G-2 or the PIB knew or the human names of Red Rose, Gardenia or Orchid. "However," Chavez added, "We are not asleep under the coconut tree." He paused. "Not too long ago, the PIB foiled the plan of a foreign agent who infiltrated Malacañang Palace with the intent of harming President Quezon and his family. That incident was kept out of the newspapers and the radio, for they would invite the public's ire. Quezon is very popular. The Filipinos love him for being a strong voice in obtaining a pledge of Philippine independence from the United States and a promise to improve the military defense of the Philippines."

Mac wondered aloud if Boris Meissner could be the Big Iguana.

"What you have just said could never be, Mac."

"Why not?" Mac's eyes were fixed on Chavez.

"Like I mentioned to you earlier. According to Walters, Meissner's obsession for anonymity would preclude what you just said," Chavez said.

"Excellent answer. Now, how about this theory? Maybe, since Iguana's headquarters could be in Manila," Mac reasoned, "wouldn't it be possible that Iguana and Red Rose, also headquartered in Manila, could be one and the same man? He who controls Manila controls the Philippines. Catch Red Rose and you'll catch Big Iguana himself."

"An outstanding answer. How about helping me make that a reality," Chavez said, smiling.

Mac changed the subject and inquired if Chavez knew what happened to all the data Walters had about Meissner.

"No. Charlie had asked me the same question. The PIB has searched everywhere and we are still searching."

Mac glanced at his watch and told Chavez that he had to go, but that before leaving he would like to borrow a history book on the Philippines.

"Yes, I have such a book," Chavez said. "It is one of the best and most complete, written by a professor at the University of the Philippines. Here, take it with you, Mac. You might want to read it one rainy night."

"That's just about every night, isn't it?" Mac smiled.

"And, Mac," Chavez continued, "Did I hear you say you would help this beleaguered bureau? We do need your expertise."

Mac studied Chavez's face for a while. Somehow, there had developed between the two men an unconscious deep respect for each other.

"You got it," Mac said and turned to leave when Chavez suddenly jumped from his chair. "Wait. Is there something you want to know about the Philippines that I can help you with? Sometimes the answer may not be in the book, or sometimes it is hard to find. Try me."

Mac again studied Chavez's face. "You might," he finally answered and took out the piece of paper from his wallet and gave it to Chavez.

"Please sit down," said the baffled Filipino.

Mac recounted how he and Poco overheard the conversation between Sonny Sollow and the cabdriver, Jim Wanabe, at the Ruby Redd's restaurant at Kapalaran. Chavez studied the piece of paper carefully and told Mac that he could not understand his scribbling. But would he mind if Director Romero's secretary transcribed it on her typewriter, that his own secretary was on maternity leave. Mac said he did not mind.

Celia, the secretary, was summoned to Chavez's office and given the notes. Within ten minutes she was back with the typewritten transcriptions. She returned Mac's notes and gave the original and the carbon copy to Chavez, who began reading his page aloud.

"Wanabe to Sollow: Did you see several different birds over the mountain, last weekend?"

"Sollow answers: No. The same types of birds as before. They continue to remain small. It's best to wait for the big ones."

"Wanabe to Sollow: Did you give to T the data on flats one, three, and five? They are very important information."

"Wanabe answers: Yes. The G-owned in L is 704 m, single T. I also included that from the very, very wide H_2O the only E to CP and M and L is through U-shaped and smaller H_2O." Sollow cleared his throat and asked,

"How about kind?"

Wanabe answers: "Yes. 2L, AW, C or AS."

Sollow asks: "Do you have a package for me now?"

Wanabe says: "Yes".

Wanabe reaches into his pocket and gives an envelope to Sollow. Wanabe says: "The photo is in there. It is the tr of two hundred ants at Bpen with fire, lightning and thunder."

They quietly sat in the office. While Chavez continued to study the typewritten notes, which did not make any sense to him, Mac was flipping through the pages of the history book. Chavez, meanwhile, raised his head and looked at Mac.

"This statement about birds over a mountain seems intriguing, but it does not make any sense."

There was a knock on the door. Celia stuck her head in.

"Mr. Chavez, Director Romero wants you in his office. It is about the Richmond."

Chavez turned to Mac and told him that he could stay in the office if he wanted to, but Mac shook his head and gathered the history book and the typewritten notes.

"You got the carbon copy. I'll be calling you. By the way, Chavez, what if we solve this puzzle? Will you arrest Sollow and Wanabe?"

"No. They will deny it. The notes are in your handwriting. Besides, they will not only blow our cover but also make a big stink publicly," Chavez explained.

When he returned to the BOQ, Mac began reading the thin history book from cover to cover. Needless to say, the data he thought he could find in the book did not materialize. Mac put the book away and studied the handwritten notes again.

Weary, he closed his eyes and doggedly continued to reason things out.

"Now," he said aloud. "Let's start with 'birds over a mountain.'" He placed the typewritten paper on the table and began to decipher the cryptic.

"What other things fly?" He asked himself aloud. "A bee. A bat. A leaf flying in the air. Balloons, they float over the earth. How about airplanes? They fly. That's it. Birds are airplanes."

"Now over the mountain. The Philippines are mountainous," he reasoned. "And there's Mt. Arayat near Clark Field. Hmmm. Planes fly in and out of Clark Field over or near Mt. Arayat. Yes. Airplanes in Clark Field."

From there, the ideas started flowing.

"Flats: Highway Routes one, three, and five," Mac said. "2L: Two lanes. AW: All weather roads. C or AS: Concrete or asphalt surface. Hot iron: trains. The R in L: The railroads in Luzon, and G: government-owned rail line.

"Single T: Single track, and about half is in CP: central plains. The very, very wide H_2O: South China Sea. The only E to CP and M and L is through U-shaped and smaller H_2O: The only entrance to central plains is through Manila and Luzon is through Manila Bay.

"Manila Bay is U-shaped!" Mac said loudly.

All at once the Sollow-Wanabe conversation made sense to Mac. It was just past 2:00 a.m. when he finished the puzzle. He was tired. He was just about to throw away the piece of paper when he realized that he had overlooked a couple of lines in his notes. He squinted and rubbed his eyes and tried to read his own handwriting and finally succeeded.

"What's this about tr of two hundred ants at Bpen. And fire, thunder and lightning?" He murmured to himself. "Wanabe told Sollow of a photo. Then he gave Sollow the photo. Okay. Sollow has the picture. But what about ants?"

Mac walked around his room, trying to solve the cryptic words.

"What do ants do?" he said.

He remembered his mother scolded him once when he was little for leaving a spoonful of honey on the floor. He remembered his mother pointing to the ants on the floor.

"'See those ants marching in line towards that honey on the floor. They are like tiny soldiers.' I got it!" he said aloud. "Two hundred soldiers are in training, firing 37-mm antitank guns and grenades at Bataan Peninsula."

He slept late that morning. At 11 a.m., he dropped a copy of the deciphered conversation at the PIB for Agent Chavez.

CHAPTER 14

If there was a single encouraging sign that the Quest mission was successful, there was no such indication. And the group's frustration over the lack of clues and a smaller staff didn't help. The month of July, and June for that matter, proved unproductive. The only thing that kept the crew going were the persistent rumors that General Douglas MacArthur was to return to active duty.

Despite the oppressive heat and very high humidity, the tempo in the city started beating faster. And when MacArthur did report for active duty on July 26, the public's attitude became energized—especially the military's.

Every day, the headline of the Manila News had MacArthur's name sprawled across its front page: "MacArthur recalled to active duty" or "MacArthur, Supreme Commander to head US Armed Forces in the Far East."

Steve Ball, a radio commentator on KMZH in Manila, reported daily on the new military reorganization that MacArthur was charged with completing.

Timed purposely with the General's recall to active duty, the United States immediately ceased all exports to Japan. The liberal Manila News, well known to support the Japanese, seized the opportunity to headline the US commercial ban against Japan: "United States commercial market closed to Japan. A big mistake."

Despite the newfound energy, the month of August was not any kinder to Quest. Losing Delgado and Golden proved tough for the remaining staff. Although Mac, Poco, Charlie, and Czestochowa continued their work, it was producing little, if any, tangible evidence. Nothing. It was beginning to take its toll on their morale.

Charlie and Mac were walking together one day when Charlie quipped that the twin months of July and August, are "plain bitches. Even the bays are a hundred degrees. Don't even bother going swimming."

On the other hand, the Philippine picture was looking rosy. By mid-August, MacArthur had established his USAFFE headquarters in Manila at the Walled City. And by September, he and his small but top-notched staff went aggressively ahead, organizing the defense for the Philippines.

Major McCord, meanwhile, viewed September as a new month and welcomed it. He hoped that it would bring a new lease to his otherwise ineffective past few weeks. Except for finding Haggarty's dog tags, he and the rest of Quest were not any further along on their mission. This was to be a new month, and the first day brought the first bit of excitement.

Mac was asleep when someone entered his room. The burglar went to his closet and rummaged through his suitcase and could not find the item he was searching for. Then he discovered that Mac was sound asleep and quietly approached the bed and shone his flashlight on Mac's hands.

Mac was finally awakened when the burglar tried to remove the blue sapphire ring from his finger with one hand while holding a dagger over him with his other. Mac waited a few seconds, and when the man relaxed the arm holding the dagger, Mac snatched him by the elbow, knocking the dagger to the floor. The man hit Mac across the forehead with his forearm, but Mac ducked enough to avoid the full blow. He kicked the man in the stomach and was able to pin his attacker by the neck against the wall and reached over to turn on the light.

"Don't hurt me. Don't hurt me, please," cried the trembling young Filipino. "If I wanted to kill you I would have already. This was not my idea. An American man gave me thirty pesos to find and steal your ring. Look, you can have the money."

He slowly took the money out of his pocket and offered it to Mac.

"I was on my way home when he approached me. I told him that I did not want to do it, but from his action, I think that he was going to kill me if I did not do as he said."

"No, I don't want your money. Keep it," Mac said. "Did he also tell you to murder me?"

"Yes," the young man said, slumping to his knees. "Please, don't hurt me. I have a wife and a child. I am a good Catholic. I was not going to kill you."

"Do you know the American?"

"No, Sir," the Filipino answered.

"Would you recognize him?"

"No, Sir. It was dark. But I could tell he was a big, tall man. I am not sure, but I think he was wearing a military uniform, and he used some German words. My boss at the shipping company was born in Germany, and I hear a lot of German words from him. So when the stranger cursed me for refusing, I knew that he was German."

Mac dismissed the Filipino.

"You can go, but don't try that on anyone again. You'll find yourself in the morgue," He gave the man a final shove before walking him out of the building.

The following morning, Mac got a telephone call from Miguela reminding him about her father's annual party that night. Mac had almost forgotten. He headed to the barber and a small store that sold linen shirts. He had never met Miguela's parents and wanted to look his best. He showered, ate a light snack, and got ready to go.

Buenavista was all lit up with Chinese lanterns. The musical band of Gregorio and Esteban was hired as they had been for the last ten years. The catering house of Magda was getting the meals ready for the two hundred expected guests. It was to be an informal gathering with food served buffet-style and plenty of drinks. About twenty long tables covered with colorful oilcloths—in reds, oranges, and yellows—were scattered throughout the garden and around the large swimming pool that had been covered with thick temporary wooden planks to serve as the dance floor. The bandstand was set up on the edge of the pool. Guests always looked forward to the beverages and delicious assortment of food— lechon, shrimp salteado, fried fish, raw oysters, and fried chicken.

In the house, the Molinas were busy tying up loose ends as guests were already arriving.

In the master bedroom, Miguela was reasoning with her mother to at least be civil with Mac and to pretend that he was a tall and handsome Filipino instead of a tall and handsome American. She told her mother that she might just grow to like Mac. Impatiently, Consolacion promised but at the same time chastised her older daughter for not having introduced Mac to her and her father, Alonso, earlier.

Miguela's younger siblings, Agrifina and Ernie, meanwhile, were sent off with the servants, Claudia and Tilde, to an 8:30 movie starring Leopoldo Salcedo.

As the band began playing their favorite music, "La Poloma," Consolacion and Alonso hurriedly went to the garden to welcome their guests. Many of Manila's prominent businessmen and their wives were there as well as high government officials, including distinguished American and Filipino Army officers. Chinese and Japanese dignitaries mixed easily with the other guests. Guests from Malaya and the Netherlands East Indies kept to themselves and especially refused to get close to any Japanese.

The party was getting started when Mac and Poco arrived in Roosie's taxicab. Miguela, who had been anxiously waiting for them, saw the cab as it was winding in towards the wide circular driveway.

Mac jumped out of the cab and kissed Miguela on her cheek.

"Miguela," he said. "You know Poco. Major North, another friend, will be joining us later. And this is Alberto, Roosie's grandson. And that's Roosie behind the wheel. Roosie, come here."

Miguela welcomed all of them, including Roosie. "Is Alberto not going to join us? Why is he leaving?"

"He has tuu make saame maaney. He weel caame back here at 11:30," Roosie answered.

Mac turned around. "Roosie, I thought that Alberto works at the Manila International Club?"

"Yes. He tuuk de apternoon oop to help me," explained Roosie and immediately made it known that he wanted a beer and excused himself.

Meanwhile, Poco, who had not been to Buenavista before, was visibly impressed with the beauty and vastness of the grounds and the big, lovely house. He was particularly awed with the panoramic view of Manila Bay.

"I imagine you can see Corregidor Island from here," he told Miguela, making small talk.

"Sometimes. It is about thirty miles on water from Manila, as you know. On clear evenings we can see some stationary lights in Corregidor, and I understand car headlights in the mainland can be seen from there," explained Miguela. "Unfortunately, it is a dark night and threatening to rain, so the view isn't its best."

Poco smiled. "It is too bad Colonel Miller, Lieutenant Colonel Rhoades, and Major North are not here or we would have the complete office."

He introduced Miguela to Purita, their secretary, and Lieutenant Czestochowa asked Purita whether Lieutenant Colonel Rhoades was coming to the party.

"Yes," said Purita. "He will be late, but he will be here. His former office at Fort Stotsenburg called him early this morning. He did not tell me the reason why he had to go," she explained. She had anticipated that question from Czestochowa.

Czestochowa moved closer to Purita and whispered in her ear, "I don't trust Rhoades or Miller. I believe that they're both spies for the Japs."

Purita looked squarely at Czestochowa. "I am not going to tell them what you just said. But if I were you, I would be more careful what I say about my superiors. You could be wrong about them."

Poco asked Miguela if Colonel Miller had also been invited.

"Your whole office was sent an invitation. However, if he does come, I would not know him. I have not met him," Miguela answered.

As the band began playing "Begin the Beguine," Mac and Miguela excused themselves and went to the dance floor while Czestochowa told Purita and Poco that he was ready for a cold beer and walked away, leaving them by themselves. They stood there for a while watching everyone with interest and played guessing games as who some of the guests were.

At one point, Sollow passed in front of them, prompting Poco to tell Purita that although he had met him, he hardly knew him. "I only know that his name is Sonny Sollow, an American. Major Mac and I think that he is a spy."

"Really? Why don't you report that to Colonel Miller, or better still, to the PIB?" Purita commented.

"I will leave that to Major Mac," Poco said and, pointing to two Japanese men standing near Mr. and Mrs. Molina, inquired, "Who are they?"

Purita Aquino let out a soft gasp as if she was surprised about something.

Poco glanced at Aquino. "Are you all right?"

"Yes," she answered. "Sometimes my throat gets dry."

"Those two Japanese men. Who are they?" Poco repeated.

"The older man is Mr. Hayakawa, Japanese consul in Manila," Purita said. "I do not know his tall companion. He could be his aide."

Poco could have sworn he had seen the aide before with another Japanese man at the Manila International Club when he and Major McCord were there several months ago. "That aide and another Jap were with a Filipina prostitute with dyed red hair, as I recall."

"Interesting, Poco," Purita said. "Excuse me. I have to join some friends."

But instead, she walked leisurely to the bar and ordered a Coca Cola and sat down on a garden chair and unobtrusively watched the Japanese aide, better known to her and the PIB as Captain Kondo, or Agent 10. By this time Kondo left the side of the Japanese diplomat. "I wonder," Purita murmured to herself, "if that diplomat knows that his companion is a spy. He must." Kondo certainly has lots of brass to show himself so openly in public. He must be here for a reason."

Purita must have glanced away because when she looked again, Kondo had disappeared.

On the dance floor, Czestochowa tapped Mac on the shoulder.

"May I, major," he said and whirled Miguela away with boyish impertinence. Mac sauntered to the beverage corner and ordered a mint julep. Then, following his deeper curiosity about Kawazaka marina, he walked across the circular driveway to the Southside of the Molina house and the tall wall. On the other side of the wall was Kawazaka's marina. Albeit he had rented a boat from there several weeks ago, he merely gave the boat livery a cursory look.

Against the cement wall were huge boulders, much like those around the cove on the north end of Buenavista. A small house, presumably the marina's office, was perched on a higher ground and almost immediately behind it was that stretch of Dewey Boulevard. Close to the boulders was a long dock where only motorboats were tied. On the adjacent dock, equally long, were native fishing boats.

"Prosperous marina," Mac murmured.

Mac walked back to the party and went inside the spacious front veranda where he had a clear view of the beverage stand nearby and the dance floor. As he stood there, he recognized Sonny Sollow a short distance away making his way to where Mr. and Mrs. Molina were sitting. They were clearly enjoying the band.

Mr. Molina pushed himself up from his chair and shook Sollow's extended left hand.

"A lefty," Mac said.

From Sollow's body language, he could only guess that Sollow was leaving and thanking the host and hostess for a fine evening. Mac moved closer to the edge of the veranda while continuing to watch Sollow. Mac knew Sollow was guilty since he spotted him at the Nagoya Emporium.

Walking away from the Molinas, Sollow began to saunter towards the beverage stand. It surprised him to see Mac on the veranda. "Wh-what're you doing Mc....McCord?" He asked angrily. "Spying on people?"

"Perhaps. Does it make you nervous, Sollow?"

Sollow ran up the steps of the veranda, grabbed Mac by the arm and tightened his grip. "You...you son of a bitch. You're...you're a f-frustrated nothing, McCord. You know what every...everybody thinks back in the States about some of those who...who are in the Army? Scums. They joined because they're not...not good for anything. And you're one of those, a...a fucking scum," Sollow said.

Mac got hold of Sollow's arm and twisted it to his back and pushed him against the wall. "I never liked you Sollow. I've got a feeling deep in my gut that you're more than just a spy. You're evil. And you were born evil and enjoy being evil," Mac said through clenched teeth. "You don't have a bit of mercy or remorse in your dark heart. You probably killed those American officers and enjoyed doing it. Furthermore, I bet you're Boris Meissner, aren't you Sollow?"

"Why don't you an...and that Filipino friend of yours, Chavez, find out? Neither of you...of you can prove anything," Sollow said glaring at Mac. "You better release my right arm, McCord. I've my revolver right on your navel."

"Go ahead. Shoot me, Sollow," Mac said.

"That's too simple. I enjoy hunting you down," Sollow declared menacingly. "Besides, I don't want for Miguela to lose you just yet."

Mac released Sollow's arm.

The music stopped, and after a few minutes Mac regained his composure and joined Miguela, who introduced him to her mother and father. Both parents appeared pleased. The band started playing, "Wang Wang Blues."

Miguela dragged Mac to the dance floor and while they were dancing, she told him that her parents liked him.

"How can you tell?" Mac asked, surprised.

"I just know. And they both smiled when they looked at you," she said. "Mac, let us dance this one."

They danced for some time when Lieutenant Stan Czestochowa appeared again and gave Mac a tap on the shoulder, and once more whirled Miguela away.

Mac went back to the veranda and stood behind several hanging, thick ferns and begonias where he could not be seen as easily by those on the ground. From there, he could see Sollow cavorting with the guests. Mac kept his eyes on Sollow, who had by then moved away from the stand and had approached two ladies sitting on a bench not too far away from the dance floor. Apparently, they invited him to join them.

Mac turned around for a moment to see if he could see Miguela among the dancing crowd. She was still with Czestochowa. But when he returned again to watch Sollow, it was then that he noticed him walking towards the driveway.

Sollow was leaving Buenavista. With speed Mac immediately worked the crowded dance floor until he reached Czestochowa and Miguela. He took her aside and whispered in her ear, "Where's your car?"

"At the end of the driveway pointing out," she answered, bewildered.

"Hurry. Give me the key. Don't tell anyone about this," Mac said, walking away in a fast pace. He had just settled in Miguela's Ford when Sollow passed by in a black Chevrolet. Keeping well behind, he followed Sollow out of Buenavista.

When Sollow turned right on Dewey Boulevard, Mac did as well. Sollow stayed on the boulevard for a short distance and suddenly turned right on Padre Faura Street and then left on Taft Avenue through the heavy traffic.

Mac continued to keep his speed and distance from the black Chevrolet, but he made certain that he did not lose sight of the car. When it slowed or stopped, he did too. But all at once, and in a high speed, the Chevrolet crossed the long bridge over the Pasig River, leaving behind Escolta, San Vicente, Dasmarinas and Ongpin streets. And there it was, they were on Binondo. The black Chevrolet was in front of him.

Suddenly the black Chevrolet stopped. The car door opened and a man approached Mac's car.

"Sir, you have been following me for a very, very long time. Are you lost? Can I help you?" the Filipino asked.

"I'm sorry. Yes. I'm lost," Mac murmured as he backed away from the Chevrolet. The party was in full swing when he returned to Buenavista. Mac grabbed a lemonade and went back to his perch overlooking the dance floor.

Roosie's behavior soon caught his attention. He was holding a bottle of beer with one hand while his other hand kept pointing to something. But from what Mac could determine, Roosie and the bartender were having an interesting conversation and appeared to be enjoying themselves.

Mac turned away and looked for Miguela to let her know that he was back, but she was nowhere to be seen. Still angry with himself for wasting his time following a total stranger instead of Sollow, he wandered toward the beach and soon felt the soft sandy beach under him and welcomed the breeze from Manila Bay. He walked until he reached the north end of Buenavista to where he knew the cove would be, but in the dark night he could only see a big hole. He stood behind the tall wire fence and stared at the big gap in front of him and wondered if the cove was really that deep or if its current was really as swift and as strong as Miguela had warned him.

"It must be pretty bad," he murmured to himself. "I've never seen Swimmer get in that water."

Suddenly, Mac heard screams coming from the dance floor. He ran as quickly as he could. Amidst the confusion, he searched for Miguela and found her sitting on the dance floor, crying, with Roosie's head on her lap.

"What happened?" he asked her and as he checked Roosie's wrist and neck for a pulse. "He's dead," Mac announced. He then pulled Miguela up from the floor, held her very close to him and walked her away from the frightened crowd and sat her down on the back steps of the house.

"Mac," she said between sobs, "while Stan and I were dancing, Roosie fell at my feet. I cradled his head on my lap to see if I could help him. I think he had been trying to reach me."

"Did he say anything to you, Miguela?" Mac asked.

Miguela nodded. "He said it ever so softly, but I heard him," Miguela said as tears fell down her cheeks. "He said, 'He is here.' And then he collapsed."

Mac took Miguela in his arms and consoled her. "I know that was hard, darling. Go upstairs, shower, and put on a clean dress. What you have on is soaked in blood. I've got to get back there."

He hurried to the dance floor where Roosie's body lay. Poco and Czestochowa were trying to move the crowd away from the dead man.

"Who do you think killed him, Major McCord?" Poco asked when he saw Mac.

But Czestochowa answered instead. "I can already tell you that poor bastard was murdered by someone in this crowd. Rhoades and Miller always act and talk so strangely. I don't like them. I know that you don't either, Major," Czestochowa rambled. "I'll put my money on Miller. He's stranger than Rhoades. But I bet you think it's Rhoades, don't you? One of them killed the old man."

"Shut up, Czestochowa," Mac shouted above the noise of the crowd. "No one asked for your opinion."

"Sorry about that, Sir, but what'd you think?"

"Hard to tell," Mac answered Czestochowa. "Appears like a professional job. I don't see any signs of struggle but the killer left his dagger. Probably didn't have time to remove it." He noticed the checkered black and red handle of the weapon. "I even doubt if our smart killer left his finger prints on that dagger." He sighed and shook his head. "Poor, Roosie. I don't think that he ever expected to see Stein's murderer again. Perhaps in some dark corners of Manila, but not here, in affluent Buenavista." Mac turned to Czestochowa. "Call the police."

Mac asked Purita, who was standing close by, whether Charlie North had arrived.

"Yes. He is over there talking to someone in the crowd. He seems to be trying to join us," Purita answered.

Mac wanted to talk to Charlie and was about to walk towards him when he almost stumbled on someone standing behind him. It was Colonel Miller.

"Good evening, McCord. Miss Aquino. What the hell happened?" Miller said.

"Colonel," Mac and Purita declared in unison. "We all wondered if you were coming to this party. We all thought you were out of town."

Miller's response was terse. "I wouldn't miss this party for anything. I got home late. Guess I missed all the action."

"Did you drive in?" Mac asked.

Miller smiled, but his eyes were penetrating and cold.

"A friend dropped me," Miller said. "Where was Czestochowa going?" Miller inquired.

"To call the police and ask for an ambulance," Mac quickly answered.

"Have you any idea who killed that poor man? McCord? Miss Aquino?" Miller asked.

Purita said that she did not know. Mac, however, said that he remembered seeing Roosie talking to one of the bartenders. He quickly excused himself and almost ran into the beverage corner, with Miller and Purita following him. He approached the young bartender.

"I saw you and that old man having a good time before he died. Did you see who killed him?"

"No, but he said something I did not understand," the bartender answered.

"Like what?" Mac asked.

"He pointed to a tall Japanese man who, he said, helped another Japanese man carry a dead American soldier out of Sergio's Bar and Grill a couple of years ago. I did not know what he meant. From where I stood, he was pointing to a man who looked to me like another Japanese-Filipino or Chinese-Filipino. There are many Chinese-Filipinos or Japanese-Filipinos in this party. "I am a Chinese-Filipino. And my partner there," he cocked his head towards the other bartender, "is Japanese-Filipino."

"Then what happened?" Mac insisted.

"Well, I asked him to point the man to me again. But he told me that the Japanese must have disappeared. He said that he would never forget him because he was tall for a Japanese."

The bartender said that Roosie got loud and said that he recognized the American who wore a gold buckle with the face of a cobra on it. That he killed the American Jewish soldier at Sergio's Bar and Grill. He said, 'dees time I knuu de keeler.' Then he walked fast to a taxicab parked near that big birdbath over there and talked to a young Filipino and came back to the bar."

The bartender paused monetarily with a questioning look on his face.

"Where is Sergio's Bar and Grill?"

"It doesn't matter. Go on," Mac said impatiently.

The bartender recounted that he failed to see the American whom the old man was pointing to.

"He drank a lot of beer. I did not take him too seriously, but I did try to help him look for his friends whom he said were named Mac and Miguela. I left the bar for a while and asked several people their names. I was not successful. Then he left and walked towards the dance floor, and that was where he fell dead. I thought he was just drunk."

"Hell!" Mac said angrily and turned to Miller. "Did you hear all that, Colonel?"

Miller nodded.

Mac further suggested to Miller that he believed the grounds should be searched, but the bartender interrupted him.

"Mister, I remember the old man mentioning something to me about the American having blond hair, if that will help you."

"Thanks," said Mac. When he turned around to further discuss the idea, Miller was gone. There was only Purita. "Where's the Colonel?"

"I do not know," Purita answered. "He must have left quietly."

Mac asked Purita if she would do him a favor.

"Of course," Purita answered.

"When you see Czestochowa again, tell him to wait for me and Poco by the boathouse. And tell Major North the same thing. I'd like to have a talk with them." Mac paused and added, "When the police and ambulance arrive, lead them to the body."

Purita nodded but explained to Mac that it would probably take the police and the ambulance some time to arrive due to the usual traffic in Manila. While she walked around looking for both North and Czestochowa, she saw Rhoades getting out of a taxicab and joined her.

"What's all the commotion, Miss Aquino?" He asked.

"A Filipino cabdriver was murdered," she answered Rhoades.

"Know who did it?" Rhoades asked.

"No, Sir. But I think Major McCord has started to search the area," Purita told Rhoades. "Major North and Lieutenant Czestochowa will probably join him."

"I believe I'll do that too, but by myself," Rhoades declared and walked away.

Several minutes after Rhoades had left, Charlie approached Purita, who imparted to him Mac's message.

"Okay," said Charlie, looking a long time at Purita. "Do you know where Lieutenant Colonel Rhoades is going?"

"To search for the murderer," Purita said.

CHAPTER 15

Mac immediately announced that no one was to leave the premises until the police arrived. If the killer was there, Mac was going to find him. He then made his way to the bathhouse where he joined Czestochowa and Poco. Charlie was with them.

"Charlie, did you hear Roosie has been murdered?"

"I talked to him before he died," Charlie answered. "Miss Aquino told me to meet you here. What do you want me to do?"

"Although it's gotten very dark, we may still have time. I don't think he has had enough time to get away," Mac told them. "We're dividing the grounds into four sections. Each of us will take a one."

Czestochowa was assigned to comb the beach and the swimming pool area. Poco was to stand guard at the gate.

"No one is to leave," Mac said loudly. "And be sure that you've got your pistol."

"Where do you want me, Mac?" Charlie asked.

"You take the middle ground while I search from the cove over to Kawazaka's. We know that area is real thick with trees and shrubberies, which are probably good places for a killer to hide. And, it's not too far from Dewey Boulevard to Buenavista's entrance either. I'll also check on the marina itself," Mac explained to the group.

One by one each man took his assigned area and painstakingly began the search. Mac, who had almost reached the wall separated the Molina property from the marina, thought he heard squish of damp leaves near the gates. He stopped in his tracks and then became motionless. There was nothing for several minutes when suddenly a large figure appeared in front of him.

Mac quickly sidestepped the shadowy form as it moved closer. With a quick burst, he adroitly tackled him to the ground and got his hands around the man's throat.

"Hold it, Mac. It's me, Charlie."

"Jeez. I'm sorry, Charlie," Mac said, releasing his grip. "Don't sneak up on me like that again."

They both started to laugh. Mac whispered that he was going to check the marina. Charlie gave Mac the thumbs up. By himself again, Mac watched as Charlie disappeared into the thick forest before approaching the marina. Instead of going through its main entrance, he decided instead to climb the cement wall separating docks from the Molina property. Using a couple of thick vines for leverage, he scaled the wall. Once on top of the twelve-foot barrier, Mac nearly tumbled over as a strong gust of wind pounded him. It was much stronger than it was when he was on the beach earlier that night. His eyes tried to penetrate the darkness. Except for the bay wind hissing and blowing, and the slapping of the waves against the boats, now tugging at their moorings at the docks, the place was eerily quiet.

Suddenly, a loud gunshot from the direction of the entrance pierced the dark night, and then a shout from Poco was heard, "Over here! Over here!"

Mac leapt off the wall, sprinted to the entrance and was there first, but there was no sign of Poco. And as he wandered around trying to find the Filipino sergeant, someone from behind a tree darted in front of him and surprised him with a strong, straight hit to his right jaw. Mac fell but quickly sprang up and ran after the fleeing man. Dodging the dangling vines and trying to keep his footing, Mac came within two feet of the man and leaped forward, clutching the man's belt and throwing him into a tree.

The attacker spun around and Mac threw two uppercuts to his chin. The man's strong arms deflected both of Mac's hits. Both men bobbed and weaved, trying to get the first blow. It was a long struggle, but finally the attacker got loose from Mac's strong grasp and began running toward the entrance of Buenavista to Dewey Boulevard. Mac, now covered in mud, again went into a flying tackle and caught his opponent's feet, dropping him to the ground.

"I got you now bastard," Mac yelled. "Who the hell are you?"

175

But his attacker rolled to one side, getting away from Mac again, although for only a short while. Once again they wrestled for sometime until Mac dealt one blow to the man's chest and gripped him by the shirt. Again the stranger extricated himself by twisting Mac's muddy, slippery fingers that were trying to tighten around his throat.

The attacker ran, zigzagging among the trees and shrubberies. Mac was in close pursuit when he stumbled over a thick limb and fell. The stranger quickly grabbed the limb and lifted it to hit Mac, who, in a bent position, moved his head ever so slightly to one side. The hard blow, however, landed squarely on his left shoulder and he folded to the ground, dazed. The attacker was trying to remove the ring from Mac's finger when he heard footsteps coming his way. He punched Mac in the face, then fled.

Now near the gate, Charlie asked in a muted voice as he came rushing from the middle ground. "Poco. Where are you? This is Major North. I heard the shot."

The reply from Poco was almost inaudible. "Over here, Sir. Over here."

"Hey, sergeant. Let me give you a hand," Charlie said as he pulled Poco from a pair of thick shrubs.

"Major North, it may have been Roosie's killer. He tried to stab me and I used my gun on him, but I guess I missed. I had to quickly hide just in case he would come back. I did not want to push my luck. He was a big man," Poco explained.

"Dammit! It's too bad you missed but then it's very dark out here." There was a long pause. "In what direction did the he go? He might have gone after Mac."

"The swimming pool, Sir. Czestochowa is guarding that area," Poco said.

"Hell. I must've just missed the crazy bastard," Charlie said, still trying to catch his breath.

"I'm sure he went that way, Sir."

"Shit. I better start looking for Mac," Charlie said and left.

A short time later, Charlie came back and told Poco that he could not find Mac.

"Get up and get back to your position soldier," Charlie said. "Use that damn gun of yours. I don't care how big he is. A gun can kill an elephant. Now get up. I'll continue to search for McCord and then look in on Czestochowa. That asshole can get into more trouble."

Charlie again disappeared into the night.

In the meantime, Mac, who had regained consciousness, tortuously dragged himself over to a circle of thick bushes and lay down, nursing his shoulder. Just as he had adjusted himself among the leaves, he again heard the squish-squish of footsteps.

"Fucking asshole," the attacker said, apparently frustrated at not finding Mac dead. "Where are you, you damn Army asshole? I know you're here you son of a bitch."

Fortunately, at the sound of the advancing ambulances and patrol vehicles, the shadowy figure decided the area was too risky and quickly disappeared. Mac lay back down and passed out.

The ambulance came to a screeching halt near the end of the driveway and the driver jumped out. "We understand someone has been murdered."

"Yes. We have been waiting for you," Poco said and directed the driver to the pool area. Shortly thereafter, two police cars also drove up into the property and asked for direction from Poco. When they reached the crowd, the police immediately asked everyone for their patience and support.

Frantically scribbling names and information on their notepads, the police interrogated many of the guests and then slowly gave people permission to leave the vicinity. However, some were held back for more questioning, while others lingered from curiosity.

The large trees at Buenavista and their long branches reached out like a thousand wide canopies, and intertwined vines draped unabashedly to the ground. The big plants, shrubbery and undergrowth that were purposely left uncut and uncleared as barriers for privacy from nearby avenues and streets and inquisitive eyes, blocked out any residual light that the trees allowed. The air hung low, close and heavy with humidity, despite the strong wind coming from the bay.

Czestochowa, avoiding the temptation to head back to the swirling police lights near the dance floor, was having great difficulty seeing where he was going as he tried to root out Roosie's killer. All at once, he heard a noise and thought he saw someone moving near a huge fire tree by the bathhouse. Step by step, he cautiously approached the tree. Suddenly he felt something sharp pressed hard on his spine. He groaned in pain and put his hands in the air.

"Put both hands behind you," the intruder whispered in Czestochowa's ear and quickly tied his hands. "Now walk."

Czestochowa marched a few hundred yards down a dark path, then was slammed head first into a tree.

"I heard that you hate the Nazis," the knife man said into Czestochowa's ear.

"I'd kill everyone of them for what they've done to my relatives in Poland. Fuck the Nazis!" Czestochowa said. "Hey. Come on. Is that a joke?"

"No," came the whispered answer, "and any call for help and I'll plunge this dagger into your spine."

"Who are you?" Czestochowa asked, at the same time trying to untie his hands.

"It doesn't matter. You'll soon know." There was a pause. "I understand a fisherman friend of yours at Olongapo gave you a description of Lieutenant Gibbs's killer. What does that killer look like?"

"If I don't tell you?" Czestochowa said defiantly.

The intruder pushed the dagger's point harder into Czestochowa's back.

"Before you stick that dagger deeper in me," Czestochowa said, "There were other officers murdered. Did you kill them too?"

"Yes," answered the intruder.

"How'd you find them?" Czestochowa asked.

The intruder explained with arrogance that he knew from a Filipino informant working for the Kempeitai, Japan's secret military police, that the American Army officers were investigating ongoing espionage activity in Cavite and Olongapo. The two places were raided and two men were taken into custody and interrogated.

"What happened to them?" the captive inquired.

"The two men later hanged themselves," the intruder said before stopping for a second. "My name must have come up during the interrogations. That's why I killed them," he added angrily, and at the same time reminding his captive that the dagger was still in his back by pushing the point of the blade a little deeper, drawing blood.

Czestochowa grimaced with pain and gasped. "Those aren't good enough reasons. Hell! You weren't sure your name was mentioned. What were your real motives?"

There was a long silence.

"Fear and revenge. And I'll kill again for the same reasons," the intruder finally answered with a cruel smile. "I feared that they knew my name and would eventually expose my identity. Yes! Fear and revenge!"

Czestochowa couldn't believe this man, who seemed to be bent on killing him, was so talkative. He couldn't understand why he was telling him all these things. But he wasn't about to ask.

The attacker began to explain in detail that he thought only Haggarty and Summers had suspected who he was. But later, he learned that Stein, who had stolen several items from his house, had confirmed their suspicions.

The attacker paused and became analytical when he spoke again. He knew, he told Czestochowa, that Stein had been following him everywhere he went. "He must have followed me one night to where I live and hid somewhere in the house during the night. The next day after I left, he must have gone through letters and pictures in my desk and other personal belongings in my house."

The attacker paused again for a second. "I was very much aware that, meanwhile, any and all information about me were being reported to their boss, Walters."

Czestochowa's arms were numbed from the clothesline tightly tied around his wrists and his throat ached from dryness. He cleared his throat. "Lieutenant Colonel Walters. Did you know him?"

"Yes," the intruder answered.

"He didn't drown, did he? I bet you killed him too. Did you kill him?"

The assailant's voice was hard and ugly when he answered Czestochowa. Walters, according to his explanation, knew well before Stein did that he was living under an assumed name he had lifted from a very, very old obituary. Walters also, aside from his own findings, had all the reports and papers from his intelligence officers about him. The assailant also conveyed that he knew Walters's plan to give all the data about him to the Philippine Department's G-2 and the military police who would have arrested him and turn him over to the United States government in Washington.

"Walters had all the evidence on me to have me jailed and executed," he said moving closer to Czestochowa. "But my destiny is yet to come. I will be recognized as a great man and a great leader. A hero."

During a brief silence, Czestochowa knew that if he continued to engage his crazed and unknown attacker to keep talking that, perhaps, Mac, Charlie or Poco would come to his rescue. He only half listened as the attacker went on a long tangent about his idea of Utopia and his hatred for America. A few minutes later, Czestochowa's pulse quickened as he heard the rustling of leaves but soon realized that it was just the wind.

"I'm curious," Czestochowa finally inquired. "How were you so certain it was Stein who followed you home that night?"

"I had to kill Stein! When I came home that evening, I was missing, among other things, an inscribed cigarette case given to me from someone I love, my mother, and a couple of pictures of me with her," He said in a maniacal tone. "He took those things which my mother gave me. I'll kill anyone who takes things given to me by my mother and those who will harm her."

"You're a real nut job," Czestochowa said. "Why is your mother so important?"

The killer elaborated that, a week later, he found a black date book in his garage. Stein's name was printed on the cover of the date book. Listed on several pages were some of the attacker's aliases including his present alias and a notation that his mother was reportedly living in Maryland.

The man added in a whisper, "I killed Stein for revenge for involving my mother!"

He gave Czestochowa a hard hit on the head.

"I'm getting very impatient with you. This time I want you to tell me who you saw killed Gibbs. I know who did it. But, hearing it from you personally would give me great pleasure."

Czestochowa could hardly speak.

"You're a weird and an insane son of a bitch. You belong in a crazy house, you motherfucker!"

The strong wind from the bay was causing the branches on the tall trees to part, giving a small amount of light on nearby surroundings. The attacker, who wore a visor cap, pushed the dagger deeper into Czestochowa's back and whispered, "It really doesn't matter if you don't tell me Gibbs's killer. I know who the fisherman was. You were the fisherman! Why didn't you report it to the police, Czestochowa?"

"I was anchored too far to be certain," he said, surprised the killer knew his name.

"You're lying! You were close enough to see me and Gibbs," the attacker said angrily and drew blood from the captive's neck with his dagger.

Czestochowa tried to turn around.

"Don't try to face me," the attacker ordered, drawing some more blood from his captive's neck. "No, tell me who killed Gibbs."

"A big, tall man with thick blond hair," Czestochowa said as he passed his dry tongue across his dry lips. "How do you know I was the fisherman?"

"I saw you when you passed by my boat. I hid so you wouldn't see me."

"Who else are you going to kill after me?" Czestochowa asked.

"McCord. He has something that belongs to me, a blue sapphire ring my mother gave to me."

"You'll kill him for a ring?" Czestochowa's said, his voice now weakening.

"McCord knows too much about me when he was in France with an intelligence group."

"Someone ought to carve your rotten heart out," Czestochowa said. "Why are you such an angry man? Your father must not have loved you."

"He did not! I hated my father and loathed him." The attacker stopped talking abruptly and started crying, tears streaming down his face. "Don't change the subject!" As he spoke, he again drew blood with his dagger, this time from Czestochowa's arm.

"Why did you kill Lieutenant Gibbs?" Czestochowa groaned in pain.

The attacker's voice hardened. "I despised him. He made fun of Hitler and called him a crazy Nazi, but I killed him primarily because he knew that I am one of the officers in Walters's group. He knew that I am one of you!"

"What? One of us?" Czestochowa said incredulously. "A spy among us!"

"Yes! One of you! He was going to expose me as a Nazi spy and a spy for the Japanese." The attacker explained.

"What are some of your aliases?" Czestochowa asked.

"Well, since I'm going to kill you anyway, I'm going to tell you. One of my names is Leon Barclay. Sometimes I pass as Sonny Sollow. I also use other aliases whenever it's convenient. And I use different disguises. The man you saw on the boat with Gibbs was Leon Barclay, and he also killed Roosie, Walters, Stein, and Gibbs. But Sollow murdered Summers and Haggarty."

"Who are you now?" Czestochowa asked.

"My real self, without a disguise. Boris Meissner. The man Quest is after. I'll surprise you however, when you see me."

With the tip end of his dagger, he pressed the sharp weapon deep enough into Czestochowa's skin and traced the dagger from below his throat down to his navel. Blood began to trickle down Czestochowa's body.

Despite the pain, Czestochowa suddenly whirled around and kicked his assailant in the groin and tried to run, but his tied hands greatly hampered his speed. He was no match with his captor's agility. Back once more in his grasp, the malefactor pushed Czestochowa roughly away from the crowd.

"You can't escape from me!"

"Why'd you wait this long to kill me?" Czestochowa asked. "You're an idiot blabbermouth. I'm going to be killed, but first let me tell you my life story. I don't give a shit about you, your dad, or your sorry excuse for a bitch mother."

"I waited for an appropriate time and place. There are people like you, McCord, and those two FBI agents, if I can find them, who must die," he said. "Now, slowly turn around and face me. And no screaming for help. The dagger is two inches from your heart."

With his right hand he took out a flashlight, flicked it on and brought it to his face.

Czestochowa's could not believe what he was seeing. His eyes bulged and his dry mouth flew wide open. Then a croaking sound came out of his throat.

"You! I...I...don't believe it! Why? I thought you liked me. I thought we were friends."

The attacker kicked Czestochowa away from the tree and shoved him deeper and deeper into the heavily forested ground.

"Face the tree," he ordered and stuffed a handkerchief in Czestochowa's mouth, and with his extremely sharp dagger, ripped Czestochowa's trousers, exposing his buttocks.

"Bend down," the assailant whispered. "Bend down." He picked up a rather large fallen limb nearby and rammed it into Czestochowa's anus. As tears again streamed down his face, the attacker continued to assault him.

Czestochowa was unsteady on his feet and was breathing heavily. His still half-conscious mind wanted desperately to call for help but knew no sound would come. His tongue clung to the roof of his mouth from dryness. Fear for his life was no longer an option. Excruciating, burning pain ran through his body. He knew that there was no escape for him. He knew that he was dying.

The attacker cut off the twine from his captive's wrists and turned his limp body to face him and jammed the dagger into his chest. Czestochowa fell face down with the dagger through his heart.

The murderer methodically took a second larger dagger from his belt and sliced off Czestochowa's head and his ten fingers and wrapped them up in Czestochowa's blood-soaked shirt. He swiftly disappeared into the pitch-black night toward the beach and tossed his bounty into the turbulent bay.

In another part of the forested area, consciousness came back to Mac once again. The pain on his shoulder had worsened, causing a strong wave of nausea and uncontrollable vomiting similar to seasickness. For five minutes, bile spewed from his mouth. Fortunately, to his surprise, he was able to stop regurgitating when he observed a shadowy figure not far from the thick undergrowths where he was hiding. Holding his breath, Mac watched as the figure paused and searched around him, then ran past his hiding place.

Mac could hear the bushes rustle in the direction of the entrance of Buenavista. Mac knew that once the man got out onto the traffic-busy boulevard, he would be gone for good.

"I've got to catch him," Mac thought, at the same time wondered why Poco did not stop the fleeing man. "Where in the hell is Poco?"

He sprung to his feet and gave chase to the fast-running suspect. But Mac ran just as fast, following on the heel of the stranger who, upon reaching Dewey Boulevard decided to veer south, passing Kawazaka's marina in the direction of Paranaque, south of Manila.

Suddenly, Mac stopped. He had lost his attacker. Although he was almost out of breath and in pain, he began to retrace his steps and decided to have another look in the marina. He began searching the docks and would stop now and then to listen for any unusual disturbances under the docks. He stood there for some time and, convinced of no such sounds, went back to the wall. He climbed the wall between the marina and Buenavista and lowered himself on Buenavista's side, where he was a couple of hours ago. Mac asked himself if the fleeing predator could have ran to the marina, left, and then decided to climb the wall and hide among the tall and thick plants of the Molina property. With that notion in mind, Mac searched carefully among the undergrowth but came to the conclusion that he was wasting precious time.

"He's not around here," he whispered to himself.

He went back to the entrance of Buenavista on Dewey Boulevard and stumbled on something large on the ground. Mac bent down and examined the object. It was Poco, unconscious on the ground. He gently shook the Filipino sergeant.

"Hey, wake up. Poco, wake up," Mac said shaking Poco's shoulders.

It seemed an eternity to Mac before the sergeant finally opened his eyes.

"Major Mac. What happened? A man passed by here and hit me on the head with a heavy object," Poco said, his voice weak.

"I believe your head is bleeding," Mac said.

He tore a strip from Poco's shirt and tied it around the sergeant's head.

"Have Miguela take a look at the wound. Don't worry about the gate. I think that the killer has left the area."

While Mac stood there contemplating what to do next, a passing car's headlights helped him spot, for a second, a male silhouette across the boulevard. Mac ran across the busy highway and began the chase. The stranger also saw Mac and, defying the fast, oncoming traffic, recrossed the boulevard. Upon reaching that portion of Dewey Boulevard that overlooked the cove, he paused for a split second and climbed on top of the balustrade and jumped into the deep, dark, swirling waters below.

Mac did likewise. As soon as he had surfaced from the depth of the cove, he knew that his attacker was no longer in the cove. There were no splashes in the water or heavy breathing, except his own. Until then he had not realized how badly he was hurting and wondered if he would be able to stay afloat in the hard swirling cove.

Mac had to think fast. He could feel the force of the vortex sucking him in. Fear gripped him, but he kept his composure, looking around for an escape from the deadly swirling water.

He could swim, he told himself, in that fast current, away from the cove, towards the Manila piers. He had trepidations, however, that the swiftness of the current would dash him against enormous boulders that were strategically placed along the edges of Manila Bay. There was also the likelihood the fast current could carry him to sharp, half submerged pilings in the shallower part of the bay, snag him, and drown him. Or he could swim to the left side of the cove and get close to the twelve-foot wire fence separating the cove from the Buenavista beach.

As he envisioned it, he could hold on to the wire fence, pull himself up, and scramble to the other side. But Mac quickly dismissed the idea. He feared that the condition of his shoulder would preclude him from accomplishing his plan. There was the dreadful consequence of him falling back, weakened, into the vortex and drowning.

Mac was proud of his ability and endurance as a swimmer, and he could not ever remember being afraid in the water. But he was afraid that night, afraid that his shoulder would fail him. He looked straight in front of him, but in the dark night, he saw only a vast black hole.

The waves on the bay had built up considerably since that morning, and the surf was heavy and pounding, pushing the water back and forth from the bay to the cove, which during the day looked mysterious, beautiful, and treacherous.

"I must swim away from the cove. I must swim away from the cove."

Mac kept repeating the words. He turned over on his back and floated. He felt a relaxation in the treacherous water. He was free. The strong undercurrent was gone. He stopped fighting. A feeling of relief came over him. He began to swim vigorously into the open bay and on to the Buenavista side and could feel his feet touch the sandy bottom.

He walked to the beached boat where he and Miguela had sat a few months before. Exhausted, he leaned on the side of the boat, determined to stay there, away from everyone, until the deep pain on his shoulder became more tolerable.

As he sat, his thoughts swung to Charlie and Czestochowa. He hoped they had fared better than he and Poco.

The guests who stayed behind were now leaving. Mac could see the long line of headlights winding their way very slowly from Buenavista like a midnight funeral procession.

When Mac, Poco, and Charlie saw each other in the wee hours of that morning, they asked each other the whereabouts of Czestochowa.

"I had concerns about that young pup. He must have encountered some foul play," Charlie explained.

"Why the past tense, Charlie? You sound like he's already dead," Mac said.

"Sorry about that, Mac. Just a premonition, that's all," Charlie answered.

They doggedly began to search the area for Czestochowa, but to no avail. To their surprise however, they found the dead body of a Japanese male between the entrance of Buenavista and Dewey Boulevard. A few minutes later, two people came screaming. They had found the headless body of Czestochowa.

After recovering the body, the Quest group handed over the reins and let the Philippine police do their job. They couldn't afford to lose anyone else that night. Mac kissed Miguela, who had been holed up in the main house most of the night, and headed back to his room.

The following afternoon, Mac went back to the cove overlooking Dewey Boulevard to contemplate how his assailant, after jumping into the treacherous cove, disappeared quickly without any trace. It was then that he found a brown army shoe on the side of the road near the balustrade. He took it home.

That night, Mac asked Miguela for directions to Miller's house. At the same time, he made her promise not to tell anyone of his interest. He hailed a taxicab and directed the driver to take him to Outrigger Lane on Dewey Boulevard, and, after paying the driver, he walked to the house to find it dark and quiet.

After deciding that Miller was not home, he stealthily went to the front door. It was locked, but Mac discovered the house key hidden under the doormat. Quickly, Mac unlocked the door and placed the key back under the doormat. He went inside, unlocked the kitchen door, and opened one of the two kitchen windows to assure his escape, should Miller catch him.

He went to the study and turned on a light. On the desk were stacks of letters addressed to Colonel Bradford Miller. A framed photograph showed Miller in a US Army uniform. All the drawers of the desk were empty, but there were magazines and newspapers scattered here and there. Mac pulled open the drawers and found a half-empty pack of Camel cigarettes, two boxes of matches, the empty shell from a Colt .45 pistol. He dropped the two boxes of matches in his pocket and examined the empty shell for a second before turning off the light.

Mac groped his way upstairs and went inside an open bedroom. Turning on the light, he was certain it was the master bedroom, but he was disappointed to find it obviously unused. Always turning off the light behind him, he proceeded to the next two bedrooms and found them in a similar condition. He was just about to go back to the first floor when he discovered a room by the stairwell. Mac pushed the door open and turned on the light. "Aha! This is where Miller sleeps. Close to the stairs," he murmured.

With haste, he examined the clothes in the closet. There was a suit, two khaki pants and shirts, and four white shirts. He glanced at the khaki shirts and found them to have all of their buttons. On the floor was a pair of brown shoes, about size twenty. Mac was shutting the closet door when a brown shoebox in the far corner of the closet caught his eye. In it was a pair of new brown shoes.

He heard a car making a turn onto Outrigger Lane. Mac instantly turned off the light. Noiselessly, he closed the closet door, raced down the steps, and ran to the kitchen window. Hopping out and quietly, he shut it behind him.

He hailed a taxicab on Dewey Boulevard.

CHAPTER 16

Early morning after the party, Agent Chavez arrived in Manila from a week's counterintelligence seminar in Mindoro Island, southwest of Luzon. Hours before his departure from Mindoro, Chavez's boss Romero, chief of the PIB, informed him by telephone about the triple murder at Buenavista.

The news media's intense interest and coverage of the rampage worried Romero. He warned Chavez that he would probably be questioned.

With hardly any sleep, Chavez was still anxious to get to work. Upon reaching the entrance to the PIB building, a journalist from the Manila News and a radio reporter from station KMZH were waiting for him. Chavez simply told them that he would let them know as soon as he had some new information. But for now, Chavez told them, there would be no comment.

A couple of hours later, he received a telephone call from Mac asking him to help find out what happened to Lieutenant Czestochowa.

That same afternoon, Mac, Charlie, Poco, and Chavez went back to the Molina compound and followed the path to the tree where Czestochowa's mutilated body was found. Leaves covered the pool of dried blood under large acacia trees. Thick hibiscus and fallen coconut tree fronds still lingered.

"Mother of God. Whoever did this is insane!" Chavez said aloud.

Mac stared at the scene, and a chilling thought crossed his mind. He recalled what the dying Duvalier had told him about Boris Meissner's style of killing.

"It's like a signature!" And as an afterthought, Mac murmured, "Meissner! He was here!"

Charlie turned around abruptly. "Did you say Meissner was here,

189

Mac?"

"Yes, Meissner was here. My gut tells me he was here, and I don't even know what he looks like." Mac rubbed his head. "I must be losing my mind, Charlie."

Chavez, meanwhile, was greatly disturbed that three men were murdered at the respected Buenavista in a single night. And why in that particular place? Because of the density of the trees, its accessibility to Manila Bay, or its proximity to spy-filled Manila? Later that afternoon, as Chavez helped Mac, Poco and Charlie search for clues. Mac told Chavez that the Japanese spy's neck, Captain Kondo a.k.a agent 10, had been twisted. Charlie suggested that only a very strong man could have done it. They all agreed.

Shortly thereafter, the PIB leadership told Chavez to relinquish his investigation on the Japanese spy's death to a colleague in the espionage division. It freed him to quietly continue his effort and direction to solving the deaths of Haggarty, Summers, Stein, Gibbs, and Walters. Included now in that effort was the murders of Lieutenant Czestochowa and Roosie. So far, the results had been bleak. He had to hold it together.

But what was really getting to Chavez was the murder of Roosie, a poor and good-natured old man who held no malice for anyone. He had known the old cabdriver ever since he was a young student working his way to college. Until he was able to find a better job washing dishes at a restaurant, Roosie used to let him drive his cab twice a week, enough time to take home some extra money to his father and mother. Chavez had never forgotten such kindness. In return, years later when he was able to repay that kindness, he loaned Roosie the money for a down payment on a new cab.

He vowed that he would find his friend's murderer. Come to think of it, Chavez never remembered his friend to have ever been young. He was certain that Roosie was born old. No one ever really knew how old he was.

A couple of days later, he secretly asked the Molinas' permission to look around the grounds again, this time by himself. He was pleased that the temporary wooden floor placed over the swimming pool during the party had not yet been removed. He had heard from the police that it was to be left there until the deaths of Czestochowa and Roosie had been fully investigated. He was especially anxious to do some investigating in the vicinity of the swimming pool, the bathhouse, and dance floor, where Roosie fell at Miguela's feet.

Chavez spent a good portion of that day quietly walking along the beach and the driveway, but for some reason, he kept focusing on the temporary bar. He also sifted through the leaves, tree limbs, and debris behind the boathouse where Czestochowa was cruelly assaulted, hoping also to find evidence that might lead to the killer.

From there, Chavez kept on walking until he had almost reached the circuitous, forested path that led to the entrance of Buenavista and out to Dewey Boulevard. Now and then, he would use a tree limb he had picked up along the way to poke the soggy leaves that blanketed the ground. He had no idea what he was looking for, but knew there had to be something—some sort of clue that would point him in the right direction.

Chavez, engrossed in his thoughts, failed to notice a clearly manmade mound of leaves and twigs.

He also failed to notice the man who had been following his every move.

Chavez stumbled and fell to the ground, catching his foot on what he presumed was a loose tree root. As he struggled to free his foot, his hand hit a solid object underneath the leaves and branches. He hastily brushed them away, and to his surprise, he uncovered a wide belt with an unusually large gold buckle. The design was impressive—the head of a cobra, with its mouth wide-open, displaying its formidable fangs. A sick feeling rushed to his stomach.

Chavez could not fathom the meaning or the importance of his finding. But at that instant, he considered it an omen. He scrutinized the buckle in his hands.

The man lurking a few dozen yards away drew closer, but in doing so, he stepped on a twig that cracked and snapped. Chavez turned to see if someone was around, thinking it was Mac.

"Mac, is that you?" he called out. There was only an eerie silence.

Chavez wandered around another few hours, then left Buenavista for his office.

Chavez gazed at the face of the reptile on the gold buckle and wondered why any man would want to display such a sinister-looking creature on his belt.

With that thought that it might be a symbol, he quickly dropped the belt into his safe to hide the evil face.

The following day, Chavez briefed his boss, Romero, other members of the PIB, and his friend Colonel Danbury, who used to be with the Philippine Department. But Danbury was now one of the staff members of G-2 in the newly established command in the Philippines USAFFE. Danbury was one of several officers from the Philippine Department G-2 chosen to join USAFFE G-2.

Everyone present concluded that the buckle was an interesting find, but no one was able to offer any meaningful advice as to what to do with it. Danbury, however, suggested that a PIB agent be immediately dispatched to Baguio, well known for its gold mining and production. A visit to the most prominent jewelry shop in the mile-high resort might shed some light on the buckle's origin. Since it was Chavez who had discovered the item, he would be the one to go. Chavez shoved the buckle in a canvas knapsack and headed out.

After surveying the shop, looking for anything in the display windows that looked similar to the buckle, Chavez approached the proprietor and showed him the buckle. He asked if he knew the jewelry shop that may have carved the cobra. The man sitting behind the glass enclosure studied the belt buckle and the imprint, and after some indecisive moments, concluded that it was probably his shop that did the artwork.

"It has been some time since we have performed this kind of work—animal faces on belt buckles. The style was very popular in the mid-thirties," he explained. "But it has been a long time since we have had such a request."

"Do you recall who ordered it?" Chavez inquired.

The proprietor gave Chavez a long look.

"I cannot remember at this moment," he said hesitantly, continuing to stare at his visitor. "The face of this cobra, however, evokes fright and repulsion, like the snake is going to strike at you and bury his fangs in your neck."

"I guess that's the idea," Chavez said softly. "Oh, well, I had better be going. I don't want to waste any more of your time."

He started to leave the shop.

"Wait," called the jeweler.

Chavez turned around and came back.

"I believe that I may be able to tell you about that particular design," the jeweler said, trying to remember. "The work on this buckle is so very unusual that I think I can say now who ordered it to be done. It was an American."

Chavez was encouraged. "Do you recall his name? Perhaps in your work order?"

"No. We only keep work orders for one year," said the jeweler.

"What did he look like?" Chavez asked.

"He was a big, tall man. Nice fellow. He said that he was from Chicago. We immediately struck up a conversation. I'm also from Chicago."

The jeweler paused momentarily, now taking out a magnifying glass to look at the buckle closer. "There was one thing the stranger said that I found rather interesting."

"Oh?" said Chavez. "What could that have been?"

"He said, 'These mountains in Baguio would make great shelters!' And with that he laughed and left."

Chavez was determined to use the belt buckle as possible evidence to the murders at Buenavista. The notion that at last he had found something important to solving the crime excited him. In the first place, although it had been buried, the buckle appeared well polished and cared for. His gut told him that whoever owned it, sooner or later, would try to trace the item.

There were only three persons who knew about it: himself, Romero, and Danbury. He wanted to add Mac to the list, but before he did, he needed approval. He convinced both men that Mac would act as a lightning rod for stalkers and spies, especially if he gave the belt buckle to Mac and had him get the word out. Both Romero and Danbury had no objections to Chavez's idea.

Chavez called Mac the next day and told him that he had something that might be of great interest to him.

"Come to my office as soon as you can."

Mac was ecstatic when he saw the belt buckle. He told Chavez about his conversation with Roosie last June about the shooting at Sergio's Bar and Grill. Roosie could not describe the killer's appearance but imparted to Mac that he would recognize the man if he saw him wearing the belt with the cobra's face on the gold belt buckle.

Mac complimented Chavez for the item.

"The perfect clue to the killer," Mac said.

Mac told Chavez what the bartender at the Molinas' party recalled Roosie yelling about before he was attacked. It was the man wearing the gold buckle.

"Mac," Chavez asked, "Who else did you know at that party?"

"Just my group," Mac answered. "And Roosie, of course. His grandson Alberto was there for a short while, but he came back later to pick up his grandfather."

"Talk to Alberto," Chavez suggested. "He might know something."

"I will," Mac said.

"Mac, do you know who our killer is? Is it Sonny Sollow?" Chavez said. "I understand he was at the party."

"Yes," answered Mac. "He's my chief suspect, and I've a gut feeling that he may also be Boris Meissner."

During their conversation about Sollow, Mac told Chavez of his encounter with Sollow that almost turned into a fight and how, shortly after that, he tried to follow him in a car after Sollow left the party.

"Unfortunately, I lost him," Mac said embarrassedly.

Mac also told him about his unknown attacker who tried to kill him and his near-death experience with the cove.

"You dove into that cove?" Chavez asked, horrified. "That was near suicide."

"Tell me about it!" Mac answered. "Anyway, Sollow is my chief suspect."

"Let's track him down. But be extra careful when covertly trailing him around," Chavez said.

As Mac walked toward the door to leave, Chavez followed him. "Mac, I was just thinking," Chavez said softly, not so sure about his thoughts. "The Baguio jeweler told me that the man who ordered that buckle was an American from Chicago." He paused. "Major North is from Chicago, isn't he?"

Mac stopped walking and faced Chavez. "Yes, he is," he answered with narrowed eyes, opened the door and left.

CHAPTER 17

The news of three murders was difficult for Filipinos to accept. It caused a terrible uproar in Manila and the sense among citizens was that law enforcement on the islands was a joke. Hundreds of phone calls and letters poured into radio stations and newspapers. But when a description of the murder of the third victim, Lieutenant Czestochowa, was leaked to the press, a strange feeling of guilt and nervousness jolted Quest. They had spent months searching for the killer and not only had they not caught the perpetrator, but the bodies continued to pile up.

The disgusting assault inflicted on Czestochowa had an immediate effect on everyone, particularly on those who knew him. A silent and uneasy fear that the killer may not be far away and could strike any one of them at any moment became an everyday reality. Mac knew that somewhere in the city was a vicious murderer and became apprehensive that the next victim would once again be one of them. They were the targets.

One day, out of nowhere, Poco stood up and said, "I wonder if I am going to be the next victim."

Clearly, it was now a matter of protecting themselves. Mac, again, tried to persuade Charlie and Poco to accept his idea of going underground. Both agreed wholeheartedly. It was obvious what they were doing wasn't working, despite all of their combined experience.

They all knew, particularly Charlie, who had known Czestochowa longer than Mac or Poco, how capable the large Polish soldier was of defending himself. No one could comprehend why a strong young man like Czestochowa could have been so easily overcome. They all concluded that the person who had committed the crime knew him, knew where to find him, and surprised him. Czestochowa was too smart and too strong to be effortlessly overpowered.

"The killer must've been at that party," Mac told Poco and Charlie. "And what's so odd about it—only the three of us knew of our individual search area."

Charlie nodded. "You're damn right about that, Mac. But we've discussed it before. This particular killer is not only smart but elusive— like Miller and Rhoades," Charlie said, laughing heartily. "At any rate, it was too bad I couldn't help my friend."

Two weeks after the incidents at Buenavista, Miller, back from one of his frequent trips to Northern Luzon, called a meeting. He was pacing up and down the briefing room floor. But now and then he would look in the direction of Rhoades and give him a veiled, accusing glance. Suddenly, he stopped his pacing and addressed Purita Aquino, inquiring if she had heard any street rumors about any of the murders. Her reply was negative. Miller turned his attention to Charlie and Poco. Their answers were both negative. Miller glanced at Mac.

"McCord. I suppose you have the answer?" Miller inquired sarcastically.

Mac's steel-blue eyes never left Miller's face. "Not yet, Colonel."

Miller walked to where Rhoades was seated. The corners of his lips were twitching. "You realize you could be implicated in Czestochowa's murder."

Rhoades jumped from his chair. He was genuinely surprised by Miller's statement. "What are you saying Colonel? Are you insinuating that I killed Czestochowa?"

Miller stared at Rhoades. "You were pretty threatening last June. Everyone in this room heard you! You didn't like him!"

Rhoades looked at everyone in the room. "Yes, I was threatening him, and yes, I didn't like him, but I didn't kill him. He didn't know when to shut up. Czestochowa was a bully." Rhoades looked around the room. "Major North? Did you like Czestochowa?"

"Yes, Sir. He and I were friends," North said.

There was an uneasy silence in the room when Miller again began pacing up and down the floor again. From the corner of his eye, he could see that McCord, North and Poco were looking at Rhoades with suspicion. "Back to Quest's mission." Miller's voice broke the silence in the room. He told the group that his request to USAFFE G-2 for at least one replacement was, in his words, "unfortunately shot down."

He further informed them, in no uncertain terms, that unless Quest could soon came up with some answers to the crimes, the task would be turned over to the PIB. "I was told that USAFFE is too involved in trying to reorganize the Philippine Defense System, and General McArthur is vehemently against being away from the defense program and wasting even one man's time. So despite our desperate need for personnel, we're not getting any more help, and we're under the gun," Miller continued, "Business, however, must go on as usual, and I want McCord to write about the incidents at the party and include whatever clues any and all of you may know of Czestochowa and the cabdriver's murders. The police will handle the Japanese spy's death."

For a couple of days after the meeting, Mac went to the office everyday to write the report. He did not, however, include the attacks on himself at Buenavista or, more importantly, the Army-brown shoe he had picked up by the cove and the button he must have unconsciously dropped in his pocket after struggling with his attacker at the party. His instinct told him to keep that information to himself. Only he, Chavez, and his attacker would have knowledge of the incidents.

Mac was convinced that the same man who had killed agent Kagan in Roosie's cab had murdered Roosie. The killer knew that Roosie had seen him kill Kagan. Mac was determined not to mention the taxicab incident in his report unless Miller insisted.

They were pondering Czestochowa's story about the fisherman seeing two men fighting in a boat and one of them killing his companion. So a couple of days later, Mac, Poco, and Charlie rented a car and drove directly to Olongapo. They checked in at the small town's hotel to do some covert investigative work on Lieutenant Gibbs's murder. Charlie told his friends that he was going to take them to Art's Café, known as far away as Batangas for its seafood and cold San Miguel beer. "You've never tasted beer as good and as cold as the beer there. In this hot Philippine weather, every swallow goes down in you like you've got wooden legs." Charlie chortled delightfully. "As you enter the café, on each side of the door are two large cut-down barrels lined with tin and filled with large chunks of ice and very cold bottles of beer. Whenever you want another beer, just fish one out and tell Art about it. He's both owner and bartender. His wife, Vera, helps him. Art is a retired American sailor. He and his wife are from Chicago."

Mac smiled. "It's that good?"

"It's that good!" Charlie chuckled and rubbed his hands together. "That's for beer drinkers like you and Poco. But my favorite is the gino. Every time I go there, Vera rushes to where I'm sitting and flops a bottle of gin on the bar and gives me a plate with a huge sweet onion from Batangas." Charlie all at once stopped talking and looked at Mac's left hand. "Where's that expensive blue sapphire ring? You pawned it?"

Mac answered that he had left it in his suitcase and that he was not much on wearing rings. "I'll tell you what I'll do for you, Charlie. I'll give the ring to you. You admire it so much."

Charlie laughed heartily.

Late that afternoon, just when the sun began to set, they walked from their hotel to Art's café at the end of a long pier that extended out into Subic Bay. Not far from the pier were fishing boats standing neatly side by side, and a thick Manila rope tied to a couple of pilings kept each boat secure.

Mac sniffed the air and opened his lungs with a deep inhalation of fresh air. "Gorgeous view."

Charlie snorted and said that it made him homesick for Lake Michigan.

Vera rushed to meet them at the door. "Charlie North! I'm angry with you," she exclaimed, planting both hands on her hips. "Someone told me you were in Olongapo a couple of weeks ago, and you didn't come to see us!"

"Divorce your husband and marry me," Charlie said, and picking up the small, slender woman, kissed her on the cheek. "Sorry, Vera," he said, putting her down. "I had a job to do. Forgive me?"

"For now! Come on in. Your friends too," Vera declared, her face beaming. She called her husband, Art, who was in the kitchen. "Guess who's here, darling."

"Don't tell me. I bet it's General MacArthur," Art shouted back.

"No, silly. Guess again," Vera pouted playfully.

"Well, from the sound of your voice it must be that lecherous, overage

Army major from Chicago," Art commented, coming out of the kitchen. "Charlie North. How are you? It's good to see you again, ol' buddy."

Before they sat down, Charlie introduced Mac and Poco to his friends. Art served Mac and Poco cold beer from the barrel and two hardboiled eggs in saltwater while Vera served Charlie his favorite gino.

"What brings you back here, Charlie?" Art asked.

Charlie shook his head. "It's on the same thing...Gibbs."

Mac took a big gulp of the cold beer. It went down easy. "Did you know Gibbs?" he asked both Art and Vera.

They answered simultaneously. "Yes."

"Gibbs was sort of a shy type," Vera added. "He had a Filipina girlfriend here."

Mac inquired how well Vera and Art knew the girl. Art shook his head. "She and Gibbs used to come here once in a while."

Mac continued his interrogation by asking when they both saw Gibbs. Art pursed his lips. "Can't remember exactly. Sometime in early June."

Charlie chimed in "Did you know that he was murdered, Art?"

"No. Vera and I thought he drowned. His body was found floating not too far from here," Art remarked.

"We've new info," Charlie said, chewing the onion and then downing it with a big swallow of gin. "We understand a fisherman here saw two men fighting in another boat. According to him, one of them killed his companion and threw his body into the bay. Of course, we can't verify that awful rumor, but it could've been Gibbs."

Art looked at his wife. "Vera, have you heard anything about that?"

"No, but old man Stabbler, ex-Army type, owns the boat livery over there. He may remember to whom he rented that particular boat. His is the only fishing marina around here for miles," Vera explained.

It was about midnight when Mac, Charlie, and Poco returned to their hotel. The next morning, they went to see Stabbler.

"Yes," he told them, "I recall renting a boat to a tall blond man. Gibbs was with him. They said that they were going fishing. I liked Gibbs. Nice fellow. Always brought me a cigar whenever he and his girlfriend, Lina, went boating. He didn't much care for fishing but enjoyed just going out there and swimming. I was real sorry when I heard he got murdered."

They were startled, Charlie especially. "How'd you know he was murdered, Stabbler?"

The old man's answer was quick. "I didn't see it or anything like that, you understand. Another person to whom I rented a fishing boat told me that from where he was, he saw two men fighting in their boat, and then the blond man killed his companion and threw his body into the water."

"Do you remember anything else about the blond man's appearance?" Charlie asked.

Stabbler paused. "I never really gave his face a good look. I recall, though, that he was tall and had a big frame." Stabbler unconsciously glanced at Charlie. "I suppose tall with a big frame like you." He paused again. "I never saw him and Gibbs come back, but I noticed that the boat was tied securely to the dock."

Charlie had an uneasy smile on his face. "You've a good memory, old man."

"Only repeating what I was told. It stuck in my mind," replied Stabbler unequivocally.

"Did the fisherman give you his name?" Charlie persisted.

Stabbler spat out tobacco juice to his side. "Nope. All he said when I asked him his name was, 'You won't be able to pronounce my name. It's too long.' That also stuck in my mind. He then walked away. Never seen him since. Young, strong-looking fellow."

Mac, Charlie, and Poco stared knowingly at each other.

"Czestochowa was the fisherman!" Mac murmured. "Did you call the police?" he asked Stabbler.

The old man shook his head. "I'm seventy years old. I've lived all over these Philippine Islands, and I've learned to keep my mouth shut." He paused and again spat out tobacco juice to his side. "I figured the police would find out about it sooner or later, but not from me."

Mac dug in his pocket. "Here are five pesos for your trouble."

"I don't want your money," Stabbler murmured and walked away to tend to his boats. Mac ran after him with Charlie following close behind. "Stabbler! Wait! I want to ask you one last question," Mac shouted.

"What about?" The old man answered without looking back.

"Where does Gibbs's girlfriend live?"

Stabbler stopped and turned around. "About a mile up the hill behind the Catholic Church. Her name is Lina, short for Saralina. Nice girl. Lives with her grandmother."

But for the breeze blowing in from the South China Sea across Subic Bay, the heat would have been unbearable. It was not yet noon, and already the strong bright sun was sending shimmering rays on the water.

On their way back to their rented Chevrolet, Charlie told his two companions, "No need for all three of us to bother Lina. I'll stay in the car and watch it. By the way, Poco," Charlie continued, "If there's anything I can do for them, don't hesitate to give them my telephone number at the BOQ."

"Come with us, Charlie. You'll learn something." Mac prodded.

"No. I've already met Grandma Fuentes." Charlie answered irritably.

Mac subconsciously turned around and gave Charlie a contemplative glance. But he shrugged his shoulders and told himself that it was probably the heat that was getting to him.

They all climbed back into their rented car and chugged up the hill. The Catholic Church and the house were easy to find, and as prearranged, only Poco and Mac got out and ran up the steps of the small, freshly painted house. Mac knocked, and a white haired Filipina opened the door. He asked her if she was Lina's grandmother.

"Yes, I am. What can I do for you?"

Poco inquired whether Lina was home. The frail old woman, with great concern in her voice, asked if something had happened to Lina. "I do not want to see anything bad to happen to my granddaughter."

Mac explained that they just wanted to ask Lina a question and that he and Poco were friends of Gibbs.

The grandmother sighed with relief. "An American man was here a week or so ago also asking to see my granddaughter. I did not like him, so I told him that Lina went to the Visayas. He became furious with me and grabbed me by the neck. I thought he was going to kill me. He was evil!" Her old eyes scrutinized their faces. "But I like you. Lina now lives in Manila. She left Olangapo many months ago to find work."

"Do you know where she works?" Mac asked.

"In her letter she said that she had found work as a waitress at the Manila International Club." She paused. "I almost forgot to tell you. The

American man who came before you was looking for photographs of himself and Gibbs taken during a party, the day before Lina and Gibbs were to be married." The grandmother related to them that the American searched all over the house and that he became angry when he could not find them. "I told him that I did not know where they were."

Poco gave Lina's grandmother Charlie's telephone number. "Just in case you do find the photo of Lina and Gibbs, or if you need help, call this number."

They rushed back to the city that same day, and that evening Poco took Mac back to his favorite nightclub in Manila in Alberto's assigned corner. Charlie could not join them due to a previous engagement.

"Hello, Major McCord. Sergeant Pocodillo," greeted Alberto and, glancing at Mac, added, "You have not been around since grandfather's death. What a coincidence that I should see you now. Today, the first of October, is my birthday. I am nineteen years old," he announced proudly. "Gentlemen, what can I bring you?" He said, whipping out his order pad.

"Two bottles of San Miguel Beer," Poco said and asked whether Alberto knew Lina.

Alberto nodded and said that he and Lina were married a week ago. "She is no longer Lina Fuentes. She is now Lina Panganiban. Her section is on the other side of the bandstand," he explained enthusiastically and went to get her. Coming back, he introduced her to Mac and Poco. Lina, however, immediately became suspicious when she was told they would like to ask her some questions. She turned around to leave. But Alberto convinced his young bride to stay. "They are my grandfather's friends."

Mac invited them both for lunch at the Manila seafood restaurant for the following day, and, since it was to be the Panganibans' day off, they gladly accepted the invitation. They agreed to meet Mac and Poco at noon. While they were making plans for lunch, Mac noticed that Sonny Sollow was in the club and had taken a nearby table from them. A wave of anger surged through him, and Mac mulled temporarily whether he was angered more by Sollow's arrogance or by the PIB's ineptness in dealing with Sollow's espionage activity. "I don't know why the hell they can't follow him, catch him in the act, and arrest him," he murmured.

Poco looked concerned. "Is something wrong, Major?"

"At the table behind you is Sonny Sollow. I'm getting paranoid about that guy. I'm beginning to believe he follows me everywhere I go," Mac said.

"I wonder what he is up to. He is a bad omen," Poco said.

Alberto had disappeared in the kitchen but was soon back and placing a pitcher of beer on Sollow's table. Shortly after Poco and Mac left the club, Sollow called Alberto back to his table. "That young waitress with you a few minutes ago is very pretty. Is she your sister?"

Alberto, pleased that one of his customers should be so complimentary about his wife, opened up to Sollow. "Lina and I just got married."

"That's wonderful!" Sollow declared and then thought a while. "Since I'm a good customer of the club—and you've always been a fine waiter, let me have your address. I'd like to send you a—a wedding gift, even if belated. My—my name is Sonny Sollow.

"Thank you, Mr. Sollow. That is generous of you. Our address is 10twenty Taft Ave., near Pasay. It is a rented house on the avenue. Easy to catch transportation to work."

Before leaving the club, Sollow gave Alberto a generous tip and insisted on knowing his family name. The young man's answer startled him. He stared at Alberto for some time and inquired whether he was related to the old man who was murdered at Buenavista."

Alberto nodded. "He was my grandfather. I am sorry he was killed."

"Were you at that party, Alberto?" Sollow inquired.

"For a short while, Mr. Sollow. I just dropped Grandpa Roosie and his passengers at Buenavista. I was to come back later. But before I left, he pointed out to me the man he said shot an American Army captain to death at the old Sergio's Bar and Grill."

Sollow was quiet for a second and then asked Alberto whether he knew the two men who had just left the club.

"Yes. Major McCord and Sergeant Pocodillo." Alberto glanced suspiciously at Sollow. "Why are you asking me all these questions?"

"No reason. Just curious. You seem to be fond of them," answered Sollow.

"I am. My grandfather was also," said Alberto. "As a matter of fact, my wife Lina and I are having lunch with them tomorrow at noon."

Sollow played with his beard momentarily. "I meant to ask—ask if you would recognize your grandfather's killer, Alberto?"

The young man nodded and said that he had gotten out of his taxicab and really given the killer a good, long look. "He was a tall man with blond hair, and his large gold buckle was imprinted with the face of a snake."

Sollow inquired why Alberto did not call the police. Alberto said that his grandfather did not want for him to be involved with the police. "He also reminded me that the killer might kill me if he knew that I knew who he was."

As planned, Lina and Alberto met Mac and Poco the following day at the designated seafood restaurant. While they were all enjoying the succulent seafood dishes, Poco asked Lina to tell them what she knew about Gibbs's death. "I hope you don't mind your wife talking to us about Gibbs," he said, glancing at Alberto.

"No. That was before she met me," said Alberto, giving his wife a fond look.

Lina was thoughtful for a second and then related to them that she and Gibbs were to be married the same day he died. Mac wanted to know how he was killed, and she answered that she did not know that he had died until some swimmers on Subic Bay found his body. "I had not heard from him in several days, so I thought that his work was keeping him busy in Manila."

Poco inquired if Gibbs had some friends in the area.

Lina hesitated, but then said Gibbs had a couple of American soldier friends from Corregidor but that they had gone back to the United States long before Gibbs died.

"However, there was one American who came to Grandmother Fuentes's house that Saturday and again the next day. The day Gibbs and I were to be married. They evidently knew each other."

Mac asked if Lina lived with her grandmother and what her name was. "I lived with my grandmother, my father's mother. She likes to be called Grandma Fuentes."

Poco prodded Lina further to tell them more about Gibbs.

She willingly related that that Saturday, the American came to her grandmother's house and insisted on seeing Gibbs. She invited him in out of politeness to join them and their friends at a house party. But she told me later that she had a strange feeling about the visitor that she could not explain. As he entered the room, he smiled, introduced himself, thanked her, and flirtatiously told her she was pretty. "When he smiled, I noticed a gap on his front teeth."

"Excuse me. Did you say, gold on his front teeth?" Mac asked.

"No. He had a gap-tooth smile," corrected Lina.

Mac and Poco listened with interest and asked her to go on with her story.

Lina continued that, during the evening, many in the house were aware of the visitor's flirtatiousness towards her and his belligerent behavior towards Gibbs. "On one or two occasions he whispered something in Gibbs's ear which made him laugh aloud and begin to make fun of the American. "I heard Gibbs say aloud, 'You'll kill me just because I think that Adolf Hitler is a crazy Nazi?'"

"What was the American's name?" Mac inquired.

Lina thought for a while.

"Leon Barclay," she finally answered and continued that Barclay came back to her grandmother's house at 8:00 a.m. the following day, the day she and Gibbs were to be married, and asked to see Gibbs again. It happened that he was not at her grandmother's house but on his way to pick them up to drive them to church for the wedding. Upon seeing Barclay when he arrived, Gibbs, instead of being happy, became angry.

"He said, 'Stop bugging me and flirting with my future wife. You're just as crazy as Hitler,'" Lina related. "And that was when Barclay pushed Gibbs to the floor, and there was a big fight. I started crying." According to her, Gibbs shouted for her to go to her room and to stay there. "From the half-way opened door, I saw Barclay pressing a dagger on Gibbs's back as they both left the house."

Mac looked intensely at Lina. "I don't want you to say anything you aren't sure of. Would you recognize Barclay if you meet him again? What color were his eyes?"

Without hesitation, she described Barclay as a big, tall man with thick blond hair, but she could not remember the color of his eyes. "They were either blue or gray. Although I did not see it, I believe he killed Gibbs."

"One more question, Lina, and I'll hush," Mac said. "Did someone take pictures of the party?"

Lina recalled that her grandmother did and that Barclay was in several of them, whereupon Poco added that they would like to see the pictures. Lina promptly answered that grandmother Fuentes had all of them, including the negatives, and that she herself did not want to keep any of them. She encouraged Mac and Poco to visit her grandmother and for them not to be discouraged if she refused to show them the pictures. "She does have the photos. She hides things she values in a burlap sack and keeps them in a cache. She can be very unfriendly with strangers, especially if she does not like them. But if she does, she is cordial. She hides most of what she considers valuable underneath the kitchen sink."

Tears swelled up in Lina's eyes as she talked about her grandmother, who took care of her after her mother died. "My father passed away when I was six years old."

Mac took a cab to Quest's office the next afternoon to submit a report on Gibbs. Charlie met him at the door while Colonel Miller and Dusty Rhoades were in the briefing room studying an oversized map of Manila. Rhoades turned around when Mac entered the office.

"Well, well. If it isn't our star pupil, Major Jake McCord. You must have something to report," Rhoades declared sarcastically.

"Yes, Sir. I do," replied Mac going straight to his desk. He told them what Lina had related to him and Poco. "Lina thinks that Gibbs was murdered by a man named Leon Barclay."

There was immediate silence in the room. Charlie stared at Mac. Purita stopped typing, and this time, Miller looked up and, turning around, asked, "Who?"

"Leon Barclay," answered Mac.

"Who in the hell is Leon Barclay?" Charlie asked.

"Leon Barclay is Boris Meissner," Mac answered.

"That mysterious man again! Where can we find him?" Miller laughed mirthlessly. He placed his fingers on the left corner of his mouth to stop its twitching.

"Dammit, McCord. Who in the hell's your source?" Charlie asked angrily.

"Alberto's wife, Lina Fuentes Panganiban," Mac answered. "Leon Barclay, who had befriended Gibbs for some time, forced him to go for a boat ride that day expressly to kill him. I'm almost certain that Barclay is one of Boris Meissner's aliases." Mac paused. "My theory is that he has several aliases, and each alias has a different disguise. Perhaps Sony Sollow, with whom I've had several encounters, is probably another alias of Meissner," Mac looked at everyone in the room. "Isn't it possible that Meissner killed all those people, sometimes disguised as Barclay or as Sonny Sollow, and sometimes as someone else?"

"How in the hell do you know so much about Meissner?" Charlie was irritated with Mac's self-confidence.

Mac gave Charlie a hard look and quietly lighted a cigarette.

"Does Meissner know you, McCord?" Charlie was sarcastic.

"He probably does, Major North!" Mac shot back. "He's probably the one who's been stalking me, disguised as Sonny Sollow," Mac paused. "What's eating you, Major North? Your conscience?"

"Hell! You—you disgusting prick! You're such a goddamned know-it-all, someone ought to crack your balls. Stop talking about Meissner." Charlie shouted angrily.

Mac was surprised at his friend's outburst. He started adding up Charlie's recent behavior. Why did he fail to meet him and Poco at Tony's lounge in Olongapo weeks ago? Why was Charlie keeping a dagger in his night table similar to the one dropped inadvertently by Mac's attacker last June? How did Charlie know Grandma Fuentes's name before he had met her? Why did he not join him and Poco when they recently took Lina and Alberto to the seafood restaurant for lunch?

Mac glanced at Charlie and unconsciously shook his head. He innately liked Charlie and, thus, refused to accept what his heart was telling him. "Sorry, Charlie," he apologized.

"Same here, Mac. You can talk about Meissner all you want," said Charlie, smiling.

"I haven't seen such belligerence between you!" Miller said.

"The girl's name sounds familiar. Any relation to the murdered old man?" Rhoades interjected, helping to keep peace in the office.

"She married his grandson, Alberto," Mac explained.

"That young woman may not be telling the truth," Miller said.

"I think she is, Sir," Mac answered Miller. "Why should she lie?"

"I'd like to talk to this woman, Mac. Where can I find her?" Rhoades asked.

"I don't think that's such a good idea, Sir. You'll scare her, and then we won't have a lead," Charlie stated nervously, turning away from Rhoades.

"McCord, I want a report on Gibbs as soon as possible. Miss Aquino, please have it ready by the end of the day." Miller turned around and went to his office.

While Mac was working on his report, Rhoades approached him and inquired whether Lina could identify Barclay. Mac nodded. "Yes, Sir."

"Mac," insisted Rhoades, "Lina's life is in danger. Do me a favor and tell me where I can find her. I can help her. Or let's both help her and her husband. If you say Alberto is the old man's grandson, he could be in danger, too." Rhoades paused momentarily. "You know, McCord, I've a feeling in the pit of my stomach that you still think I'm the one who tried to kill you at the pier when you arrived last June." Rhoades moved close to Mac so that Mac was the only one who could hear him. "I thought that you're equipped with more brains than you're showing. I don't expect you to love me, but look around you, McCord, and stop imagining me as your enemy. I'm not your Meissner!" The hard-hitting, tough Lieutenant Colonel Dusty Rhoades, whispered.

"Look," Mac said. "She's a waitress at the Manila International Club with Alberto. I don't know where they live. The club will know," Mac said and stood up to leave. He had a bitter taste in his mouth when he left the office. Seeing Miller and Rhoades reminded him once more how he mistrusted them. He regretted acquiescing to Rhoades's request. "That was stupid on my part," he told himself as he hailed a taxicab to take him to the Army/Navy Club off Dewey Boulevard for some fresh air from Manila Bay, some swimming, and a chance to be by himself to do some thinking.

It was a hot afternoon, but then, according to Mac, it was always hot in Manila. Upon entering the swimming pool room, he found it so surreal that the Army officer who was responsible for him being in the Philippine capital drowned in the same pool that he was about to jump into. Fate is unquestionably mysterious, he thought. Reluctantly, he walked closer to the oversized pool and wondered where exactly in the water Walters drowned. He had an odd feeling about being there at all. But, despite his reluctance, he jumped in, swam a couple of laps, and got out. He pulled a lounge chair towards him and sat down. Soon, Mac was enjoying himself while the breeze from the Manila Bay reminded him that, if it were not for its pleasant and invaluable gift, everyone might die from the heat of the Philippine sun.

With his eyes closed, Mac feigned sleep, but his mind was busily wondering again about Charlie's puzzling outburst at the office. He had never seen him act with such uncontrollable anger. Charlie acted as if he loathed Mac telling everyone in the room that Meissner was the killer.

And then there was Rhoades. He sounded like he was trying to protect Mac from someone. With those thoughts, Mac fell into a deep sleep.

CHAPTER 18

The entire time Mac was at the Army/Navy Club, he was chiding himself for telling Rhoades where Lina and Alberto worked. He wished that he used his better judgment. At the same time, he had a strong urge to inquire around the club whether there had been someone there who may have witnessed Walters's drowning at the club's pool four months earlier. Before leaving the health facility, he approached several people there and asked whether they knew Lieutenant Colonel Walters or if any of them saw him drown. All answers to both his questions were negative.

Meanwhile, after he had left the military club, his intuition kept reminding him to get hold of either Alberto or Lina. That was when he made a point to pass by the Manila International Club for a quick supper. It was crowded that evening, and Lina and Alberto were unusually busy. But by luck, the hostess led Mac to Alberto's table. During a hasty conversation, Mac casually asked the young waiter whether his grandfather had ever discussed with him a certain murder at the former Sergio's Bar and Grill. Alberto nodded and said that his grandfather did and had pointed out the guilty American at the Buenavista party. Alberto's description of the murderer echoed that of what Roosie had told Mac, as well as Lina's description of Gibbs's killer. Without any doubt, they were both describing Leon Barclay. After he had talked to Alberto, Mac became convinced that both newly-weds knew too much about Barclay. Why in the hell didn't it occur to him that Roosie would eventually tell his only grandson of his secret? Mac questioned himself. He quickly advised the young man that he and his wife not let strangers in their house, and if a suspicious man knocks at their door to not let him in and immediately call Mac at the BOQ. Mac gave Alberto his telephone number.

Mac allowed two days to pass, and then he called Alberto at the club and inquired if he had encountered any problems. His answer was cheerful, and he said that he and Lina were about the happiest two people on earth and for Mac to stop worrying about them. Despite the cheerfulness, Mac was fearful that the newly-weds were unaware of the danger they were in. He was so perturbed that he called Chavez at his home that same evening and discussed with him in detail the reasons why Alberto and Lina were in danger.

Chavez, after listening carefully, assured Mac that the Panganibans would be all right. "Do not worry. But if it will make you feel better, I will send an agent to see that they get home safely from work for at least a week."

Mac had a difficult time sleeping that night. And when finally he did fall asleep, he had nightmares.

The telephone on the night table awoke him. He awkwardly reached out and picked up the receiver. "Hello. Who's this?" Mac asked, wiping his face and chest with his pajama top. He had been sweating profusely during his sleep.

"This is Chavez."

"Chavez? Where are you? Jeez. I thought that I was still having nightmares," Mac said. He was now sitting on the edge of his bed. "Is something wrong?"

"Yes. Lina has been murdered and Alberto is dying outside of his house. He must have ran after the killer, caught up with him, and had a fight before he was stabbed. He is not going to last much longer." Chavez paused. "The police and I are at their home doing some investigations. I know how fond you were of them, but you need not come here. I just wanted you to know about it from me and not the newspapers."

"Oh," was all Mac could say. His stomach twisted inside. He wanted to cry. He was profoundly saddened.

As he sat there listening to Chavez on the telephone, tears rolled down his face for Alberto and Lina. "Mac, are you all right?" Chavez asked.

"Yes. Are you sure you don't want me to join you, Chavez?" Mac finally answered, trying to keep his voice from quivering.

"Yes. The place is crawling with cops. Where can I meet you later?"

Chavez inquired.

"I generally have an early breakfast at the Manila Café." Mac answered. "But today I'll be there at lunch time."

"Fine. I'll see you there."

The young waitress who most often served Mac, asked, "Lunch, Sir?"

"Just coffee," answered Mac. Meanwhile, the newspaper boy cried out in front of the café, "Extra, Extra! Newly-wed couple murdered on Taft Avenue!"

"Hey, newsboy, over here," Mac said and paid him. He quickly glanced at the front page. "Poor kids," he murmured.

As Mac sat there trying to figure out who took his young friends's lives, making them two more statistics in Manila, a taxicab stopped in front of the café, and Poco and Charlie rushed to where he sat.

"We thought we would find you here, Major Mac," Poco said. "But is this not late for you?"

In the meantime, Charlie asked Mac if he had seen the front page.

Mac nodded. "I've a copy." He paused. "More murders."

Charlie glanced at Mac and theorized that perhaps Lina and Alberto knew too much. "That killer is clever. He strikes and disappears."

Mac concurred with Charlie but added that he was glad Lina told him and Poco about some photographs before she died.

"What photographs?" Charlie asked in a surprised tone.

"Tell the good major about those photographs, Poco," Mac said.

The Filipino sergeant related everything Lina had told them during lunch about Leon Barclay being in some of the pictures taken before Gibbs's death.

"Why didn't you tell me about those photographs, Mac?" Charlie inquired with a slight anger in his voice.

"I don't really know, Charlie." Mac replied. "I didn't think you'd be interested."

"Have you stopped trusting me, McCord?" Charlie asked angrily.

Mac did not say a word.

To keep peace between the two friends, Poco added that the whole thing about the photographs were not really that important. Charlie, eventually, shrugged his shoulders and told Mac to forget it. "I'd say this, however: Manila is getting to be a hell hole. I'm just glad that my wife and children are back in the States."

True to his words, Chavez took time to meet Mac at the Café, which surprised Poco and Charlie.

"What's Chavez doing here?" Charlie asked, glancing at Mac.

"He called me very early this morning, and I told him I'd meet him here. He was at the Panganiban's house doing some investigation," Mac explained.

"Found any clues, Chavez?" Charlie inquired with interest as soon as Chavez got comfortable and had ordered a cup of coffee.

Chavez pursed his lips and shook his head. "No. It is another one of those mysterious and heinous crimes."

"How did they die?" Mac inquired.

"Killed by a dagger, decapitated, and completely finger-less," Chavez answered and added almost in a whisper, "Mac, Lina was raped before she was killed." He pressed his eyes with his fingers. "I received a call about 4:00 a.m. According to the police they were murdered somewhere around 2:00 a.m. this morning." As an afterthought, he said, "One of their neighbors called the police and reported that he became alarmed when he heard screaming coming from Panganiban's house."

Chavez looked at his watch and drained his last drop of coffee. He got up and told them that he had to leave.

They followed Chavez as he walked to his car, and Charlie asked the PIB agent if he found any fingerprints on the dagger. He explained that although no fingerprints were found, the dagger that was used to kill the Panganiban's was similar to the daggers found on Roosie and on Czestochowa. "If it is the same killer, he is causing the bureau an awful lot of headaches and embarrassments."

"I know that you're tired, but let me quickly throw at you an idea before you leave," Mac said, his steel-blue eyes dug deep into Chavez's.

"Go ahead, if it is not too long," Chavez answered, showing signs of fatigue.

"For background," began Mac, "Roosie told me last June that he had witnessed Stein's murder at the old Sergio's Bar and Grill. He told me then that he would only recognize Stein's killer if he saw him wearing that belt with the gold buckle which you recently found. He must have recognized Stein's murderer at the Buenavista party. And when Poco and

I met Lina and Alberto during lunch a week or so ago, she told us that she knew the name of the male visitor with whom Gibbs left the house that morning, and that she could describe his appearance."

Chavez was suddenly alert. His eyes were fixated on Mac's face. The PIB agent took a deep breath and asked Mac casually, "What did Lina say his name was?"

"Leon Barclay. Alberto also told us the man has blond hair." Mac explained that Lina's description of Barclay was in-depth, also recalling the blond hair.

Poco asked Chavez. "But why was Alberto killed also?"

Charlie joined the conversation and answered for Chavez. "Alberto knew the killer. Perhaps Roosie, feeling he might get killed, confided in Alberto that night at the party. I'm guessing, of course. Like I have said before, he must be a very clever guy. I think this Barclay killed Roosie, Czestochowa, Lina, and Alberto. Same killer. Same style, same weapon. Barclay is probably one of Meissner's aliases. Isn't that right Mac?" He paused. "Meissner disguised as Barclay."

Mac said, "Yes. Barclay, I believe, is one of Meissner's aliases. And yes, I believe that Barclay is one of Meissner's disguises. But then again, Meissner may have changed his disguise from that of Barclay to another disguise."

"I see," Chavez murmured. "I feel like I know Meissner—first from Walters, then Mac, and now from Charlie. Walters never doubted Meissner's presence in Manila. Meanwhile, though, the PIB has assiduously checked around and encountered a blank wall. The PIB is hemorrhaging from constant public doubt and criticism for its seeming lack of inaction in catching this serial murderer, spy, and saboteur." Chavez paused. "He is so evil that if I were to draw blood on any part of his body, ninety-nine little devils would come out."

"Yes, he is that evil," Poco added.

"Other than having blond hair, does anybody have any idea what Barclay looks like, disguise and all? Do you, Charlie?" Chavez asked.

"Nope! But he sounds so meticulously clever, it'll probably take PIB covert agents and human intelligence, combined with good detective work to flush the son of a bitch out of hiding," Charlie declared and added, "All these killings are probably spy-related, with the exception of the newly-weds, all the others knew their killer was a spy for the Japs."

Chavez announced again that he had to go. "I have to go back to the office for a meeting with my boss." He thanked them for the information they had given him about Barclay. He neared his car but turned around and shouted to Mac, "Could you come over here, I forgot to ask you something else about Barclay." When Mac reached his side, Chavez quietly told him, "I want you to come to my office by yourself as soon as you can. Be discreet. Do not tell them, especially Charlie." He paused. "I don't trust him."

After he joined Poco and Charlie again, both men asked Mac what Chavez wanted to know more about Barclay. "Not much. Just that he's pretty sure Barclay killed Lina and Alberto. Chavez had a good point. After all, why not? He killed Gibbs." Mac paused momentarily and glanced at his watch. He told them that he had an errand to do and had promised to see Miguela.

As soon as Mac entered the office, Chavez pulled out the belt and buckle from the safe and said, "A big man owns this belt." He then gave it to Mac for him to show it to Charlie, Poco, and anyone else who might be interested. "Relate the belt and buckle's history." It was agreed that they would both spread the news around; meanwhile, they just had to wait and see who would come and claim it. Before Mac left, Chavez inquired how Mac was coming along, tracking down Sonny Sollow.

"With great difficulty," Mac answered and began to explain that several weeks ago at the Manila International Club, he and Poco saw Sollow talking to Alberto. "My gut tells me that Sollow killed those two young people. I realize I told you, Charlie, and Poco that Barclay killed them. But you see, Barclay and Sollow are one and the same man: Meissner. Gut feelings do not count, Mac. Only tangible evidence. And that is one more reason why you and I should continue our vigilance on Sollow." Chavez paused. "I prefer for us to watch Sollow because at least we know what his disguise looks like. I think we do, but all we know about Barclay is that he is blond. So what! Many American's and Europeans in the Philippines are blonds. The three people who actually saw Barclay are dead. And no telling who it was who killed Roosie. From what you have told me about Sollow, his role seems different from that of Barclay's, even if they are Meissner's disguises. Barclay appears only to kill. Of course, I am only guessing. He may be active as a saboteur and as a spy. While Sollow, we think, maybe spying for the Japanese. He is probably also a killer and a saboteur." Chavez smiled. "Anyway, end of my preaching."

A couple of weeks had passed. One evening, while Mac, Poco, and Charlie were having supper at Charlie's favorite restaurant just outside the military center, Mac brought up his idea about their current style of investigating, that of leading them to another perpetual fool's errands. "I've been on this mode since June, while you guys have been in it longer. We can't catch a shadow," Mac continued. "One of us will have to become that elusive creature." He explained to them his plan of approach. He was to assume a new name and detailed what his disguise would be. "And I don't think it would be wise for us to be seen together in public."

Charlie was pleased with the plan and declared that they use code names on the telephone when addressing each other. "You, Mac, will be UG-1. UG for underground. I'll be UG-2, and Poco will be UG-3."

Mac was to reside at Kapalaran while Charlie and Poco were to continue to make their presence known at Quest. But no reports, they agreed, would be submitted about their underground covert activity. And the rented house at K Strip would be his clandestine residence and their meeting place.

Big Redd and Ruby, Charlie explained, owned a two-story house that was furnished and unoccupied, and, he was certain, they would only be too happy for them to rent it.

Charlie went to the telephone and talked to Big Redd. When he came back to the table he told Mac the house was ready for occupancy, and they could stay there until the end of December, for a minimal fee. "There's a permanent renter come January." He paused. "I told Big Redd we'll pay in advance. The three of us will split the expense, so the Army won't get suspicious of a big expense on our reports."

Mac inquired where the house was located. Charlie exploded in laughter. "In the midst of Sodom and Gomorrah. It's between Fat Mama's Hibiscus, and Uncle Billy's Girls. Across the street is the Periscope Club where pansies and the sinful frequent."

"The whole strip is beyond bad," interjected Poco.

The following night, in a designated remote area in the town of

Paranaque, south of Manila, there was a loud explosion. Flames from a burning car were leaping to the sky with no one able to get close to the vehicle. The town's police and the local newspaper, along with a large crowd witnessed the disaster.

"Do not get close to that flame," the policeman warned the crowd. "There could be another explosion. And do not try to save anyone inside that car. It is impossible."

A young man foolishly picked up dogtags and a man's wallet lying about twenty feet from the now melting car. He promptly gave them to the policeman and told him and a member of the town's daily paper where he had found the items. Not far away, an elderly woman asked the man standing next to her, "Is there someone trapped in that car?"

"Yes. He must have been a drunk American soldier or sailor," answered the man.

On a dirt road nearby behind tall bamboo trees, a car was standing still with its headlights turned off and its motor running. The driver was waiting nervously while his eyes pierced the darkness. After a while he heard footsteps, and when the silhouettes of two men became clear and he was certain who they were, he made a move. "Psst. Major Mac. Major North. I am over here. Hurry!"

Mac and Charlie jumped into the car. "Step on it, Poco. Let's get the hell out of here," Mac urged. He was out of breath.

No one uttered a word until they were out of Paranaque and heading towards Kapalaran in Sampaloc to drop Mac off at his new residence on Horseshoe and Ace Streets.

Mac turned to Poco. "Where did you find that old beat-up Ford?"

Poco explained that his brother was in the car wrecking business, pressing the pedal of his Chevrolet. "He also sells second-hand Chevrolets."

"How about finding me a second-hand Chevy, Poco," Mac asked, keeping his eyes on the road.

"I do not know, Major Mac. Those kind of cars get bought quickly," Poco answered, "but I will let you know."

Mac turned to Poco. "As soon as you get home, telephone Chavez that you want to see him and explain our plan."

"What the hell, Mac. We're supposed to keep this just among the three of us," Charlie said.

"Chavez is okay, Charlie." Mac paused momentarily. "Poco did you hear what I said?"

"Yes. I heard you. Chavez is a good man to keep as a friend. I will also tell him that you will contact him. How about Miss Molina?"

"Tell her that I'll give her a call." About eight o'clock the following night, Mac called Miguela. "Hello. Do you know who this is?"

"Yes…"

Mac interrupted her. "I don't want you to say anything other than yes or no, just in case someone is wire-tapping the telephone. Understood?"

"Yes."

Mac inquired whether his Filipino friend came to see her and if he explained the whole situation to her.

"Yes, this afternoon. He said that you would contact me."

Mac told Miguela to listen to him carefully and to keep to herself what was discussed between them. "It'll be about a week before I can see you. Take good care of yourself."

"Are you all right?" Miguela asked.

"Yes. I love you," Mac answered and hung up.

Mac was now deeply tanned like most Americans who have lived in Manila for some time, and his hair was longer, no more crew cut style. He added a pair of wire-rimmed non-prescribed eyeglasses to his new nighttime look. During the day, he wore dark sunglasses. To complete the disguise, he grew a moustache and dyed it dark brown to match his dark brown wig.

He had earlier acquired a map of Kapalaran from a newsstand in Manila, and for the next day or so he studied it, read books and magazines about the Philippines, and listened to the radio about Major Jacob Victor McCord's tragic "death in a burning car." He ventured out of the house only to eat. At night, he would sit by the second floor window that overlooked the main road of the strip, Longshot Street. From that window, he had a clear view of the Periscope Club, Uncle Billy's Girls Club, and Fat Mama's Hibiscus.

On the third day, Mac walked around the blocks to get himself acquainted with the streets and the area. On the night of his fourth day, he walked to El Oro gambling casino, which was about a quarter-mile from his house, and sat at the bar quietly drinking his beer and listening to nearby conversations. But not finding any leads there, Mac soon left and went to another gambling casino, a block from El Oro.

A uniformed doorman politely greeted him at the entrance door. "Good evening, Sir. Welcome to Lara's."

Inside, Mac could hear revolving sounds of roulette daises. Nearby, he observed six men playing blackjack in deep concentration. He sauntered to a table close to the bar and sat down, where he was immediately attended by an attractive Filipina waitress. "What will it be, Sir?" she asked, looking him over.

"Ham and cheese sandwich and a beer," Mac said, realizing he was hungry.

When the waitress came back she placed the sandwich and beer on the table and gave Mac a good scrutiny. "You look like you could stand a friend. Are you married?"

Mac shook his head. "What's your name?"

"Teresita."

Mac invited the waitress to sit down. "I cannot. Against club regulation." Teresita paused momentarily. "You work here in K Strip?"

"No. Downtown Manila." Mac answered.

"Say, there was a terrible dual murder on Taft Avenue, near Pasay, not too long ago, young married couple. I saw it in the newspaper," Teresita said.

"Yeah," Mac said, taking a swallow of his beer. "I also read about it. Know anything about it?"

Teresita shook her head. "But Anna might know."

"Who's Anna?"

"She owns the Coconut Tree Cocktail Lounge. It is very popular with the Filipinos and a stop over for karetelas, taxicabs, and jeepneys going to Kapalaran and out of Kapalaran. We hear all kinds of rumors here," the waitress added smiling. "Any more beer?"

"No." Mac paid the bill and left Lara's. On the way out, he glanced at his watch. It was midnight, and he was exhausted.

The following night, about 8:00 p.m., Mac strolled out of his house and stopped a karetela and told the driver that he would hire him for six hours. "From now until 2:00 a.m., how much will you charge me?"

"Are you an American?"

"Yes, I am."

The driver straightened his back and thought a while. "Okay, twenty pesos, plus my supper tonight." He paused. "Get in. My name is Salvador, but you can call me Badong. Where do you want to go?"

"Coconut Tree Cocktail Lounge."

"You want to go there? Only Filipinos go there. You like Filipinos?" Badong asked.

"Yes."

"Good!" Badong was pleased. "I like that place also. It has cockfights and betting. And you will like Anna."

"Say, Badong. Since you and I will be together for several hours we might as well be on first name basis. Call me Mac."

Badong turned the horse carriage around towards the entrance of Kapalaran, in the direction of Manila.

"Do you know Anna, Badong?" Mac asked.

"Everybody knows Anna," Badong answered, now and then encouraging the horse with the soft tip end of the whip to run a little faster, and announced to Mac that they would be at the lounge in about ten minutes.

The smoke-filled room was crowded and very noisy. The walls were lined with signed photographs of Filipino movie stars such as Leopoldo Salcedo, Rogellio de la Rosa, Fred Cortez, and others. Mac stood by the bar, and Badong, before disappearing in the back, told him that behind the closed door was an arena where cockfights went on.

A young and pretty Filipina in a tight dress soon approached Mac. "Are you interested?"

Mac shook his head and went to the bar and ordered beer. The Filipino bartender gave him a belligerent and suspicious stare. "Say, Joe. I have not seen you here before."

Mac stared back. "So what! Are you going to serve me beer or not?"

The bartender reluctantly served Mac his beer. "That is what is wrong with you white foreigners, you bully everybody."

The same woman who propositioned Mac earlier followed him to the bar. "What is a handsome Americano doing in a Filipino night club? Are you looking for a sleeping partner?"

"No." Mac turned away and sat on the other end of the bar and lighted a Chesterfield. Soon, he and a Chinese-Filipino sitting on the next bar stool, struck a conversation. "Do not mind the bartender. He is really a friendly guy. He just thinks all American men in Manila are troublemakers and after their women." He paused. "My name is Loo. What is your name?"

"Mac. Short for MacTaggart. Victor MacTaggart."

Loo asked Mac if he was in the US Army and if he lived in Kapalaran. Mac answered that he was a civilian and that he had just moved to Kapalaran.

"How about you, Loo?"

The Chinese-Filipino took a swallow of his beer. "Now in Manila. I used to live in Corregidor, at the barrio of San Jose. I was a cashier in a little shop for three years. About a couple of years ago I got a better job at the Army and Navy Club on Dewey Boulevard."

Mac became interested in what Loo had just told him. "Did you know a Lieutenant Colonel Walters?" I understand he was found drowned at the swimming pool there."

Loo closed his eyes in order to prod his memory. "Oh, yes," he finally answered. "I do remember him. They said he had a heart attack and drowned. Funny thing he came to the club at least two or three times a week for his exercise. Strong swimmer."

Mac asked Loo if Walters was by himself the day he drowned, but their conversation was interrupted by a female voice with a pleasant Filipino accent. "Loo, is this Americano bothering you?" She inquired, feigning deep concern.

"Why, hello, Anna," Loo greeted. "Mac, I would like for you to meet the owner of this club. Anna, this is Mac."

"How do you do, Mac?" Anna gave him a long but friendly look. "New to the club?"

"Yes. My first time."

Anna explained that she could not help hear Mac ask Loo about Bill Walters. Proudly, she related to Mac of her friendship with Walters and his wife. He had made it known to her that he was sending his family back to the States because of frequent political and ideological differences between Japan and the United States that could lead into a dangerous eruption between the two countries. Anna was silent as a look of suspicion slowly crept on her face. She asked Mac why he was asking about Walters.

Mac shrugged his shoulders. "Just curious. Been hearing ugly rumors about how he died," he answered casually.

"If you are a detective, a policeman, or a secret agent of the government snooping around for information, you will not find it here." Anna's voice was terse and belligerent. "They are nothing but trouble!"

"I'm neither, but I'm interested."

Anna kept her eyes on Mac for a long time and then she finally said softly, "Let us move to that corner table and have a friendly visit."

Having settled in a quiet corner of the club, Anna inquired what Mac wanted to know about Walters's death.

"Whatever. If you want to talk about it." Mac tried to maintain his casualness.

The fifty-year-old Anna took a deep breath. She told Mac point blank that she generally did not talk to anyone about anyone, especially to white strangers. "I have found it always spells trouble. But, I seem to feel that you really like Filipinos, and for some strange reason, I like you. So I will tell you what I know. Bill was murdered!"

The unequivocal information startled Mac. "Really?"

Anna nodded. "Really. I want you to know I like Americans. Most Filipinos do. Americans have done so much for the advancement of this island nation, in education, health, and freedom of speech. Most Americans respect Filipinos." She paused and sighed deeply. "That is why," she continued, "I felt very sorry when Haggarty, Summers, and Captain Stein all met their terrible fates."

"You knew them also?" Mac was surprised.

Anna nodded and related that Bill Walters used to frequent her club on Saturday nights when fried fish and boiled all-you-can-eat shrimp were served. Mac lighted a Chesterfield cigarette. "Do you know who murdered Bill and the other three officers?"

"Bill Walters only."

"Can you tell me who?"

Anna glanced at Mac and narrowed her eyes. She was not certain if it was wise for her to discuss Walters's murder. But her woman's intuition told her that she and Mac could easily be friends. "First let me tell you something to remember. Once I have given you the information I wish for you to honor the source. While Anna was talking, a man at a nearby table left the club with a slight nod from her.

"I think you were about to tell me the name of the person who murdered Bill Walters."

"I was. I have to think about it."

The telephone rang a Filipino waiter motioned to Anna that the call was for her. Anna excused herself.

Mac pushed back his chair. "Still having your special Saturday nights?"

Anna smiled and with great pride explained to Mac that it had been the club's tradition started by her father twenty years ago. "He was a commercial fisherman fishing Lingayen Gulf and the South China Sea. Come by any Saturday. You will enjoy it."

"Well, Anna," said Mac, "before I go. Have there been other Americans who've come here aside from myself and our dead friends?"

To her recollection there was an American by the name of Sonny Sollow. Now and then, she said, he dined there on Saturday nights. She paused and told Mac what was in her mind, that it would be better if he did not mention to anyone he talked to her about Walters or that he, Mac, even knew her. "It could be dangerous." She paused again. "Visit the Periscope Club. It is popular with both men and women. Go there and listen. Some of them might know something regarding the other three officers. Talk to the bartender. He hears many things, and the customers like to confide in him." There was a pleasant grin on her face. "He is not what he appears to be. I know his wife." Anna turned around and disappeared behind a closed door marked Private.

CHAPTER 19

Mac learned from previous intelligence reports that Meissner has an obsession for women and to couple that with Anna's advice that he should go to The Periscope Club because of its popularity with women, prompted Mac to visit the club.

It would be a gamble, he told himself. And again, he might just be lucky and catch the German spy in person. "Of course, it's easier said than done, but the consequence could be to my favor," he murmured. His thought process continued that, should his luck fail him, someone in the club might know something that could lead him to the elusive spy. With that up-beat reasoning, Mac was determined to make the Periscope his next stop.

Mac found the karetela driver, Badong, in the cockpit arena and asked to be taken to the Periscope Club. Badong was taken aback by Mac's request. "Do you know who goes there, Mac? Many bad men, rich and glamorous women, and whores."

"Just take me there. I've a good reason," Mac insisted as they were driving away from the lounge. And, upon reaching the club he paid Badong his twenty pesos plus two pesos extra for his supper until he had located the bar where he pulled up a barstool and sat down. Mac observed that some men there were hugging, kissing, and flirting with some women, and one or two couples were in lascivious positions, while others were merely standing around enjoying their drinks and music. The bartender, wearing a shoulder length blond wig, dangling gold earrings, a tight-fitting red dress with well-defined falsies, was not difficult to find. He was the bartender Anna had mentioned to Mac.

On another area of the club, a glamorous Eurasian woman with long straight black hair and dressed in white-sequined, tight, long gown approached the microphone on the dance floor and announced that the song she was about to sing would be her last for that night.

"Dance time, friends," she said with a slight French accent, "Until tomorrow night." And in a low, sexy, and provocative rendition, sang "Besame Mucho."

The large dance floor was immediately filled with men and women dancing to the melodious music from the all-Filipino band and the exotic singing. At the bar, the bartender with the blond wig asked Mac in a friendly baritone voice, "What'll it be, handsome?"

"San Miguel beer." Mac answered.

With the efficiency of an experienced bartender, the friendly man came back quickly and gently placed the glass of beer in front of his customer. "I'm Johnson. What's your name?"

"Vic MacTaggart. Call me, Mac." He noticed that the bartender spoke with a lisp.

"Mac, what'd you think of Ginger, our singer?"

"Good voice. Beautiful woman."

"Yes. Gorgeous," added Johnson.

"How'd you like the band?"

"Excellent," answered Mac. "Why all the commotion over in that corner, Johnson?"

"They're getting ready for the revue," lisped the bartender. "You'll love the 'girls.'"

Johnson paused and smiled. "They're men. Our women customers love the show."

The stage was set, and the lights were dimmed but simultaneously four bright stage lights came on. The drums began the low beat. It was exactly 11:00 p.m. Two blonds dressed in gorgeous female costumes came out from behind the silver silk curtains and walked provocatively around the stage to the music of "Night and Day." Then, two performers, both redheads, joined the two blonds on the stage. As the "girls" walked gracefully around, they dropped to the floor pieces from their elaborate costumes, exposing little by little to the rambunctious audience their well-muscled male bodies until they had nothing left except G-strings. The female audience clapped and shouted delightfully, "More off! More off!" Other acts, just as people-pleasing, followed the first performance.

Mac, meanwhile, had been keeping his eyes on the entrance door and observed several latecomers to the revue. One late customer especially caught his attention, not because, upon entering the club, the man immediately stumbled into the vacant table by the door and fell to the floor but because he was very small, a dwarf. Mac rushed to help him, but the dwarf jumped up with agility and quickness and disappeared in the crowded room. When Mac was leaving the entrance area to return to the bar, he noticed a small white-covered date book on the floor. He picked it up and examined it for a second and quickly dropped it into his pocket. Now back at the bar, he turned to the bartender. "Johnson, I'll be back in a couple of minutes, but fill up my glass again." In the men's room, he turned the date book from page to page, and to his astonishment, the fourth page contained words he had heard or seen before—"Birds over a mountain." He kept on turning the pages and found some cryptic writings which, he told himself, he would later study in the privacy of his house.

"Say, Johnson, did you see that dwarf enter the club?"

"Sure, I did, Mac. I make it a point to disappear whenever he shows up here. I don't like that son of a bitch," answered the well-built Johnson, who could well stand for the club's bouncer. His lisp was very pronounced at that moment.

"Why?"

"He's a nasty motherfucker. He told me once in front of my customers that I couldn't have an erection if two nude women made love to me at the same time. The asshole! I could've clipped him then. But I kept my temper. I didn't want to go to the slammer."

"Why should that rile you?" Mac was amused. He could hardly keep from laughing.

"Hey. When someone questions my masculinity just because of this stupid red dress, I get pissed off. I get good tips here." Johnson paused. "That dwarf was really talking about my penis! If it hangs right! You bet it does! And it isn't short either!" He got close to Mac and whispered, "My wife loves it!"

"What's the dwarf's name?" Mac asked.

"Dwarf!" Johnson paused momentarily and looked around to see if anyone was near them. He lowered his voice. "Mac. About Dwarf. If I were a secret service man I'd arrest that guy just for being a suspicious character and have him interrogated for allegedly spying for the Japs."

Mac did not say a word but found Johnson's statement interesting and might mention the possibility to Chavez.

Johnson continued, still in a low voice. "He and another of my customers, Mr. Sollow, are good friends."

"Sollow?"

"Yes. Sonny Sollow."

Mac casually asked Johnson if he knew Sollow well. Johnson frowned and answered that he really did not know Sollow that well. "But he's a heavy tipper. And tells a good story about Hitler and the war in Europe." Johnson continued to tell Mac that Sollow seemed to know a good bit about the deficiency of the Philippine military system. "According to Sollow, the Philippines is ripe for a take-over by Japan. He thinks MacArthur is too late in trying to spruce up the military."

"Sollow tells you all of those things?" Mac asked.

"Why not? Freedom of speech. Half the time I don't listen to him, though."

Johnson paused. He moved closer to Mac. "You know what, Mac, there are times when I think that Sollow is an officer in the US Army here in Manila, and many times, I can almost swear that he's a spy for the Japs. Now and then, I see him here with a Jap or two. Real friendly like. To be honest with you, I don't really like Sollow. He strikes me as weird. There're times when I'm almost afraid of him."

A look of interest appeared on Mac's face. "What makes you say that he's in the US Army and a spy for the Japs, Johnson?"

"Just the way he talks and carries himself. But, hey, I've no reason to prove it." Johnson apologized to Mac that what he just said was due to his vivid imagination. "I enjoy reading murder and spy stories," Johnson confessed to Mac that he liked to listen to Sollow's deep, fluid voice, without any speech impediments like he had.

"Sollow stammers badly," Mac said.

"Listen, I know my cutomers! Maybe he's faking it with you, Mac. I know something else that you don't know. Sollow likes to sleep with very young girls." Johnson smiled. "Me, I prefer mature women. Not that I sleep around. My wife takes good care of me."

"Where'd you think Sollow gets his money to be such a big tipper?" Mac asked.

"He told me once he was in some kind of big business." Johnson suddenly stopped talking. "Speaking of the devil. Sollow just walked in."

Mac turned around and saw Sollow kissing the young Filipina girl with him. "Does he come here often, Johnson?"

"Yes. I heard him once tell one of my customers at the bar that he either has a permanent suite at the Far East Hotel, or it belongs to a friend of his. I'm not quite certain. The conversation drifted off."

"The hotel next door?" Mac asked.

Johnson nodded.

"Interesting," Mac said. Before paying for his two drinks and leaving a tip, he asked Johnson if he knew of a man by the name of Meissner. Johnson's answer was negative, and with that, Mac left the bar and walked around the Periscope Club, wondering how Dwarf could have disappeared so quickly. He knew deep down it was useless at the time to look for Dwarf but, nevertheless, he walked the entire length of the club and wandered into a long narrow alley shared with the Far East Hotel. Mac pushed one of the back doors and found himself in the hotel's dimly-lit bar, grabbed a barstool and this time ordered a Johnny Walker Red Label with water.

The Filipino bartender was soon back. "Your drink, Sir."

"Say, does someone called Dwarf comes here?" Mac inquired of the bartender.

The bartender was slow in answering. In the meantime, a customer elbowed his way to the crowded counter, giving Mac a push with his right hand just as Mac was about to take a sip of his drink. The glass fell to the floor. Mac turned around and was startled to see it was Sonny Sollow who had pushed him. He felt a sudden surge of anger. He hated his guts the first time Miguela introduced them at the Manila International Club.

"Clumsy fool," snapped Sollow derisively, and Mac quickly grabbed him by his shoulder and dug his strong fingers into his skin until Sollow winced in pain. "You'll pa...pay for this," he hissed in Mac's ear and turned to the bartender. "Have you...you seen Dwarf?"

"He is sitting at the corner table, Mr. Sollow," the Filipino bartender answered and, after Sollow had left, he turned to Mac. "Does that answer your previous question, Sir?"

Mac nodded. "Know Sollow well?"

"Sort of," answered the bartender. "Sollow is here often with Dwarf. But now and then Dwarf comes here with a blond American named Barclay. I do not know him at all. He does not say much." The bartender paused. "I think Sollow has a room in the hotel, or a friend of his has a room at this hotel."

While Mac was telling the bartender that he had heard from someone else that Sollow may have had a suite at the Far East Hotel, he changed his sitting position in such a way as to be able to easily watch Sollow and Dwarf. But the next time he glanced in their direction, they were gone. "Dammit," he murmured, paid for his drink, and sauntered to the lobby of the hotel, where he saw Sollow, without Dwarf, take the elevator with the same young Filipina girl he saw with him at the Periscope Club.

Mac approached the desk clerk. "Excuse me. I'm a friend of Mr. Sonny Sollow. I'm to see him. May I have his room number please?"

The clerk sifted through the pages of the registration book in front of him. A blank look appeared on his face. "I am so sorry, Sir, but we do not have a Sonny Sollow as a guest here."

"Excuse me. I must have misunderstood him on the telephone," Mac apologized. He left the hotel lobby and decided to walk home. In a dark and narrow street corner barely illuminated by a nearby streetlight, not too far away from the plush hotel, Mac heard footsteps. He looked around, but there was no one. He took several fast steps, and so did the stalker. Mac concluded then that he was being followed. He quickly turned around to see who was following him, but the stalker quickly hid behind a building. Mac continued to walk, mindful of the danger he could encounter. Suddenly, he felt a strong arm around his neck. Then he heard a voice whisper in his ear, "I understand you've been looking for me. Well, here I am, and I'm going to kill you."

The voice was masculine, but the tone had a strange ring to it, like it had not quite developed. Mac tried to extricate the strong arm that was choking him, and hit the left side of his attacker's eye and face with his fist, again and again. Meanwhile, Mac tried to hit the body of his attacker with his right and left elbows once or twice. But they were empty hits.

There was no solid body behind him. Failing in that effort, Mac grabbed the muscled arm with his two hands and flipped his unknown attacker to the ground.

It clearly surprised Mac to see, through a sliver of light, his opponent. Dwarf had no problem getting to his feet, and the explosive way he hurled himself at Mac's torso caused him to fall backwards to the ground. The hard fall momentarily caused Mac to lie there immobile, at which time Dwarf adroitly jumped on top of an upside-down empty oil barrel and, with full force, feet first, descended on top of Mac. Somehow, Mac's eyes opened just in time to see the hurling body coming down towards him. In a split second he was able to lift both of his hands and feet, cushioning Dwarf's fall on him and at the same time enabling him to repulse the strong midget away from him, to the ground. But Dwarf just rolled over and, with an easy sommersault he had learned as an oddity in the circus, landed on his feet, once again attacking Mac, who was still in a horizontal position. Sensing that Dwarf was on the verge of attacking him again, Mac forced himself to get up and went into an offensive mode. He jumped on his attacker, who fell to the ground. Mac picked him up, hauled him over his head, and flung him against the upside down empty oil barrel. Hitting the barrel did not appear to hurt Dwarf, who, with agility, ran between Mac's legs and hit his testicles with such force that it doubled Mac to his knees. Whereupon, Dwarf jumped on Mac's back and tried to choke him once more with his strong arm around Mac's throat. With Dwarf still hanging on him, Mac intentionally fell backward and began to move his head forward and back, again, and again and again, each time pounding Dwarf's body and head against the concrete street. The action went on until Mac felt Dwarf's arm become limp around his neck. Suddenly, Mac realized that Dwarf was on top of him jabbing his face and eyes with his hard, strong fists. Dwarf left Mac unconscious on the corner of the dark street near the Far East Hotel.

Mac's whole body was throbbing with pain, with the left side of his face bleeding and his eye swollen, he wondered if he could get home at all without folding on the ground, unconscious. He remembered vividly how Dwarf's hard fist kept on hitting the left side of his face, while his right arm was like a tight vise around his neck, intending to choke him to death. Weary from his encounter with Dwarf, Mac forced himself to walk to his newly rented house. He felt as if each leg weighed a ton. Each step was difficult. Coughing and trying to clear his throat, he eventually reached his house. Since it was still dark, he hardly could bend to insert the key into the lock of the door to open it. Once inside the house, he first pulled down the bamboo shade, a ritual he had developed when one day a store clerk informed him that one night he saw a suspicious-looking man surveying his rented house. Mac, since then, became mistrustful of the area and came to believe that Kapalaran Strip had a thousand eyes and ears.

He sat down on the edge of his bed, opened the bottle of San Miguel beer, and drank it thirstily, stopping only to catch his breath. Having emptied the bottle, Mac removed his disguise, placed it on his night table, took off his shoes, and laid down on his bed, moaning in aching pain. As soon as his head hit the pillow, he was asleep.

The Phillipine sun that particular morning was stubbornly playing on Mac's immobile face, displaying blinding bright rays streaming shamelessly through the slats of the bamboo shade. At times, the presence of cumulus clouds here and there would change the tone of rushing bright rays, encouraging the hide-and-go seek game—now bright light, now dull light; now dull light; now bright light. That went on, until the mischievous game of the sun and the clouds, accompanied by the loud banging on the front door, eventually awakened Mac from his deep sleep.

Without putting on his shoes, he scampered down the long stairs and asked before he opened the door, "Who is it?"

"It is Poco, Major Mac."

"Come in." Mac looked at the Filipino sergeant, bewildered. "I wasn't expecting you. Have you been outside a long time?"

The sergeant answered that he had been standing outside for twenty minutes. "I thought that something might have happened to you, Major Mac." He hastened to add that it was Major North who insisted on meeting him at Mac's place. "Major North was to meet me here a little earlier. He told me it would be better for both of us to come unannounced. He was afraid your telephone might be wire-tapped." Both men simultaneously turned around when they heard a gentle knock on the door.

"Is that you, Charlie?" Mac asked loudly.

A deep voice answered, "No other."

Mac invited Charlie to come in. Once inside, Charlie observed that Mac appeared disheveled and noticed his black eye and swollen face. Unlike Poco, who preferred not to notice Mac's appearance, Charlie wondered aloud if Mac was in some sort of accident. "What happened, Mac?" Charlie inquired.

"I'll tell you both later," answered Mac and gave his two friends a quizzical look. "I wasn't expecting either of you. Both of you must have darn good reasons for being here this early in the morning."

"We certainly have good reasons, Major Mac. First, the good news." Poco began to explain that he was leaving for Northern Luzon for three weeks as of tomorrow. The reason for the assignment was that Rhoades wanted for him to help in the investigation of arms smuggling from an Army unit in a small town near Aparri. At a short briefing session, Rhoades imparted to him that the US Army Command had called him, requesting a Filipino Scout with experience in intelligence and who was fluent in both English and Tagalog. "The second good news. I parked your 1938 second-hand Chevrolet in the back of your house. My brother said that he would sell it to you at cost price. Here is his address and the key to the car; you can pay him later." Poco was pleased with his second message and gave Mac his tight-lipped quick smile.

Mac was surprised but happy to know about the car.

Charlie took a drag from his cigar. "Now, the bad news. Three Jap saboteurs tried to dynamite the POL at Sangley Point in Cavite Province."

Mac was taken aback. "I didn't hear about it! Much damage?"

"The three saboteurs were killed before they could accomplish their plot but, unfortunately, the two American sailors guarding the compound also died."

"When did it happen?"

"Two nights ago." Charlie took a deep breath. "Also, the east end of Corregidor was infiltrated the same time the sabotage in Cavite occurred. I understand two coastal patrols caught the two infiltrators whereupon a bloody fight ensued. One coastal patrol was wounded. He was a friend of mine. He was rushed back to the States yesterday. Mike and I were to be homebound this coming December."

What happened to the infiltrators, Charlie?"

"They both escaped."

"Too bad," Mac murmured.

"Now that we have given you our reasons for being here, what's the excuse for the black eye?" Charlie asked.

Mac wearily told his friends how glad he was to see them and that he had some information that would be of interest to them. "But first, let's all have some coffee, now that we've cleared the air as to why you're here."

Poco jumped up and announced that he would do the brewing. While they were drinking their morning coffee, Mac related how a guy called Dwarf attacked him and left him unconscious.

"What happened to Dwarf?" Charlie asked.

For a moment, Mac thought that Charlie sounded concerned about Dwarf's well being. But he shrugged his shoulders as just his imagination playing tricks on him. Then he heard Charlie asked again, "What happened to Dwarf?"

"He left me unconscious on the street, not far from the Far East Hotel." Mac paused. "Do you know Dwarf, Charlie?"

"I see him around now and then in some bars," Charlie answered.

Mac changed the subject. He was still fatigued and in no mood to go into an open debate with Charlie about Dwarf. He then revealed to both men that during a visit to Chavez some months ago, the subject of espionage in the Philippines came up, and Chavez had asked Mac to help him do some surveillance on Sollow. "Have you ever met, Sollow, Charlie?"

"Haven't had the pleasure. But why did Chavez want your help with Sollow?" Charlie inquired curiously.

"He had long suspected him of spying for the Japanese," Mac answered.

"Those ineffective bureaucrats!" Charlie thundered. "They can't catch a spy or a criminal even if he stood in front of them. I don't know why in the hell they don't do their own homework. I bet they don't have any evidence to even say that Sollow is a spy."

Mac smiled. "I didn't know that you disliked the PIB so much."

Charlie looked a Mac a long time and lighted a cigar and blew out smoke rings. "I do, but there could be serendipity if you do help the PIB with Sollow," he finally said calmly. "Who knows? One thing could lead to another. Sollow might be your ticket to Meissner. You certainly can do much more now in your reincarnated state." He cleared his throat. "Heard of any leads on our dead friends?"

Mac shook his head and reached into his pocket for the small date book he had found. "Take a look at this." Mac paused. "As soon as I decipher all those notations I'll turn Dwarf in to the PIB."

"If you can catch him." Charlie said, smiling. He showed an unusual interest in the date book and began examining it carefully, then he stopped. "Here's a page which says 'Call Barclay.' Where in hell did you get this?" Charlie asked, intrigued.

"Periscope Club. It belonged to Dwarf. It fell out of his pocket." Mac explained.

Charlie quietly inquired if Mac frequented the club. Without looking up from Dwarf's date book, he added that the club "is too wicked a place for a God-fearing man like you to even get near it, much less get inside it." He then continued reading the contents of the little book.

Mac answered that it was his first time there. "Sometimes, though, one gets results from unexpected places, such as that date book."

"Here's a page that looks like a grocery list, some with dates and check marks." Charlie began reading slowly from the page. "NE/T: 11 Jun; A10: 18 Jun; W: 25 Jun: LR: 30 Jul: BOAM: 6 Aug: Tadpole: 13, 20, 27 Aug: LB: 22 Sep; SP: 22 Sep; Tadpole: 4, 11, 18, 25 Oct; BOAM: 8 Nov; LB: 15 Nov; BI: 22 Nov; LM: 30 Nov."

"What do you think of it?" Mac asked.

Charlie answered that it was his guess NE/T stood for Nagoya Emporium, and T for Tanaka, who managed the shop. W could be for Wanabe, the cabdriver's name. "Remember him?" He glanced at both Mac and Poco and continued to give meaning to the letters. LB, 15 Nov, at the bottom of the line, he said, stood for a name. "He gave Mac a quick look. "Could the letter B stand for Barclay?" Charlie hesitated and told both of his companions that he could not even guess what the letter L stood for. "But the rest can be analyzed by anyone if given enough time."

But Mac interjected that if B stood for Barclay, "then 'L' should stand for 'Leon.'" Mac paused momentarily and lauded Charlie on his knowledge regarding the cryptic words on Dwarf's date book. "You seem to know so much about that date book."

"Of course I do!" Charlie cut Mac off, not bothering to hide his irritation. "Hell, I've lived in Manila a long time, and intrigue has become second nature to me."

"Excuse me, Charlie for roughing up your feathers," Mac said sarcastically.

Sensing antagonism rising between the two Army officers, Poco interrupted, "Pardon me, Sir. I think we should stick to the real issue, that of trying to decipher Dwarf's notations."

"You're right, Poco," Mac said and paused momentarily. "Let me take another look at that diary. Yes. This NE/T, 11 Jun has already passed. The dates that have check marks have already occurred. The rest are not checked, starting from LB, Tadpole and SP, all dated 22 Sep, and those following them, in October and November. They have yet to happen. Now, Tadpole...."

"Corregidor," promptly responded Poco.

"Of course!" Mac exclaimed. "Now the two sabotages you just mentioned happened two nights ago at Corregidor and at Sangley Point at Cavite. That was the twenty-second of September. Today is the twenty-fourth of September. So those recent incidents were masterminded by Leon Barclay, and Dwarf chose the infiltrators, who then carried out the orders." Mac added that Barclay and Dwarf were following their plans very closely.

"It appears that way, Mac," said Charlie. "I'm checking 22 September and leaving unchecked Corregidor on 4, 11, 18 and 25 Oct and BOAM on 8 Nov; LB on 15 Nov; BI: 22 Nov and LM: 30 Nov."

As an afterthought, Mac asserted that last night he saw Dwarf and Sonny Sollow together at the Far East Hotel. Later, he said, they disappeared again together. Shortly thereafter, Dwarf attacked him. He further added the bartender at the hotel also told him Dwarf was sometimes seen with Barclay. Mac paused and seriously said, "Barclay and Dwarf. Sonny Sollow and Dwarf. Jeez, guys, don't you both find it too coincidental? I know that I've been sounding on this for sometime, that Leon Barclay and Sollow are one and the same man—Meissner's two different disguises."

"Hell! You've got to be out of your mind, McCord. I know this is Southeast Asia where the leading story everyday is about intrigue and murder. But Barclay and Sollow disguises of Meissner's? I don't think so. Where the hell is Meissner?" Charlie exploded.

"I'm going to stick to my hunch. I could be right," Mac argued.

"Let me have that book again, Mac." Charlie's voice was conciliatory. "Here they are—'BOAM, 6 Aug' and 'BOAM, 8 Nov.' They intrigued me. I bet they're important acronyms."

"They are. Turn to page 4. BOAM. Birds over a mountain. Airplanes in Clark Field"

Hold it right there, Charlie," Mac all at once said. "I've a piece of paper with the same words, BOAM: Birds over a mountain. Poco and I overheard it in a conversation between Sollow and Wanabe, whom I also suspect is a spy for the Japs. We followed them to Ruby Redd's restaurant last June."

Charlie was clearly irritated. "Give me that piece of paper." He studied it and then glanced at Mac. "BOAM sounds like a code name. The rest of the information you've written down looks like Greek to me."

Mac applauded Charlie for having quickly recognized Birds over a mountain was a code name. "Generally, only the FBI, the police and those in intelligence would catch its underlying cover."

"How about adding, a spy, to your list, Mac." Charlie burst into laughter. "Hey, don't give me that suspicious look, McCord. I'm an avid reader of spy novels. By the way, have you been able to decipher what you've written down?"

"Yes. I've turned it all in to Chavez" Mac said.

Charlie gave Mac a long and angry look. "Why the hell did you do that? They're depending on you to do their dirty work." Charlie cleared his throat. "Shit. I might as well join in. Mac, about Sollow. Can I help you and Chavez? I can always get from the PIB a photo on Sonny Sollow so that I, too, can shadow him."

Mac was adamant that Charlie and Poco not do any surveillance on Sollow. "You've enough work to do, Charlie and so does Poco," Mac explained. Turning to the Filipino sergeant, Mac inquired about the condition of Quest. The sergeant disgustedly explained that Miller and Rhoades were seldom at the office but that the secretary, Purita Aquino reported for duty everyday.

Charlie interjected and noted that Miss Aquino was wasting her time because for all intents and purposes, Quest might just as well shut down that there was no one who managed the office since Miller and Rhoades were constantly traveling. In addition, continued Charlie, pointing to Mac, that since he had "died" in a car wreck there was really no one to go after spies and saboteurs except himself and Poco. "We've been unsuccessful before Quest and I don't see how we can be successful now. Furthermore, all that reporting and investigating are useless. We've caught no one and the reports handed in have been, were and are useless. Who reads them? Miller? Rhoades? Hell. They're never around." Charlie paused. "When Walters died, the idea of searching for Meissner and the murderers of those officers died with him."

"They've not died with me," Mac said.

Poco cleared his throat and made it known that since Quest was in the conversation, it reminded him of something he had been wanting to tell Mac and Charlie. It appeared that one early morning, on his way to the building to jot down some information he did not wish to forget his report, he saw a man hurrying out of the Quest building. Since he sensed that it was Colonel Miller, he called out his name but the man kept on his fast pace but slightly tilted his head to the right. He soon disappeared from sight. Poco noted that the individual wore dark sunglasses and wore a white visor cap. "I wondered then how he got in the office if he was not anyone from Quest." Poco paused momentarily. "He was about the same height of Colonel Miller or about your height and build, Major North!"

Mac stared at the Filipino sergeant. "Well, was it Colonel Miller or Major North?"

"I really thought at first it was either Major North or Colonel Miller." Poco narrowed his eyes and corrected himself that perhaps the stranger he saw coming out of Quest building could have been Sonny Sollow, disguised as someone else. "I became suspicious and went inside the building and opened Colonel Rhoades's safe and found that the schematic on Corregidor was gone."

Charlie emphatically voiced his previous concern to Mac and Poco. "I knew then it was dangerous to have the map of Corregidor. I was afraid that it would eventually be stolen."

Charlie gave his watch a quick glance. "We've got to be going."

Mac told them that before they left he had something to show them. "Chavez gave it to me to keep." He went to his closet and came out with the belt and the buckle. "Here it is!"

Charlie was stunned. "Where'd Chavez get that?"

"At Buenavista." Mac expounded that unknown to all of them, Chavez went back to the Molina property to do some investigating of his own on the three murders.

"I'll be damned," said Charlie, trying to keep his equilibrium. "That cobra's face on that buckle certainly look threatening."

Mac agreed.

"As he neared the door to leave, followed by Poco, Charlie turned around and told Mac, "Why don't you sometimes go to Uncle Billy's. There's some really beautiful women at that club. It'll relax you."

"I'll think about it," Mac murmured.

Poco reminded Mac of the redhead woman who bumped into him last June at the Manila International Club. "Do you remember her, Major Mac?"

"Sure I do," Mac answered. "What about her?"

"I was right about her then. She is a waitress at Uncle Billy's and I think she's whoring on the side." Poco said.

"We've got to be going," Charlie repeated.

That coming Saturday night, Mac went back to the Coconut Tree Cocktail Lounge as he had previously planned. Anna, who was happy to see him again, greeted him at the door and jokingly added, "Are you here because of the all-you-can-eat seafood tonight, or did you really wanted to see me again?"

Mac smiled. "Both. I can't resist ladies with soft brown eyes, and I enjoy seafood."

Anna grinned and motioned for Mac to follow her to her office. Seafood and a pitcher of beer was already on a table. "Let us sit down, Mac," she said and gave him a long look. "I do not really think that you came back to eat. You have that intense look in your eyes. You came back to find out the name of Bill Walters's killer." She paused momentarily. "Although I hardly know you, there is something about you that tells me I can trust you. I will tell you what my source had told me—he thought then that the name of the man who killed Walters was Leon Barclay," as she poured beer in his glass.

Mac was silent for a while. When he heard Anna mention the name of Barclay, he was convinced of her veracity. He had to ask her how her source could have known the killer's name.

"He found a business card in the men's room with that name."

"Did your source actually see the act? From what I've heard, Walters drowned accidentally."

Anna looked intensely at Mac. "Bill Walters was murdered! My source is trustworthy! The murderer held Walters's head under water until he died. There were no other swimmers in the pool that afternoon. Just Walters. The killer must have come in later." Anna paused. "My source said that the killer had blond hair, was tall and strong, and had a strange-looking tattoo on the back of his upper-left shoulder." She continued in a whisper, "If you can find the man with such marking, you will find Walters's killer."

Mac's pulse quickened. "Your source must have been at the Army and Navy Club's swimming pool."

Anna unfolded to Mac that her source dispensed towels at the club and kept the pool clean. "He knew Walters and followed him to the pool, and he recalled how pleased Walters was to have the pool to himself. 'Come back in about forty-five minutes,' he told my source, 'I've a gold bracelet I brought back from Baguio for your little daughter. But I forgot it in the car.'" Anna paused. The source, according to Anna, had left but went back to the pool twenty-five minutes later to tell Walters that he had to leave early and that he would get the bracelet from him the following afternoon. As he was leaving, he saw a man with a white visor cap and dark sunglasses get into the pool, knocked Walters unconscious from behind and then held his head under water until he drowned. Fearful that the killer would see him, Anna's informant quickly hid and waited until the killer drove away in his car. The informant got on his bicycle and followed the stranger, only to lose him on the crowded downtown streets.

Mac was quizzical and asked how a man in a bicycle could follow someone in a car.

"Evidently, you have not been in Manila long. The traffic in this city is always snarled up. A turtle can go faster," Anna explained. "And the next thing he saw, from a short distance, was a blond-haired man with a white visor cap and dark sunglasses go inside La Rose Hotel, a second-rate hotel. I asked him if it was the same man at the swimming pool. He said, yes."

"Did your confidant tell anyone at the Army and Navy Club of the incident or go to the police?"

"Neither. I do not think he ever will. He has since quit the club for fear that this Barclay will also kill him. It is a jungle out there, Mac, especially for inquisitive Filipinos. Only the careful survive in Manila."

"Who's your source, Anna? Let me talk to him."

"No, Mac. I promised to keep that a secret. I am now your source!" Anna gave Mac a straight look. "I noticed a slight reaction on your face when I mentioned the tattoo. Do you know of a man with such markings?"

"Not personally. Only from someone I used to know. And it's not a tattoo. It's a birthmark." Mac paused momentarily. "Anna, thank you for your trust. Let me now be honest with you. My real name is Jake McCord and I'm a major in the United States Army. The nick-name is the same, Mac." He began to explain to her, from beginning to end, the reason why he was primarily in Manila, and now in Kapalaran. He exposed his true identity to her, by removing his disguise.

Mac glanced at his watch and pushed back his chair. "It's late, and I've taken enough of your time."

Anna opened her desk drawer and gave Mac the card with the name Leon Barclay printed on it and that he could keep it. Mac then wondered aloud why a careful man like Barclay would have his name printed on a card. "Ego," Anna retorted. "It is a real trap for most criminals." She continued to tell Mac that there was something else she wanted to impart to him. "Be careful of Kapalaran Strip. Be very careful with whom you befriend or ask questions," she said. "For example, there is a very small man, a duwende, Tagalog for dwarf, who is a very dangerous person. Do not fool with him." Her eyes narrowed. "There are rumors in the Strip that he is not only a spy for the Japanese but that he is also a murderer. He is one of those who makes the jungle so very vicious." Anna paused and added that she could tell from the look in Mac's eyes that he, Mac was going to the La Rose Hotel and search for a blond American wearing a white visor cap and dark sunglasses. "Be careful, Mac; you just might find him. I do not wish to see you hurt!"

Mac smiled and thanked Anna for her help and her trust. "I'll keep in touch with you."

CHAPTER 20

Mac did not have to look at his watch as he approached his house. He knew what time it was. He could hear the band at Uncle Billy's playing its regular finale music—"Three o'clock in the morning."

He should have been exhausted and ready for bed, but he was neither. As a matter of fact, he felt strangely exhilarated. The events of the last couple of days, gave him reason enough to be encouraged. For one thing, Dwarf's date book and his definite affiliation with Sollow and Barclay bolstered his optimism. And Anna's revelation about the death of Walters, which furthered his belief that the murder was connected with that of the other Army officers, only intensified his expectation that the unsolved incidents would be solved. At last, he thought, there was a light, though still dim, at the end of the tunnel. Charlie could be right, Mac told himself, that there could be serendipity in helping Chavez find Sollow's true identity.

Once inside his house, Mac pulled down all the bamboo shades and turned on the ceiling fans upstairs and downstairs. Before he sat down, he grabbed the history book Chavez loaned him, the belt and buckle, Dwarf's date book, and any other items that pertained to Sollow and Barclay. He took out Meissner's blue sapphire ring. He laid everything on the dining room table, pulled up a chair and sat down.

Mac first studied the cryptic conversation of Wanabe and Sollow that he and Poco had written down. Placing that to one side, he opened Dwarf's date book and turned it slowly until he came to the page that Charlie had aptly called the "grocery list." In deep thought, Mac walked to the kitchen, slipped off the calendar from the nail on the wall, and took it back to the table. He was aware that certain dates on the list still had to be fulfilled by foreign enemy spies and subversives in October and

November. Mac first studied the month of October and noticed there were no other words listed except the word tadpole, which he already knew was code name for Corregidor. He further noted with exasperation that the word tadpole was followed by similar calendar days in October— four, eleven, eighteen, and twenty-five. All of them fell on a Friday. He sat there puzzled as to why there were four different dates with similar days. His sense was that it was thought out deliberately and that it was a well-intended diversionary tactic in case the plan accidentally fell into the hands of the American Army or the PIB. His gut feeling told him that his analysis was right.

"It would be a bad move to follow Dwarf's military agenda on Corregidor," Mac mumbled to himself.

He studied the whole plan of October again, this time more in-depth, and he came to a definite conclusion that only one day out of the four days should be allotted to reconnoitering the area, and only one night to sabotage all the important military elements at Corregidor. Otherwise, he reasoned, if the four-day plan on the date book for October was to be followed and exercised, obviously every soldier in Corregidor would be hunting or on the lookout for the saboteur. According to Mac, it would be a foolish idea to apply intermittent destruction on the fortress island.

Mac closed his eyes and tried to recall the schematic of Corregidor done by Czestochowa and Golden for Quest. He recalled especially Kindley Field and some armaments on a place called Topside that the two officers accentuated with asterisk on the map. Although everything on the schematic, presented about three months ago, was believed to be accurate, somehow Mac could not convince himself that the two junior Army officers were given all of the information.

"They must have had some sort of surreptitious control from some senior Army officers at Corregidor as to what they could and could not put on paper, as important as that fortress is to the defense of the Philippines," Mac murmured.

His recollection of what was on that map had mostly faded from his memory. Nevertheless, he went ahead and envisioned himself as a spy for the Japanese by following explicitly his earlier thoughts about entering Corregidor and how he could destroy several essential weapons there.

Mac knew that if he were the Japanese spy to destroy Corregidor, he must see the island fortress by himself to be able to establish a credible plan to infiltrate Corregidor in the month of October and reconnoiter the area. Having clandestinely entered General MacArthur's jewel defense fortress, he would mentally take notes of all of the primary locations of the island's formidable weapons, such as coastal guns, anti-aircraft equipment, types of guns like the 155-mm and the 12-inch guns, their range capabilities, and other types of armament, including the indispensable searchlights for use against air attack and enemy landings. He remembered from the schematic that on the tail end of the tadpole was the small but important Kindley airfield. On the eleventh of that month, during his second infiltration of Corregidor, he would see to it that the airfield was destroyed along with the sixty-inch Sperry searchlights. He would go back to Corregidor on the eighteenth and strategically place heavy explosives around the power plant, knowing that without it most of the facilities, the fortress would cease to function. On the last day indicated, the the twenty-fifth, the demolitions of the north and south docks of Corregidor would be imperative.

He went down the page of the date book. The acronyms listed on the eighth, fifteenth, twenty-second and the thirtieth of November appeared to be challenges for him too. Starting with the acronym BOAM, which Mac had earlier decrypted as "birds over a mountain," or airplanes in Clark Field. Then there was LB, Leon Barclay, on the fifteenth. He wondered what Barclay planned to do on that day and wished that he could find him. Mac's mind went blank as to what BI on the twenty-second and LM on the thirtieth of November meant. Adding to his frustration was his inability to think of a reason why all the dates in October and November fell on a Friday, with the exception of the acronym LM, on Saturday, November thirtieth.

Mac grabbed a piece of paper and began drawing a button to a man's shirt; a man's left shoe and a dagger. But on a separate sheet, he drew the belt and buckle. Then underneath the drawing, he wrote down in big letters the word, SOLLOW, and stared at it.

Meanwhile, a sense of inadequacy was fast mounting inside him. He rubbed his eyes. They burned with fatigue. "This doesn't make any sense," he murmured disgustedly, removed his wig and beard, and went upstairs to bed.

A bright ray from the sun manifested into Mac's bedroom through the center of the bamboo screen where several sticks were missing, and the telephone's ringing finally awakened him after just a few hours of shut-eye. He crawled out from under the mosquito net and answered the phone. The small clock on the credenza by the telephone showed past noon. "Hello," Mac answered, his voice still tight from a deep sleep. He did not remember falling asleep.

He instantly recognized the voice of Miguela's at the other end of the line.

"How about lunch today? I know an excellent seafood restaurant: Benito's in Paranaque. I will be waiting for you at my parents' house," Miguela said.

"Great. I'll pick you up at 2:30," Mac said.

Mac arrived at Buenavista slightly late and blamed the heavy downtown traffic. Inside the car he kissed Miguela.

"I've missed you," he told her and kissed her again.

Miguela stroked Mac's dyed-brown moustache. "You look different with a moustache. Poco said I wouldn't recognize you."

Mac laughed heartily. "You wouldn't have if I had these on," he told her, putting on his dark brown wig, beard and dark glasses. "Now, would you have known me?"

"No! Your disguise is absolutely astonishing."

"Sonny Sollow brushed into me at the Far East Hotel's bar, and he didn't recognize me. Now I know Dusty Rhoades and Bradford Miller won't know me either." Mac chuckled. "I've a new name also—Vic MacTaggart. Same nickname, Mac."

Miguela was amused. "I am glad to meet you, Vic MacTaggart. It is strange, but I think I have fallen in love with you. It must be your wavy brown hair and beard."

They both laughed.

At Benito's, they took a corner booth. "Darling, I love you," he told Miguela, taking her hand to his. "I'm sorry that my work is keeping us from seeing each other more often."

"I am sorry too. Mac, I am worried about you. Why Kapalaran Strip, of all places? That is such a dangerous and rough place." Miguela paused and gave Mac a long look. "You mentioned a few minutes ago that Sonny

Sollow did not recognize you. I find him so evil. My own mother thinks he is evil. Please keep away from him."

"Do you think that I follow him around? He's the one following me. Everywhere I go, there he is," said Mac, visibly irritated.

"I did not mean to anger you," Miguela said.

"Where do you think I'd find this serial murderer and spy? In a peaceful neighborhood like Pasay, Mandaluyong, or affluent Taft Avenue and Dewey Boulevard?" The look on his face was intense, and his voice was terse.

Miguela was puzzled as to why Mac had such an abrupt and displeased reaction to what she had said. But she feared that what she was going to say next would once again be disagreeable. She hoped, nevertheless, that he would consider the possibility of her reasoning.

Quietly, she told him that, yes, perhaps, he should look for that murderer and spy, who may or may not be Sollow, in a peaceful and affluent neighborhood where he may be hiding. She continued to explain to Mac what she read in the newspaper not too long ago about a wealthy woman who was killed in a less fortunate area of Manila in a place called Tondo. "The police carried on a dragnet in that poor place, only to find that the killer had dropped his victim's body there. They later learned that he lived just a block away from her house in Makati. People who live in Makati are very wealthy."

Mac stared at Miguela. "Yeah! Sure. For all I know, Sollow could even be living in the Manila Hotel or in a plush hotel in downtown Manila," he said irritably.

Neither spoke, but after a while, Mac apologized.

"I am so sorry. I shouldn't be this upset or even raise my voice with you, regardless of my job getting to me," he said rubbing her hand.

"I understand, Mac. Tell me a little about your work."

He told her that Dwarf was a spy for the Japanese and about his date book and the significant information within. "He's also a good friend of Sonny Sollow."

Miguela reminded Mac that while they were boating a couple of months back, she had pointed out two houses on Dewey Boulevard—one was rented from the Molina Corporation by Sonny Sollow, and the other by an Army Colonel whose name she did not know.

Mac nodded. "I recall you saying that you were moving in Sollow's house as soon as he vacated it."

"He called the office one day and told them he was definitely going back to Maryland at the end of December."

"Hmm. I know someone else who's leaving by the end of December," Mac said.

"Who is he?" Miguela inquired.

"Major Charlie North," Mac answered.

"That is a strange coincidence," Miguela uttered thoughtfully.

"What do you mean?" Mac asked, surprised at Miguela's choice of words.

"I do not really know, Mac. I just found it extremely coincidental that your friend Charlie North and Sonny Sollow should both be leaving for the United States at the same time," Miguela remarked.

Mac was quiet for a moment, and then he gave Miguela a long look. "What do you think of old Charlie?"

She explained that, although Charlie was charming and friendly, he sometimes behaved as if he did not really want for anyone to get too close to him. Miguela paused and added apologetically, "Mac, I know how fond you are of him, but he strikes me as odd and calculating. I think that if you really look deeply into Charlie, you will not find a man you admire but a man you despise. I hope that I have not hurt your feelings."

"No, darling," Mac said with a sober look on his face. "Perhaps, you're right about Charlie. I think I'm going to hire you as my intuition gauge."

Upon reaching Buenavista, Miguela invited Mac to stay. It was a hot afternoon in late September and perfect for bathing in the large pool. After a brief swim, they left the pool, and walked on the beach, and plunged into the briny Manila Bay. Still full of energy, they walked as far as the cove. Standing there with his arm around Miguela's waist, the swirling water once again mesmerized Mac, and a slight shiver ran through his body. His thoughts had strayed to the man who jumped into the cove while being pursued and how astonishingly quickly he disappeared from sight. He turned to Miguela and asked if a man could survive in that cove. He failed to mention that he survived it after the party.

"He has to be strong and an excellent swimmer," she answered.

It was about 9:00 p.m. when Mac returned to Kapalaran and reflected that he had not seen the sky so vividly clear and the stars so unusually bright. He decided he would walk to Uncle Billy's. As he neared the club, he stopped suddenly when a Ford cut in front of him. The car stopped behind the club. Mac, meanwhile, thought the silhouette of the man driving the car looked familiar. He crouched behind an empty vehicle close to the Ford and tried to see who the driver was. About that time, the man got out of the car and helped a woman get inside the car. The lights on the parking lot behind the club, though dim, enabled Mac to recognize the driver of the Ford car and the woman. "It's Dusty Rhoades! And that woman who went inside the car..." he murmured. "Where have I seen that redhead before?" Recognition came back to him. It was the same woman whom he and Poco saw at the Manila International Club that June. It was the same woman who had accidentally bumped into him when they were coming out of the club's entrance that night, causing him to fall to the floor. Poco insisted that she had deliberately thrown herself at Mac to save him from the male stranger standing by, who clearly intended to kill him. "Poco had said that she was probably a whore," Mac murmured to himself. "I wonder why Rhoades is with her. Could he be interested in her?"

After a long conversation in the car, the redhead woman stepped out, but she and Rhoades continued to talk to each other for about a minute, then he handed her a large brown envelope, which she promptly dropped into her bulky cloth bag. She turned around and went inside the club while Rhoades drove away.

Mac pushed the door open to Uncle Billy's, where the hostess instantly met him at the door. "Good evening, Sir. Welcome to Uncle Billy's. Are you new to our establishment?" she asked engagingly. "I do not think I have seen you here before."

"First time," Mac answered.

"Well, you will not regret it. Please follow me." The hostess led Mac through another door and into a dimly lit, crowded, and smoky room. "A waitress will take you to your table. Enjoy!" She whispered.

A scantily dressed waitress, who appeared from nowhere, took charge of Mac.

"Hello, handsome. My name is Sophie. I am going to seat you at one of those ringside tables, where you will have a better view of our girls," she said smiling. "And as soon as you give me your drink preference, I will bring it to you."

"Scotch. Johnnie Walker Red Label and water," Mac said and told the waitress it was an excellent table. Sophie thanked him and left.

The platform where the girls were performing was about three times as large as a boxing ring but only slightly elevated from the floor. Across from where the customers were allowed to sit were steps to the boxing ring-shaped stage. There was a curtained door nearby where the performers entered and exited. The on-stage equipment consisted of three stripper poles, a couple of cages, barbells, and leather whips. Backed by a three-piece band, the whole stage looked like a three-ringed circus, but in this case, all of the performers were semi-nude and each doing her own naughty act.

Mac turned to order a second Scotch and water when he saw the waitress with red hair. She was waiting on two Filipino-Japanese men a couple of tables away from his. After she had deposited the pitcher of beer and two glasses on their table, she started chatting almost intimately with them. Mac moved his chair so as to be in a better position to observe them. He was convinced that it was the same woman whom Poco saw at the Manila International Club.

The ten-minute intermission finally ended, and the second act was about to begin. Five separate wrestling pads were rolled to the center ring, where ten bare-breasted women, whose bodies were heavily oiled, went in pairs and began wrestling each other. It was by far the most popular part of the show. During the attention-grabbing spectacle, Mac noticed the redhead waitress slip the same large envelope she had received from Rhoades to one of the Filipino-Japanese men at her table. In the meantime, Mac became so distracted by the wrestling acts and loud cat calls from the customers, that when he glanced at the redhead's table again, the two men and the redhead waitress had left.

Mac rushed outside, hoping to see where they went. The two men were nowhere in sight, but he saw the waitress pacing up and down the sidewalk. Soon, the same Ford car that he had seen earlier that evening stopped to pick her up. The bright lights from the club's entrance identified Rhoades as the car's driver.

He went back inside and approached the hostess. "That redhead waitress who just left—what's her name? Is she coming back?"

"In answer to your first question. Her name is Cookie. And, to your second question, it is her time off. Are you a friend? Give me your name, and I will leave a note for her. Cookie works five hours a day. She has been on an early shift. Did you want for me to leave her a note from you? What is your name?"

Mac shook his head. "No."

The following evening, Mac went back to Uncle Billy's before the show was to begin at ten o'clock. This time he came in his car, though it was just a short walk from his house to the club. He might have a need for the car, he told himself, and he parked it behind the club. When he entered the club, Mac looked around the crowded room and at the same time requested the hostess for a table in Cookie's area. He noticed that the same erotic acts of the night before were to be on again that night, and he observed that some of the men who were there last evening were there again. Then he heard a female voice moaning a comment—"Men cannot get enough of our sexy girls' show."

Mac turned around. The redhead was standing by his table. "Hello, handsome," she greeted, smiling. "I guess you heard what I told those guys over at that table."

Mac nodded.

"I am your waitress, and my name is Cookie," she said, giving Mac a come-on look. "I have not seen you at Uncle Billy's before. Are you new in town?"

Mac's thoughts raced. She's very clever, he thought. "I'm visiting some friends in Paranaque," he told her.

"Oh, I am familiar with that place," Cookie said. "There is a popular restaurant there which American servicemen from Sangley Point Naval Base frequent."

Mac gave a sigh of relief. He had to thank Miguela for taking him there. "Benito's," he answered Cookie.

She continued the conversation by mentioning the terrible car accident at Paranaque. "I understand the police could not find any clues on the man who burned to death in the car. He was by himself."

"I heard," Mac murmured.

"Do you wish to order a drink, Sir?"

Mac scrutinized her face. He wanted very badly to thank the brash waitress with the heavy makeup for saving his life last June, but he could not, knowing it would uncover his disguise. "Bring me Scotch and water," he finally answered.

When Cookie came back with his drink, Mac paid her with a heavy tip and told her, "You've a number of tables to attend to. I may be gone by the time you come around to my table again."

"If you are coming back to Uncle Billy's tomorrow night, come at ten. It is my late shift for the next three nights." She glanced at her watch. "It is now quarter of ten," she said rather nervously. "I am off soon."

Having said that, she quickly turned around to attend to another of her customers.

Mac stood impatiently in the shadow of Uncle Billy's, waiting for Cookie to come out of the club. He could not believe that fifteen minutes could be so very long. His mouth was dry from smoking too many cigarettes, and his patience was starting to get the best of him, when he saw Cookie coming out of the club and walking towards the end of the building. He followed her and observed the same Ford car waiting for her, and as soon as she got in the car, Rhoades drove away.

Mac's suspicion of Rhoades deepened. He jumped into his own car and followed them, heading for the city. But he soon discovered that following Rhoades through the streets of Manila was not easy, especially with the help of Cookie. After an hour of intense tracking, Mac lost sight of Rhoades's car in the community of San Marcelino. Furthermore, Mac did not see where Rhoades had dropped Cookie. But, instead of turning around, he slowly drove through the area, scrutinizing each house, hoping to see Rhoades again. He remembered Rhoades telling him last June that he was moving to San Marcelino from Fort Stotsenburg. When he had almost reached the end of the road he noticed Rhoades talking earnestly to a Filipino with a folder under his arm standing in front of the house. After a few minutes, the Filipino gave the folder to Rhoades, and both drove off. The chase began again.

Mac lost them through a series of crooked streets in San Marcelino. Rather than waste more time, he turned around and drove back to

Kapalaran. On the way to his house, a couple of police cars, blaring their sirens and flashing their lights, passed him. The telephone was ringing as he entered his house. Mac picked up the receiver.

"Hello, UG-1?" The voice sounded amused.

"Who's this?" Mac reluctantly asked, not recognizing the voice.

"On his way to Aparri, UG-3 called me and said that you have something that might interest me." There was a pause. "Now do you know who this is?"

"Yes. I do! You son of a gun! It's good to hear from you. Are you in trouble, Chavez?" Mac inquired. "Where are you?"

"At Lara's Casino investigating a homicide. Since I am not far away from where you live, I would like to see you when I get done here."

Mac was delighted to hear from Chavez. "I'll leave the door unlocked," he said, stretched himself on the sofa, and immediately fell asleep.

A couple of hours later, Chavez awakened Mac.

"What happened at Lara's?" Mac asked.

"It has all been very intriguing," Chavez said. He explained that Lara's assistant manager and another man began a heated argument with each other. Each took a gun and went into a shooting match. The dead man, a white man who had been living in Singapore, turned out to be a well-known gun smuggler and saboteur, whom the Philippine government had been trying to apprehend for some time. Furthermore, in the last two years, he had been known to incite the Moros against the government in Mindanao.

"Where did the smugglers get the guns?" Mac inquired.

"This is not confirmed information. Probably all the guns and other types of weapons, initially, are coming from Russia into China and are being distributed to Macao, Shanghai and Hong Kong." Chavez expanded that those weapons and guns from those three areas were then smuggled to the Philippines. "That smuggler, Erik Graz, Austrian by birth, had been suspected of dynamiting several military arsenals in Iloilo, Cebu, and Leyte. It is probably the same guy who had been stealing guns from Army posts and selling them to foreign spies in some parts of Northern Luzon and to the Moros in Mindanao."

"How is the assistant manager?" Mac asked.

"Badly wounded, but he will live. It was acting in self defense, according to witnesses."

"Poco and those Army units in Aparri will certainly be happy to know of the gun smuggler's demise," Mac said.

"Yes, he told me he was going on TDY to Aparri to help investigate who is stealing Army guns from military units in that Northern region." Chavez told Mac. "How is your underground investigative work doing, Mac?"

"It's moving along, but Charlie and Poco have not been as lucky." Mac glanced at Chavez. "I've something you might find useful."

"Do you have it here with you?"

Mac nodded and walked to the credenza. He took out the date book and handed it to Chavez. "Here, look through this."

"What is it?" Chavez asked, turning the pages of the book.

"I believe it contains important information that you want, agenda to espionage activity against your country."

"That sounds like it was a formidable task!" Chavez remarked worryingly. "Do you know who owned this date book?"

"His name is Dwarf." Mac elaborated how he got a hold of it.

Chavez looked pleased, adding that Dwarf was also on their suspect spy list. "We could throw him in jail, but we would rather let him lead us to the big fish," he said, continuing to flip through the pages with increasing interest and stopping on the "grocery list," reading it aloud. After a while, he glanced at Mac. "Have you deciphered any of these yet?"

"Most of it. Do you remember the acronym BOAM? It's in there also," Mac answered.

"Indeed. I do remember," Chavez said. "It was in the Wanabe-Sollow conversation regarding the highway and railway systems you shared with me last June. The PIB sent several agents to northern Luzon to check for any tampering or sabotage."

"Now go back to either page two or three. Take a look at the note," Mac urged.

"Yes, here it is. It says, 'Call Barclay.'"

Mac looked at Chavez. "Ever heard of that name?"

"I recall you telling me about it," answered Chavez.

"Now go back to 'grocery list' and focus only your attention on the months of October and November." Mac began to describe in detail his analysis of the dates in the two following months and the implications that could have on the national security of the Philippine government.

Chavez sounded alarmed. "That must never happen. The PIB must act on all of these dates immediately! Director Romero must be made aware of these planned sabotages. Do you mind if I keep Dwarf's date book, Mac?"

"Keep it. I've made notes for myself."

"I see that some of these dates have already passed," Chavez noted.

"Yes," Mac answered and added that although he was on track with the notations on the month of October, he had difficulty deciphering BI and LM on the November espionage plan. "I'll also discuss with you my hypothesis on Corregidor in the month of October when you've more time and not so tired. I'll call you at your office." Mac paused. "I've something else to tell you."

"I am interested," Chavez answered.

"I know who killed Walters."

"Sollow," Chavez said.

"Do you know the owner of the Coconut Tree Cocktail Lounge?" Mac asked.

Chavez nodded. "Yes. Anna."

"She informed me that it was Leon Barclay who killed Walters. Why don't you go and see her. She might also be able to help you about Sollow and Dwarf. They go there sometimes," Mac explained to Chavez.

Chavez smiled and told Mac that it would not be such a good idea. "Anna hates policemen and nosey people like me. I knew that she was a good friend of Walters. I went to see her after he drowned to find out if she knew who might have done it. She would not talk to me. Even refused to see me." Chavez paused. "I would like to thank you again for sharing this very important information with me. The PIB will forever be grateful to you." He paused. "Where can I find Barclay?"

"At the La Rose Hotel. But you won't find him, Chavez. I tried. If you can catch him, put him in the slammer. He's Meissner."

"Are you certain?" Chavez asked.

"Yes. But before you go, Chavez, I'd like to put on my disguise so you'll recognize me in case we do meet somewhere else. And my name is

Victor MacTaggart. Still the same nickname, Mac."

Chavez glanced at his watch and smiled. "Next time I visit you, MacTaggart, it will not be this late." He walked towards the door but turned around as an afterthought. "Pass by my office in a day or two, and let's see if we can make some sense out of Dwarf's date book. I will bring in another agent who could help us analyze the meaning of these letters. You can brief me then on what your plans are about the month of October on Corregidor."

Mac gave Chavez a thoughtful look. "Chavez, I want you to do me a favor."

"Okay," Chavez answered.

"Before we all meet to discuss Dwarf's date book, I'd like for you to give me a tour of Corregidor. What I know about it is vague and only based on Czestochowa and Golden's schematic."

"I would be happy to be your guide. When?" Chavez asked.

"Today," Mac answered.

Chavez glanced at his watch. "I have not had much sleep, but it would be my pleasure. Give me a couple of hours," he told Mac. "I need to go back to the office and report the death of the Austrian. I will meet you at the Manila Hotel dock in a couple of hours." Chavez explained to Mac that the PIB had a small office at the hotel managed by two Filipino civil servants whose sole duty was to run government officials, PIB agents, and important businessmen to and from Corregidor.

As he promised, Chavez met Mac at the Manila Hotel dock and immediately secured a twenty-foot motorboat. Rather than have one of the PIB employees take them to the fortress island, he insisted that he would navigate the boat himself, since he and Mac did not know exactly when they would return to Manila.

Except for the roaring of the motorboat going at top speed and the wind on their faces, there were few words exchanged between them. Each man was deep in his own thoughts.

At one instant, Mac shouted a question to Chavez over the strong wind, "How far is the fortress from Manila?"

Chavez shouted back, "Twenty-six or thirty-two nautical miles west of Manila. There are differing opinions. My bet is twenty-six. A short distance from Corregidor is the southern tip end of Bataan Peninsula,

Mariveles." He paused. "The Mariveles Naval Base has the drydock Dewey. It was moved there in July."

It was a beautiful day. Chavez remarked that mother nature was showing off her pleasant side; he had not seen the weather as good as it was that day. Then there was silence again. And as they neared Corregidor, Chavez mentioned that he was going to tie up the boat at South Dock on the South Channel and pick up a couple of ham and cheese sandwiches and two bottles of San Miguel at a small café at barrio San Jose. While they were eating, Chavez glanced at Mac and said that there were several sights he would like to point out to him and hastened to add that since time was not on their side, he would show Mac only the important ones.

As they were walking away from the barrio San Jose, Chavez explained that Corregidor, the site of Fort Mills, was the largest of the four islands lying across the entrance to Manila Bay. He pointed to the fortresses: Caballo, El Fraile, Carabao, and La Monja. "There is another fortress, Grande Island in Subic Bay, which is not far from here. They are all known as Harbor Defense of Manila and Subic Bay."

"Corregidor and those other fortified islands would almost make it impossible for an encroachment by an enemy to take Manila and the Subic Bays," Mac said. He quickly asked Chavez the size of Corregidor.

"It is three and a half miles in length and half a mile wide at that large head, known as Topside," Chavez explained, pointing to the western portion of the tadpole-shaped area. He continued to explain to Mac that the large area was five hundred feet above the sea, and on top of the cliff were the headquarters, barracks, officers's quarters, and parade grounds of Corregidor. Chavez further informed Mac that where they stood was known as Bottomside with South Dock on the South Channel and the barrio of San Jose. "That other dock on the north side is the North Dock on North Channel. "If you turn around, west of Bottomside is the power plant."

Mac asked the name of the hill east of Bottomside.

"Malinta Hill. There is a tunnel there completed in 1922, and it's bomb proof," Chavez said proudly. "Philippine history books always point out that Malinta Tunnel was first used as a hospital, warehouse, and arsenal."

"Looks like a good underground hideaway also, in case of a war," Mac added.

Before leaving Bottomside, Chavez pointed to a small plateau called Middleside. But because of time, Chavez gave Mac a cursory briefing of Middleside, the narrow neck of the tadpole-shaped island connected to the big head. Middleside had barracks and schools for children.

Chavez was anxious for them to reach Topside, the big head of the allegorical form, via reinforced wide steps built there many years ago. He wanted for Mac to see for himself the coastal weapons of Corregidor made up of fifty-six guns and cannons. Among them were many batteries, such as Batteries Hearn, Geary, Crocket, and Smith. "Batteries Hearn and Smith have twelve-inch guns with top range of twenty-nine thousand yards and can fire on all directions." He added that there were other guns such as 155-mm; antiaircraft guns; .50-calibre machine guns. The defense of Corregidor also included sixty-inch Sperry searchlights.

As they left Topside, Chavez again pointed to the power plant west of Malinta Hill and Malinta Tunnel. From Bottomside, they went directly eastward to the tail of the tadpole where navy radio intercept station and the small Kindley Airfield were located.

It was a beautiful evening, and the Manila Bay was calm as Mac and Chavez left Corregidor Island behind them. The combination of air, water, and pleasant weather made them both hungry. Upon reaching the Manila Hotel, they had a bite to eat and a couple of San Miguel beers at a small café near the famous hotel where General Douglas MacArthur and his family occupied a small penthouse overlooking the crescent-shaped bay. It was while they were eating that Mac discussed his hypothetical spy scenario with Chavez, who expressed his approval. "If you were the spy assigned to destroy Corregidor, how would you do it?" Chavez asked.

Mac thought a while and answered that, first, he would have to enter Corregidor covertly a day ahead of what was the first day in the date book. "Instead of going in on the fourth of October, I'll go in on the third to realign my thoughts and strategy."

Mac continued that, since he knew the security maintained at the fort, "I'd first destroy Batteries Smith and Hearn at Topside. They appear to be the most sophisticated of all the weapons systems. Furthermore, Mac informed Chavez that he would dynamite the power plant located west of Malinta Hill. And since he would be in that vicinity, he would find it imperative to destroy both the North and South Dock. "The last on my wish list would be to rush to the tail of the tadpole, east of Malinta Hill, and destroy Kindley Field and the radio intercept station."

The more Mac discussed his plan with Chavez, the better it sounded to him than he had at first imagined. When he had finished, he stretched his long legs, and a pleased look came to his face. Both he and Chavez were amazed at the clarity and the soundness of the October hypothetical plan.

CHAPTER 21

Poco's temporary duty in Aparri was short-lived. After about a week there, he was sent back to his old job in Manila.

True, all guns and weapons were coming from Russia to China, but all suppositions, rumors and unconfirmed reports of where smugglers were getting their weapons in China were finally erased from the Army's and the PIB's books. It became clear to both parties through mutual exchange of classified information that there were two confirmed distribution points in China. One was from Macao, a Portuguese colony in southeast China, not far from Hong Kong. From Macao, the weapons were taken to Aparri, the northeastern region of Luzon in the Philippines. The other Chinese distribution point was the small town of Mengzi, which had a direct route to Saigon French-Indochina, where they were taken to British Singapore in Malaya. The weapons were transferred to Cotabato, one of the seaports in Mindanao, Philippines. Most of the weapons were then sold to the renegade Moros cell, which had political, religious, and cultural ambitions for taking over that island. A majority of the Moros were Muslims. According to G-2 and the PIB intelligence, the remaining weapons and guns had been sold to the Japanese spy cells in Manila and the provinces. In addition to bringing weapons in from other countries, the contrabandists also stole guns from other Army units in Aparri and sold their booty to enemy spy cells in the Visayan Islands too. But, after the capture of ten Filipinos, weapons smuggling and stealing had temporarily stopped. The death of their leader had a far-flung effect on the smuggling of weapons from Luzon to Mindanao. Shortly before he died, the PIB, under the guidance of Agent Chavez, was able to extricate the names and addresses of Graz's trusted aids in Manila, Cebu, Iloilo, Leyte, and Mindanao. With a well-planned and accelerated strategic

259

action, the PIB, with the help of the US Army, was able to capture the criminals.

Shortly after Poco's return, Mac met him and Charlie by the Quiapo Church. They were on their way to Olongapo.

"How do you like your car, Sir?" Poco asked Mac as he flopped himself into the passenger seat.

"It has changed my entire life here," Mac answered and, turning to Charlie, said, "I see you've got your faithful thermos of cold coffee with you."

Charlie nodded. "Can't survive the day without it. Hard to find in restaurants. I guess not many people appreciate cold java."

For the first few minutes of their fifty-mile drive, they were all quiet and deep in their own thoughts. The silence was broken only by the annoyingly loud squeak of the windshield wipers. Finally Charlie, who was in the back of the car, tapped Mac on the shoulder. "Why don't you remove your disguise? It's damn hot and humid in this car."

"I'm getting used to it," Mac said staring at the road. "No one told me before I left Washington that when it rains in the Philippines, it really pours. I just hope we don't get bogged down."

"Yes, this kind of rain sometimes washes away part of the road," Poco noted.

There was another silence as the rain, now heavier, began hitting the windshield faster, causing a blinding effect and prompting Mac to drive even slower.

Poco, on the passenger side, asked Mac if he had heard from Agent Chavez.

"Yes. Talk about a man in a hurry. Chavez is everywhere these days," Mac said, avoiding a more in-depth answer. Besides, he was tired of talking about Dwarf's date book. He then looked at Charlie from the rearview mirror.

"Charlie, when did you say Lina's grandmother called you about the photo?" Mac asked.

"Yesterday morning, but I didn't know about it until last night."

"What happened?" Mac asked.

Charlie took a puff from his cigar. "I wasn't in when she called. Jones, who lives three doors down, answered the phone and forgot to tell me about it. Probably figured it wasn't important."

Mac swerved the wheel of the car to avoid a deep rut in the road. "I'm anxious to see that photo," Mac said.

"According to Jones, the old lady had told another American whom she thought was a friend of her granddaughter about the photograph," Charlie said.

"She made a mistake. She shouldn't have said anything to anyone about it," Mac noted. "Do you happen to know who that American was?"

"No," answered Charlie and quickly added, "I do wish we could complete our mission before the thirty-first of December. You know, Mac, this whole thing is so damn discouraging and really impossible to solve. I've decided that when my time comes up for a change of assignment at the end of December, I'm going back to the United States." Charlie said then paused as he stared outside. "The security of the Philippines is alarmingly porous. It appears spies and criminals enter the country without any difficulty, but the PIB and the police appear incapable of doing anything about them."

"Are you sure you don't want to tough it out until we find the answer to our mission, one way or another?" Mac said.

Charlie ran his hand to his bald head and said he would probably stick around. "It just keeps getting harder and harder," he said. "But we'll see."

He then remembered that two days ago Miss Aquino had telephoned him regarding a meeting Colonel Miller scheduled for everyone next week. Attendance, Charlie said as he rolled his eyes, was mandatory. "She hinted he's going to disband Quest."

Mac shrugged his shoulders. "For all intents and purposes, we're disbanded already."

"Exactly," Poco said.

"And another thing. Miller is giving a farewell party at his house at the end of the month. According to Miss Aquino, Poco and I are invited," Charlie explained.

"Did you ask who else is going to the party, Charlie?" Mac inquired.

"No," answered Charlie.

"It's okay. I'll call Miguela when we get back to Manila," Mac said as he glanced at Charlie in the rear-view mirror.

By the time they arrived in Olongapo, the rain had stopped. They were within sight of the house when Poco exclaimed, "Major Mac. Major North. Look over there! Is that not Colonel Miller with a Filipino?"

Mac stopped the car abruptly. "Yes! That's Miller!"

"What the hell!" Charlie declared. "They're coming out of Lina's grandmother's house!"

"Could they have been after the same thing we are?" Mac asked. "Miller may be the American whom the grandmother told us visited her."

"Yes, I am wondering about that myself," Charlie mused. "Mac, let's stay back. We don't want them to see us."

"Let's confront Miller," Mac said emphatically.

Charlie shook his head. "No, Mac! The son of a bitch will just deny whatever questions you ask. Besides, we still have our careers to think about. Never put your superior on a defensive situation."

Mac took a deep breath. "You're probably right, Charlie. I'm highly suspicious of him and Dusty Rhoades."

Charlie moved close to Mac and whispered, "Which of the two do you think is Boris Meissner?"

Mac waited a while to answer. "I don't know yet. Maybe neither."

"No?" Charlie was barely audible.

As soon as Miller and his Filipino companion were out of sight, Mac started the car and stopped in front of the house. They all jumped out. Poco knocked on the door, but there was no answer. He knocked again and eventually turned to Mac. "She must not be home, Sir."

"Try again, Poco," Mac encouraged.

This time Poco banged on the door and at the same time jiggled the doorknob. He turned abruptly to look at Mac. "It's unlocked!"

"Knock again," Charlie advised.

Since there was no answer, they all decided to go inside. The small house looked neat and normal, except for the fact that all the curtains were drawn, including the colorful bamboo blinds in the bedroom.

"Hello. Is anybody home?" Mac shouted. "Hello. Is anybody home?" He repeated.

In the meantime, Charlie and Poco went from room to room, searching under the bed, behind the tables and chairs, and around the sofa. Charlie opened the kitchen door that led outside with Poco following close behind. He walked around the house and did not see anyone. Both men got on their bellies and crawled under the house that was supported by three-foot stilts. Finding nothing, both men crawled away from under the house. They were about to go back inside, when Charlie turned to Poco.

"Wait," he said, "Do you see those old clothes over there? They seem to be covering something." He lifted the clothes with an old broom handle.

"It's a dead body! Poco, get McCord! I think we've found Lina's grandmother."

Mac rushed to the scene and found Charlie covering his nose with a handkerchief. "Take a look at this, Mac."

"How in the hell were you able to find that body behind those steps?"

"I'm just a good sleuth, Mac. And from the odor, too," Charlie answered.

"Jeez," Mac exclaimed, staring incredulously at the body. "He's struck again—no head and no fingers."

"Yes, like what the murderer did to Major Haggarty and Lieutenant Czestochowa," softly intoned Poco.

Charlie's voice was urgent.

"Mac, I'm going to that church to call the police. The telephone wires here have been pulled out of the wall."

"Before you go, Major North, help us look for a burlap sack. Do you recall me telling you what Lina had told us about some photographs we think are important to our mission?"

Charlie nodded. "Yes. According to your story, Lina's grandmother had a habit of keeping things important to her in a burlap sack under the sink."

"Those pictures still might be in that sack," answered Poco.

They searched the kitchen extensively and even lifted several planks off the floor from around the sink pipes.

"You needn't go any further," Mac exclaimed after a while. "I found the burlap sack stuffed behind the stairs to the kitchen, not far from the dead body. But it's empty. Evidently someone was ahead of us. Charlie, before you go, where can we meet you?"

"Meet me at Tony's, a hole in the wall-type bar less than half a mile away. Poco knows where it is."

He then glanced at the Filipino sergeant, "Poco, you go back with Major McCord. Take the car."

"Are you meeting us at Tony's, Major North?" Poco inquired.

"Yes, I'll walk there from the church," answered Charlie, turning around and facing Mac. "Hell, Mac. No one knows you here. Why don't you take off your disguise? You'll be more comfortable," Charlie said irritably, kicking a dog that had been growling at him.

"Dammit, Charlie!" Mac became angry at Charlie's unnecessary cruelty. He looked at Charlie. "It's 7:00," said Mac. "A couple hours at Tony's should quench our thirst and drown our disappointment. I'll give you both a signal when to leave the bar."

Mac entered the popular club, went directly to the bar, quickly decided he could use a stronger drink than beer, and ordered a Scotch and water. As he sat there, he began to wonder if anyone in town knew about the murder of the old woman. But, judging from the behavior of those in the club, he concluded that no one was aware of the heinous incident. It's good that Charlie is calling the police, Mac told himself. At the other end of the bar across from him, he noticed that Poco, drinking beer, was looking directly at him. He began to wonder where Charlie was.

It was about 8:30 when a man approaching the bar recognized Poco and sat down next to him. "Sergeant, may I join you?"

"Lieutenant Colonel Rhoades! Of course!" Poco tried to keep from looking surprised. "What brings you here?"

"Oh, I had some business here, and then I'm on my way to Clark Field. How about you, Sergeant?"

"Visiting a friend," said Poco.

Rhoades nodded. "I see. Are you here by yourself?"

"No, Sir. With Major North. He finds Olongapo interesting. And he also has friends here."

Rhoades nodded again. "I see."

The bartender had by this time noticed Rhoades and asked what he wanted to drink. "Beer," he answered and then turned his attention back to Poco. "Where's Major North?"

"He said he was going to meet a friend of his," Poco answered.

Rhoades paused momentarily. "Does Major North take you on many of his assigned trips?"

"No, Sir."

"Do you find him friendly?" Pursued Rhoades.

"Not exactly, Sir. He is rather aloof. He tends to be a loner and keeps things to himself." Poco wanted to change the subject and did. "I understand that Colonel Miller is going to close shop shortly."

"Yes. Probably next week. Are you sorry, Sergeant?"

Poco shook his head. "No, Sir. I am anxious to go back to my old unit."

"How about Major North? Has he ever voiced to you what he's going to do?"

"He did say something about going back to the States at the end of December."

"Sergeant Pocodillo," continued Rhoades, "When McCord was alive, did he ever describe Boris Meissner's appearance to you?"

"I do not recall, Sir," Poco paused. "I do not think he knew."

Rhoades continued to stare at Poco. "By the way, how did McCord die?" He inquired suspiciously.

Poco was momentarily taken aback but did finally managed an evasive answer: "Car accident." Poco took a swig of his beer.

"Ah. Well, it was nice bumping into you, Sergeant. I'll be at Clark Field for a couple of days," Rhoades said and left Tony's Bar and Grill.

Poco was relieved to see Rhoades leave. A man of few words, he disliked being interrogated. Like Mac, he had a deep mistrust for Rhoades and found him suspiciously nosey. He was just beginning to enjoy his beer and garlic-fried peanuts when he felt fear come to him upon glancing in Mac's direction. "Oh, no!" He murmured.

"Did you say something?" asked a stranger sitting on a bar stool next to him.

Poco shook his head but kept his eyes on a familiar figure—it was Sonny Sollow. Sollow grabbed a bar stool next to Mac's and sat down. When Poco eventually turned his eyes on Mac, he got a discrete signal from him to leave, and with that Poco paid his bill and left Tony's.

Meanwhile, Sollow ordered Bourbon and Coca Cola and turned to Mac. "Are...are you at Subic Na...Naval Station?"

"No, just visiting my brother. I'm a business man."

The bartender placed Sollow's drink in front of him. Sollow took a swig of his drink. "In what?"

"I'm a manager of a rice company in Crowley, Louisiana. I came here to see why Philippine rice has bigger grains."

"Is… is Crowley near New…New Orleans?"

"It's a good distance."

"I've ne…never been there. I'd like to…to go there someday." He glanced at Mac. "What's your…na…name?"

"MacTaggart. Victor MacTaggart."

"Which do you pre…prefer. Vic or Ma…Mac?"

Mac shook his head. "It doesn't matter."

"Well, Mac, my…my name is Sollow. Sonny Sollow. You can call me Son…Sonny." Sollow looked fixedly at Mac. "I'd like to give you a…a good advice. Go back to Lou…Lou…Louisiana and tell your brother to… to ask for re…reassignment in the States. Listen to the radio and read the newspapers. They all think Japan is acting awfully aggressive. I think Japan is itching for a war with the US."

Mac finally excused himself and met Poco at the designated place behind Tony's Bar and Grill.

"Jesus Christ, Major Mac," Poco whispered. "What were you trying to do for the last five minutes, get recognized? You scared the shit out of me, Sir."

"I'm okay. What went on between you and Rhoades?"

"He asked one or two questions about you, like how you died or if I had ever heard you describe Boris Meissner. But many of his questions were surprisingly about Major North. One of his questions I found strange: 'Does Major North take you with him on many of his assignment trips?'"

"That is strange! But so is Rhoades." Mac paused momentarily. "Where's Charlie?"

"I noticed he took his thermos with him when he left us. He told me before leaving that if he is not back with us by 10:00 p.m., for us to go on without him. He is probably visiting some friends."

"It's almost ten," Mac said. "How's he going back to Manila?"

"By train, Sir."

Suddenly, a ringing shot from a gun splintered the dark September night, barely missing Mac's head. Mac dropped to the ground when another shot rang out, shattering the windshield of his car, the bullet going through the roof.

"Poco, go inside the bar and wait for me."

"I do not want to leave you, Sir," said the loyal Filipino sergeant.

"Just go, Poco," Mac insisted. "I believe those shots came from behind the building adjacent to Tony's."

Just as soon as Poco left, Mac saw a shadowy figure run towards a lonely boat graveyard. Mac got up and ran past old wooden buildings and fishing huts until he had reached an open beach. Another shot rang out. He could feel the hot zing of the bullet pass by his left ear. He rushed up the hill and made a quick dive for the nearest clump of undergrowth to wait for his assailant, whom he was certain was not too far away.

While he stayed in that crouched position, thoughts flashed through his mind that it could be Sonny Sollow, but then, he reasoned that he had just talked to Sollow, and he had no idea who Mac was. Suddenly, he saw something flashed in the dark that looked like a wristwatch or a shiny metal. There was another quick flash, and this time it was much closer to him. He did not move even when he heard footsteps. He told himself that he must be sure to grab the figure. But, realizing that the sound was coming from behind him and not in front of him, Mac whirled around and grabbed his assailant by the shoulder. The man quickly extricated himself and landed a strong blow on Mac's stomach, forcing him off-balance. Regaining his composure, Mac returned his foe's attack with a hard hit on the right jaw, causing him to fall to the ground. Sensing that he was at an advantage, Mac jumped on the downed attacker with a strong drive for the jugular, when he was met with an effective kick on the midrib.

Mac quickly scrambled to get up and gave the man, who was now standing over him, a hard tackle. They fought for a while, and then it was over. The assailant had escaped.

"Major Mac! Major Mac! Where are you?" Poco was frantically shouting. He had been looking for his friend.

"Up here, Poco." Mac answered, while massaging his ribs. In the distance, to the south, he could see car lights and streetlights at Corregidor

Island. He was out of breath as he ran down the hill to meet Poco. "Let's pick up my car and get the hell out of here."

On their way to the car Mac told Poco how strong his attacker was. "I don't recall having told you that the night we searched Buenavista for Roosie's killer, a man attacked me and tried to kill me. That guy was as strong as this one tonight."

Poco did not answer immediately, but he eventually ventured, "Maybe it was the same man." It startled Mac.

"Could be!" Mac was barely audible.

Mac stepped on the gas and left Tony's behind them. Neither said a word for a couple of miles, when Mac glanced at the Filipino sergeant. "I think my attacker knew me despite my disguise."

"Yes, Sir. I would definitely say that," Poco said. "I know you have been suspicious of Colonel Miller and Lieutenant Colonel Rhoades. And, of course, there is Sonny Sollow. Have you given it any thought that it could be Sollow who has been after you?"

"I don't know, Poco. I'll just have to continue playing detective. I must have something in common with those other murdered officers and Roosie. I'm a threat to whoever that person was."

Both men were in deep thought for several minutes, then Poco glanced at Mac. "By the way, you seem to have come out well with Sonny Sollow. Neither he nor Colonel Rhoades recognized you."

"Good," Mac said almost absentmindedly. "After I told him that I'm here visiting my brother, Sollow said something to me at the bar that gave me a cold shiver: to get out of the Philippines and for my brother to ask for reassignment in the States."

Poco whistled. "Those are eerie statements. Maybe he was bragging that he knows something that we don't know."

"You may be right, Poco. He was probably trying to tell me that there's going to be trouble in paradise and that General MacArthur's USAFFE won't be strong enough to save the Philippines from an attack."

When they reached Manila, Mac dropped Poco at his house and called Miguela at her apartment. She asked him to stay for the night. "You have a long way to drive to your house in Kapalaran."

When he got there, Mac gathered Miguela in his arms and told her how much he had missed her. They were elated to be together again after so many weeks of not seeing each other. Certainly sleep was not in their minds.

The following morning, Mac related to Miguela the shooting incidents in Olongapo and also told her about Colonel Miller's farewell party.

"My parents and Uncle Jose were invited. But my parents will be out of town. I am going with Uncle Jose."

A day or two later, Mac drove to an automotive body shop in Manila to leave his car for windshield repair and other damages.

"My, my. Did someone try to kill you?" The American auto body repairman asked matter-of-factly.

"Yes," Mac answered.

"Know who?"

"I wish I did."

"Well, you've got to be careful these days. Seems like many happenings like this have been occurring in the last several months. Come back in three days."

CHAPTER 22

There was a knock at Mac's door. It was Chavez. Earlier that evening, he had called Mac about discussing a couple of things with him. Mac was delighted to see his friend and invited him in. Their friendship had developed into a deep trust and respect for one other. There was something about the Filipino agent that Mac liked—his straightforwardness, his veracity, and his integrity.

"Make yourself comfortable while I get us a beer," Mac said and was soon back with two bottles of San Miguel beer.

Chavez had by that time pulled out a folder from his briefcase and laid it on the table. "I brought along the pictures I mentioned, but before you look at them, let me first brief you about them."

According to Chavez, PIB agents working along with British intelligence agents in Hong Kong and Shanghai had been covertly following the activities of two notorious spies, dubbed by the British as the "Twins" because they were always assigned together. They were known to be two of the most effective and cunning foreign agents. Chavez fixed his brown eyes on Mac.

"Of course, not as effective or cunning as your friend, Boris Meissner."

He further explained that, a couple of years ago, there was an extensive manhunt for the "Twins" in Great Britain because they were believed to be spying for Germany.

"They were never caught, as you can probably guess," Chavez said as he leaned his head against the back of the chair. Meanwhile, he continued, they were advised to be on alert that the Philippines could be one of their destinations in Southeast Asia. The bureau immediately went to work, selecting and training some of the brightest and the best

270

agents on counterintelligence. About a month ago, the PIB received highly classified information from their own group in Shanghai that the Twins had been seen in Tokyo and Peking. Not long after the reports were received, PIB agents in Shanghai dispatched a classified letter notifying the PIB headquarters in Manila that, although the Twins were in Shanghai harbor posing as stevedores, they may have already left China and could be on their way to Singapore in Malaya to enter the Philippines via Mindanao. Shortly thereafter, subsequent reports confirmed that they had indeed disappeared.

"But the Mindanao notification did not materialize," Chavez said. "PIB agents believed that the twins may have quietly left China, leaving no traces of their whereabouts, but, nevertheless, Manila was instructed to be ready."

According to more recent and secret reports—and Chavez agreed with their findings—Manila may be their primary area of interest.

"They likely slated the Philippines as a great place to aid the Japanese intelligence network," Chavez said. "And, as you can see by what's been happening around here lately, the Philippines was ripe for the picking."

"Where is the best area to enter the Philippines if one is a foreign spy trying to get in?" Mac asked Chavez.

"The islands have a number of accessible places to illegally enter. But the best two routes would be via Hong Kong or Formosa, each less than seven hundred nautical miles from Aparri. Or Laoag to the northwest. Or at the town of Lingayen, also on the western part of Luzon." Chavez further elaborated that another route was Mindanao, in southern Philippines, with a deep seaport in Davao.

"It is a very busy sea lane for ships and freighters coming from Malaya and the Netherlands East Indies. The magnate is Manila."

Chavez added that Japan had always been interested in the United States colony because of its agricultural wealth and strategic location for Japan's overall geopolitical scheme. He pushed back the chair and walked to the window and watched the well-lit, busy streets.

"It is my opinion that the Twins, Pfeiffel, and Oberti are already in the Philippines," Chavez said.

Mac joined Chavez at the window. He generally lowered the window blinds whenever he was in the house for security purposes, but that evening he reasoned that whoever was following him probably already knew his visitor.

"What do you know about these jokers?"

"Very little. According to informants, the blond with blue eyes is Pfeiffel. German. And the swarthy one is an Italian by the name of Oberti. I am sure that in time we will know more about them," Chavez explained, walking back to his chair.

"You definitely think they are already in the Philippines, Chavez?"

"I suppose I am jumping the gun. I am a naturally suspicious man when it comes to foreign spies and saboteurs in the Philippines."

Chavez handed Mac some faded photographs of the pair, forwarded by British Intelligence.

Mac studied them and inquired if there was something he could do to help.

Chavez told Mac no because he was already busy with his own commitments.

"I think the PIB can take care of these two men. But if you happen upon them, let me know." Chavez paused. "It might please you to know that I am going to northern Luzon to see, among other notations on Dwarf's date book, the effectiveness of our surveillance in the Mt. Arayat area. The PIB also has assigned agents to see to it that our rail lines and highways are not sabotaged."

Chavez added that, from there, he was driving to Aparri to find out how well the PIB's surveillance was on Pfeiffel and Oberti.

"According to a top secret report, they could be in Aparri rather than Laoag or the town of Lingayen. We want to catch them." His voice was tense. "Come with me, Mac. I will call Rhoades and tell him that you are coming with me, but I want him to keep the information to himself and Miller."

Mac nodded. "Okay." He glanced at Chavez. "I wish they did not have to know. I think one of them is Meissner."

Chavez did not say a word.

It was dark when they arrived at the small town of Arayat. Chavez turned right on a small isolated road at the edge of town and pulled up in front of the white cottage. A Filipino appeared at the open door, beaming pleasantly upon seeing Chavez. "It is good to see you, Chief."

"Mac, this is my good friend, Ignacio," said Chavez. "He supervises a team of ten PIB agents who do surveillance of Mt. Arayat and the rail lines and highways throughout Luzon. They are part of PIB's northern Luzon field office in Aparri."

Ignacio invited Mac and Chavez to come in, leading them to the small dining room. "Please sit down. I know you are both hungry and tired. The native woman who cooks for all of us has set aside some fried chicken, mongo beans, and rice. I have eaten, so dig in."

While Chavez and Mac were eating, Ignacio briefed Chavez on the Mt. Arayat situation. "As you know, we keep in close contact with the natives here. My men and I work in shifts. Five are based here, and the other five are in other parts of Luzon. Two of the men with me are in town relaxing on a day off."

Ignacio paused momentarily but continued to tell Chavez that the only thing that occurred during his group's watch happened three days ago. He was on his way to the foot of Mt. Arayat to join his men when he observed a man some distance away surveying the mountain with a pair of binoculars.

"Who was he?" Chavez inquired.

"He said that his name was Major Charles North and that he worked for a Colonel Miller in Manila."

"Did he show you his identification?" Mac inquired.

"Yes, Sir," answered Ignacio. "We talked a while, and he said that whenever he was at Clark Field he always visits the small town of Arayat to eat Philippine cooking and admire the beautiful mountain. Nice man. He even offered me some cold coffee from a thermos."

A frown creased Chavez's face. "I have often wondered about North. He is not just a loner. He is a loner's loner."

Mac glanced at Ignacio. "You did meet Major North. Charlie doesn't go anywhere without his silver thermos bottle. He's okay, but he does often travel to Clark and other areas by himself. He told me once he likes to work alone." Mac looked at Chavez. "There have been many instances that caused me to suspect Charlie. Even Poco has been justifiably suspicious of him, but, so far, no reasons have been evident."

Chavez's interest in Charlie heightened after hearing Mac. "How often does he travel?"

"Because of our current assignment, I would say frequently. Cavite Naval Station, Clark Air Base, Olongapo Naval Station, and sometimes Fort Wint. Sometimes he's gone for a week or so," Mac explained.

"That is very interesting!" Chavez murmured to himself. "I wonder if North has traveled to Iloilo?"

"Iloilo?" Mac inquired, perplexed at Chavez's statement. "Iloilo?" He repeated. "I don't know." Mac paused. "What's in Iloilo, Chavez?"

"We at the PIB believe that Iloilo is one of a very important divisional Japanese espionage headquarters, code name Gardenia. The chief is a woman known among Japanese intelligence as Gardenia. She is a beautiful but cunning Eurasian. According to some Filipino informants, she is the mistress of a major in the US Army." Chavez cleared his throat. "Seems to fit Major North."

Mac gave Chavez a surprised look. "You're making Charlie sound like a romantic figure. Well, I'll start monitoring his actions more closely. He does travel extensively."

Ignacio interjected. "Would you both like to join me and my men tomorrow about 5:00 a.m.? It is cooler at that time." He got up, yawned, and said he was turning in. "There are two bedrooms adjoining the living room," he told them. Before he left, he mentioned to Chavez something he almost forgot, about two Japanese-Filipinos who were caught in Angeles trying to sabotage the railroad tracks there. "They were arrested and sent to Manila for questioning and possibly imprisonment."

Mac glanced at Chavez, who was smiling. Chavez thanked Mac again and told him, after they were by themselves, that the PIB was able to decipher his and Poco's note on the Sollow-Wanabe conversation at the Ruby Redd restaurant.

The following morning, Chavez and Mac followed Ignacio and his four men to the foot of Mt. Arayat. Ignacio pointed to Mac their observation hideaway. He was proud of the fact that the hideaway was not visible from the ground, elaborating that it was six hundred feet from the base of the mountain to their hideaway. "We built a rough passage to the observation point and reach it by truck. It offers us a clear view of Clark Field, Fort Stotsenburg, and the areas around here."

"I'm sure," Mac responded. "Mt. Arayat appears like an excellent lookout point for a spy."

They did not stay long in the town of Arayat, as Chavez was expected in Aparri the following day. The drive there was hot, long, and tedious. The highway was narrow and crooked, and the terrain was rocky and mountainous. They arrived there late in the afternoon, giving Chavez a chance to drive down to the coastal fishing village.

Since there were still many hours left in the day when they arrived, Chavez drove down to the small coastal fishing village, where a PIB agent posing as a fishing guide met him. "We can talk better in that fishing boat," the covert agent whispered to Chavez, glancing suspiciously at Mac.

"This is Mac. An American. He is a friend," Chavez said, gaining the confidence of the agent.

After they were all aboard, the PIB agent pushed the boat hard from the dock and guided it about two hundred feet away and dropped his anchor. He quickly briefed Chavez. Evidently, the US Naval Patrol arrested a Japanese in the Japanese community in Aparri.

"Reason?" Chavez asked.

"He allegedly took part in that explosion at the Cavite Naval Yard," the agent answered.

Mac quickly added that he had heard about that explosion. "It happened two or three months ago. Chavez, could that be the same incident Miguela mentioned to us during supper at her house last June?"

Mac continued that Miguela was quite emphatic about noticing a blond man rushing in his boat toward the area. "In retrospect, now that we know more about Leon Barclay, perhaps that was him?"

"It could have been Barclay, Mac," Chavez said. He then glanced at the agent. "Who was he?"

"No one really knew. Some said he was a Japanese," answered the guide, who elaborated that the official leader of the Japanese community, when approached, insisted that they did not know him and had no knowledge of the incident. But after the arrest, for lack of proper security, the alleged bomber escaped to Davao, the capital of Mindanao. The guide paused and quickly said that some informants allegedly mentioned that it was a Caucasian with blond hair who was guilty of the sabotage.

"I am more inclined to say it was the Caucasian with blond hair,"

Chavez said.

"I hate to speculate," answered the fishing guide, who added that he had a strange bit of information that might interest Chavez also.

There was a dead silence. The only sounds were those of the waves hitting against the bow of the native fishing craft while Mac and Chavez listened to the agent. "From Lingayen to Aparri, a rumor is going around that a German spy posing as an American Army officer has infiltrated the military center in Manila."

"Interesting!" Chavez said.

"Yes!" Mac intoned, a surprised sound in his voice. "Your source?"

"A Filipino working in a shipping company has been talking in bars in Manila and the town of Lingayen, and the rumors have spread as far as here about the imposter. From what I have heard, the Filipino seems to know what he is talking about," explained the fishing guide.

"I've met that man. He tried to kill me one night while I was still at the military center. He told me that an Army officer paid him to murder me." Mac explained.

Chavez changed the subject and told the fishing guide, "Let me discuss a more recent subject. I really came here to find out if Pfeiffel and Oberti did get here, as stated in those secret reports we sent you."

"After a couple of months of doing covert work on them, my men and I heard a suspicious story that, last night, a Japanese freighter, delivering food and fuel and coming from French Indo-China on her way to the Netherlands East Indies had engine trouble in the middle of the night between Batan Islands and Babuyan Islands on the Balintang Channel," the agent said. "A Philippine shrimp boat from Aparri went to the aid of the freighter. Allegedly, a number of people were quietly transferred aboard the shrimp boat and were taken to Escarpada Point, where a Philippine commercial fishing boat headed back to Aparri picked them up. I immediately set up a tight surveillance at the Aparri dock."

"Let me guess," Chavez said, "Pfeiffel and Oberti were not among the passengers."

The agent shook his head. "If they were on that fishing boat, they must have escaped our dragnet. I personally followed the freighter's passengers for some time after they left the boat."

The agent paused, looked squarely at Chavez, and explained his mystification as to why the "Twins" were not among the rest of the passengers. According to him, those secret reports Chavez had sent him, including highly classified information from the PIB agents in Hong Kong, Shanghai, and the British intelligence, had stated that "the twins" would be in that freighter. "The freighter was scheduled to dock at Aparri overnight before proceeding to the Netherlands East Indies, but engine trouble occurred. Nevertheless, they should have been in that ship. They could not have just disappeared into thin air." The agent paused. "Intelligence reports from our Hong Kong and Shanghai agents are generally excellent. For example, the information we had received from them about the Austrian smuggling guns from Macao, Hong Kong and Shanghai have been confirmed." Chavez paused.

"No, only Macao and a small town in China, Mengzi, were confirmed."

"I know about the Austrian gun smuggler. Forget him. He is dead," Chavez said. "Let us go back to the Twins."

The agent shook his head in dismay.

"If they had been on that Philippines fishing boat, they must have escaped. Some of the passengers were French Indo-Chinese, Malayans, and Chinese. There were two whom I followed—an old man and an old woman. I think they said they were from French Indo-China, specifically Saigon, based on what little French I knew. They spoke only French. What attracted me to them was that they were so bent with age that I wondered how in the hell they were able to travel. I offered to help carry what little luggage they had. They both said no, that what they had was very light. I then decided I was following the wrong people. All the passengers from the freighter registered at the same hotel. In the meantime, boat mechanics had been working on the freighter's engine since last night. I was told the trouble was not serious. The ship, with most of its passengers, left very early this morning. Some stayed behind to visit relatives here."

"What happened to the two geezers?" Mac inquired.

"After I met them, I had a strange feeling that I should reconnoiter around the vicinity of the hotel and around the wooded area near the hotel. As I walked away from the wooded area to get back to the dock, I encountered the two oldsters again. I asked them by signs and body language if they were lost. They answered with their hands that they were taking a walk so they would sleep better. With that explanation, I walked away. I am sorry, Chavez. I tried. I guess intelligence is not perfect."

The fishing guide's explanation was very disappointing to Chavez. He took a deep breath and let out a heavy sigh, as if to wrench out the deep frustrations that had been building up inside him. "We're following old people now, huh?"

Mac, sensing Chavez's mental unhappiness, asked if his friend was all right. Chavez smiled, shook his head, and explained that the men assigned to the Pfeiffel and Oberti case were some of the best in Philippine Investigative Bureau. The capture of the two European spies was important for a number of reasons. One, the PIB would have been able to extract from them the information regarding the espionage network in the Philippines, which could further result in finding who murdered the American Army officers and whether their murders were spy-related. Chavez then turned to the fishing guide.

"You and your men fine-combed the Japanese community?" Chavez inquired, still visibly agitated at the agent's failure.

The agent nodded. "Thoroughly and discretely but with negative results. You know yourself how non-committal the Japanese are. Nice citizens, but they keep their lips sealed."

"Are there other nationalities, other than Japanese, who live in that Japanese community?" Mac asked.

"Very few," answered the agent. "Some French Indo-Chinese, some Malayans, and some Chinese."

"Before we go back ashore," Chavez said, "perhaps you may have learned the identity of the leader of the espionage group in Luzon, cover name Red Rose."

"I was going to include them in my report. During the clandestine meeting with our group, an informant from Ilocos Norte told me that he thinks there is a Japanese espionage network operating in the Philippines. I do not have any information about Red Rose and who he is. But as I understood from the informant, the real brain behind the network operation is a Caucasian. He was unable to provide me with a name." The fishing guide paused. "The Ilocos Norte informant also added that our own code name for the Japanese network intelligence establishment, the Network, might not be correct. He thought he heard insiders of the organization referring to it as the "Saber." Allegedly, Big Iguana will visit the Japanese community here in Aparri on the twenty-second of November to visit friends. A man named Dwarf will accompany him. Perhaps we can learn something from that visit."

Mac asked the fishing guide whether his informant was trustworthy.

"Yes. He is," said the guide.

Mac turned to Chavez to remind him that the information the fishing guide just gave them was in Dwarf's date book, including BI (Big Iguana) and LM.

"Yes. He just confirmed the information we have," answered Chavez who turned to the fishing guide and told him to watch for the twenty-second of November.

The fishing guide nodded and continued with his reporting. "On November thirtieth, BI and Dwarf will leave Manila. Destination unknown. My informant, a Filipino who speaks Japanese, further told me that General Sonoda, code name Red Rose, was the head of the espionage arm in Luzon but that he had gone back to Japan. He did not know who took his place. According to him, Red Rose's headquarters is somewhere in downtown Manila. He insisted that the PIB keep an eye on the Nagoya Emporium."

The agent paused momentarily, but quickly added, "Mr. Chavez, this is just a suggestion. I would send a couple of covert agents to Iloilo to find out more about Gardenia." He elaborated by saying that a Visayan informant had told him that Gardenia was a quiet individual who disliked being mentioned in newspapers and radios. She was allegedly an important and dangerous member of Saber and highly feared by Japanese intelligence agents and informants.

"What makes her so important and dangerous?" Chavez asked.

"According to my informant, she has a straight shot to the Saber organization, whereas Orchid of Mindanao has to go through channels to see Big Iguana," the fishing guide explained.

Chavez smiled. "You have more than made amends for your failure regarding Pfeiffel and Oberti. I shall inform Director Romero about your excellent report and begin infiltrating the emporium as soon as we know a little bit more of what is going on in there." He added that the PIB would have to do it slowly but surely. "We want to capture Big Iguana and Red Rose. Send your report to Manila anyway. Thank you. You are a fine agent."

It was later that night when Chavez decided to drive Mac around the Japanese community in Aparri and then drive back to Manila.

Meanwhile, the old man and the old woman left their small hotel room and walked to the nearest thicket of undergrowth that they had surveyed the night before after meeting the fishing guide. The old man first dug a deep hole, proceeded to remove his eyeglasses, white wig, and the life-like mask, and dropped the disguise into the hole. He slowly straightened his back, flexed his arms, and massaged his thighs and legs. The old woman did likewise with her disguise.

"Hurry up and fill up the hole," the transformed old man commanded. "We must leave Aparri quickly for Manila. The car over there is for us. I've already checked us out. I told the desk clerk that we have some relatives in the Japanese community and that there was a sudden death in the family. The desk clerk was helpful."

"Pfeiffel, do you have the key to our hotel in Manila and the key to the car?" Oberti asked.

"Yes. In my pocket. They were in an envelope when we registered at the hotel. The clerk gave them to me then."

"Are you sure?"

"You've always been a pain in the ass, Oberti. Of course I'm sure. I've both the car key and the key to our hotel in Manila. Let's hurry and leave this mosquito-infested place. I don't know how these Filipinos stand it. I'm sure it's this uncomfortable in Manila. I understand from a Nazi operative in Hong Kong that the whole country is full of snakes, lizards, and iguanas as big as dogs." Pfeiffel paused and glanced at Oberti. "I thought that fishing guide would never go away. And then he scared me when we met him again while we were walking to do some reconnoitering in the woods."

"Shit, you're nothing but a yellow-bellied, thick-headed German. You're always pretending you're so brave. I understand iguanas eat Germans alive." Oberti added sarcastically. "Do you know who that man was you're talking about?" Oberti asked.

"No," answered Pfeiffel.

"He was a Filipino secret agent. I heard another man telling him that he did not think the "Twins" are here in Aparri," Oberti explained. "Before we left Kagoshima for French Indo-China, an intelligence agent there told me that you and I are known as the Twins in Allied intelligence."

CHAPTER 23

"Hell! We've been in Manila for three days. And for three days, it has been blowing and raining, and the streets have been flooded. These Filipinos must have webbed feet," Oberti said.

"Shut up, Oberti! You talk and complain too damn much!" said Pfeiffel, the blond, blue-eyed German driving the 1939 Ford Standard Coupe. "I hope we are going the right way."

Oberti snapped back that he did not trust Japanese intelligence personnel. "They make too many mistakes. They directed us to the wrong hotel in Hong Kong, and maybe again this time."

"Hey, Oberti, we've been at this for over an hour," Pfeiffel said impatiently. "Turn your damn flashlight on that notebook and the building numbers again, and see if they match the numbers the Hong Kong agents gave us before we left."

Oberti flipped feverishly through several pages of the notebook. "Here it is," he snapped, "Nagoya Emporium, 500 Escolta, Manila. But this dark night and heavy downpour makes it extremely difficult to see the numbers on the buildings." He further added that the strong wind was about to flip their car over.

"Shit!" Pfeiffel exclaimed, "Stop complaining about the miserable weather and pay better attention to the building numbers. We're on the right street."

"Fuck you!" Oberti shouted. "You're not my boss! We're equal on this Philippine job. You Nazis treat us Italians like servants. Many times I wish Mussolini wasn't so dumb and cowardly as to side with Hitler."

"Shut up, Oberti!"

"Screw you, Pfeiffel! And why the hell are you stopping?"

Pfeiffel answered back angrily that he could not see the road through the heavy rain. But Oberti urged him to keep on going. "I know we're on the right track," he said, adding that he saw number 446 Escolta on one of the buildings.

"We can't be that far from the emporium."

"Yeah. Sure," Pfeiffel said, giving Oberti a condescending look. "Stupid Italian."

After a while, Oberti excitedly pointed to a parked 1940 Chevy and a 1939 Buick. "Stop! Slide in behind that Buick," Oberti directed Pfeiffel and aimed his flashlight on the building. "We're here! The Nagoya Emporium! And there's the side door."

They both jumped out of the car and knocked on the narrow side door of the emporium. A deep, harsh voice inquired in English, "Who is it?" the voice said as the door cracked open slightly.

"Birds over a mountain," Pfeiffel answered in English.

"Purpose?" the harsh voiced asked.

"We've an appointment with Red Rose," Pfeiffel answered.

"Are you alone?" The harsh voice again inquired.

Pfeiffel shook his head. "No I'm with an Italian gentleman."

The door opened halfway. "Come in," the man told them and shut the door behind his visitors.

"I'm Pfeiffel. I'm from the German foreign infiltration group in Hong Kong. And this is Oberti, with compliments from Benito Mussolini's Italian operatives, also in Hong Kong."

"Follow me," the man said. He was burly with a stern face.

Pfeiffel's eyes narrowed. "No! We must see some identification."

The man uttered something in Japanese and reached into his back pocket, pulled out his passport, and handed it to Pfeiffel, displaying a missing little finger on his right hand.

"I am Colonel Matsumuto."

"Your passport also," Pfeiffel told the other Japanese with Matsumuto.

The much taller but thin Japanese with buckteeth did what was asked of him and introduced himself. "I am Lieutenant Ikeda. Now, we want your passports, please."

Matsumuto and Ikeda, in turn, carefully studied their passports. Ikeda turned to Matsumuto.

"Both British citizens born in Hong Kong?"

Matsumuto nodded. "It is okay. Our operatives in Peking and Hong Kong had warned us it would appear that way."

Pausing momentarily, Matsumuto gave the visitors a searching look before handing them back their passports.

"Follow me," said Ikeda, leading Pfeiffel and Oberti up the stairs while Matsumuto followed behind. They went by some empty rooms until they reached a closed door. Ikeda knocked. No human voice answered the knock. But a low, vicious growl was heard coming from the room. Matsumuto then told Ikeda that it was all right to open the door. Matsumuto, however, insisted on going in first in order to control the dog in the room. Evidently, some time in the past, Ikeda had some difficulty in getting obedience from the dog that consistently showed its dislike for strangers. Matsumuto gestured for the dog to sit and stay, invited everyone to enter the impressive war room, and immediately went to leash up the dog, who grew increasingly excitable upon seeing Oberti and Pfeiffel. It was just a few seconds when the adjoining door clicked open.

A small man of just over five feet, even smaller than most Japanese, emerged. He had strong jaws and a thick chin. But, unlike most Japanese who are known for their straight hair, he possessed beautiful dark, wavy hair that he kept rebelliously long with tacit approval from his superiors. His tight lips, which tended to curl upward on each corner, gave him a good-natured look. His soft voice complimented his facial attributes, lending an appearance of kindness and benevolence.

"Do not stand by the door. Come in, gentlemen. Come in. I am Tanaka," he greeted. The dog had followed him and stood by his side. As Pfeiffel and Oberti moved to the invitation, the dog gave another vicious growl.

"Hoshi! Be Quiet! These are my guests!"

Pfeiffel said, "We came to meet and report to Red Rose."

Tanaka smiled. "I am Red Rose."

Matsumuto interjected, "General Tanaka, your guests from Hong Kong, Pfeiffel and Oberti."

"We came to meet and report to you, Red Rose."

Tanaka turned to Matsumuto who slightly nodded his head.

Tanaka smiled. "I prefer to be addressed as General Tanaka."

Pfeiffel made a movement to come forward to shake Tanaka's hand but stopped when Hoshi bounded alertly in front of Pfeiffel.

"Hoshi," commanded Tanaka. "Stay near me," he said as he extended his hand to Pfeiffel.

Pfeiffel took Tanaka's hand. "General, it's good to meet you. The Axis covert operatives in Peking told us that you and your men are doing a very good job here in Manila."

"Thank you, Mr. Pfeiffel," Tanaka said with a smile. He removed his gold-wired eyeglasses, wiped them with his handkerchief, and placed them carefully back on his nose. "I am sure our guests are thirsty and hungry. Bring some wine and crackers for our European guests, and please bring some towels so they can dry themselves," Tanaka ordered.

After Pfeiffel and Oberti had dried themselves, Tanaka sat down and told his visitors to sit as well. "Messrs. Pfeiffel and Oberti, please enjoy the wine and crackers. Let me apologize for bringing you here so late at night and in this torrential rain. But I had no choice."

Pfeiffel lit a cigarette. "Oberti and I were also hoping, perhaps, sometime during our stay, to also meet the chief of the Japanese espionage network in the Philippines."

Tanaka again turned to look at Matsumuto, who stood near him. This time, Matsumuto answered for Tanaka. "Gentleman, allow me to explain. General Tanaka holds two important positions. In other words, he has two code names—Iguana and Red Rose. The code name Iguana refers to being chief of the entire Philippines intelligence establishment. His other code name, Red Rose, is because he is in charge of the Luzon intelligence division. The Japanese intelligence network is divided into three intelligence operations in the Philippine archipelago. Their code names are Gardenia, for the Visayan Islands or central Philippines, Orchid for the Mindanao area or southern Philippines, and Red Rose, of course, you already know."

Matsumuto paused and specifically glanced at Oberti. "The whole intelligence organization in the Philippines carries the code name Saber. We had a good reason to hold back the code name from you because our informant in Macao heard that PIB agents are stationed along the coastal area of northern Luzon from Lingayen to Apparri. We were afraid you

285

might be caught and would be forced to talk." Matsumuto paused.

"We have suspected for a long time that the PIB and the American G-2 are not quite certain if Network is the correct code name for our intelligence establishment." Matsumuto paused momentarily. "We have been aware of their wiretapping and eavesdropping activities."

"Well, what do you know about that? An iguana is a dangerous animal," Oberti observed sarcastically. "The man has two titles. Pfeiffel, it's a good thing you asked." Oberti paused. "We understand Gardenia and Orchid are not as well managed as Red Rose. You are a pure genius, Tanaka," he added mockingly. "We heard a white man formed this spy network, and he's also running the show for you."

"Were you also born insolent, Mr. Oberti?" Matsumuto inquired disdainfully.

Oberti glanced at Matsumuto. "And you're a son of a bitch. I don't like condescending Japs!"

"I apologize for my friend's behavior," interrupted Pfeiffel, with his hand on Oberti's shoulder. "We have had a difficult time dodging the PIB in Aparri, and we've been shut in the hotel since we arrived here because of the extremely bad weather. We also had a hell of a time finding your address in the rain. We're tired and irritable."

"How can you stand all this rain?" Oberti asked Tanaka.

Matsumuto again answered for Tanaka. "Take your pick. Suffocate in heat and high humidity or swim in the streets of Manila."

Pfeiffel looked at Tanaka. "Tell us the truth, General. How are Gardenia and Orchid operations doing?"

Tanaka was pleased with Pfeiffel's question. "Unlike what Mr. Oberti thinks, they are doing fine."

Pfeiffel continued. "General, your men in Hong Kong told us that you wanted us here on Wednesday at dawn. Oberti and I tried, but our previous assignment precluded that. We were in the midst of covert work on Chang Kai Shek's Kuomintang Nationalist Army. They're very strong."

"Why'd you send for us, Tanaka? And why particularly on Wednesday?" Oberti inquired.

"Wednesday happens to be General Tanaka's lucky day of the week," answered Matsumuto.

Oberti gave Matsumuto a snarling look and then turned to Tanaka. "Why'd you send for us?"

Tanaka cleared his throat and explained that, since MacArthur's arrival in late July, things have been changing fast in Manila. "Japanese secret agents have been reporting almost daily on the military reorganization known as US Army Forces Far East—USAFFE—for the defense of the Philippines against enemy attacks. He took off his spectacles, wiped them and then placed them carefully back on his nose. "Time is passing very fast. We must work hard. I had to see you tonight instead of waiting for the weather to clear. I have urgent jobs for both of you to do."

Lieutenant Ikeda, meanwhile, had left and returned with a woman walking by his side. He whispered something in Tanaka's ear and then left. Tanaka smiled and got up from his chair abruptly. "You can come out from behind that curtain. I apologize. I have forgotten that you were waiting for me to invite you to join us," Tanaka paused, smiling. "Did you hear me tell these gentlemen that I am both Iguana and Red Rose?"

"Yes," the woman answered.

Tanaka introduced the woman with the bright red hair, heavy makeup, a very short dress with a belt of many stones of varied colors, and a pair of red shoes with spike heels.

"Messrs. Pfeiffel. Oberti. This is Cookie. She is one of our underground agents in Manila. She has been providing us with the nation's defense secrets and is loyal to me and Japan." Tanaka paused momentarily and added, "I am so sorry that our American connection here has not yet arrived."

Oberti stared with interest at Cookie. "What do you know, a Filipina Mata Hari. Does she speak English?" He inquired, giving Cookie a suggestive wink.

"All Filipinos speak English," Matsumuto interjected gruffly.

"Can she be trusted?" Pfeiffel asked.

"Of course, Pfeiffel! The great Iguana, Director of the Japanese spy network in Asia, and Red Rose, all rolled into one, will tell you that she is to be trusted," Oberti said.

Tanaka again cleaned his eyeglasses and slowly placed them back on his nose. He fixed his eyes on each person in the room as if ordering each one, mentally, to pay attention to what he had to say because what he was about to impart to them was important as to why they were all there. They were there to help pave the way for a Japanese invasion of the Philippines. The acquisition of the American colony was ancillary to Japan's dream of an Asiatic and Pacific conquest.

"Yes, Cookie has already been of great help to our mission. She has provided us with a detailed plan of proposed naval forces in the Philippines and as soon as it becomes available to her, Cookie will give us the strength and composition of the USAFFE units in the Philippines."

He gave her a pleased look. "Heretofore, she has been supplying us with important information through our agents. Cookie has often been in our headquarters but this is the first time she has joined us in our meeting. I thought I would invite her tonight and probably to our future meetings." Tanaka glanced at his two visitors. "Cookie is a waitress in one of the night clubs on the Kapalaran Strip, Uncle Billy's Girls, a strip tease joint and a fine place for obtaining national defense secret data." Tanaka paused. "Many talkative American soldiers and sailors go there."

Oberti laughed raucously. "Cookie probably does whoring on the side." He grabbed Cookie by the arm. "What'd you say, Cookie? Can I take you home tonight and have a little piece of you know what? Italian men know how to sexually satisfy a woman."

"Let go of my arm," she told Oberti. "Even a whore recognizes a swine."

Pfeiffel, meanwhile, abruptly turned around and looked Cookie squarely to her face. "Who are you? You don't smell like a whore. I can smell one a mile away," he told her suspiciously.

"It is because I have a PhD on how not to smell like a whore," she snapped at Pfeiffel.

There was laughter in the room.

"Gentlemen. The photographs I am about to hand to you," continued Tanaka, came from Cookie. She has a number of friends in the US Army who pay her, when they run out of money, with military secrets in exchange, shall we say, for her attention." Tanaka paused momentarily and opened the briefcase on his desk and handed to Pfeiffel three photographs. The back of the photos were marked with "Assignment No. 1." One was the dry-dock Dewey, the second was that of a US minesweeper and the third picture had two cargo vessels—the Yorktown and the Orleans. "They arrived from the United States two or three days ago. These are Cookie's contributions to our goal."

To Oberti, Tanaka gave three photographs marked on the back— POL sites. Assignment No. 2. "Here is a military pamphlet on POLS in Luzon. Study them carefully in your hotel room."

Colonel Matsumuto came forward. "Are there any questions?"

Pfeiffel inquired where the dry-dock was.

"The dry-dock Dewey was moved to the southern tip of Bataan at Mariveles," Matsumuto said. "The minesweeper is anchored near Corregidor Island but the cargo vessels Yorktown and Orleans are anchored in Manila Bay, loaded with supplies, artillery and ammunition slated for the Army units. We understand from Cookie the Army will still start unloading it in a couple of days after the high wind subsides and the bay calms down." Matsumuto then gave Pfeiffel a chart of Manila Bay. "This chart will give you the ships's positions. We want these four objects destroyed. Be careful. The Americans have mined Manila Bay as well as Subic Bay. Wanabe, one of our agents, will lead you to Mariveles first, then Corregidor and on to Manila Bay for the destruction of the two vessels." Matsumuto paused. "You must destroy all four."

While Oberti was studying the three photos he had in his hands, Matsumuto handed him a small map and began to give him the highlights. Petroleum, oil and lubricant installations were circled in red, namely. A POL camp 10 kilometers north of Olongapo is another red target in Angeles, Pampanga. According to him, the Japanese espionage unit in Pampanga told them that there was a large POL reservoir being built for Clark Field, a major air base with B-17's and some P-40's. And, there was Iba highly rumored to be a fighter base only in Zambales Mountains, about 64 kilometers west of Clark Field, on the South China Sea and not far from Lingayen Gulf. "We understand that the Americans have already begun building Iba's POL camp in anticipation of P-40's delivery. It is going to be a small air base but very important to us. We must keep those B-17's and P-40's dry, without access to fuel. We want them destroyed!"

Tanaka interjected. "Other agents will take care of a shipyard site at Sangley Point where the Cavite Naval Base is located. South of the Naval Base, in Batangas, is a large ammo dump. That must be destroyed.

Those agents will also sabotage the fuel camps at Nielson and Nichols Fields, the fighter bases in suburban Manila." He paused. "It takes time to rebuild a POL complex. We must keep on the destruction." Tanaka studied the faces in front of him for a while before he spoke again. "I specifically requested for white male bomb experts and who speak fluent English. Albeit, many US military installations in the Philippines are rather lax still, it would even be much easier for a white, tall man to pose as an American soldier or sailor," he said.

Tanaka fixed his eyes on each person in the room for a long time.

"Mr. Pfeiffel, one of our agents, Agent 5, is Jim Wanabe. He poses as a taxicab driver and will meet you at your hotel, Quiapo Hotel, in a week. Next Wednesday at 1:00 p.m. and take you to the Kawazaka fishing marina."

"How will I know Jim Wanabe? Ask him if he's Agent 5, a spy for the Japanese?" Pfeiffel asked sarcastically.

Matsumuto answered tartly for Tanaka. "He will have a tattoo of birds over a mountain on his upper right arm. He already knows you!" Matsumuto went on and told Pfeiffel that everything necessary to do his job would already be in the boat he was to use and that the two motorboats would be tied at the end on the marina. "You will be met by three of our Filipino agents who had been guarding the boats. They have been instructed to go with you and help you. Let Campos pilot your boat in case you encounter some American or Filipino sea patrols. He is a good talker. The two other Filipinos with Campos, are Silvio and Munoz. There are fishing equipment in both boats."

"What's the travel time to dry-dock Dewey?" asked Pfeiffel.

This time Tanaka answered and estimated that it would take them approximately two hours of open throttle from the boat livery to Mariveles but a short time to the minesweeper near Corregidor. "But going back to Manila Bay for the cargo vessels would probably take two to three hours."

"Do you have a detailed map of Corregidor?" Pfeiffel inquired. "I might as well do some damage while near there."

Tanaka shook his head. "We are waiting for a better layout. We want to know more about the fortification system at Corregidor and where the camouflaged artilleries are located on the landing beaches, about the sentries guarding the beaches and the island's power plant, the Kindley Landing Field, and a radio intercept station. Meanwhile, I want these other assignments accomplished first."

Pfeiffel lighted a cigarette. "Okay. Just trying to get things to go faster. Back to Agent 5. Where does he fit in on the boat ride?"

"Tell Campos to follow him. He will lead you to those places," Tanaka said. "He will be your lookout while you and the Filipinos work. When those jobs are finished, Wanabe will guide you to the anchored freighters. Both of you should be back to the city by daylight." Tanaka paused and smiled. "I see a puzzled look on your face, Mr. Pfeiffel."

"Does Agent 5 know where on the bays the mines were planted?"

Matsumuto answered for Tanaka. "Agent 5 has been following the operation when the Americans began in April, eight months ago. He has a chart indicating where they are."

"So, why did you bother to give me a chart?" Pfeiffel asked sharply.

"In case your boat gets separated from Wanabe's. It is, of course, better to be prepared than to be sorry," Tanaka answered in his naturally soft voice. "But, I do not think that will happen. Agent 5 knows Subic and Manila Bays too well." He turned to Oberti and told him that Agent 30, a Filipino, would come in his car and pick him up at the Quiapo Hotel, also at 1:00 p.m. Agent 30, according to Tanaka, was to lead and help Oberti to the POL sites that were pinpointed to be destroyed.

"Where'd this Filipino agent get his info?" Oberti asked Tanaka suspiciously.

It was Matsumuto who answered him. "Agent 30 has a younger brother who is an employee of USAFFE and has an easy access to their military plans. Your job, Oberti," Matsumuto continued, "may take a week because of the traveling and what you have to do."

While Oberti and Matsumuto were talking, Cookie, meanwhile, approached Tanaka.

"General may I use your telephone," she asked. "I would like to call the manager at Uncle Billy's and tell him that I would be there in about 45 minutes for the second shift. I am already an hour late."

Before Tanaka could answer Cookie, his attention was taken by Pfeiffel's question. "General, since you're the master spy Iguana, you might help me with this question—How many foreign agents does

Iguana control in the Philippines?"

"Over a thousand, scattered throughout the Philippine archipelago and about 5,000 throughout Asia. We are very active in Burma and are especially watching the Dutch Borneo's port of Tarakan, which I believe is strategically important to our Navy. All are under the jurisdiction of Iguana," Tanaka answered. He then turned to Matsumuto and directed him to pull back the curtains that covered a wall across from his desk. It opened to a wall of maps of Manila and the Philippines, and a chart of Manila Bay. "Mr. Pfeiffel. Mr. Oberti. These big maps and charts will give you better ideas of where your targets are. Please feel free to study them and familiarize yourselves with your locations."

Cookie, meanwhile, edged closer to Tanaka and this time got his attention. "General, may I use your telephone? I must call Uncle Billy's."

Tanaka apologized. "I am so sorry. I forgot all about your problem. There is a telephone in the next room."

Cookie came back from her short telephone call, and again approached Tanaka and in a whispered voice asked, "General, would you mind if I leave? I do not think you will need me anymore tonight. You also have the photographs I have promised to give you. As soon as my Army friend gives me the data on the strength and composition of the US Army units, I will contact Colonel Matsumuto or Lieutenant Ikeda like I have done before."

Tanaka nodded, looking pleased. "I need the information badly. Do you think you can have it, say, by tomorrow?"

"Perhaps next week?" Cookie answered.

Tanaka shook his head. "I am afraid that will be too late. Shall we say tomorrow night?"

Cookie nodded. "Tomorrow night."

Tanaka smiled. "Good," he said and quietly slipped 200 pesos in Cookie's hand and told her that he wanted for her to meet a very important American member of Red Rose's networks of agents in Luzon. "I am sorry he is not here but wait 5 minutes. Then you can go if he does not show up."

CHAPTER 24

A tall bearded man entered the Iguana/Red Rose control room and strode arrogantly to an empty chair. "Good evening," he said. His voice was hard and behind the eyeglasses his eyes were furtive and hostile. "I'm sorry...sorry I'm late. I've just driv...driven from Olongapo."

"Ah, Mr. Sollow. It is good you have finally arrived. Messrs. Pfeiffel and Oberti, and Cookie. This is Mr. Sonny Sollow."

Sollow shook Cookie's hand first. She felt strangely uncomfortable when he touched her hand. Something about him told her that she had seen him before but could not recollect where. She intuitively cautioned herself to be very careful and not to cross him. While Sollow stood there shaking hands with Pfeiffel and Oberti, she studied his face from the corners of her eyes and concluded that he exuded evil. He is evil! And I am afraid of him! She told herself. Then she heard Tanaka telling them that Sollow was Red Rose's American connection, for a while, in Washington, DC and in Manila shortly after his arrival there. Tanaka took off his spectacles and cleaned them.

"Mr. Sollow prefers to be called Sonny," Tanaka said, placing his eyeglasses back on his nose and continued. "Mr. Sollow, also, is our only connection with Boris Meissner."

"Oberti and I heard rumors Meissner is in the Philippines or in some part of Asia," Pfeiffel stated.

"He's in...Manila," Sollow offered the information without being asked, "but he comes and...and goes."

Tanaka smiled and turned to Sollow. "We also heard. Please correct me if I am wrong." He paused for a second. "Meissner entered Manila, according to our intelligence, in August 1940, a month before the Axis Alliance was signed, did he not?"

Sollow fixed his gaze on Tanaka. "Why ask me? You're running one of the biggest spy networks in Asia!"

Tanaka continued. "It was Mr. Boris Meissner, I was told, who was the architect of the Philippines espionage network. He presented the idea to General Tani, our top Army General, who liked it. I understand the same general offered him the top job, that of Big Iguana and Red Rose, but Meissner turned it down. However, he is still helping us through Mr. Sollow."

"Tanaka, are you sure Meissner is not the real Iguana and also Red Rose?" Oberti said with great sarcasm.

Tanaka's faced paled but he ignored Oberti.

"Meissner is the best covert spy and intelligence agent Nazi Germany will ever produce," Pfeiffel stated admiringly.

Oberti laughed derisively. "I heard throughout the intelligence in Europe that Meissner is a womanizer. That he especially likes very young girls if he can get them."

Oberti pursed his lips and looked at Pfeiffel. "I also heard that he likes to torture women after he finishes with them, sometimes he kills them. He's known as the 'butcher.'"

An angry retort came back from Pfeiffel. "I don't believe any of that. You know, Oberti, one of these days someone meaner than you will cut off your balls. So what if Meissner prefers young girls. That doesn't make him less of a super spy. No one will ever out smart him, not even any of the best British spies. He's an excellent spy."

Pfeiffel stopped talking and glanced at Tanaka. "No one knows what Meissner looks like. He's known in Europe as the phantom spy. I don't know of anyone who has ever seen him. Have you, General?"

Tanaka shook his head. "Not any of us. But, perhaps Mr. Sollow can describe Meissner to us."

Sollow shook his head. "I ha...have never seen him. He only discusses th...things with me by telephone or by mail."

Tanaka cleared his throat. "Anyway, gentlemen. It was Meissner, through Mr. Sollow, who suggested that we ask help from our European friends. That is why you are both here." He glanced at Sonny Sollow. "You called me yesterday and said you will have something important to give me. Do you have it with you?"

Sollow nodded and opened his briefcase and handed to Tanaka a rolled heavy paper. "I...I'll do it. I know the place."

Tanaka studied it very carefully for a long time and lifted his head and thanked Sollow.

"This is a fine piece of work," he said, and gave it to Pfeiffel. "This is a layout of Corregidor Island known as the Rock. If you will notice it is shaped like a tadpole. I am showing it to you because the dry-dock Dewey is not far from the Rock. It is at the tip end of Bataan, in Mariveles. Mr. Sollow is right. The infiltration of Corregidor has to be accomplished by someone already familiar with it. Mr. Sollow has inside knowledge of the island regardless of what Japanese intelligence had told you and Mr. Oberti in Hong Kong that you would be the infiltrators of Corregidor.

"Excuse me, General," Matsumuto said and bowed, "I...believe that you had earlier mentioned that Sollow and a Filipino agent should do the job."

Tanaka nodded.

"Sollow, contact Marcelo and brief him as to what we want done. And tomorrow night, you will be met by another Filipino agent in the lobby of the Manila Hotel. He will lead both of you to your boat tied at the hotel's boat dock. It will have all the necessary explosives and weapons you will need," Matsumuto elaborated.

"Marcelo?" Sollow said disgustedly. "Why Marcelo? Several months ago we were on assignment together to steal some explosives and rifles from an Army stash. We were discovered by Military Police. Instead of helping me fight the MP, Marcelo disappeared. I had to fight my way out without alerting the rest of the American camp. Marcelo is a coward."

A few minutes later, Pfeiffel passed the map to Oberti, who, after studying the drawing declared that the head of the tadpole was well fortified. "Where exactly is it located and how big is the island?"

"It is one of the islands across the entrance to Manila Bay and only two miles from Bataan. It measures three and a half miles long and one and one half miles at the widest point," Tanaka said, turning his attention to Sollow. "Did you have a message for me from Meissner?"

"Yes. Mei...Mei...ssner told me by tele...telephone to tell you, General Ta...Ta...naka, that US sh...ship he blew up last June in Ma...Ma...nila Bay will be hi...his last in that line of work since you've Pfei...Pfei...ffel and Oberti to help you. Mei...ssner is going to north Luzon and stay ther...there for a while. He'll be studying that part of Lu...Lu ...Luzon from...from Lin...Lingayen to...to...Aparri. He...he...will be sending you reports on his fin...findings through me." Sollow paused momentarily. "I'll also be gone but for only a...a couple of we...weeks. I'm going to Olongapo again to ...to snoop around and see what type of coastal defense USAFFE is developing there. After that I'll be going to Bataan. I understand they're building up the southern tip of Bataan, Mariveles." Sollow cleared his throat. "Dwarf left for Pampanga a couple of days ago. He'll be taking pictures of areas around Clark Field and will be watching Clark for the arrival of additional B-17 bombers and P-40 fighters he has been hearing about. He'll be back in a couple of days with a re...report."

Oberti started to laugh raucously. "A spy who stammers."

He looked at Tanaka. "How'd you ever get anything out of that guy?" He began mimicking Sollow.

Instantaneously and noiselessly, Sollow had his dagger's tip end on Oberti's cheek and his left hand was tight like a vise on the Italian's throat. "I don't li ...like people who la...laugh too easily," he growled in a low angry tone and a maniacal look on his face. "I ...I ...I've k...k...killed for less offense," he said, and at the same time drawing blood from a fine line he had slowly etched on Oberti's cheek.

"You warped son of a bitch! I'm going to kill you!" declared Oberti, placing a handkerchief on his cheek and jumping from his chair to go after Sollow.

Pfeiffel grabbed his friend by the arm. "Sit down, Oberti."

Sollow quietly went back to his chair but while still glaring at Oberti, he wiped his lips with his handkerchief and then also wiped the tip end of his dagger.

"Mr. Sollow," Tanaka asked, "is it true you will be leaving the Philippines?"

Sollow did not answer Tanaka immediately but, instead, stroke his moustache for a few seconds and then he nodded. "At the end of December or earlier," Sollow answered. "I've some personal bus...business in the United States. Baltimore, Maryland, to be exact."

Tanaka glanced at Matsumuto and asked if he had something to say.

Matsumuto reminded Pfeiffel and Oberti that they had to coordinate everything with either him or Lieutenant Ikeda. He did not want for them to call the office unless it was urgent and that Ikeda was going to give them the telephone numbers before they leave the building. "When calling, please identify yourselves as "Saber." Our enemies call our intelligence establishment as the Network. I do not believe that they are yet aware that our code name is Saber. We know that USAFFE G-2 and PIB agents are monitoring telephone calls of suspected foreign spies and fifth columnists. The telephone system of the emporium could be wiretapped." Matsumuto cautioned them to refer to the general, to him and Ikeda as Mr.

"We are supposed to be Japanese civilian merchants." He continued on to say that their rooms at the Quiapo hotel had been paid in advance through the end of January."

Tanaka approached Matsumuto. "Give our Axis friends 1,000 pesos each." And, to Pfeiffel and Oberti he said, "Enjoy yourselves but be very careful. Mr. Oberti, try not to talk too much."

Tanaka turned his attention to Sollow again. "Do you recall the three FBI agents who entered Manila in late May of this year? Our current intelligence information indicates that two of the agents, whose names we now know, Edward Martin and William Lucas seem to have disappeared from the scene. And, of course, the third agent, James Kagan, through his own indiscretions and talkativeness in bars and nightclubs soon uncovered his own identity."

According to Tanaka, through Agent 10 a.k.a Captain Kondo, they knew that Kagan had been surveying their espionage cell in Pasay. Kondo, who was later murdered at Buenavista along with Army Lieutenant Czestochowa and an old cabdriver, began following Kagan around Manila and found that aside from being an FBI agent, he was also connected with the PIB.

"You were assigned to take care of Kagan quietly, Mr. Sollow. Why did you not do as you were assigned to? Why did you kill him in a taxicab going downtown Manila in a clear day?"

Sollow glanced disdainfully at General Tanaka. "I didn't kill him. It was another American and the only one who knew who killed Kagan, was the taxicab driver who also got murdered. Rumors had it that Kagan was going to surrender the American to the police. Thus, he killed Kagan."

"Do you know that American? For whom does he work?" Tanaka inquired.

"No one knows him or his employer," answered Sollow. "You should be happy Kagan got killed or you would have already been hanged, Tanaka." He licked his dry lips.

"By the way," Tanaka said, "Kondo was a trusted member of our group." A cloud of anger appeared on Tanaka's countenance as he imparted tersely to Sollow that Kondo was highly regarded in Japan for his exceptional talent as Kempeitai who spoke good English and had charisma. Kondo was to infiltrate Intramuros known also as the Walled City particularly Fort Santiago, located on the mouth of the Pasig River. Kondo's purpose was to find a place that could be turned into a prison for Filipinos who turned against Japan when the Japanese preconceived war erupts between Japan and the United States. Tanaka's eyes never left Sollow's face. "Did you kill him, Mr. Sollow?" He paused. "I believe you did, you despised his faithfulness to me."

"You're crazy, Tanaka!" Sollow said. "He kept on shadowing me at the Buenavista party. You assigned him to kill me, didn't you? I won't tell you if I killed Kondo but if I did, I wouldn't regret getting rid of one son of a bitch Japanese secret police better known as Kempeitai."

Tanaka continued as if he didn't hear Sollow. "Kagan, according to Kondo, was very close to identifying the Pasay cadre to the PIB and was overheard by him telling someone at a bar that a certain house in Pasay was a nest of Japanese spies.

"I am so very sorry that you killed him," Tanaka said.

"So what!" Sollow growled.

Tanaka just continued. "My predecessor's sudden call back to Japan was most interesting. Evidently, according to rumors the white man who masterminded this entire spy organization did not like him. General Sonoda made it quietly known to me that he had the entire Luzon's Red Rose intelligence division, for that matter the whole Iguana organization in the Philippines division questioned because Sonoda thought that someone in the organization had murdered the American Army officers. Everyone denied having anything to do with the murders. Such acts has the PIB and the American intelligence snooping around looking for the murderer and in doing so they could very well stumble into Iguana's activities." He shook his head with displeasure. "I want it understood Mr. Sollow. I do not want to see or hear any more problems with the United States or this colony." Tanaka stared coldly at Sollow for a long time. "I wonder who it was that killed those officers? Would you happen to know?"

"Are you accusing me? How should I know? Listen General," Sollow exploded angrily and jumped from his chair, pointing threateningly at Tanaka. "Be careful to whom you direct your innuendos."

Matsumuto suddenly came forward and stood between Tanaka and Sollow. His right hand dug inside his shirt and pulled out a gun and laid it on the general's desk. "Mr. Sollow, you misunderstood the General. Those were no innuendos. We believe you killed those officers," Matsumuto explained in a low voice but his eyes were smoldering with hatred for Sollow. "He was also reminding each one of us to be careful with our personal adventures, that they are not traced to Iguana, Red Rose, Gardenia or Orchid. After all, Mr. Sollow, we are all here to help Japan attain her goal and anyone who disrupts that process will naturally, shall we say, know about it?"

"Are you threatening me, Mr. Matsumuto?" Sollow hissed.

"No, Mr. Sollow. I never threaten."

"Mr. Sollow, tell us about Lieutenant Colonel Rhoades," interrupted Tanaka.

"He's hard to read. Very careful with his actions and speech," Sollow said.

"We are aware Sergeant Pocodillo is a Filipino and we saw in the papers that Major McCord died in a car accident. How about Colonel Bradford Miller?" Tanaka continued.

"I hardly think he's an FBI agent. He's too nervous and openly suspicious," Sollow said.

"That leaves Major Charles North," Matsumuto tersely stated.

Sollow straightened his shoulders and was quiet for a while. "Very smart and travels a good deal between Manila and the provinces," he said, again running his tongue over his dry lips.

"You seem to want to protect this Major North, Mr. Sollow," Matsumuto said.

Sollow glared at Matsumuto. "Yes! He is the key to finding FBI agents

Edward Martin and William Lucas." He then glanced at Tanaka. "I will deal with them myself! I don't want you and your killer team to tamper with them." He paused. "I'll hold you personally responsible. I hope you understand, Mr. Tanaka." Sollow emphasized threateningly and then added to soften his threat and to please the Japanese general. "They're all dangerous to Iguana's goal. It would be better if I alone handle them. If I get caught you won't get implicated."

Tanaka's face was inscrutable but his voice rolled in acid. "Your dedication," he said, " is highly commendable, Mr. Sollow!" He got up, took a long breath and thanked everyone. "Gentlemen, we shall meet here again in two weeks at 10:00 p.m. And, good luck to you Mr. Pfeiffel and Mr. Oberti." Tanaka motioned to Ikeda. "Take Cookie back to Uncle Billy's."

Sollow turned around and gave Cookie a long look. "No. Let me have the pleasure of accompanying the young lady there."

"Oh, no! I already called a taxicab. It is probably waiting for me now." Cookie glanced at her watch. "Besides, Uncle Billy's will soon close. I might as well go home."

"As you wish," Sollow said.

Cookie walked briskly away from the emporium until it was out of her sight. She was glad the heavy downpour had ceased. She stopped temporarily and took off her high spiked-heel shoes, started to run for a quarter of a mile, and disappeared between two buildings. She opened the door of the car and jumped in, started it, and did not slow down until she was a safe distance from the Nagoya Emporium.

She had finally reached her street on San Marcelino and could see her house and the light in the living room that she had turned on as a habit before leaving the house. As soon as she had shut the door behind her, Cookie took off her carrot-red wig and removed her long false eyelashes and her dangling earrings. She unbuckled her wide belt with the distinctive colorful stones and placed it on the sofa along with her wig and her large handbag. She walked to her bedroom and spread Pond's face cream on her face and began wiping the very red rouge and lipstick off her face. Once that was done, she picked up the telephone and asked the operator for a connection to a certain telephone number."

A male voice on the other end answered, "Hello."

"I know it is late, but you told me I should call you as soon as I got home."

"I did. You must be tired," the man said.

"I am. You know, Chavez, these late night assignments are getting to be a pain in the derriere."

"How did it go, Purita? Did General Tanaka buy the photos? And the data on the naval forces you gave them last week?"

"Yes. Both," Purita paused. "Have you heard of the two European spies named Pfeiffel and Oberti?"

"Yes. I see they got through our intelligence dragnet at Aparri," Chavez said.

"Big assignment for them. It will cripple our national defense if they are not stopped. They are going to make their move next week at 1:00 p.m."

"Good! That gives us just enough time to prepare. I must call Director Romero and FBI agents Edward Martin and William Lucas immediately."

"I certainly would not have been successful in transferring all those documents to the Japanese without Martin's help."

"Try and get some sleep. I will see you at the headquarters at 8:00 a.m. for a briefing. We'll all be there."

"Chavez, when you gave me this assignment, I was only to help the Philippine Deaprtment G-2 in the murder case of the Americans, Purita breathed deeply and then exhaled slowly. The Philippine Department is now a subordinate command to USAFFE, the new command. "Tanaka wants the USAFFE's Order of Battle in the Philippines tonight."

"We will make up a fake copy for him. Pick it up from my office and deliver it to Tanaka personally before you report for work at Uncle Billy's."

"Chavez, I will also brief you about Sonny Sollow."

"By the way, Purita. Do not expose your true identity to Major McCord. Not yet. I do not wish to unravel his own agenda. I will brief him about you eventually."

"Very well."

Sollow left the emporium the same way he had entered, by the back exit door and the alley fence gate. He got in his Cadillac and slowly eased out of the alley and headed in the direction of Kapalaran Strip. This time he parked his car a block away from Mac's house. With brisk steps he crossed the road and entered the Periscope Club and went directly to the bar. "Bourbon. Straight," he told the bartender. "Sure thing, Sonny Sollow," lisped Johnson the bartender, wearing his usual blond wig and long gold earrings.

"Say, is the Guys Revue over?" Sollow asked. "I bet I missed it," he added, snapping his fingers. "Hell! I had some late work to do."

"You sure did, Sonny," Johnson answered. "Starts at 11 and folds at 1. It is 2 now, prowling time," he added, giving Sollow a wink.

"Still early though, Johnson. I know the club itself doesn't close until 3." Sollow paused. "Say, this place is empty. Where's everybody?"

"The heavy rain. Kept customers away."

"You know what, Sonny. I wish I didn't lisp so. And, sometimes I stammer when I get nervous. I wish I could speak like you, so clear and decisive, no stammering or lisping like I do."

"Thanks, Johnson." Sollow downed his drink and whispered. "Were you able to find someone for me?"

Johnson nodded.

"Nationality?"

"Filipina. Pretty and only 15 years old, like you prefer."

"Where is she, Johnson?"

Johnson's head moved on the direction of a young girl sitting at the other end of the bar. "Over there."

"Hmmm." Sollow gave the girl a long look. Pleased, he took some money out of his pocket and gave it to Johnson. "You did well. Here's 10 pesos. Save up for another red dress." Sollow then approached the girl and sat near her.

"What's your name?"

"Felipa," the girl answered. "The bartender said you were looking for someone my age."

Sollow nodded. "Yes. Are you a whore?"

"No."

"Your first time?"

"Yes."

Sollow cleared his throat. "I like that."

"I want 25 pesos now," the young girl said. "My family needs the money."

Sollow nodded and instantly reached in his pocket. "Okay. Here it is."

"My name is Sonny," he said, swallowing hard. "Let's go up to my hotel room, the Far East Hotel."

"Do you live in the Far East Hotel?"

"No. The room belongs to a friend, Boris Meissner. I live in a house, 1000 Outrigger Lane, Dewey Boulevard. In a couple of days I want you to take a taxicab and come over to my house and be my guest for a couple of days. It's more private there." Sollow paused momentarily. "Here's an extra 5 pesos for the cab ride. I'll meet you at the house," he said and pressed hard on the girl's young breasts.

The youth's face remained immobile.

"Come on," said Sollow. "Let's go to my friend's hotel room. Room 219."

Many hours later Felipa, clearly afraid to be seen, emerged from the room and used the stairs instead of the elevator to leave the hotel. On her way to the back door of the hotel, she briskly straightened her dress, opened the door, and quietly closed it behind her. Felipa started to run away from the building but stopped. She winced in pain and began rubbing both of her thighs. She started crying. "I hate him! I hate him!" She said aloud.

The alarm clock by Purita's bed was ringing incessantly, reminding her that she had better get up. She turned off the noisy apparatus, and while still groggy from a deep but short sleep, she took a shower and quickly dressed for the 8:00 a.m. briefing at the PIB building.

Chavez met her at the entrance of the building. "We still have about ten minutes before the director arrives."

"Are agents Martin and Lucas back from Clark Field, Chavez?"

"I don't think so. The director told me when I called him about your briefing that they will be unable to hear it. They have an early-morning meeting to attend. Generals MacArthur and Wainwright will be there."

"Is something going on at Clark Field?"

"I understand it is going to be about airplanes and better fortification of Corregidor, from what Romero told me," Chavez said. "The natives at the small town of Arayat have reported a man asking questions about the airfield and taking pictures of the Calumpit bridges, the Candaba Swamp, and Mt. Arayat."

Purita took a sip of her coffee, "Very interesting."

Chavez continued. "Anyway, the two agents will probably be going on a surveillance mission around those places I just mentioned, to find out, I am sure, if the man the natives have reported watches for the number types of US airplanes fly in and out of Clark. That is BOAM. Birds over a mountain, bird watching at Mt. Arayat."

"Sounds definitely like a foreign spy hard at work." Purita glanced at Chavez. "Where did you get the date book? From someone here at PIB?"

"McCord."

At exactly 8:00 a.m. Director of PIB Romero, PIB director of counterintelligence Brisco, and Manila Chief of Police Gomez entered the room. "Good morning, Chavez. Purita," greeted Romero. You both know Mr. Brisco and Chief Gomez. Let us go on with the briefing. I will brief Martin and Lucas when they get back from Clark."

Purita opened her briefing by handing Romero an official paper stamped URGENT. " I covertly picked up this document at Red Rose's headquarters last night."

Romero read it silently to himself first and then read it aloud to those in the room—Planned Objectives. We must determine the bases for advance landings in northern Luzon, including in Batan Islands, which are between Formosa and the northern tip of Luzon, for Japanese aircraft, as well as deep water for our naval ships. Orchid has designated Davao in Mindanao and Jolo Island as places that would make attacks on Borneo much easier. We attach a great deal of importance on those vital areas for obvious strategic reasons. Meanwhile, Gardenia in Iloilo had informed us of excellent landing bases for our navy and air in the Visayan Islands: Iloilo, Cebu, and Leyte.

"Very interesting," everyone murmured.

With urging from Romero, Purita proceeded to describe the men called Tanaka, Matsumuto, and Ikeda as posing as civilian clerks at the emporium, but in actuality they were Japanese Army officers. She informed them in great detail about the espionage network. "The code name of the Japanese intelligence in the Philippines is Saber, not Network as we have assumed," Purita said then paused. "Tanaka's code names are Red Rose as Chief of the Luzon Division and Iguana as the big chief of the entire organization Saber." She confirmed the PIB's suspicions about the divisions' code names.

Director Romero inquired as to whether the exact locations of Gardenia's headquarters in Iloilo and that of Orchid's in Mindanao were mentioned during the meeting, to which Purita said, "No." But she added that she would try and find out their exact locations.

Purita's briefing about Tanaka's espionage empire reminded Chavez of what Mac had told him months ago, "Catch Red Rose, and you'll catch Iguana." She continued about the spies Pfeiffel and Oberti and what their assignments entailed. "Each will be picked up by Agents 5 and 30, respectively." She began briefing the group about Sonny Sollow.

Chavez interjected. "Sollow is elusive and influential. He has many friends and acquaintances in high places in Manila. If I may make a suggestion, Sir," he said directing his gaze at Romero. "We should deal with Sollow separately. He appears to work by himself and only joins Tanaka's meetings at certain times. He is a loner."

Romero nodded. "Excellent suggestion, Chavez. Do you have photographs of Tanaka and his two aides?"

"I will check, Sir." Chavez came back with a thick folder and handed it to Purita, who went carefully through each photograph."

"Here they are. These look like newspapers and enlarged passport photos," Purita told the men and passed the photographs to them. "Unlike Matsumuto and Ikeda," she continued, "Tanaka very seldom shows himself in the store itself, but he is at his office at the emporium nearly every night from 7:00 p.m. to 1:00 a.m. Matsumuto and Ikeda are generally with him. They are all well armed all the time. I have been to Tanaka's office a number of times, but last night was the first time he invited me to their meeting. In their inner sanctum." Purita paused. "I forgot to mention the Boxer. His name is Hoshi. Vicious dog. He will attack to kill if you make the slightest move towards Tanaka."

"Where do they keep Hoshi when he is not with Tanaka?" Gomez inquired.

"Behind the emporium. It has a six foot wire fence, and the gate is most often locked," explained Purita. "There is dog house near the door facing the gate."

Romero gave Purita a hard look. "Will you be able to identify the German and the Italian foreign agents, Pfeiffel and Oberti?" He asked.

Purita nodded.

"How about Agents 5 and 30. Do you know what they look like, and their names?" Romero asked again.

"Yes," Purita answered. "Agent 5, James Wanabe, is a Filipino, born in San Francisco. He drives a 1939 Chevrolet repainted blue and white, which he had turned into a taxicab."

Chavez added, "And Agent 30 is Flores, also a Filipino but born in Angeles, Pampanga. He is short, about five feet two inches, and has a definite limp on his right leg when he walks. He drives a black Ford, also a 1939. We have photos of both of them. I have them here with me."

Romero studied the photographs for some time and passed them to Brisco and Gomez. "What do you think, Brisco? Chief?"

Brisco, PIB's Chief of counterintelligence, answered for both of them, "I think we have all the information we need." He paused and looked at everyone in the room. "I believe we are all well aware of what Japan has in mind. Everyday the newspapers and radio commentators in Manila speculate about Japan's intentions in Asia, and everyday they report on the American drive to improve the defense of the islands. Also, the heightened international developments have considerably increased tension between the US and Japan." Brisco took a deep breath. "The Americans are especially very suspicious of Japan's increasing air and naval power in French Indo-China."

"Yes. I am just grateful the general Filipino population is not, as of now, thinking of Japan one way or another, or we would have problems. It could start a riot against the Japanese living in this country," added Romero. He pursed his lips. "We must not waste time. We must brief our men and prepare them for their task." He gave each person in the room a hard look. "How do you think we can best go about capturing Tanaka and his spies? This intelligence network Saber—it has been giving the PIB a headache."

After many hours of intense discussion, they arrived at their plan of strategy. But before they left the briefing room, Romero approached

Purita with a frown on his face.

"Purita, I do not want you to go with the men to the Quiapo Hotel."

"Why not, Sir?" Purita asked, surprised at her boss's decision.

"Too dangerous," answered Romero. "They will recognize you."

"But Pfeiffel, Oberti, and Wanabe only know me as Cookie, the whore and waitress at Uncle Billy's. Flores has never seen me as either Purita or Cookie. I am the only one who can identify all four men."

"She is right, Sir," both Chavez and Brisco said.

"Sir," Purita said, "I really think I can help."

Romero was thoughtful for a while. "Very well," he finally replied, "you can join them, but sort of stay behind." Romero glanced at Chavez. "Any additions?"

"Yes, Sir. We must keep our plans from leaking to the newspapers and radio."

"Of course. Keep the number of people involved to a minimum. And only tell them what their specific assignment is. Only those who have the need to know."

Romero left the room, followed by Brisco and Gomez.

Meanwhile, very early that morning, Sollow left his fashionable house on Dewey Boulevard, drove to Binondo, and stopped in front of a tenement house. He knocked on the door. "Marcelo. Let me in."

As soon as Marcelo had opened the door, Sollow told him to get dressed. On their way to Kawazaka to rent a motor boat equipped with fishing gear, Sollow told Marcelo that Red Rose wanted for them to sabotage Corregidor that morning. But Sollow insisted that he would prefer that he and his companion first survey the area with binoculars and then sabotage the island fortress later that night.

Upon reaching Corregido they immediately exchanged views with each other to review how much knowledge each knew about the fortress. They discussed only the formidable weapons at Topside, and many other armaments including Sperry searchlights.

Sollow turned to look at Marcelo. "The plateau called Middleside contains buildings not critical to the defense of Corregidor. Look at the low area," he said emphatically.

"Yes, the 'Bottomside,'" Marcelo said. "To its east is Malinta Hill. Do we need to go to into all those tunnels? Or should we destroy it?"

"No," Sollow answered. "But to the west is the power plant. It's vital that we get that to help break their communications. If we blow up the power plant, Corregidor is finished." Sollow sounded sure of himself.

Marcelo nodded. "We'll have to enter it from the North Dock."

From North Channel, Sollow proceeded east to North Point, towards the tail of the tadpole shaped island where they could see Kindley Field and the radio intercept station.

From there they entered South Channel while they studied South Dock and the barrio of San Jose. They also studied the roads and the electric rail lines that led to the barrio and the two docks. After several hours, they went back to Manila.

That night the rain had started again and a mean west wind was whipping from the South China Sea but as planned, Sollow and Marcelo arrived at the Manila Hotel where they were met in the lobby by another Filipino undercover agent for the Japanese. He led them discretely to the motorboat tied to the hotel's dock.

Before leaving, Sollow told Marcelo to be certain there were guns, bombs and dynamites in the boat.

Marcelo nodded but his mind was on the weather. "This looks bad. They bay is getting rough," he told Sollow. "I do not think this small boat can take these big waves especially at the entrance of the bay. Maybe we should not go tonight."

Without answering Marcelo, Sollow opened the throttle and guided the boat across Manila Bay. By the time they had reached the open entrance, five foot waves were rushing in from Subic Bay causing the boat to bounce up and down and started taking on water.

"We're going to tie up at Corregidor's South Dock," Sollow shouted above the strong wind, "and get to the power plant from there instead. Then we're going back to the tail of the tadpole and take care of the airfield and radio station. And then go home."

"No!" Marcelo shouted back. "We must go back now. These big waves will sink us! We will not be able to swim this. The current here is too strong."

"We'll make it. We're almost there. I'm going to head for South Dock. We'll be protected there," Sollow insisted. "These wind and rain should soon subside."

Marcelo angrily reached for the steering wheel. "You'll kill us!"

Sollow took out a knife from inside his jacket and stabbed Marcelo in the arm and shoved him into the dark water. "Go down deep you disgusting man," Sollow howled. "Go down deep to your liquid grave. Cowardice begets destruction."

As soon as Sollow regained his composure he turned starboard, the boat dropped down from atop a wave and then was immediately lifted up by the next. Sollow held on to the steering wheel and turned the boat in the direction of Corregidor. Two or three more waves carried the boat to the shores of the barrio of San Jose where he stayed hidden until the following early morning where he hopped on a large commercial fishing boat on its way to Cavite. That same day, Sollow reported the incident to Tanaka who commented that the mission would have to be accomplished another day. But soon, he said.

A week later, on a beach in Cavite, south of Manila, the local marine police discovered an unidentified man's body. The death was deemed as a drowning.

The week passed quickly as Romero had predicted. That Wednesday, twenty men from the Manila police and the PIB were geared up and ready to go. By noon, they quietly and methodically arrived at the Quiapo Hotel. Two well-armed police detectives, dressed in civilian clothes, along with Chavez and Purita, entered the lobby of the hotel. One detective mingled with the guests in the lobby, while the other sat, comfortably but alert. Chavez and Brisco each pulled a chair. Brisco grabbed a magazine from a nearby table and sat near the front entrance of the hotel, while Chavez, newspaper in hand, positioned himself between the elevator and the stairs, close to Purita, who stayed behind one of the columns in the lobby, within full view of Chavez and Brisco. She passed her time reading a book about Rudolph Valentino.

On the street, near the entrance, seven PIB men, two posing as beggars and the others as loiterers and bystanders were waiting for Wanabe's blue and white taxicab and Flores's black Ford. The others surrounded the hotel. Everyone was now in place according to plan—inside and outside.

At five minutes to one, Wanabe was the first to drive up and enter the lobby. He stood near the door with a newspaper. He was followed a minute later by Flores, who looked nervously around the large room until he saw Wanabe. The two spies made signs of recognizing each other before Flores sat down not far from the elevator and the stairs.

Pfeiffel and Oberti emerged from the elevator to the lobby at about the same time the grandfather clock struck one. Wanabe and Flores immediately joined them, and they all left the hotel. With a slight nod from Purita, Chavez and Brisco followed them outside, and with the help of the undercover PIB agents and police detectives, they were all grabbed and arrested for espionage.

At 8:30 that night, other PIB agents raided the emporium. Unfortunately, Tanaka, Hoshi, and Matsumuto had escaped, carrying with them important military papers. That same night, a body was found in a closet that Purita later identified as Ikeda.

Somehow, the Manila News got hold of the information about the raid and printed the story, front page, the very next day, congratulating the PIB but bemoaning the fact that the two top level spies escaped.

That same day, the emporium was shut down, and the digging operation in the backyard produced an unidentified male corpse. Meanwhile, Steve Ball, the radio commentator reported: "Yesterday must have been spy day, and a good day it was for the Philippine Investigative Bureau. While the Nagoya Emporium was being raided, an American spy for the Japanese, Dwarf, was taken into custody. En route to Clark, Dwarf killed the MP guarding him. While trying to escape, a PBI agent fatally shot him. Clark's commander refused to give the name of the PIB agent. Perhaps lady luck is at long last smiling on the long-beleaguered PIB. Will their next captive be the patterned killer who has wreaked havoc in Manila, leaving at least four, maybe five American officers dead and mutilated? Let us hope. Good night!"

CHAPTER 25

One morning, while they were having breakfast at her apartment, Mac asked Miguela about Sollow's rented house and the neighborhood. She did not hear his question, but instead she commented how much more relaxed Mac was since Miller officially closed shop and discontinued Quest.

She did not answer but lowered her eyes, perhaps embarrassed that he might read her thoughts racing through her mind about him.

Mac glanced at Miguela and said, "Many people who live on Dewey Boulevard are affluent and the streets are generally quiet, including Outrigger Lane, where Sollow rents. Coming from downtown, Sollow's house is to the left, and Colonel Miller's is to the right."

Miguela looked at Mac quizzically and wondered why he should be so interested about the two houses, but she shrugged.

"Those houses are only about a fourth of a mile from your parents's house, are they not?" inquired Mac.

"Yes. And the cove."

"What did you say, Miguela?"

"I said, yes. And the cove. That cove seems to be identified with Buenavista." She paused. "Miller's farewell party is tonight. Are you coming with us?"

"I can't. Miller thinks I died in a car accident. Besides, there's something I must do. But I'll meet you at your car later."

That night, Mac eased his car from the driveway of Miguela's apartment on Taft Avenue and drove as far as the public playground on this side of the Pasig River. He turned left on Magallanes Drive, then turned left again on Bonifacio Drive. Deciding to park his car on the side street off Muelle San Francisco, Mac shut the car door and walked on South Port Harbor's busy Pier 7, which he had heard was the longest pier in the world. He inhaled deeply, filling his lungs with the fresh air from Manila Bay, a deep inlet of South China Sea, which he thought was one of the prettiest bodies of water he had seen and admitted to himself, with a sudden feeling of homesickness, that it was probably as colorful and beautiful as his beloved Chesapeake Bay. Squinting to sharpen his gaze, Mac focused his eyes beyond the large commercial vessels tied along the docks. In the distance, lighted US ships lying at anchor looked like tiny toys. He stood there a while enjoying the breeze and taking in the surroundings.

Mac drove away from the harbor and stopped at the Luneta. He had been there a number of times before during the day.

He stopped his car and scampered up the huge boulders, placed there years ago by the US Army Corps of Engineers, separating miles of the shorelines of Manila Bay from the land. A sudden thought came to him. It would not really be difficult for anyone with strong arms and legs to climb those high rocks from below. It would be made easier by high tide, too.

Mac left the Luneta. He passed the Army and Navy Club and went slowly on, turning on a dirt road and again parking his car, this time behind a clump of trees. He began walking between the boulders and the edge of Dewey Boulevard and estimated that, although the boulders were only about four feet high from the ground along the edge, they were widely and gradually slanted down, making it approximately ten feet or higher from the water's edge.

It was dark but there was ample illumination from the reflections of the many lights on the bay, the bright moon, the stars, and car headlights. Suddenly he stopped. A natural arch-like passage, which only time and nature could create, caught his attention. He got on his hands and knees and crawled through the passage, ending on a lower ledge on the other side, about two feet above the beach.

Since the tide had receded, Mac jumped down on the sandy beach and stayed there a while, mulling over an idea. Suddenly, he had a great urge to leave the beach. Not too far away, he could see Colonel Miller's house glowing with party lights and could even hear, now and then, music from a phonograph drifting through the air.

Mac ran to his car and drove until he could see lights shining through the thick trees of Buenavista. He knew that a couple of yards at the north end of the property was the cove he was forced to dive into while going after his attacker. He stopped his car by the side of the road, close to the cove, and looked down, mentally trying to penetrate the extreme depth and the vicious current of the water below and reconstructed the puzzling cove incident. After he had plunged into the water that night, he could not find the man who had attacked him. At that moment, his attacker's immediate disappearance then became clear to Mac. Since there was no report the next day or even in the days that followed of a man having drowned, there was a probability that his attacker, who also could have been Roosie's murderer, could either be Sollow or Miller, since their houses were across the street from each other, and the two houses were but a short distance from the cove. His attacker could have either swam below Kawazaka's marina and went home, or swam upstream towards the Army and Navy Club or the Manila Hotel and walked back home.

Mac walked back to his car and went directly to Outrigger Lane. But, instead of parking on the area Miller allotted for guests, he turned left and stopped a block away from Sollow's rented house. The two-story stucco house was surrounded with ornate cement walls. He tried the front and garage doors and found them both locked. He walked around, also found the back door locked, and assumed that the windows of the house by the swimming pool were also securely locked. He came upon a permanent cement bench situated behind the shadow of the house, facing the pool with small flowering plants near it. Behind the bench were a couple of tall, bushy gardenia plants growing close to the house. Mac sat down, happy to rest his feet. His eyes soon rested on a spacious veranda facing Manila Bay and thought enviously that Sonny Sollow certainly had a magnificently clear view of the bay and all the activities and ships lying at anchor. He got to his feet and began circling the large house, still searching for an opening into it. After a time, he found himself, once again, by the swimming pool. His eyes wandered to the tall gardenia plants behind the ornate cement bench. Curiously, he inspected behind the plants and was amazed to discover a narrow door. It was unlocked. Mac quietly opened it and stepped inside the house, and, while groping in the room, his hand fell on a matchbox on a nearby table. He dared not turn on the electric light but struck a match to see in what part of the house he was standing. He was in the kitchen. He quickly blew out the match and dropped the matchbox in his pocket.

Mac entered the dining room, where he found a candelabrum. Mac took a candle with him. But before lighting it, he closed all the curtains and briskly crossed over to a big living room adjacent to the study that he hoped would not be as bare as the other rooms he had gone through. In a corner was a large desk. He inspected each desk drawer, but found them empty. On the other side of the room was a floor to ceiling, wall-to-wall library stand. Here and there were old books, Saturday Evening Posts, Esquire Magazines, and old newspapers piled high. He leafed through some of the magazines, hoping a card or a piece of paper might fall out of the pages, giving some clues about Sonny Sollow. He picked up a newspaper with a front page that attracted his attention. The bold black title read—"US Army Lieutenant Murdered." The story was about Stan Czestochowa's murder. What further drew his attention was that the title of the article was underscored three times and heavily circled in red crayon. He winced, recalling the brutal killing of the young officer. He tore the page, folded it, placed it in his pocket, and immediately inspected the whole room. Underneath the full-length curtain, he picked up what he assumed was the key to the house.

Mac was about to leave the room when he heard faint footsteps coming from the kitchen headed toward the study. He blew out the candle and fanned the smoke away with his hands so as to diffuse the odor and hid behind a lounge chair. The door to the study slowly opened, and a man came in and went directly to the same window where Mac had found the key. The man began feeling with his hands underneath the same window curtains. From there, he went to the desk, searched every desk drawer, and left the room. It seemed to Mac that the stranger was familiar with the house from the way he moved about in the dark with ease.

From the sounds of the footsteps, Mac could tell that the man was on his way upstairs. Without hesitation and not wanting to have any confrontation with the stranger, Mac left the house from where he had entered and closed the door softly behind him. He hid in the bathhouse to wait for the stranger, whom he just knew would also use the kitchen door. After waiting for about five or ten minutes, Mac saw him emerge from the kitchen door. He tried to follow the stranger, but the man seemed to know the neighborhood and soon disappeared into the darkness.

Miguela was standing by the Molina car in the designated parking place for guests.

"Where have you been, Mac? It is midnight," she whispered. "I have been waiting for you."

"I'm sorry, darling. I had some important work to do. How's the party?"

"Lots of people and lots of champagne. I told Uncle Jose that I would go back with a friend and for him to go on home when he decides to do so."

"Let's go to the Manila International Club. I'll treat you to a Coca-Cola and a sandwich."

On the way there, Mac asked Miguela who else was at the party that he knew.

"Senator Magal and his wife, Dr. Longo and his wife, Lieutenant Colonel Rhoades, and Chavez."

"How is Colonel Miller?"

"Fine host, but he seemed to have his eyes on someone in that group."

"Like who?"

"I am not certain, Mac. But it seemed to me that everywhere Charlie went, Colonel Miller was nearby. I think he was shadowing him."

"That's interesting," mused Mac. "What else can you tell me about Miller?"

"That he has paid his rent through the end of the year, but I heard that he will be leaving for California in a day or two. Might just be a rumor, or I would have heard from my father."

"You'd make an excellent spy, darling," Mac said and kissed Miguela.

Although they did not get back to Miguela's apartment until 3:00 a.m., Mac was up by 5:00 a.m. The whole time they were at the Manila International Club, he felt the compunction of going back to Sollow's house to finish what he was doing.

Without waking Miguela, Mac hailed a cab instead of driving his car. When he was a block away from Sonny Sollow's rented house, Mac told the driver to stop and began walking the long block. It was early, and the fog coming from the bay was heavy. He went to the front door and tried the key that he had found last night. It did not fit, but to his surprise, the door was unlocked. He stepped inside and shut the door behind him.

Even though it was very quiet in the house, and it appeared that no one was there, Mac instinctively walked lightly. All at once, a loud gunshot from upstairs shattered the quietness of the empty house. Mac was more anxious to see about the shot than to go after the man whom he saw fleeing from the house. The first bedroom he looked into showed no signs of human presence. The master bedroom, though, was different. The dresser drawers and the closet door were wide open, and the mattress had been lifted.

The whole room looked like someone had been searching for something. By the bed, a male body was lying immobile and face down. He was bleeding. Mac turned over the body.

"Jesus! Chavez!" He placed his fingers on his friend's neck to feel his pulse. "Chavez! Chavez! Can you hear me?"

Chavez opened his eyes. "McCord!" He tried to smile but his face reflected pain. "Is it bad, Mac?"

"It's a bad wound, close to your heart. Whoever shot you thought he got you."

"Help me up, Mac," said Chavez, lifting up his right arm.

"No! You must lay still!" Mac came back with a couple of towels. He wadded one and placed it under Chavez's head and the other on Chavez's shoulder. "This should temporarily keep the blood from rushing out. I'm calling a taxicab to take you to the Hospital."

Chavez's eyes fluttered. "The key to my car is in my shirt pocket. I parked it behind the house."

On their way to the hospital, Mac asked, "Did you see who took a shot at you?"

Chavez shook his head. "I am not sure. It happened so fast. May have been Sollow," he said and then lost consciousness.

At the hospital, two nurses expertly placed Chavez on a gurney and wheeled him to the emergency room.

Three hours passed, and the doctor awakened Mac, who had insisted on staying at the hospital. "I'm Doctor Fletcher. I understand you are a friend of Mr. Chavez."

Mac nodded. "How is he?"

"Fine. He is tough and stubborn. We found the bullet lodged in his collarbone. That saved his life. He should be out of here in a couple of days," the doctor answered. "His wife and children are with him. But you can go in and see him."

"No. He should be alone with his family." The next day, Mac went back to the hospital.

"How's the patient?" he asked Chavez.

"I hate being in the hospital. I feel well enough that I will ask the doctor if I can leave tomorrow. My wife is a nurse. She will take good care of me. Mac, I want to thank you for saving my life. I could have bled to death." Chavez paused momentarily. "That was my second time in that house."

Mac pulled a chair near Chavez's bed. "I've been thinking what you told me on the way to the hospital. You thought it might have been Sollow who shot you. Could it have been Sollow?"

"I do not know. According to our intelligence, Sollow seems to have disappeared," Chavez explained. "Romero has directed undercover agents to be on the lookout for him at transportation points—roads, railroads, waterways."

"That Nagoya Emporium raid must have forced him to go underground for a while." Mac paused. "Why did you go back to Sollow's house? Find anything?"

Chavez smiled. "Looking for clues, I guess, that might have led me to arrest him. I found nothing on both trips. My theory is that Sollow is either very neat, or he only lives in that house occasionally. He is so clever, I sometimes wonder if he is real."

"What do you mean, Chavez?"

"It appears that Sollow is only in that house occasionally. I think he uses it only as an address. Listen, Mac, during my fifteen years of service, I have inspected a million homes. That house is too neat! We know he is a spy. But we have to catch him red-handed."

"I have a strange feeling about him. You say that he is a spy, but I think he's more than just that."

Chavez closed his eyes and when he opened them, he looked squarely at Mac. "Mac, I am glad you are here. I have something to tell you, and

I guess this is as good a place as any. I know that you are suspicious of Colonel Bradford Miller. You are also suspicious of Lieutenant Colonel Dusty Rhoades. You think that he was the one who had been trying to kill you. Furthermore, you cannot decide who, between the two men, is Boris Meissner. You have been doing your best to trap them. Am I right, Mac?"

"Yes. But, what's all this about, Chavez?"

"Let me finish. Mac, I know why you came to Manila. You yourself told me why. Walters told me about you. He, somehow, was convinced that you could succeed where we failed." Chavez leaned his head back on his pillows. "I should not tell you this. It is supposed to be top-secret information, but I feel, as a friend, that you must know the truth in order for you to rearrange your agenda and place your utmost effort in completing your mission. I know that you want to do that."

Mac nodded, curious to know where Chavez was going.

"Mac, Lieutenant Colonel Rhoades' real name is Edward Martin, FBI agent. He works at the FBI headquarters in Washington. Colonel Bradford Miller's real name is William Lucas, an agent from the FBI branch in Los Angeles. They are here, coincidentally, for the same purpose, but each to find different murderers," Chavez explained. He continued why they were invited to the Philippine Department, albeit the two men were after two different killers. "The PIB and the U.S. Army obviously, are after the murderer of four American Army officers and also searching all over Manila where the Japanese spy network could be located. Danbury told them that the Army and the PIB are after one man or two men. Martin and Lucas stated that they were initially after the murderers including the culprit who killed the Americans." Chavez paused. According to his briefing to me, Danbury asked Mr. Lucas, "Why did you find yourself in Manila?"

FBI agent, William Lucas related to Danbury why he was in Manila. Evidently, a spy who sabotaged a U.S. vessel at Port San Pedro, California was able to escape from the first FBI agent who had been following him. During a gunfight, the saboteur killed the second agent and then disappeared from sight. Later, informants reported to the FBI branch in California that the saboteur and killer was seen in Honolulu and later in Hong Kong and then in Manila. Lucas was then assigned the job of tracking down the spy in the Philippines. At the nation's capital he met with G-2 staff officer, Colonel Danbury and together they planned a strategy. In addition, Lucas agreed to assume the name of Colonel Bradford Miller as his cover name. "The man I'm after is Maurice Olivier, a Frenchman fluent in German. He's spying for the Germans. He parts his black hair in the middle," he explained.

It was Martin's turn to explain, but first he thanked Danbury for suggesting that he too assume a cover name of Lieutenant Colonel Sonny Rhoades, a.k.a. Dusty Rhoades. He continued that Lucas and he had not known each other but he was glad to see another FBI agent in Manila." He and his assistant, Agent James Kagan, who unfortunately got murdered recently in Manila, came to the city by the invitation of Mr. Romero, chief of the PIB, via his boss in the Federal Bureau of Investigation in Washington. They were to aid the PIB in a covert mission to uncover a Japanese spy network in the Philippines. Chavez told Mac that Martin mentioned some time ago that "he had heard about me from his boss. He spoke very highly of me and Mr. Romero, and of course, the PIB." He also said, "Kagan and I were also briefed about Mac, by Army Colonel Duncan in Washington." Martin stated, "The invitation from the PIB came first before the murders in Baltimore." He narrated to Danbury that at the same time he was anxious to find the man responsible for mutilating the bodies of two FBI agents in Baltimore, Maryland. According to FBI analyses, the killer made a quick trip from Manila to Baltimore where the agents were on temporary duty during that time. The two agents killed were experts in German and on Germany and were slated to sail for Great Britain to aid the British in anything related to Germany and Hitler. It was determined from early on through British intelligence and informants that the person he and Kagan were looking for left the United States for Canada. There he boarded a ship for Australia and on to the Philippines. "The man we wanted had reportedly entered Manila unnoticed," Martin said. "I don't have the name of the man I'm after or his physical description. I know, however, that he's in possession of two passports. One, that of FBI Agent Donald Phillips and the other passport belonged to FBI Agent Vincent Dell, both residents of Maryland."

Mac, embarrassed by what Chavez had told him, murmured, "One of these days I'll have to apologize to agent Martin and thank him for saving my life two or three times." Mac took a deep breath. "Have they left Manila?"

Chavez shook his head. "No. Not yet. They had an urgent call from General MacArthur's headquarters to report to Clark as soon as possible. I suppose, in time, they will have to go back to where they came from, or they will separately accept an assignment here to help MacArthur."

"Did Martin and Lucas know each other?"

"Not from the beginning."

"Jeez. I feel like an idiot, Chavez. I suspected both men because they have the same coloring as Boris Meissner, according to intelligence reports given to me in Washington—blond hair, blue eyes, and tall. A good start I thought. So, I guess Meissner is still in Manila masquerading as someone else with an assumed name."

"He may be," answered Chavez, clasping Mac's arm.

"Thanks again for helping me." He paused temporarily. "Be careful. I would hate to see you become another casualty. There are many evil and murderous people in Manila."

"I know," Mac whispered back. "But there are an awful lot of good ones."

Chavez smiled. "If you need help, call the PIB and ask for Cookie."

"Cookie?"

Chavez nodded and smiled devilishly. "I forgot to tell you. Cookie is also Miss Purita Aquino! Your former secretary at Quest. She is a PIB undercover agent. I think that Poco has told you that she is always followed by her pimp," Chavez laughed. "That pimp he was talking about is a covert PIB agent." Chavez paused momentarily. "I also briefed Martin and Lucas about Purita, a.k.a Cookie. And, Purita about the two men.

"Damn! Chavez! You're full of surprises. You should be in the hospital more often. Why in the hell didn't you tell me earlier?"

"I couldn't, Mac. Keep what I just told you about Martin, Lucas, and Purita to yourself, though," Chavez said, placing his index finger to his lips. "We do not want to compromise their safety." Chavez sipped some water. "And Mac. Get away for a little bit. Take a short vacation. Lake Taal is a beautiful place. Stay at the Lake Taal Hotel."

Outside the hospital, Mac lit a cigarette, walked to the nearest café, and ordered beer. The unexpected information he received from Chavez unnerved him.

"So who the hell is after me if it's not Rhoades or Miller?" he asked himself under his breath. He had earlier planned to again investigate Miller's house and continue to monitor Cookie and Rhoades's activities at Uncle Billy's.

He shook his head. "They're no longer in my game plan, and I must thank Purita for saving my life last June," he murmured, discouraged. Putting his hands into his pants pocket, he took out the key and matchboxes he had found in Miller's and Sollow's rented houses on Dewey Boulevard. He contemplated as his next move what Chavez had suggested about taking a vacation.

While Mac was with Miguela that night, he had a call from Charlie, who told him that he had learned from the PIB that morning that Chavez was in the hospital with a bullet wound.

"How is he, Mac?"

"He isn't dead."

"Where'd it happen?"

"At Sollow's rented house."

"He's lucky. Did he find something there?"

"No, nothing."

"Who shot him?"

"He thought it was Sollow, but he wasn't sure."

Charlie then inquired how Mac knew about Chavez.

"I was in the house when it happened."

There was a long silence before Charlie made any comment.

"How about you, Mac? Find anything?"

"Nothing," Mac answered.

At that moment, he could not understand why he said that he had found nothing. He was not cerebral in his deductions. This time, Charlie's question, though innocent it may have sounded, left a knot in his stomach. "How's Poco?" he asked, adroitly changing the subject.

Charlie explained that the Filipino sergeant had received an order from USAFFE to go back to his old unit. "And, as for me, I told you before, the end of December is it." There was a pause. "Care to have supper at Chinatown's Peking Duck tomorrow night, Mac?"

321

"I'm sorry, Charlie," Mac answered, "I'll be on my way to Lake Taal. I'm about burned out with all these futile investigations. I need to be by myself for a couple of days."

"I don't blame you. Where in Lake Taal are you staying?"

"Lake Taal Hotel," Mac answered.

CHAPTER 26

Several weeks had passed since the Philippine Investigation Bureau raided the Japanese emporium. During that raid, General Tanaka and Colonel Matsumuto had escaped. The Philippine watchdog was immediately accused of flawed strategy and lack of discipline to stop information leaks.

For a time, however, since that raid, there were no known occurrences of sabotage in Manila and nearby provinces. But early one evening there was a loud and deadly explosion at a large POL depot at nearby Clark Field. The USAFFE intelligence operatives at the airfield base hastily went to work and brought the PIB into the midst of the flurry to find the perpetrators.

Late that night at Kapalaran, a loud knocking on his door awakened Mac. His visitor was a covert agent from Romero's office. Shortly after he had presented his credentials to Mac, the agent briefed him on the nature of the incident at the depot.

"I am very sorry to have awakened you, Sir. But Mr. Chavez, with the consent of the Chief of the PIB, Mr. Jesus Romero, very highly recommended you to USAFFE for help in the investigation based on your previous experience in France."

"How is Chavez?" Mac inquired.

"Improving fast," said the agent, smiling with fondness upon hearing Mac's inquiry about the popular Chavez. The agent continued with his briefing. "The horrible explosion at first was suspected to be the work of the underground Japanese spy organization, under the continued leadership of Tanaka, whom, you may recall, escaped but whose modus operandi, the PIB believes, will of course continue in helping Japan's takeover of the Philippines and other Southeast Asian countries."

"That all sounds positive. But how did I get into the picture simply because of my assignment in France?" Mac said puzzled at the agent's story.

"Well, Sir, as I understood from Mr. Chavez, when it was discovered the type of deaths the two Army guards encountered at the depot, your name immediately came up, that you would know for whom to look."

"Where's the depot?" Mac asked.

"It does not belong to Clark. It is near it. It is sort of a POL reservoir depot accessible to any military base that runs out of, say, petroleum, oil or lubricant in nearby provinces or Manila," the covert agent explained. "It's under Clark's jurisdiction."

"How did the men die?"

"They met strange and unusual deaths. Their heads were found about ten feet away from their bodies, and their fingers were missing," said the agent. "They were on their way home from the small base."

"I see," Mac said softly. "That appears to be the ritual signature of a serial killer I have long suspected." Mac glanced at the agent. "Is that all?"

"Another thing, Sir. Four Filipino civilian workers also were killed. They were on their way home from the base as well when shrapnel hit them. They were rushed to the infirmary, but they could not be saved," the agent said, then he paused. "One more thing, Sir. You are to depart for Clark Field now. Your name has already been cleared with the authorities there. You will be briefed of the incident when you get there. Here is your top-secret ID. Both USAFFE and the PIB are cautioning you not to discuss anything with anyone except designated personnel, to whom you will be introduced." The agent paused. "We are all afraid of leaks and a possible danger to yourself. The proper military echelon at the airfield has been notified of your background, and you are to submit your report to Lieutenant Colonel Dougherty." The agent paused momentarily. "The PIB and USAFFE's intelligence group will be anxious to hear from you."

"I understand," Mac said.

"I shall be leaving now, Sir. Good luck!"

Two officers from Clark's intelligence unit were assigned with Mac. But the three days of intensive sleuthing on the deaths of the two Army guards did not yield them any clues as to the identity of the culprit. It did not, however, surprise Mac that the incident became another unsolved crime. The reason: no witnesses and the overwhelming cleverness of the criminal. But Mac was certain that Meissner committed the crime, which he indicated in his report, but catching him was another story.

Mac was only too happy when Lieutenant Colonel Dougherty called the investigation at the small base closed. He considered his assignment frustrating. "Another unsolved crime," he murmured to himself. But despite his disappointment, he decided to stay at Clark Field where he was assigned a BOQ until the next day. With permission from the colonel, he checked out a Jeep from the Transportation Unit and reconnoitered the area. It soon relaxed him and he saw some interesting things he otherwise would not have known about the area. And, Clark Field was more than like any other military airfields he saw in the Philippines. It was not only a vast place but several of its runways were very wide and long, fit for big bombers and a multiplicity of different size hangars. Barracks for the personnel were evident some distance away from the airfield.

Mac stopped when he reached an isolated, well cared for wooded area within the confines of Clark with the sign Section F and inroads going somewhere. He followed the one closer to him. He got out of the Jeep and was immediately encountered by two tough looking Filipino guards who seemed to have appeared from nowhere and asked for his ID. Upon getting their approval, Mac drove on and stopped at a well-hidden enclosure with about ten large storage tanks with big letters written on their sides, 'Petroleum.' Not too far away were about twenty storage tanks marked 'Oil.' And over a hundred standing barrels, each was marked with red letters, 'Lubricant.' They were covered with thick tarpaulins. He diverted his eyes to several sheds built among the trees. He walked to where the sheds were and discovered that each door was locked. But one of the shed's door had a hole in it. Mac peeped in and saw rifles, pistols, machine guns, mortar and hand grenades. In buildings shaped like garages were tanks, motor trucks, passenger cars and some Jeeps.

"Jeez," Mac said softly, "wouldn't a Japanese spy love to see this place." He turned around and sat on one of the barrels for some time and became aware that the sun had receded and cooler air had prevailed over the heat and humidity. Instinctively, he was wary of impending danger. He looked around him and quickly got on his feet and walked towards the Jeep when a hard fist hit his jaw and downed him on his back.

When the attacker tried to stab Mac with a dagger, perceptively Mac rolled to one side and grabbed the stranger's legs, causing the attacker to fall backward. With speed, Mac pulled himself up from the ground and grabbed his attacker by the shirt to pull him up but the stranger forcefully freed himself and ran, disappearing among the trees.

The Manila traffic was literally at a standstill. Drivers of karetelas tried to bully others by shouting obscenities, while cars and taxicabs sat on their horns. But nothing moved.

"Hey," Mac called to the driver whose karetela was standing near his car. "Suppose a typhoon occurs suddenly?"

"We will all be swept away," answered the driver casually.

Mac took a deep breath and steadied himself. He stuck his head out of his car window and asked the same karetela driver, "What's going on?"

"Everybody is in Manila," answered the driver and paused. "See over there?" He said pointing. "It is that procession. The Catholic churches and Catholic schools are rehearsing for December eighth, the holy day of the Immaculate Conception. There is going to be a fiesta in Manila. This traffic is nothing. Wait till December eighth. All the Catholic schools and churches will be opened to the public, and they will serve food and drinks. There will be music and merriment. People will be dancing on the streets."

After a couple of hot and miserable hours, the procession finally turned right on a less busy street, easing the traffic. Meanwhile, Mac noticed that the big altar that was under construction several weeks ago appeared finished, with carpenters putting finishing touches to the giant platform. Benches for the faithful were being installed.

On the way to Kapalaran to pick up his clothes, Chavez's previous suggestion to Mac about going to Lake Taal was making more and more sense. True, he told himself, he was in a rut. He asked himself seriously if he should continue with his disguise as Vic McTaggart. The latest incident at the POL should convince him, he told himself, that, despite his disguise, he was still known to whoever it was stalking him.

"Cunning son of a bitch. I've become the hunted!" Mac murmured incredulously. He realized then, more than ever, that no one could help him—not Poco, not Charlie, not even Chavez. He had to help himself.

"I must get away by myself, sort things out, and develop a better strategy before he kills me," he said under his breath. Suddenly, a loud whistle jolted him out of his thoughts. He looked around and soon discovered that a city policeman, standing on a traffic platform under a wide yellow umbrella, was impatiently urging him to move on.

Once Mac passed the Quiapo Catholic Church, the traffic became unsnarled and he was able to go a comfortable speed.

The Coconut Tree Lounge, the one and only establishment at the arched entrance of Kapalaran, was now in sight. Mac glanced at his wristwatch. It showed 3:00 p.m. It was hot and humid, and his disguise contributed a great deal to his discomfort. He parked his car, went inside, and ordered beer. Very soon, he heard a soft, familiar female voice behind him.

"Hello, Victor McTaggart. Long time no see."

Mac turned around and was delighted to see Anna.

"Have you found the murderers yet?"

"I wish," Mac said softly. "To make it worse, I've not heard or seen my prime suspect, Sonny Sollow. I hope he hasn't left Manila."

Anna appeared surprised. "Oh?"

"What's that supposed to mean?"

"Mac, this is Kapalaran. The underbelly of Manila. Remember? Everything that happens in the city flows through here." Anna fixed her eyes on Mac. "He is still around."

"Hope you're right. Do you know where he is?"

Anna nodded. "Yes."

"Sollow is a spy and possibly a murderer, Anna. You should tell the police."

"You know I keep away from the police. They are bad news. Besides, many of them are corrupt and can cause me problems." Anna paused. "Come with me to my office. I will show you on the map where you will most likely find Sollow."

In the office, she unfolded a map of Manila. "Here, near the Manila railroad in Binondo. Right here," she said, pointing to the map.

"Doesn't that rail line go as far as San Fernando, La Union?" Mac asked.

Anna nodded. "Yes. Almost over nine hundred and sixty-five kilometers from Manila through the Central Plain. It stops at La Union in northern Luzon and goes way down south of Manila."

"He has immediate access to transportation. He can easily get lost either going north or south by railway or road. Thanks for the tip. I'll pass it along to a very good Filipino friend."

"Chavez?

"Yes. Do you mind? It's important that he knows."

"I will not be the bearer of the information," she paused. "You look discouraged, Mac."

"I've tried to be optimistic about eventually catching the killer or killers of the officers. It has been an unsuccessful venture."

Mac continued to say that he had asked himself many times whether he should keep using the disguise, and the answer was always yes until a recent incident.

"I had my disguise on recently on an assignment and someone still tried to kill me. The thought of discarding it didn't convince me until now, when I saw you, Anna, and talked to you."

"This is a very interesting story, Mac. A person has tried to take your life a couple of times earlier, before your disguise. And I recall you telling me, the group you joined had been disbanded."

Mac nodded. "Some of the members have gone back to the United States. "Poco has since joined his old unit." He went on to say that Major Charlie North, whom she also knew, might still be working on the case. "I don't know that for certain. However, we're each on our own." He took a deep breath and stated that he would like to be reassigned if he did not accomplish something soon.

Anna thought for a while with half-closed eyes, and then she quickly opened them and fixed her eyes on Mac. "This person must know you with or without your disguise and probably knows your every move. Obviously, your disguise is not working, for you are still a known and important factor to that someone, who, since you arrived here, checked you out as his target." She inclined her head to one side. "Move away from where you are now living and do not tell anyone in your former group where you are going. It is difficult to tell who is a friend and who is an enemy anymore." She glanced at Mac. "You will think clearer without that disguise. Manila is too hot and humid."

"Sounds like a good idea." Mac glanced at his watch. "I've got to go, Anna. Thanks for the suggestion."

Mac could hear the telephone ringing in his house as he parked his car by the front door. He rushed inside and grabbed the receiver. "Hello." He answered. There was a long silence, and then he heard a soft click at the other end. A sudden knot formed in his stomach.

The next day, he called the Ruby Redd restaurant and asked for either Ruby or Big Redd. A female voice answered and said that she was Ruby's cousin, and she and her chef husband were attending to the restaurant until the Redds came back from their vacation in Cebu.

Relieved that he did not have to explain himself, Mac said that he was a renter of the house adjacent to the Periscope Club and Fat Mama's Hibiscus but that he planned to move out immediately. He further explained that the rent had been paid in advance through the end of December.

With the help of Anna, Mac moved to a small, one-story house several blocks from Lara's Casino.

One evening at his newly rented house, Mac pulled out a box from under his bed and poured out the contents, which he called his "informants" on the dining room table, as he had done on several occasions. Perhaps by some magic they would reveal to him the identity of the killer. He stared at the items and reviewed in his mind the importance of each object. There was the sapphire ring that seemed to attract so much attention, especially from Charlie North, who wanted to buy it. He recalled Duvalier whispering that the ring belonged to Boris Meissner.

Mac leaned his head against the chair and closed his eyes to help his memory. What his friend Stone at the FBI in Washington had said about Meissner rushed to his mind. Then his eyes settled on the evil-looking buckle with the face of a cobra.

And there was the dagger with the checkered handle. His eyes fell on a brown shirt button and the brown shoe he had found on the street near the cove. They all seemed to whisper to him that they were important, yet they yielded no results. He turned his head slightly to his right.

"Ah," he murmured to himself. "My most recent informants."

The matchboxes and the key somehow gave him a slight hope that perhaps they would lead him to the murderer. He picked up the matchboxes; both had the Periscope, the Club's logo. The third one he had found at Lara's Casino. He especially liked its logo, the ace of spades.

"A winner," Mac thought.

While almost absentmindedly toying with the matches, he became all at once aware of number 219 someone had written on one of the matchboxes. Mac looked at the other matchbox he had picked up at Sonny Sollow's house and discovered that it, too, had the number 219 written on it. He studied both matchboxes.

"Damn strange," he murmured.

He gathered the matchboxes and the key, dropped them in his pocket, got in his car, and drove to the Periscope Club, which was now over a mile from his newly rented house. Instead of going inside the club, Mac stood outside for a few minutes in the darkest part of the street and watched for anyone suspicious loitering near the house he had recently vacated. As he watched the house located across the street from the Periscope Club and Fat Mama's Hibiscus, Mac hoped that he had permanently escaped the person who had been following him. But, as he stood there, he saw a silhouette of a tall man wearing a hat get out of a car, gave the house a quick look, walked around it once, and peered through the first floor windows. Satisfied that the house was empty, the stranger hurriedly walked across the street and disappeared down in one of the back alleys.

Mac wondered whether that tall man was his stalker or merely a person interested in renting the house. He turned around, went inside the club, and walked directly to the bar. While Hoagy Carmichael's "Star Dust" was softly playing in the club's Nickelodeon, workers were carrying props to the stage, obviously getting ready for their eleven to twelve male show.

"What will you have, handsome?" the bartender asked.

Mac recalled the lisp, the red dress, and the blond wig. On the other hand, Mac doubted whether Johnson would recognize him. Mac did not answer.

"I don't believe you heard me. What's your pleasure?"

"Beer," Mac said and, remembering Johnson's fondness for red, added, "I like your red dress."

"Thanks," Johnson chuckled, pleased with the stranger's compliment. "I'm Johnson. What's yours?"

"Mac."

"That's a friendly name," Johnson retorted, smiling. "There was a man by that name who used to come here. Nice guy."

Mac took a sip of his beer. "Say, Johnson," he said. "Did you know—" But just about then, another customer interrupted him.

"Hey, bartender," a young man shouted impatiently from the far end of the long bar, "How about some service over here?"

Johnson immediately excused himself. "Let me take care of that young virgin," he whispered to Mac. "I'll be back with you." He was back a couple of minutes later, "You were saying?"

"Johnson, is Sollow still around?"

"Come to think of it, I haven't seen him for some time. He was an interesting man. I enjoyed listening to him talk. He was such a fluent speaker."

"Say Mac, talking about Sollow, I found him a young girlfriend like he wants. Young kid by the name of Felipa, works at Lara's, what do you think of that, Mac?"

Without answering Johnson, Mac decided to drive to Lara's to meet Felipa. Once inside the gambling casino, he was determined to see the young Filipina and the bar, ultimately, was a more adequate place to meet because of its informal atmosphere. Mac ordered beer and began to quietly ask the bartender if a young woman by the name of Felipa worked there, when a man, who appeared to be a cook, rushed to the bar out of the kitchen, shouting excitedly, "She needs help! She needs help!"

Mac hurriedly left the bar and ran to the kitchen. He bent down and placed his fingers on the young woman's throat feeling for a pulse. That was when he noticed the dagger through her neck. The checkered handle of the weapon was similar to the other daggers he had come to recognize, including the one in his possession. He stayed in that crouched position for some time, almost mesmerized by the dagger, when a male voice asked him, "What in the hell is going on?"

Mac answered without looking up, "Someone murdered this girl."

"Mac! You're not wearing your undercover disguise!"

"It really doesn't matter," Mac said automatically, not realizing at first that it was Charlie he was talking to.

"I was on my way to the gambling room when I heard commotions back here," Charlie explained hesitantly, staring down at the young woman. "Whoever did that meant to kill her." He bent down and ran his hand through the dead girl's hair and gently touched her face. "Poor kid," he softly said.

A frown broke out on Mac's face. "Did you know her?"

"Hell, no!" Charlie sounded angry at Mac's question.

Mac asked the cook, who was by now standing next to him, to cover the corpse and to call the police. "What was her name?"

"Felipa," answered the cook.

On their way to the bar, Charlie told Mac that the killing appeared to have been done by an expert and voiced his doubt about the police finding any witnesses or fingerprints. "They'll chalk up the incident on their long list of unsolved homicides. Take that explosion near Clark Field and the two decapitated soldiers. They'll never catch the perpetrator."

Mac turned around in surprise. "How'd you know about that, Charlie?"

"Hell. You can't keep a loud explosion and two murdered soldiers a secret," he said before a long pause. "I also heard about the four Filipinos who died from shrapnel. I happened to be around the area," Charlie added softly.

He ordered a dry martini for himself and scotch and water for Mac. "Poor Felipa," he said as an afterthought. "I wonder who killed her, Mac."

Mac glanced at Charlie. He hated his guts. He hated his cultivated image of friendliness and easy-going manner. Most of all, he hated his extreme self-confidence, which was nothing but suppressed arrogance. With the tiniest bit of provocation, Mac would beat him until he bled.

"I don't know who killed her, Charlie. Perhaps Sonny Sollow? I understand he was sweet on the young girl," Mac finally answered. "Maybe she two-timed him. I don't know. Just an assumption."

Charlie's eyes narrowed, "Hmmm," he murmured and took a sip of his martini. "Say, Mac. I thought you were going to Lake Taal."

"I might leave tonight or early tomorrow morning," Mac said and changed the subject by asking about Poco. Heard any more about him?"

"He and his unit got transferred to Lingayen. And as far as Miller and Rhoades go, they seemed to have disappeared from Manila," Charlie paused momentarily. "Do you think they're still in the Philippines?"

Mac shook his head. He recalled Chavez telling him to keep the information to himself regarding the two men. "I don't know," he firmly answered.

Charlie took another sip of his drink. "If they left, that leaves just you and me. That whole Quest thing seemed like a front. Like it was set up to catch someone. Don't you think so, Mac?"

"Yes. It was strangely short-lived and unfocused." Mac's thoughts were still on Felipa. He glanced at Charlie. "I wonder why anyone would kill someone that young."

Charlie shrugged his shoulders. He stared at Mac. "Still looking for the phantom murderer or murderers?"

"Trying to. How about you, Charlie? Or has your passion for the search gone cold?"

"I guess it finally did. Just enjoying paradise till the end of December, then back to Chicago. How about you, Mac? When do you plan to leave?"

"Probably the end of December also. But, like I said, I'm still trying."

"Give up, Mac. You're wasting your time."

"You're probably right," Mac answered irritably.

"Come on, Mac. Let's go. The police have arrived. We don't want to be implicated in this murder case." He was outside before Mac could utter anything.

"Charlie, Wait! What the hell is the matter with you? We won't be implicated! We haven't done anything wrong!"

"In this Army uniform? I hope you noticed that I'm wearing a uniform. The police in Manila seem to judge soldier boys as troublemakers. Besides, I've other more important things to do than listen to cops. Look me up when you're in the city." Charlie explained hurriedly.

By the time he got home, Mac felt tense and restless. He was above all displeased with himself for his zero accomplishments in his mission, and his stalker was constantly at his heel. He made up his mind to leave Kapalaran permanently. It no longer held the promise of an eventual success to his work, as he had earlier perceived. He was glad that he had rented the small house for only a week and had paid in advance. After he had packed his clothes, Mac called his landlord and told him of his decision. He placed his suitcase in the back of his Chevrolet and drove to the city, where he planned to stay that night.

Before checking in at the Quiapo hotel, he dropped in at a nearby bar and grill. After he had been there for some time, Mac approached the bartender.

"Let me ask you a question. What do people write on matchboxes?" He showed him the two boxes with number 219 written on them.

The bartender looked at Mac a while and said, "A girlfriend's name; a birthday; a telephone number; a betting number if you are a gambler, a hotel room number...."

From his own experience Mac knew that many people did use matchboxes, lacking a ready piece of paper, to make a note of something important so as not to forget it. He toyed with the idea that the number 219 could be a room number in a hotel. He also toyed with the thought that, perhaps, the key that he had found in Sollow's rented house could be the key to room 219. After leaving the bar and grill, he went to some of the nearby hotels and found that nearly all of the bigger establishments had a room 219, but the key he had with him did not fit any of the locks. Albeit he was disappointed with another unproductive search, Mac, nevertheless, decided to keep the key.

CHAPTER 27

Before leaving for Lake Taal, Mac called the General Hospital to inquire about Chavez. He was told that his doctor had released him. Aware of his friend's workaholic habit, he called his office.

When Mac entered Chavez's office, he was surprised to find his friend looking so well and hard at work, though his left arm was in a sling.

"It is all this rice and fish I have been eating," Chavez said, happy with his fast recovery. "It is good to see you again, Mac." He paused. "Thanks for your help at that POL depot near Clark Field."

"I wish we had been successful. I'm pretty sure that Meissner did that job, but then, where is he?"

"Do not feel so badly about it, Mac. One of these days he is bound to get careless. I think he is in Manila. Just a feeling," Chavez said.

"I was on my way to Lake Taal but decided to first see how you're doing."

Chavez was pleased by Mac's concern and thanked him.

During his visit with Chavez that morning, Mac learned that shortly after the emporium was raided, PIB workers began digging in the backyard, specifically that area underneath the cement slab that Mac had earlier told him about. After a few hours of excavating, a male corpse was uncovered and taken to the laboratory, but, so far, no identification could be found.

"How about dog tags?" Mac asked.

Chavez shook his head. "No dog tags."

Disappointed with Chavez's report, Mac temporarily postponed his trip to Lake Taal. He drove to Olivia Street and parked his car between his former office building, the old Sergio's Bar and Grill, and the fenced backyard of the now-boarded emporium. The gate was wide open, and

335

he noticed that PIB men had thrown the doghouse to the far corner of the backyard. He searched around for a shovel and found one near the pulverized cement slab, left there by the workers, and he began to dig in and around the hole where the corpse was found. Although it could not be identified, he was almost certain that the skeleton the PIB discovered was Stein's. After all, it was a straight shot from the former Sergio's Bar and Grill to the emporium's backyard.

In broad daylight, by a busy street and alley, he told himself, the dead body could not have disappeared without a nearby and ready place to be disposed. He further theorized that, possibly, the cement slab was there first but was removed, and a hole was dug, then the slab was placed back until that predetermined day when Stein's dead body had to be disposed of. He was disappointed that the PIB agents were unable to find any identification and equally as disappointed that Sollow, according to Chavez, seemed to have vanished.

For over an hour, Mac dug deeper in the same hole and carefully placed the soil away from the previous mound. He kept on at that until he had a circle of fresh earth around the big mound the men from the PIB had left behind. Sifting carefully through the dry and compact dirt with his hands, he found nothing. Then, as methodically as he did before, he shoveled some more dirt and created another fresh mound and to his disappointment, he found nothing there either. Just as he was about to give up on what he thought a useless effort, he unconsciously grabbed a ball of hard dirt the size of a plum and automatically began breaking it with his fingers. Much to his surprise, there on the palm of his hand was a West Point ring.

He looked on the inside of the ring and murmured, "Bingo!"

Knowing Chavez's habit of working late, Mac called his office. "Chavez?"

"Yes. I thought you had left for your R and R."

"I'm glad you're still there." Mac paused. "Don't say anything. Just listen. For the last six months I've been hitting nothing but dry holes, but an hour or so ago I hit oil! That skeleton at the lab is Stein! I've found a West Point ring, and his name is etched on it—A. B. Stein. Poco told me once that they called him Abe." Mac cleared his throat. "I also have something else to show you. A piece of paper. I forgot I had it with me when I saw you this morning."

"Excellent, Mac. Come by the office tomorrow afternoon. I will be going to Cavite in the morning for a meeting."

At 1:00 a.m. that same day, a tall man jumped out of a taxicab, "Wait here, and turn off those damn headlights," he commanded. He ran to the house on Dewey Boulevard and went around to the back and entered the house through a small, unlocked door. He promptly raced up the stairs, and, going directly to a bedroom, he began searching in all the dresser drawers, but he found nothing. Without hesitation, cursing under his breath, he went to the study, and there he searched the desk and other furniture in the room including the full-length window curtains. "Where in the hell is that damn key!" he angrily said aloud. Exasperated, he went back to the waiting taxicab.

"Where to now, Sir?" the cabdriver inquired suspiciously, still trying to catch a glimpse of his mysterious passenger's face.

"South Port Harbor! Step on it!" he demanded, glancing at his watch. "We have just enough time." When they arrived at the port, the passenger paid the driver. "I won't need you anymore," he said, jumped out of the taxicab, and raced to the cargo ship Lotus. He rushed up the gangplank but was stopped by a Filipino sailor at the entrance.

"Name?" the sailor asked.

"Sonny Sollow."

The sailor checked the bunch of papers on a clipboard he was holding. "Okay." "Welcome aboard, Sir," he said. "You have the forward stateroom number three."

"Thank you," Sollow replied as he sauntered off, but, instead of going to his stateroom, he walked to the stern of the freighter. He first carefully studied the harbor below. Satisfied that no one was around, he began to lower himself into the briny water by a thick Manila rope hanging on the side of the vessel and swam to the nearby Manila Hotel and climbed out of the turbulent and murky bay. He stood under a low hanging tree, his breath short and rapid, and watched the Lotus being guided away from Manila harbor by tugboats Paul Bunyan and Babe. He walked away only when the cargo ship became indistinguishable in the early morning fog.

Sollow approached a taxicab from among those waiting in line for passengers in front of the exclusive Manila Hotel. "Where to, Sir?" Asked the driver, giving Sollow's wet clothes a quick look.

"Military center, BOQ."

"Oh, you are in the US Army. Did you know that General MacArthur lives up in that penthouse?" explained the proud taxicab driver, pointing up to the penthouse.

"I don't like MacArthur! He's a pompous son of a bitch! Now, drive me to the BOQ! And hurry!"

"Okay, Sir," answered the driver nervously.

The sentry stopped the taxicab at the gate of the BOQ. "ID for you," he told the cabdriver, "and the passenger also."

The cabdriver pulled out his ID and gave it to the sentry while Sollow stuck his arm out of the vehicle's window with his ID, staying as much as possible in the dark corner of the cab, at the same time discretely covering his face with his right hand. The sentry saluted and waved them on.

"Stop here at this building. How much do I owe you?" Sollow asked the cabdriver.

"Fifty centavos."

"Here's one peso. Keep the change," Sollow said. He walked to the front of the door with the name Major Charles J. North, Jr. painted on a block of wood nailed to the door. He quickly unlocked the door to the room, and, once inside, he locked it. Before turning on the lights, Sollow pulled down the shade first. He opened the closet door, picked up a brown briefcase hidden behind the hanging clothes and opened it. Inside was a box marked number one. A pleased look came to his face. He was about to pick up a similar box from the floor marked number two and place it in the briefcase when he heard a knock on the door. It startled him and he hastily pushed the box marked number two in the far corner of the closet and covered it with a newspaper. There was another knock, followed by a male voice.

"Major Delaney. The car is waiting for you for Clark Field."

"This isn't Delaney's room. Three doors down," Sollow answered, glancing at his watch. He hurriedly grabbed his briefcase and called a taxicab and demanded a prompt service.

It was already hot and humid at six o'clock in the morning. At the gate, the lackadaisical sentry saluted and casually waved the taxicab with its passenger out of the military compound.

"Where to Sir?" The cabdriver inquired.

"Kapalaran. The Far East Hotel," Sollow directed. "And hurry!"

"Yes, Sir. We will get there fast. It is still early and the streets are not yet crowded with people, cars and karetelas."

"That didn't take very long. Here's your fee and keep the change," Sollow said as he got out of the cab with his briefcase. Instead of walking directly to the desk, he stealthily waited until the desk clerk had disappeared into another room. Whereupon, he ran up the stairs and rushed to the hotel door marked room 219 and expertly picked the lock with a narrow blade especially designed for jimmying door locks.

Inside the hotel room, Sonny Sollow took off his still wet clothes and proceeded to eyeball his image in the mirror. How he had murdered Czestochowa and those others he had killed flashed before him. He relished the way the images in front of him made everyone believe, especially those inefficient PIBs and equally inefficient Customs that he was still in the Chinese cargo ship as a passenger on her way to Hong Kong when all the while he had cleverly manipulated an escape from the ship and swam to shore. A deep, soundless laughter gurgled in his throat. He had always considered himself a master artist on disguises but congratulated himself on this particular masterpiece of an escape.

Entranced with his cleverness, he slowly, very slowly became enamored with the masquerade he had created and when pleased with his work, as in the past, he began to feel his blood rising and his face and neck getting red and hot. He clutched the edge of the washbasin tightly with both hands until his knuckles turned white while his body uncontrollably began to shake and commence to move to and fro. A sound like a soft sob escaped form his throat. His body stopped shaking. He took a deep breath. His orgasm was completed. He grabbed a towel and began to wipe the perspiration running down his face and neck and splashed cold water on his face.

Once again he studied his face in the mirror. "Sonny Sollow," he murmured emotionally to his image, "I'll always miss you. You've been a perfect disguise and have saved my life many times. You've been my alter ego. Goodbye. I love you," and kissed his own image in the mirror.

Like an artist at work, he first took off his eyeglasses and then his wig.

Carefully, he removed his false eyebrows, his beard then his moustache. From his mouth, he pulled out the dental prosthetic appliance covering the gap in his front teeth. He reached down on the back of his neck and pulled up over his head and face a lifelike thin and delicate rubber mask, a mask that was Sollow, and folded it neatly. And gathering all the items, he placed them in a packet in the box marked number one and shut it.

He stared at himself in the mirror and examined his true teeth with the gap between the two front teeth and a slight smile came to his face. He noticed that his naturally blond hair had grown slightly longer through the dark brown color that he used to dye his hair.

"Boris Meissner," he chided the image, "We can't let you be a blond just yet, which is your natural color and we won't let your hair grow longer. For now, you must continue to be Major Charles J. North Jr., United States Army! Bald with dark hair!" He paused and told his image in the mirror "You can't be Meissner until the Japanese bomb Manila."

Before putting on dry clothes, Meissner carefully examined his baldhead and ran his hand on it. Feeling the hair growing back, he took out a razor from his medicine cabinet and began to shave the bald area smooth and applied dark brown dye to his blond hair that had slightly grown through the previous dye. He scrutinized his appearance in the mirror. A slight smile of approval crossed his face and he began to address himself.

"Ah, Major North! You're a good-looking devil! You look sexy with that bald head!"

A deep laughter echoed throughout the hotel room.

Major North left the hotel room by the side door, took a taxicab and directed the driver to stop at a small wooden house in Binondo, not far from the government-owned Manila Railroad Company. North was in one of his rented houses for only a few minutes and coming out instructed the driver to take him to the railroad station

The next afternoon, both Mac and Chavez studied Stein's ring. Chavez glanced at Mac.

"I hope you realize that you have found something very important. This ring definitely belonged to Stein, and that skeleton at the lab is Stein. The killer must have removed his dogtags and forgot to remove his ring. You have not only helped us identify Major Haggarty's body, but now Captain Stein's. The PIB is very grateful to you, Mac. However, the case is not yet closed, as the criminal has yet to be brought to justice. Naturally, that is not always possible."

"Chavez, do you think the killer is still in Manila?"

"I think so. But, whoever he is, he covers his tracks with meticulous care," Chavez paused. "Oh, and by the way. I thought I would do some more sleuthing at Sollow's rented house this morning on the way to Cavite. The house appeared empty. Strange about an empty house, it gives itself away. I immediately became suspicious that Sollow has skipped Manila, or worse, the Philippines. I have not heard any report on him. He has been awfully quiet."

Mac breathed deeply. "I have that same feeling."

Chavez's eyes narrowed. "I called a friend of mine at Customs, but I have not yet heard from him."

"Jeez. You've got everybody watching the guy, and yet you can't catch him."

Chavez cleared his throat. "He is clever!" The telephone rang. Chavez picked up the receiver.

"Hello, may I speak to Mr. Chavez." The male voice sounded serious and urgent.

"This is Chavez. Javier?"

"Yes. This is Tony Javier at Customs Service." He paused. "I checked around and finally called the Manila International Shipping Organization, and I am afraid I have very bad news."

"Well, Javier, has Sonny Sollow left Manila?"

"I am afraid so. The man in charge of MISO verified that Sollow's name is on the passenger's list of the Chinese freighter, Lotus."

"When was departure time, Javier?" Chavez inquired.

"On schedule at 2:00 a.m. this morning, loaded with rice, copra, and dried fish. Seventeen hours ago. Chavez, are you still there?"

"Yes."

"I am sorry we could not help you." There was a pause. "Perhaps next time."

"Wait! Javier! What is the cargo ship's destination?"

"It is first enroute to Hong Kong to unload its cargo, and then it will turn around for Singapore."

"Very good! I will send a Western Union telegram to the United States FBI office in Hong Kong. As I told you the other day, Sollow is a Japanese agent engaging in espionage in the Philippines."

"Chavez," Javier said, "I am sure you are aware how easy it is for a person to get lost in Hong Kong."

"I know, Javier. Thank you for trying to help."

"Listen, Chavez. I will give you a call if I have better information for you, but I doubt it."

"Okay, Javier," Chavez sounded tired. "Well, Mac. You no longer have to help with Sollow."

"Why not?"

"That was Customs who just called. Sollow has escaped Manila."

"Hell! That's too damn bad!" Mac took out a piece of paper from his pocket and handed it to Chavez. "Aside from Stein's West Point ring, I had this to show you also. Before you unfold it, let me ask you a question. Have you ever played words backward? Map becomes pam and golf is flog."

Chavez grinned. "And dog is god. Sure. I and an American friend growing up in Cebu played that game."

"Fine. Now, unfold that paper. On it you'll see the word Sollow. See that mirror over there? Stand in front of it and hold the paper across your chest, if you want to be dramatic. Or, you can just spell the words backward, sitting there."

Chavez pushed his chair back and told Mac he wanted to be dramatic. "Mac, am I reading this correctly? Sollow is Wollos spelled backward?"

"Chavez, you and I have let the most wanted German spy in the world, Boris Meissner, elude us. I don't know why it didn't occur to me before that Sollow is Wollos. Sollow is Boris Meissner!"

"Purita Aquino went undercover as Cookie and personally saw Sollow at Tanaka's meeting. He is a spy."

"Excellent. This will confirm it. Back to that piece of paper," continued Mac. "According to the office of Naval Intelligence, Wollos is Meissner's mother's maiden name—Ann Wollos—and she called him Sonny instead of Boris. This sapphire ring on my finger belongs to Sonny Sollow, given to him by his mother."

"How did you come to this spelling backward thing about Sollow?"

Mac mused that it was strictly by accident and not by inspired genius. He could not recall when he scribbled Sollow's name on the piece of paper, nor could he remember when he laid it on the dresser in front of the mirror. "I was getting ready to call the hospital about you yesterday morning when I noticed the name reflected on the mirror. It escaped my mind until I found Stein's West Point ring."

CHAPTER 28

Mac was only too glad to be in Cavite's Tagaytay City, away from Manila with all its intrigues. At Lake Taal, he distanced himself from the newspapers and the radio.

The beautiful lake resort had such a definite relaxing effect on him that, instead of staying a couple of days as he had previously planned, he stayed a week, enjoying swimming and sailing. The frolicking in the sun, plus the exhilarating and unique splendor of the island-within-an-island atmosphere soon erased Mac's disappointments. He resolved once again to pursue the reason why he was in the Philippines but decided to be more secretive about his plans with Charlie North. Being open seemed to have horrible consequences.

In his last night at Lake Taal, Mac was ambushed while coming out of a seafood restaurant. It was a stormy, dark night, and he was hurrying back to his lakeside hotel when he saw a shadowy figure of a man trailing him. As he walked faster, so did the man. Upon reaching the corner of a small souvenir shop, Mac stepped behind the building and waited to accost the person following him. But, unbeknownst to him, the man must have read his strategy and went, instead, around the small shop and attacked him from behind by encircling his arm around Mac's neck. Struggling to extricate himself from his attacker's vise-like strength, Mac eventually was able to do so by jabbing his right elbow into the pit on the man's stomach, causing him to relax his hold around Mac's neck. With a swing of his right fist, Mac landed what he thought was a crushing blow on the man's jaw. But with agile movement seldom seen in a big man, the attacker was able to deflect some sting from Mac's blow that could have downed him. He retaliated by hitting Mac on the head with a 2x4 he grabbed from the ground, causing Mac to be in a partial state of unconsciousness. Aware of Mac's physical condition, the attacker whipped out his dagger and was poised to stab Mac to death.

But the heavy rain on his face brought Mac back to, and he was able to catch a glimpse of the weapon on his attacker's hand. Readying himself for the dagger to plunge into him, Mac pulled back his legs and landed a kick on the stranger's crotch.

Groaning with pain, the assailant, whose face Mac was never able to see in the darkness, dropped his dagger and disappeared into the stormy night. Now by himself and still on his back, Mac began to feel for the weapon. A passing car splashed more mud on him, but its bright headlights enabled him to find the dagger. He grabbed it and placed it in his pocket. He then massaged his head, his neck, and the back of his legs, hoping to ease the sharp pains that shot through him. He forced himself to get up from the muddy street and rainwater that had by then created deep puddles around him. He straightened and, massaging his neck again, looked around to make certain his attacker was not around. Mac took the weapon back to the hotel with him and washed it. To his amazement, it was similar to the other daggers in his possession. He contemplated the episode and wondered if he was a magnet for trouble. He found it ludicrous to imagine that it could be the same man who had been trying to kill him since his arrival in Manila back in June. And yet, why not? The weapon was like the others he had picked up after the fights. Were it not for the aches in his body, he was almost ready to say that it really did not happen, that he was just being paranoid. He was tired and restless, and he could not sleep.

But when sleep finally came, his sweet and peaceful dream about Miguela suddenly turned into a nightmare. He found himself in the jungles of Bataan being chased by three very large iguanas. The faster he tried to run, the deeper his feet sank into the muddy ground. He tried to scream, but no sound came out of his throat. His mouth was very dry from fear that the giant iguanas would catch him and devour him alive. There was neither water nor food to be found. As he sank deeper into the mud and the powerful animals fought amongst themselves for his body, an unusually long arm, not attached to a body, stretched out to help him.

He was jolted from his sleep by a loud clap of thunder close by, or was it the sound of an explosion? He jumped from the bed and looked out the window. Everything was quiet and still dark. Mac lit a cigarette and sat on the edge of his bed. As if urged by an inner voice to leave, he packed his suitcase. For the last several days he had had an unexplained perception of an impending disaster, as if the sky would fall on him. He walked again to the window and wondered when the heavy rain would stop. But, having lived in the Philippines for the last several months, he knew that it would probably stop as fast as it had started, like many of the rains he encountered. Shortly after he had left the hotel, the heavy rain turned into a drizzle.

Mac glanced at his watch. Dawn had still a long travel before it could break through the cloudy sky. And as he drove away from the resort, he made up his mind to take in a quick, early breakfast at the Cavite Naval Station, if they served breakfast at all that early. He was hungry. The previous night's incident kept him from even thinking about supper.

As he neared the Naval Base, he immediately observed that the base was in total darkness. In addition, the alert siren was on. Mac stepped on the gas. As soon as he entered the base, he noticed the nervousness and tension among the men, and many of them were placing machine guns on the gunboats. He soon learned the startling news.

"The headquarters in Manila has informed us that Japan attacked Pearl Harbor yesterday morning," someone told him.

As if he did not understand his own statement, the man said again. "Pearl Harbor has been attacked by the Japanese."

Mac was shaken by the news. As he drove back to Manila, he repeated over and over again the dreadful news he had learned from the sailor. A terrible anger towards the Japanese swelled inside him. The anger was so deep that Mac's stomach twisted inside him. Determined to get back to the city, he decided to stop at the USAFFE headquarters to get updated information. The mind-boggling report infuriated him. He shouted to the open air, "The Japanese will also attack the Philippines! It's inevitable!" He recalled what his stoic mother, Helen, told him when his father died. "Mac, there are three things that can change one's life—marriage, war, and death."

Mac reached Manila faster than he had anticipated. He was now on the north end of Taft Avenue and could see the public playground off the road. In another two minutes, he would reach the busy and thriving area of Escolta in downtown Manila. It was only the first week in December, and many of the shops, including his favorite Manila Café, were already decked out in colorful tinsels, trimmings, and strings of different colors of Christmas lights. He told himself that, before going to USAFFE, hot coffee and a hot meal would shake off the bad feeling he had had since leaving Cavite.

The Escolta was teeming with so many people that Mac could hardly find a place to park. After ordering his meal, he asked the waitress the reason for the big crowd on the streets.

"I think it is the radio," answered the waitress. "Radio station-connected loud speakers were installed so that everybody can listen to radio commentators reporting on the Japanese attack on Pearl Harbor. The report comes every ten minutes."

"Say, I thought there was going to be a Catholic feast and procession today," Mac said.

"It has been cancelled," the waitress answered.

Meanwhile, the owner of the café turned on the restaurant's Philco radio, and the voice of Steve Ball came on the airwaves. "This is December 8, 1941. Japanese planes have bombed Clark Field. It was a surprise attack. Reports are coming in fast, and they are not pretty. The whole camp is an inferno. The fighter base Iba has also been attacked. The U.S. Army's Fort Stotsenburg, an artillery training ground near Angeles is practically obliterated. The sky fifty miles from Manila is dark with Japanese planes. More reports soon."

The first wail of the siren sounded not long after the news report. There was chaos on the streets. Confused and scared, people ran here and there. Within a short period, the transportation system on the streets of Manila became a liability. The traffic was bogged down, and fear was rampant. In the distance, bombs could be heard.

In the café, everyone was either taking cover or leaving the restaurant to hide. Mac, after leaving some money on the table, got in his car but could not move. He decided that, instead of going to USAFFE, he would see Charlie North. Meanwhile, a couple of young men who were looking for a ride to Pasay helped Mac get out of the parking area and directed him to another street with less people.

"Are you going to Pasay?" One of the young men asked. Mac shook his head. "Not any farther than the Walled City. I'm seeing a friend who may be able to shed light on the Japanese attack of Clark Field. You can hitchhike from there."

He parked in front of the BOQ, ran up the steps of the building, and knocked on Charlie's door. There was no answer, but the door was unlocked. Once again, Mac knocked, and this time he pushed the door open. "Hello?"

A frightened Filipina maid came out of the bathroom. "I was cleaning the room when that siren made me afraid and I hid. Are the Japanese coming here to kill us all?" she asked almost hysterically. "Sir, tell me the truth. Are the Japanese coming?"

"It'll be all right. Don't worry," Mac said.

The maid became even more upset, gathered her things together, and started to leave the room.

Mac looked around the room. It was bare. "Wait. Have you seen Major North?"

"No, Sir," said the maid. "Major North has left."

"Do you know when he's coming back? I'm a friend of his."

"No, Sir. I was told Major North has left the base for good. No one here knows where he has moved to."

Mac shook his head. "Strange! Just like that!"

Before the maid left, she gave Mac a small metal box. "Sir, I think this belongs to him," she said, handing the box to Mac. "Your friend will probably call you," she smiled uneasily. "I must go home to my children. I am sure they are frightened."

On his way to his car, Mac decided he was going to see Chavez at his home, and upon reaching his car he causally threw the box, marked with a number two, on the passenger seat. The lid flew open, displaying its contents.

Curious, Mac began to examine the items. There was the large, gold belt buckle with a cobra's head. He picked up a picture of an older woman that was also in the box. Under the photograph of the woman was the inscription "To Sonny, love, mother." Mac studied the woman's face. "This must be Ann Wollos," he murmured. He remembered Johnson the bartender at the Periscope Club telling him once about Sollow knowing a friend who had a suite at the Far East Hotel. The next item that fell out of the box was a checkered dagger, torn brown wig, fake beard, eyeglasses, and dogtags. He picked up the dogtags and read the engraved name. "These are Stein's!" he whispered as if afraid someone would hear him.

Perplexed, he quickly placed the items back and shut the top down. As he continued to stand there, Mac said under his breath, "My God!"

His surprise was so overwhelming; it was like someone just hit him in the stomach, knocking all his air out. A chilly thought gripped him. "I've got to get the hell out of here!" Charlie is Boris Meissner, disguised as Sonny Sollow.

About a mile from the center, Mac stopped his car at the nearest restaurant and called Miguela at her apartment on Taft Avenue. Not getting an answer, he called Buenavista and finally connected with Miguela there. Without waiting for her to speak, he told her that he would meet her at her apartment. "I must see you alone. This is urgent!"

Because of the heavy and chaotic traffic, the drive to Miguela's apartment took longer than Mac wished, but when he arrived, she was waiting for him. "Mac, where have you been? I was worried about you. I heard on the radio Clark Field had been bombed."

"Sorry. I couldn't get here any faster. The traffic was a nightmare. Let me in! I've got something to show you!" Mac explained and walked straight to the bathroom and hurriedly put on the brown hair, the moustache, the beard, and the eyeglasses. "Do you recognize this, Miguela?"

"Sonny Sollow?" Miguela whispered, breathless. "Why, those spectacles and the rest are unmistakably Sonny Sollow's. I have never seen him without those. Never without them! Where did you get them? Are you playing games, Mac?

"They were in Charlie's room at the BOQ, and I'm not playing games. Look at these dogtags. They're Stein's. The PIB has his skeleton and West Point ring, but they couldn't find these. And here's a picture of Sonny Sollow's mother." Mac paused. "The maid at the BOQ gave me this box to return to Charlie. He must have forgotten it."

"Is your friend, Charlie North, Sonny Sollow?" Miguela inquired incredulously.

"Yes, and if he's Sonny Sollow, he's Boris Meissner. I don't have much time. I've got to get back to Kapalaran. What's the best way to get out of the city? All hell is breaking loose out there."

Miguela directed Mac to Kapalaran.

Before Mac left the apartment, he made Miguela promise that she would immediately go back to her parent's home. "You'll be safer there. The Japs will soon bomb Manila Harbor, and your apartment isn't too far away. I'll see you at Buenavista."

Mac was about to leave when the telephone rang. Miguela answered it. It was a hurried call, and Miguela soon hung up. "Mac, it was Edward Martin. He said that he is an FBI agent and that he was not in a position to talk to you personally, but he says for you to call the PIB. Chavez knows all about it. It's about a telegram from a Mr. John Stone in Washington about Charlie North." Miguela searched Mac's face. "What's going on, Mac?"

"I'll explain everything later. I must go, darling!" Mac gave Miguela a peck on the cheek and rushed out the door.

"Where will you be, Mac?" she shouted.

"The Far East Hotel in Kapalaran," Mac shouted back. On the way there, every nerve in his body warned him to be alert. He was now entering the world of big spies, murderers, and cold, calculated actions and reactions with deadly results. All of a sudden a sensation came over him like a big wave had rolled in, carrying him out in the deep, blue sea. He gasped for breath, like a drowning man. Charlie North's face kept flashing in front of him. There was no stopping the images going through his mind—Meissner killing Duvalier, Meissner murdering Haggarty, Summers, Stein, and Gibbs; Meissner pushing down Walters's face in the water until he could no longer breath; Meissner killing Roosie, Alberto and Lina; grandmother Fuentes. And those others he had killed before them.

"Charlie killed Czestochowa," Mac said aloud.

Unconsciously, he slammed hard on the brakes. The glass entrance to the Far East Hotel was only inches away from the front of the car. He backed the car a couple of feet away and sat there for a second, breathing heavily, perspiration running down his face. Every fiber in his body was tense, and he knew that at last he had the answer.

"The son of a bitch was my stalker!" He murmured. He wanted to scream until his lungs burst. He wanted to hit something with his fists until his knuckles bled.

Mac took a deep breath to clear his mind and lungs. He jumped out of the car and rushed inside the Far East Hotel, ignoring the desk clerk's polite, "Sir, may I be of help?"

He ran up the stairs and did not stop until he had reached the second floor. He carefully checked his gun, placed it back in his belt, and began to search for the room.

The key easily fitted the lock to room 219. Mac pushed the door open and looked around, but no one seemed to be there. He stepped inside what appeared to be a kitchenette. Near the kitchen sink was a stainless steel thermos bottle. Mac picked it up and poured a bit of the content into the sink.

"Cold, black coffee. Boris Meissner, a.k.a. Major Charles North," he told himself.

Leaving the tiny kitchen, Mac cautiously entered the bedroom and opened the closet door. There were shirts and trousers on clothes hangars. His eyes fell on a khaki shirt missing a button. On the floor was a lone brown shoe, and leaning against the wall were Mac's stolen briefcase and suitcase. The lock to the briefcase had been broken. He noted immediately that the copy he had made of Walters's letter to his friend, Colonel Polson, had been laid on top. Knowing by heart what was in the suitcase, Mac did not bother to unlock it. When it was stolen from him last June at the pier, Meissner probably surmised it contained important papers rather than just clothes.

As Mac stepped out of the closet, he caught a glimpse of the infamous three-ringed blue binder on the table. He bent down and opened it. Mac quickly turned the pages and concluded that it was an impressive document. The title page, "The Spy Ring in The Philippines. Code name Saber," conveyed exactly the contents of the pages. Mac was aware that a thick black line had been drawn across the word NETWORK, and the word SABER was written over it.

Most of what he read he had already heard from various sources. Towards the end of the document, however, a paragraph attracted his attention. Someone had underlined the paragraph in red crayon. 'After months of research and collating data received from many reliable sources, and keeping him under surveillance, I can report to G-2, unequivocally, that there is a foreign spy in our midst. This spy is an expert on disguises. His real name is Boris Meissner the German master spy who murdered Major Haggarty, Major Summers, Captain Abe Stein. Meissner is also masquerading as Major Charles J. North, Jr. North is also a member of my small group trying to find Meissner, the spy and murderer. The real Major North was an American Infantry officer who fought and died in battle in Europe during World War I. The physical appearance on the fraudulent Major North is actually Meissner's own true identity."

Mac was so engrossed, he was unaware that someone had entered the room.

"Well. Well. I have a visitor, the intelligence officer extraordinaire, Major Jacob McCord. Enjoying reading Walters's Opus Magnus, Mac? Good to see you."

Mac looked up, but, although startled, he kept his composure.

"Yes, I am Charlie North, or Boris Meissner, whichever name you prefer. But Meissner will be just fine," he told Mac dryly. "Would you believe, McCord? Charlie North's face is my real face. Walters was right. The Philippines became my playground." He paused. "My hatred for you, McCord, has been consuming me. I could have escaped from the Philippines a hundred times and not be heard again."

"But, why didn't you?"

"You saw my face in Paris when Duvalier was dying. I did not want you to tell the authorities here."

"Believe it or not, Meissner, I didn't see you. What disguise were you using? A Hitler look-alike?"

Meissner paused momentarily. "McCord, for a super spy, you really astound me. I am surprised at your lack of observation. All this time, despite my dyed hair and shaved head, I assumed one day you would recognize me for the differences in the color of my eyes. The left eye is blue and the right eye is gray. The deep scar on my right cheek should also be a dead giveaway for an observant spy. As I stood at the door outside Duvalier's apartment, watching you talking to him while he was dying on the floor, I carelessly hit the door with my foot. You looked up, turned your head, and you stared right at me. I vowed then to kill you. I was afraid that in time you would write an essay about my appearance and distribute it to the British, French, and later American intelligence. I knew that Duvalier told you a copious amount of details about me."

"To reiterate, I didn't see you." Mac explained. "But Duvalier told me you cut off heads, legs, and fingers," he paused. "Let me tell you what you are—a coward."

"Not so!" Meissner said, smiling. "I'm really very brave."

Mac's steel blue eyes were unblinking on Meissner's face. He tried straightening up but Meissner stopped him by pointing his gun at Mac. "Drop your gun. Drop it! That's good!" Meissner picked it up and stuck it in his belt. "What took you so long to find me?"

Without waiting for Mac to answer, Meissner, with his gun in his hand, waved for Mac to stand against the wall and commanded him to put his hands behind his head. "Don't you think experience counts in our field, McCord? I've known all along who you are. What's so fascinating about the intelligence world is that the bad guy is always called a spy, and the good guy is a covert intelligence agent engaged in counterintelligence. It all depends, of course, on which side of the coin one happens to be." Meissner paused momentarily.

"And you're a spy, McCord! I'm doing covert intelligence. Don't you think I did a splendid job setting up the spy network for the Japanese in Manila? You see, my group is about to take over your group! He paused once more. "Spies are such egomaniacs, don't you think so, McCord? And they do get away with murder."

Mac tried to take a step forward.

"I wouldn't try that! Keep your back against the wall!" He paused. "I'm certainly glad you're wearing that blue sapphire ring today. Drop it on the sofa. It belongs to me. My mother gave it to me."

Mac did as he was asked. "Before you kill me, Meissner, I want to hear from you personally that you murdered those four officers, and Walters."

"Yes! And I stabbed Czestochowa and Roosie to death."

"And Duvalier?" Mac added.

"He was a fool. Double agents are useless to the country that hires them. They don't have any loyalty to either country. They only try to protect their own interest. They're scums of the earth!"

As Meissner was speaking, the roar of airplanes in the sky, though distant, distracted him.

"They're here sooner than I had anticipated."

He looked out of the window for a second, and when he did, Mac tackled him, and the gun flew out of Meissner's hand. Mac crawled to it, but Meissner stomped on his hand. Quickly, Mac retaliated by pulling both of his opponent's feet, causing him to fall to the floor. Mac began to hit Meissner's face left and right with his fists. It occurred to him then that his opponent, fighting with almost superhuman strength, was the same man who attacked him in Olongapo and Buenavista, who jumped into the swirling cove on Manila Bay.

After a long and hard struggle, Meissner extricated himself by kicking Mac in the ribs, temporarily downing him. But with an Olympian leap and agility he did not know he possessed, Mac knocked Meissner to the floor. More struggle ensued until Meissner was in a better position and forced Mac to stand up and face the wall. Picking up his gun, he placed it on Mac's head.

"You were a quick target. I should have killed you in Paris."

"Why didn't you?"

"You presented a challenge. That intoxicating feeling to let the difficult prey go, even if it means that the prey escapes. But not for long. You see, I've caught you. You're under my control, and I won't let you escape again." Meissner laughed a dry laugh. "McCord, have you ever been in hunter's position? Full of strength and dominance?" He half-closed his eyes. "Ah it's a sweet feeling. It's better than sex."

"You're a crazy murderer and a sadist!"

Meissner looked at Mac for a while. "Murderer and sadist? Yes. But crazy? No. I've never been as sane as I am now, knowing that I'm going to kill you. Then, I'm going on to new challenges."

"Before you kill me, grant me a last request by telling me where general Tanaka is hiding. He just disappeared from the face of the earth."

Meissner's eyes narrowed. "Very well. Tanaka and Matsumuto have fled to Davao. Many Japanese there. Chavez will never catch them, nor will any of MacArthur's men. The Japanese are clever and here to stay. Clark Field has been bombed heavily. Finished!" He paused. "But don't worry. The Japanese will repair it when they conquer the whole country."

Meissner continued to gloat that the successful attack in Hawaii the day before gave momentum to the attack of the Philippines that following day, and that the time was right, in that the US Department of War was indeed extremely vulnerable to foreign hostilities.

Suddenly, they heard a plane approaching above them.

"A Japanese fighter plane," Meissner said. He became curious, but, before he left Mac for the window, he struck him on the head with the butt of his gun. Mac folded to the floor, dazed.

Meissner grabbed a pair of binoculars. He stood there for some time while targeting his sight on the plane. It was a Japanese Zero. Meissner smiled. When he came back from the window, he pulled the trigger of his gun and aimed at Mac. Suddenly, there was a slight noise at the door. Meissner quickly turned around and recognized Martin, whom he knew to be Lieutenant Colonel Dusty Rhoades, aiming his gun at him. Meissner pulled the trigger of his gun and fired, hitting the FIB agent's hand, dropping the gun to the floor. Meissner went forward and pummeled the agent's abdomen with his fists. The agent fell to the floor, unconscious. Meissner then approached the downed and helpless FBI agent and began kicking him in the head. Unknown to Meissner, Mac, who was still weak, had been watching the episode, slowly forcing himself to get up and quietly moved to where Meissner was still insanely kicking the agent. Mac encircled Meissner's neck with his strong arm and tightened it until the German spy fell to the floor face down, dead with a broken neck. Mac tore Meissner's shirtsleeve and tied it around Martin's arm. He then ran to the bathroom and grabbed a towel and wiped his bloody face. He was still alive, but just a little woozy. He went to get a glass of water for Martin.

"Raise your head and have a little water," Mac said.

The FBI agent could not. Mac subsequently parted the agent's lips and dripped water into his mouth.

"Thanks, Mac," Martin said weakly.

"Come on, let's get out of here," Mac said. "But before we go...."

Mac walked to Meissner's body and ripped the last bit of fabric from his shirt.

"There it is," Mac said as he glanced at the birthmark that Duvalier had described. "No wonder he always wore a shirt on the beach."

As they left the hotel, Martin glanced at Mac.

"Thanks," he said.

"No. Thank you," Mac smiled wryly. "Miguela told me that you had something to tell me," Mac said.

Martin shook his head. "It was about Charlie North. It's no longer important."

"Those Japanese aircraft bombers are getting awfully close," Mac said.

They were a mile away from the Far East Hotel when they heard two loud explosions behind them. Mac could see in his rearview mirror a line of fire and black smoke rising to the sky.

ABOUT THE AUTHOR

Dorothy Fleming was born in Iloilo, in the Visayan Island, Philippines. She began her career as an intelligence analyst for the U.S. Air Force Security Service in San Antonio, Texas, and later joined the Air Force Intelligence in Washington, D.C. Over a thirty-one year career, she continued to serve in a variety of positions in military intelligence with the Defense Intelligence Agency. She retired in 1980 and now writes from her home in Arlington, Virginia. Ms. Fleming is working on her third novel, *The Longing in the Heart*, which takes place on one of the many islands off the coast of Florida.